SIDNEY SHELDON

NOTHING LASTS FOREVER

TELL ME YOUR DREAMS

Grafton

This omnibus edition published in 2003 by
HarperCollins*Publishers*

HarperCollins*Publishers*
77-85 Fulham Palace Road,
Hammersmith, London W6 8JB

The HarperCollins website address is:
www.**fire**and**water**.com

ISBN 0 00 768308 1

Set in Times

Printed and bound in Great Britain by
Mackays of Chatham Ltd, Chatham, Kent

NOTHING LASTS
FOREVER

To Anastasia and Roderick Mann,
with love

The author wishes to express his deep appreciation
to the many doctors, nurses, and medical technicians
who were generous enough
to share their expertise with him.

What cannot be cured with medicaments is cured
by the knife, what the knife cannot cure
is cured with the searing iron, and whatever
this cannot cure must be considered incurable.

HIPPOCRATES, 5th century B.C.

There are three classes of human beings: men,
women, and women physicians.   SIR WILLIAM OSLER

PROLOGUE

*San Francisco
Spring, 1995*

District Attorney Carl Andrews was in a fury. 'What the hell is going on here?' he demanded. 'We have three doctors living together and working at the same hospital. One of them almost gets an entire hospital closed down, the second one kills a patient for a million dollars, and the third one is murdered.'

Andrews stopped to take a deep breath. 'And they're all women! Three goddam women doctors! The media is treating them like celebrities. They're all over the tube. *60 Minutes* did a segment on them. Barbara Walters did a special on them. I can't pick up a newspaper or magazine without seeing their pictures, or reading about them. Two to one, Hollywood is going to make a movie about them, and they'll turn the bitches into some kind of heroines! I wouldn't be surprised if the government put their faces on postage stamps, like Presley. Well, by God, I won't have it!' He slammed a fist down against the photograph of a woman on the cover of *Time* magazine. The caption read: *Dr Paige Taylor — Angel of Mercy or the Devil's Disciple?*

1

'Dr Paige Taylor.' The district attorney's voice was filled with disgust. He turned to Gus Venable, his chief prosecuting attorney. 'I'm handing this trial over to you, Gus. I want a conviction. Murder One. The gas chamber.'

'Don't worry,' Gus Venable said quietly. 'I'll see to it.'

Sitting in the courtroom watching Dr Paige Taylor, Gus Venable thought: *She's jury-proof.* Then he smiled to himself. *No one is jury-proof.* She was tall and slender, with eyes that were a startling dark brown in her pale face. A disinterested observer would have dismissed her as an attractive woman. A more observant one would have noticed something else—that all the different phases of her life coexisted in her. There was the happy excitement of the child, superimposed onto the shy uncertainty of the adolescent and the wisdom and pain of the woman. There was a look of innocence about her. *She's the kind of girl*, Gus Venable thought cynically, *a man would be proud to take home to his mother. If his mother had a taste for cold-blooded killers.*

There was an almost eerie sense of remoteness in her eyes, a look that said that Dr Paige Taylor had retreated deep inside herself to a different place, a different time, far from the cold, sterile courtroom where she was trapped.

The trial was taking place in the venerable old San Francisco Hall of Justice on Bryant Street. The building, which housed the Superior Court and County

2

Jail, was a forbidding-looking edifice, seven stories high, made of square gray stone. Visitors arriving at the courthouse were funneled through electronic security checkpoints. Upstairs, on the third floor, was the Superior Court. In Courtroom 121, where murder trials were held, the judge's bench stood against the rear wall, with an American flag behind it. To the left of the bench was the jury box, and in the center were two tables separated by an aisle, one for the prosecuting attorney, the other for the defense attorney.

The courtroom was packed with reporters and the type of spectators attracted to fatal highway accidents and murder trials. As murder trials went, this one was spectacular. Gus Venable, the prosecuting attorney, was a show in himself. He was a burly man, larger than life, with a mane of gray hair, a goatee, and the courtly manner of a Southern plantation owner. He had never been to the South. He had an air of vague bewilderment and the brain of a computer. His trademark, summer and winter, was a white suit, with an old-fashioned stiff-collar shirt.

Paige Taylor's attorney, Alan Penn, was Venable's opposite, a compact, energetic shark, who had built a reputation for racking up acquittals for his clients.

The two men had faced each other before, and their relationship was one of grudging respect and total mistrust. To Venable's surprise, Alan Penn had come to see him the week before the trial was to begin.

'I came here to do you a favor, Gus.'

Beware of defense attorneys bearing gifts. 'What did you have in mind, Alan?'

'Now understand—I haven't discussed this with my client yet, but suppose—just suppose—I could persuade her to plead guilty to a reduced charge and save the State the cost of a trial?'

'Are you asking me to plea-bargain?'

'Yes.'

Gus Venable reached down to his desk, searching for something. 'I can't find my damn calendar. Do you know what the date is?'

'June first. Why?'

'For a minute there, I thought it must be Christmas already, or you wouldn't be asking for a present like that.'

'Gus . . .'

Venable leaned forward in his chair. 'You know, Alan, ordinarily, I'd be inclined to go along with you. Tell you the truth, I'd like to be in Alaska fishing right now. But the answer is no. You're defending a cold-blooded killer who murdered a helpless patient for his money. I'm demanding the death penalty.'

'I think she's innocent, and I—'

Venable gave a short, explosive laugh. 'No, you don't. And neither does anyone else. It's an open-and-shut case. Your client is as guilty as Cain.'

'Not until the jury says so, Gus.'

'They will.' He paused. 'They will.'

After Alan Penn left, Gus Venable sat there thinking about their conversation. Penn's coming to him was a sign of weakness. Penn knew there was no chance he could win the trial. Gus Venable thought about the irrefutable evidence he had, and the witnesses he was going to call, and he was satisfied.

4

There was no question about it. Dr Paige Taylor was going to the gas chamber.

It had not been easy to impanel a jury. The case had occupied the headlines for months. The cold-bloodedness of the murder had created a tidal wave of anger.

The presiding judge was Vanessa Young, a tough, brilliant black jurist rumored to be the next nominee for the United States Supreme Court. She was not known for being patient with lawyers, and she had a quick temper. There was an adage among San Francisco trial lawyers: *If your client is guilty, and you're looking for mercy, stay away from Judge Young's courtroom.*

The day before the start of the trial, Judge Young had summoned the two attorneys to her chambers.

'We're going to set some ground rules, gentlemen. Because of the serious nature of this trial, I'm willing to make certain allowances to make sure that the defendant gets a fair trial. But I'm warning both of you not to try to take advantage of that. Is that clear?'

'Yes, your honor.'

'Yes, your honor.'

Gus Venable was finishing his opening statement. 'And so ladies and gentlemen of the jury, the State will prove — yes, prove beyond a reasonable doubt — that Dr Paige Taylor killed her patient, John Cronin. And not only did she commit murder,

5

she did it for money . . . a lot of money. She killed John Cronin for one million dollars.

'Believe me, after you've heard all the evidence, you will have no trouble in finding Dr Paige Taylor guilty of murder in the first degree. Thank you.'

The jury sat in silence, unmoved but expectant.

Gus Venable turned to the judge. 'If it please your honor I would like to call Gary Williams as the State's first witness.'

When the witness was sworn in, Gus Venable said, 'You're an orderly at Embarcadero County Hospital?'

'Yes, that's right.'

'Were you working in Ward Three when John Cronin was brought in last year?'

'Yes.'

'Can you tell us who the doctor in charge of his case was?'

'Dr Taylor.'

'How would you characterize the relationship between Dr Taylor and John Cronin?'

'Objection!' Alan Penn was on his feet. 'He's calling for a conclusion from the witness.'

'Sustained.'

'Let me phrase it another way. Did you ever hear any conversations between Dr Taylor and John Cronin?'

'Oh, sure. I couldn't help it. I worked that ward all the time.'

'Would you describe those conversations as friendly?'

'No, sir.'

'Really? Why do you say that?'

'Well, I remember the first day Mr Cronin was brought in, and Dr Taylor started to examine him, he said to keep her . . .' He hesitated. 'I don't know if I can repeat his language.'

'Go ahead, Mr Williams. I don't think there are any children in this courtroom.'

'Well, he told her to keep her fucking hands off him.'

'He said *that* to Dr Taylor?'

'Yes, sir.'

'Please tell the court what else you may have seen or heard.'

'Well, he always called her "that bitch." He didn't want her to go near him. Whenever she came into his room, he would say things like "Here comes that bitch again!" and "Tell that bitch to leave me alone" and "Why don't they get me a *real* doctor?"'

Gus Venable paused to look over to where Dr Taylor was seated. The jurors' eyes followed him. Venable shook his head, as though saddened, then turned back to the witness. 'Did Mr Cronin seem to you to be a man who wanted to give a million dollars to Dr Taylor?'

Alan Penn was on his feet again. 'Objection! He's calling for an opinion again.'

Judge Young said, 'Overruled. The witness may answer the question.'

Alan Penn looked at Paige Taylor and sank back in his seat.

'Hell, no. He hated her guts.'

*   *   *

Dr Arthur Kane was in the witness box.

Gus Venable said, 'Dr Kane, you were the staff doctor in charge when it was discovered that John Cronin was mur—' He looked at Judge Young. '. . . killed by insulin being introduced into his IV. Is that correct?'

'It is.'

'And you subsequently discovered that Dr Taylor was responsible.'

'That's correct.'

'Dr Kane, I'm going to show you the official hospital death form signed by Dr Taylor.' He picked up a paper and handed it to Kane. 'Would you read it aloud, please?'

Kane began to read. '"John Cronin. Cause of Death: Respiratory arrest occurred as a complication of myocardial infarction occurring as a complication of pulmonary embolus."'

'And in layman's language?'

'The report says that the patient died of a heart attack.'

'And that paper is signed by Dr Taylor?'

'Yes.'

'Dr Kane, was that the true cause of John Cronin's death?'

'No. The insulin injection caused his death.'

'So, Dr Taylor administered a fatal dose of insulin and then falsified the report?'

'Yes.'

'And you reported it to Dr Wallace, the hospital administrator, who then reported it to the authorities.'

'Yes. I felt it was my duty.' His voice rang with righteous indignation. 'I'm a doctor. I don't believe in taking the life of another human being under any circumstances.'

The next witness called was John Cronin's widow. Hazel Cronin was in her late thirties, with flaming red hair, and a voluptuous figure that her plain black dress failed to conceal.

Gus Venable said, 'I know how painful this is for you, Mrs Cronin, but I must ask you to describe to the jury your relationship with your late husband.'

The widow Cronin dabbed at her eyes with a large lace handkerchief. 'John and I had a loving marriage. He was a wonderful man. He often told me I had brought him the only real happiness he had ever known.'

'How long were you married to John Cronin?'

'Two years, but John always said it was like two years in heaven.'

'Mrs Cronin, did your husband ever discuss Dr Taylor with you? Tell you what a great doctor he thought she was? Or how helpful she had been to him? Or how much he liked her?'

'He never mentioned her.'

'Never?'

'Never.'

'Did John ever discuss cutting you and your brothers out of his will?'

'Absolutely not. He was the most generous man in the world. He always told me that there was nothing I couldn't have, and that when he died . . .' her voice broke, '. . . that when he died, I would be a wealthy woman, and . . .' She could not go on.

Judge Young said, 'We'll have a fifteen-minute recess.'

Seated in the back of the courtroom, Jason Curtis was filled with anger. He could not believe what the witnesses were saying about Paige. *This is the woman I love*, he thought. *The woman I'm going to marry*.

Immediately after Paige's arrest, Jason Curtis had gone to visit her in jail.

'We'll fight this,' he assured her. 'I'll get you the best criminal lawyer in the country.' A name immediately sprang to mind. *Alan Penn*. Jason had gone to see him.

'I've been following the case in the papers,' Penn said. 'The press has already tried and convicted her of murdering John Cronin for a bundle. What's more she admits she killed him.'

'I know her,' Jason Curtis told him. 'Believe me, there's no way Paige could have done what she did, for money.'

'Since she admits she killed him,' Penn said, 'what we're dealing with here then is euthanasia. Mercy killings are against the law in California, as in most states, but there are a lot of mixed feelings about them. I can make a pretty good case for Florence Nightingale listening to a Higher Voice and all that shit, but the problem is that your lady love killed a patient who left her a million dollars in his will. Which came first, the chicken or the egg? Did she know about the million before she killed him, or after?'

'Paige didn't know a thing about the money,' Jason said firmly.

Penn's tone was noncommittal. 'Right. It was just a happy coincidence. The DA is calling for Murder One, and he wants the death penalty.'

'Will you take the case?'

Penn hesitated. It was obvious that Jason Curtis believed in Dr Taylor. *The way Samson believed in Delilah.* He looked at Jason and thought: *I wonder if the poor son of a bitch had a haircut and doesn't know it.*

Jason was waiting for an answer.

'I'll take the case, as long as you know it's all uphill. It's going to be a tough one to win.'

Alan Penn's statement turned out to be over-optimistic.

When the trial resumed the following morning, Gus Venable called a string of new witnesses.

A nurse was on the stand. 'I heard John Cronin say "I know I'll die on the operating table. You're going to kill me. I hope they get you for murder."'

An attorney, Roderick Pelham, was on the stand. Gus Venable said, 'When you told Dr Taylor about the million dollars from John Cronin's estate, what did she say?'

'She said something like "It seems unethical. He was my patient."'

'She admitted it was unethical?'

'Yes.'

'But she agreed to take the money?'

'Oh yes. Absolutely.'

*   *   *

Alan Penn was cross-examining.

'Mr Pelham, was Dr Taylor expecting your visit?'

'Why, no, I . . .'

'You didn't call her and say, "John Cronin left you one million dollars"?'

'No, I . . .'

'So when you told her, you were actually face to face with her?'

'Yes.'

'In a position to see her reaction to the news.'

'Yes.'

'And when you told her about the money, how did she react?'

'Well — she — she seemed surprised, but . . .'

'Thank you Mr Pelham. That's all.'

The trial was now in its fourth week. The spectators and press had found the prosecuting attorney and defense attorney fascinating to watch. Gus Venable was dressed in white and Alan Penn in black, and the two of them had moved around the courtroom like players in a deadly, choreographed game of chess, with Paige Taylor the sacrificial pawn.

Gus Venable was tying up the loose ends.

'If the court please, I would like to call Alma Rogers to the witness stand.'

When his witness was sworn in, Venable said, 'Mrs Rogers, what is your occupation?'

'It's *Miss* Rogers.'

'I do beg your pardon.'

'I work at the Corniche Travel Agency.'

'Your agency books tours to various countries and

12

makes hotel reservations and handles other accommodations for your clients?'

'Yes, sir.'

'I want you to take a look at the defendant. Have you ever seen her before?'

'Oh, yes. She came into our travel agency two or three years ago.'

'And what did she want?'

'She said she was interested in a trip to London and Paris, and, I believe, Venice.'

'Did she ask about package tours?'

'Oh, no. She said she wanted everything first-class—plane, hotel. And I believe she was interested in chartering a yacht.'

The courtroom was hushed. Gus Venable walked over to the prosecutor's table and held up some folders. 'The police found these brochures in Dr Taylor's apartment. These are travel itineraries to Paris and London and Venice, brochures for expensive hotels and airlines, and one listing the cost of chartering a private yacht.'

There was a loud murmur from the courtroom.

The prosecutor had opened one of the brochures.

'Here are some of the yachts listed for charter.' He read aloud. 'The *Christina O* . . . twenty-six thousand dollars a week plus ship's expenses . . . the *Resolute Time*, twenty-four thousand five hundred dollars a week . . . the *Lucky Dream*, twenty-seven thousand three hundred dollars a week.' He looked up. 'There's a check mark after the *Lucky Dream*. Paige Taylor had already selected the twenty-seven thousand three hundred a week yacht. She just hadn't selected her victim yet.'

13

'We'd like to have these marked Exhibit A.' Venable turned to Alan Penn and smiled. Alan Penn looked at Paige. She was staring down at the table, her face pale. 'Your witness.'

Penn rose to his feet, stalling, thinking fast.

'How is the travel business these days, Miss Rogers?'

'I beg your pardon?'

'I asked how business was. Is Corniche a large travel agency?'

'It's quite large, yes.'

'I imagine a lot of people come in to inquire about trips.'

'Oh, yes.'

'Would you say five or six people a day?'

'Oh, no!' Her voice was indignant. 'We talk to as many as fifty people a day about travel arrangements.'

'Fifty people a day?' He sounded impressed. 'And the day we're talking about was two or three years ago. If you multiply fifty by nine hundred days, that's roughly forty-five thousand people.'

'I suppose so.'

'And yet, out of all those people, you remembered Dr Taylor. Why is that?'

'Well, she and her two friends were so excited about taking a trip to Europe. I thought it was lovely. They were like schoolgirls. Oh, yes. I remember them very clearly, particularly because they didn't look like they could afford a yacht.'

'I see. I suppose everyone who comes in and asks for a brochure goes away on a trip?'

'Well, of course not. But —'

'Dr Taylor didn't actually *book* a trip, did she?'

14

'Well, no. Not with us. She—'

'Nor with anyone else. She merely asked to see some brochures.'

'Yes. She—'

'That's not the same as *going* to Paris or London, is it?'

'Well, no, but—'

'Thank you. You may step down.'

Venable turned to Judge Young. 'I would like to call Dr Benjamin Wallace to the stand . . .'

'Dr Wallace, you're in charge of administration at Embarcadero County Hospital?'

'Yes.'

'So, of course, you're familiar with Dr Taylor and her work?'

'Yes, I am.'

'Were you surprised to learn that Dr Taylor was indicted for murder?'

Penn was on his feet, 'Objection your honor. Dr Wallace's answer would be irrelevant.'

'If I may explain,' interrupted Venable. 'It could be very relevant if you'll just let me . . .'

'Well, let's see what develops,' said Judge Young. 'But no nonsense, Mr Venable.'

'Let me approach the question differently,' continued Venable. 'Dr Wallace, every physician is required to take the Hippocratic oath, is that not so?'

'Yes.'

'And part of that oath is . . . ,' the prosecutor read

15

from a paper in his hand, '"That I shall abstain from every act of mischief or corruption"?'

'Yes.'

'Was there anything Dr Taylor did in the past that made you believe she was capable of breaking her Hippocratic oath?'

'Objection.'

'Overruled.'

'Yes, there was.'

'Please explain what it was.'

'We had a patient who Dr Taylor decided needed a blood transfusion. His family refused to grant permission.'

'And what happened?'

'Dr Taylor went ahead and gave the patient the transfusion anyway.'

'Is that legal?'

'Absolutely not. Not without a court order.'

'And then what did Dr Taylor do?'

'She obtained the court order afterward, and changed the date on it.'

'So she performed an illegal act, and falsified the hospital records to cover it up?'

'That is correct.'

Alan Penn glanced over at Paige, furious. *What the hell else has she kept from me?* he wondered.

If the spectators were searching for any tell-tale sign of emotion on Paige Taylor's face, they were disappointed.

Cold as ice, the foreman of the jury was thinking.

Gus Venable turned to the bench. 'Your honor, as you know, one of the witnesses I had hoped to call

16

is a Dr Lawrence Barker. Unfortunately he is still suffering from the effects of a stroke and is unable to be in this courtroom to testify. Instead I will now question some of the hospital staff who have worked with Dr Barker.'

Penn stood up. 'I object. I don't see the relevance. Dr Barker is not here, nor is Dr Barker on trial here. If . . .'

Venable interrupted. 'Your honor, I assure you that my line of questioning is very relevant to the testimony we have just heard. It also has to do with the defendant's competency as a doctor.'

Judge Young said skeptically, 'We'll see. This is a courtroom, not a river. I won't stand for any fishing expeditions. You may call your witnesses.'

'Thank you.'

Gus Venable turned to the bailiff. 'I would like to call Dr Mathew Peterson.'

An elegant-looking man in his sixties approached the witness box. He was sworn in, and when he took his seat, Gus Venable said, 'Dr Peterson, how long have you worked at Embarcadero County Hospital?'

'Eight years.'

'And what is your specialty?'

'I'm a cardiac surgeon.'

'And during the years you've been at Embarcadero County Hospital, did you ever have occasion to work with Dr Lawrence Barker?'

'Oh, yes. Many times.'

'What was your opinion of him?'

'The same as everyone else's. Aside, possibly, from DeBakey and Cooley, Dr Barker is the best heart surgeon in the world.'

'Were you present in the operating room on the

17

morning that Dr Taylor operated on a patient named . . .' he pretended to consult a slip of paper. '. . . Lance Kelly?'

The witness's tone changed. 'Yes, I was there.'

'Would you describe what happened that morning?'

Dr Peterson said reluctantly, 'Well, things started to go wrong. We began losing the patient.'

'When you say, "losing the patient . . ."'

'His heart stopped. We were trying to bring him back, and . . .'

'Had Dr Barker been sent for?'

'Yes.'

'And did he come into the operating room while the operation was going on?'

'Toward the end. Yes. But it was too late to do anything. We were unable to revive the patient.'

'And did Dr Barker say anything to Dr Taylor at that time?'

'Well, we were all pretty upset, and . . .'

'I asked you if Dr Barker said anything to Dr Taylor.'

'Yes.'

'And what did Dr Barker say?'

There was a pause, and in the middle of the pause, there was a crack of thunder outside, like the voice of God. A moment later, the storm broke, nailing raindrops to the roof of the courthouse.

'Dr Barker said, "You killed him."'

The spectators were in an uproar. Judge Young slammed her gavel down. 'That's enough! Do you people live in caves? One more outburst like that and you'll all be standing outside in the rain.'

Gus Venable waited for the noise to die down. In

18

the hushed silence he said, 'Are you sure that's what Dr Barker said to Dr Taylor? "You killed him."'

'Yes.'

'And you have testified that Dr Barker was a man whose medical opinion was valued?'

'Oh, yes.'

'Thank you. That's all, doctor.' He turned to Alan Penn. 'Your witness.'

Penn rose and approached the witness box.

'Dr Peterson, I've never watched an operation, but I imagine there's enormous tension, especially when it's something as serious as a heart operation.'

'There's a great deal of tension.'

'At a time like that, how many people are in the room? Three or four?'

'Oh, no. Always half a dozen or more.'

'Really?'

'Yes. There are usually two surgeons, one assisting, sometimes two anesthesiologists, a scrub nurse, and at least one circulating nurse.'

'I see. Then there must be a lot of noise and excitement going on. People calling out instructions and so on.'

'Yes.'

'And I understand that it's a common practice for music to be playing during an operation.'

'It is.'

'When Dr Barker came in and saw that Lance Kelly was dying, that probably added to the confusion.'

'Well, everybody was pretty busy trying to save the patient.'

'Making a lot of noise?'

'There was plenty of noise, yes.'

'And yet, in all that confusion and noise, and over the music, you could hear Dr Barker say that Dr Taylor had killed the patient. With all that excitement, you could have been wrong, couldn't you?'

'No, sir. I could not be wrong.'

'What makes you so sure?'

Dr Peterson sighed. 'Because I was standing right next to Dr Barker when he said it.'

There was no graceful way out.

'No more questions.'

The case was falling apart, and there was nothing he could do about it. It was about to get worse.

Denise Berry took the witness stand.

'You're a nurse at Embarcadero County Hospital?'

'Yes.'

'How long have you worked there?'

'Five years.'

'During that time, did you ever hear any conversations between Dr Taylor and Dr Barker?'

'Sure. Lots of times.'

'Can you repeat some of them?'

Nurse Berry looked at Dr Taylor and hesitated. 'Well, Dr Barker could be very sharp . . .'

'I didn't ask you that, Nurse Berry. I asked you to tell us some specific things you heard him say to Dr Taylor.'

There was a long pause. 'Well, one time he said she was incompetent, and . . .'

Gus Venable put on a show of surprise. 'You heard Dr Barker say that Dr Taylor was incompetent?'

20

'Yes, sir. But he was always . . .'

'What other comments did you hear him make about Dr Taylor?'

The witness was reluctant to speak. 'I really can't remember.'

'Miss Berry, you're under oath.'

'Well, once I heard him say . . .' The rest of the sentence was a mumble.

'We can't hear you. Speak up, please. You heard him say what?'

'He said he . . . he wouldn't let Dr Taylor operate on his dog.'

There was a collective gasp from the courtroom.

'But I'm sure he only meant . . .'

'I think we can all assume that Dr Barker meant what he said.'

All eyes were fixed on Paige Taylor.

The prosecutor's case against Paige seemed overwhelming. Yet Alan Penn had the reputation of being a master magician in the courtroom. Now it was his turn to present the defendant's case. Could he pull another rabbit out of his hat?

Paige Taylor was on the witness stand, being questioned by Alan Penn. This was the moment everyone had been waiting for.

'John Cronin was a patient of yours, Dr Taylor?'

'Yes, he was.'

'And what were your feelings toward him?'

'I liked him. He knew how ill he was, but he was

21

very courageous. He had surgery for a cardiac tumor.'

'You performed the heart surgery?'

'Yes.'

'And what did you find during the operation?'

'When we opened up his chest, we found that he had melanoma that had metastasized.'

'In other words, cancer that had spread throughout his body.'

'Yes. It had metastasized throughout the lymph glands.'

'Meaning that there was no hope for him? No heroic measures that could bring him back to health?'

'None.'

'John Cronin was put on life-support systems?'

'That's correct.'

'Dr Taylor, did you deliberately administer a fatal dose of insulin to end John Cronin's life?'

'I did.'

There was a sudden buzz in the courtroom.

She's really a cool one, Gus Venable thought. *She makes it sound as though she gave him a cup of tea.*

'Would you tell the jury why you ended John Cronin's life?'

'Because he asked me to. He begged me to. He sent for me in the middle of the night, in terrible pain. The medications we were giving him were no longer working.' Her voice was steady. 'He said he didn't want to suffer anymore. His death was only a few days away. He pleaded with me to end it for him. I did.'

'Doctor, did you have any reluctance to let him die? Any feelings of guilt?'

22

Dr Paige Taylor shook her head. 'No. If you could have seen . . . There was simply no point to letting him go on suffering.'

'How did you administer the insulin?'

'I injected it into his IV.'

'And did that cause him any additional pain?'

'No. He simply drifted off to sleep.'

Gus Venable was on his feet. 'Objection! I think the defendant means he drifted off to his death! I —'

Judge Young slammed down her gavel. 'Mr Venable, you're out of order. You'll have your chance to cross-examine the witness. Sit down.'

The prosecutor looked over at the jury, shook his head, and took his seat.

'Dr Taylor, when you administered the insulin to John Cronin, were you aware that he had put you in his will for one million dollars?'

'No. I was stunned when I learned about it.'

Her nose should be growing, Gus Venable thought.

'You never discussed money or gifts at any time, or asked John Cronin for anything?'

A faint flush came to her cheeks. 'Never!'

'But you were on friendly terms with him?'

'Yes. When a patient is that ill, the doctor-patient relationship changes. We discussed his business problems and his family problems.'

'But you had no reason to expect anything from him?'

'No.'

'He left that money to you because he had grown to respect you and trust you. Thank you, Dr Taylor.' Penn turned to Gus Venable. 'Your witness.'

23

As Penn returned to the defense table, Paige Taylor glanced toward the back of the courtroom. Jason was seated there, trying to look encouraging. Next to him was Honey. A stranger was sitting next to Honey in the seat that Kat should have occupied. *If she were still alive. But Kat was dead*, Paige thought. *I killed her, too.*

Gus Venable rose and slowly shuffled over to the witness box. He glanced at the rows of press. Every seat was filled, and the reporters were all busily scribbling. *I'm going to give you something to write about*, Venable thought.

He stood in front of the defendant for a long moment, studying her. Then he said casually, 'Dr Taylor . . . was John Cronin the first patient you murdered at Embarcadero County Hospital?'

Alan Penn was on his feet, furious. 'Your honor, I —'

Judge Young had already slammed her gavel down. 'Objection sustained!' She turned to the two attorneys. 'There will be a fifteen-minute recess. I want to see counsel in my chambers.'

When the two attorneys were in her chambers, Judge Young turned to Gus Venable. 'You *did* go to law school, didn't you, Gus?'

'I'm sorry, your honor. I —'

'Did you see a tent out there?'

'I beg your pardon?'

Her voice was a whiplash. 'My courtroom is not a circus, and I don't intend to let you turn it into one. How dare you ask an inflammatory question like that!'

24

'I apologize, your honor. I'll rephrase the question and —'

'You'll do more than that!' Judge Young snapped. 'You'll rephrase your attitude. I'm warning you, you pull one more stunt like that and I'll declare a mistrial.'

'Yes, your honor.'

When they returned to the courtroom, Judge Young said to the jury, 'The jury will completely disregard the prosecutor's last question.' She turned to the prosecutor. 'You may go on.'

Gus Venable walked back to the witness box. 'Dr Taylor, you must have been very surprised when you were informed that the man you murdered left you one million dollars.'

Alan Penn was on his feet. 'Objection!'

'Sustained.' Judge Young turned to Venable. 'You're trying my patience.'

'I apologize, your honor.' He turned back to the witness. 'You must have been on *very* friendly terms with your patient. I mean, it isn't every day that an almost complete stranger leaves us a million dollars, is it?'

Paige Taylor flushed slightly. 'Our friendship was in the context of a doctor-patient relationship.'

'Wasn't it a little more than that? A man doesn't cut his beloved wife and family out of his will and leave a million dollars to a stranger without some kind of persuasion. Those talks you claimed to have had with him about his business problems . . .'

Judge Young leaned forward and said warningly, 'Mr Venable . . .' The prosecutor raised his hands in a gesture of surrender. He turned back to the defendant. 'So you and John Cronin had a friendly chat. He told you personal things about himself, and he liked you and respected you. Would you say that's a fair summation, doctor?'

'Yes.'

'And for doing that he gave you a million dollars?'

Paige looked out at the courtroom. She said nothing. She had no answer.

Venable started to walk back toward the prosecutor's table, then suddenly turned to face the defendant again.

'Dr Taylor, you testified earlier that you had no idea that John Cronin was going to leave you any money, or that he was going to cut his family out of his will.'

'That's correct.'

'How much does a resident doctor make at Embarcadero County Hospital?'

Alan Penn was on his feet. 'Objection! I don't see —'

'It's a proper question. The witness may answer.'

'Thirty-eight thousand dollars a year.'

Venable said sympathetically, 'That's not very much these days, is it? And out of that, there are deductions and taxes and living expenses. That wouldn't leave enough to take a luxury vacation trip, say, to London or Paris or Venice, would it?'

'I suppose not.'

'No. So you didn't plan to take a vacation like that, because you knew you couldn't afford it.'

'That's correct.'

Alan Penn was on his feet again. 'Your honor . . .'

Judge Young turned to the prosecutor. 'Where is this leading, Mr Venable?'

'I just want to establish that the defendant could not plan a luxury trip without getting the money from someone.'

'She's already answered the question.'

Alan Penn knew he had to do something. His heart wasn't in it, but he approached the witness box with all the good cheer of a man who had just won the lottery.

'Dr Taylor, do you remember picking up these travel brochures?'

'Yes.'

'Were you planning to go to Europe or to charter a yacht?'

'Of course not. It was all sort of a joke, an impossible dream. My friends and I thought it would lift our spirits. We were very tired, and . . . it seemed like a good idea at the time.' Her voice trailed off.

Alan Penn glanced covertly at the jury. Their faces registered pure disbelief.

Gus Venable was questioning the defendant on re-examination. 'Dr Taylor, are you acquainted with Dr Lawrence Barker?'

She had a sudden memory flash. *I'm going to kill Lawrence Barker. I'll do it slowly. I'll let him suffer first . . . then I'll kill him.* 'Yes. I know Dr Barker.'

'In what connection?'

'Dr Barker and I have often worked together during the past two years.'

27

'Would you say that he's a competent doctor?'

Alan Penn jumped up from his chair. 'I object, your honor. The witness . . .'

But before he could finish or Judge Young could rule, Paige answered, 'He's more than competent. He's brilliant.'

Penn sank back in his chair, too stunned to speak.

'Would you care to elaborate on that?'

'Dr Barker is one of the most renowned cardio-vascular surgeons in the world. He had a large private practice, but he donated three days a week to Embarcadero County Hospital.'

'So you have a high regard for his judgement in medical matters?'

'Yes.'

'And do you feel he would be capable of judging another doctor's competence?'

Penn willed Paige to say, *I don't know.*

She hesitated. 'Yes.'

Gus Venable turned to the jury. 'You've heard the defendant testify that she had a high regard for Dr Barker's medical judgement. I hope she listened carefully to Dr Barker's judgement about her competence . . . Or the lack of it.'

Alan Penn was on his feet, furious. 'Objection!'

'Sustained.'

But it was too late. The damage had been done.

During the next recess, Alan Penn pulled Jason into the men's room.

'What the hell have you gotten me into?' Penn demanded angrily. 'John Cronin hated her, Barker hated her. I insist on my clients telling me the truth, and the whole truth. That's the only way I can help them. Well, I can't help *her*. Your lady friend has given me a snow job so deep I need skis. Every time she opens her mouth she puts a nail in her coffin. The fucking case is in free fall!'

That afternoon, Jason Curtis went to see Paige.

'You have a visitor, Dr Taylor.'

Jason walked into Paige's cell.

'Paige . . .'

She turned to him, and she was fighting back tears. 'It looks pretty bad, doesn't it?'

Jason forced a smile. 'You know what the man said—It's not over till it's over.'

'Jason, you don't believe that I killed John Cronin for his money, do you? What I did, I did only to help him.'

'I believe you,' Jason said quietly. 'I love you.'

He took her into his arms. *I don't want to lose her*, Jason thought. *I can't. She's the best thing in my life.* 'Everything is going to be all right. I promised you we would be together forever.'

Paige held him close and thought, *Nothing lasts forever. Nothing. How could everything have gone so wrong . . . so wrong . . . so wrong . . .*

Book One

1

San Francisco
July, 1990

'Hunter, Kate.'
  'Here.'
  'Taft, Betty Lou.'
  'I'm here.'
  'Taylor, Paige.'
  'Here.'
They were the only women among the big group of incoming first-year residents gathered in the large, drab auditorium at Embarcadero County Hospital.

Embarcadero County was the oldest hospital in San Francisco, and one of the oldest in the country. During the earthquake of 1989, God had played a joke on the residents of San Francisco and left the hospital standing. It was an ugly complex, occupying more than three square blocks, with buildings of brick and stone, gray with years of accumulated grime.

Inside the front entrance of the main building was a large waiting room, with hard wooden benches for patients and visitors. The walls were flaking from too many decades of coats of paint, and the corridors were worn and uneven from too many thousands of patients in wheelchairs and on crutches and walkers. The entire complex was coated with the stale patina of time.

Embarcadero County Hospital was a city within a city. There were over nine thousand people employed at the hospital, including four hundred staff physicians, one hundred and fifty part-time voluntary physicians, eight hundred residents, and three thousand nurses, plus the technicians, unit aides, and other technical personnel. The upper floors contained a complex of twelve operating rooms, central supply, a bone bank, central scheduling, three emergency wards, an AIDS ward, and over two thousand beds.

Now, on the first day of the arrival of the new residents in July, Dr Benjamin Wallace, the hospital administrator, rose to address them. Wallace was the quintessential politician, a tall, impressive-looking man with small skills and enough charm to have ingratiated his way up to his present position.

'I want to welcome all of you new resident doctors this morning. For the first two years of medical school, you worked with cadavers. In the last two years, you have worked with hospital patients under the supervision of senior doctors. Now, it's *you* who are going to be responsible for your patients. It's an awesome responsibility, and it takes dedication and skill.'

His eyes scanned the auditorium. 'Some of you are planning to go into surgery. Others of you will be going into internal medicine. Each group will be assigned to a senior resident who will explain the

34

daily routine to you. From now on, everything you do could be a matter of life or death.'

They were listening intently, hanging on every word.

'Embarcadero is a county hospital. That means we admit anyone who comes to our door. Most of the patients are indigent. They come here because they can't afford a private hospital. Our emergency rooms are busy twenty-four hours a day. You're going to be overworked and underpaid. In a private hospital, your first year would consist of routine scut work. In the second year, you would be allowed to hand a scalpel to the surgeon, and in your third year, you would be permitted to do some supervised minor surgery. Well, you can forget all that. Our motto here is "Watch one, do one, teach one."

'We're badly understaffed, and the quicker we can get you into the operating rooms, the better. Are there any questions?'

There were a million questions the new residents wanted to ask.

'None? Good. Your first day officially begins tomorrow. You will report to the main reception desk at five-thirty tomorrow morning. Good luck!'

The briefing was over. There was a general exodus toward the doors and the low buzz of excited conversations. The three women found themselves standing together.

'Where are all the other women?'

'I think we're it.'

'It's a lot like medical school, huh? The boys' club. I have a feeling this place belongs to the Dark Ages.'

The person talking was a flawlessly beautiful black woman, nearly six feet tall, large-boned, but

35

intensely graceful. Everything about her, her walk, her carriage, the cool, quizzical look she carried in her eyes, sent out a message of aloofness. 'I'm Kate Hunter. They call me Kat.'

'Paige Taylor.' Young and friendly, intelligent-looking, self-assured.

They turned to the third woman.

'Betty Lou Taft. They call me Honey.' She spoke with a soft Southern accent. She had an open, guile-less face, soft gray eyes, and a warm smile.

'Where are you from?' Kat asked.

'Memphis, Tennessee.'

They looked at Paige. She decided to give them the simple answer. 'Boston.'

'Minneapolis,' Kat said. *That's close enough*, she thought.

Paige said, 'It looks like we're all a long way from home. Where are you staying?'

'I'm at a fleabag hotel,' Kat said. 'I haven't had a chance to look for a place to live.'

Honey said, 'Neither have I.'

Paige brightened. 'I looked at some apartments this morning. One of them was terrific, but I can't afford it. It has three bedrooms . . .'

They stared at one another.

'If the three of us shared . . .' Kat said.

The apartment was in the Marina district, on Filbert Street. It was perfect for them. 3Br/2Ba, nu cpts, lndry, prkg, utils pd. It was furnished in early Sears Roebuck, but it was neat and clean.

When the three women were through inspecting it, Honey said, 'I think it's lovely.'

'So do I!' Kat agreed.

They looked at Paige.

'Let's take it.'

They moved into the apartment that afternoon. The janitor helped them carry their luggage upstairs.

'So you're gonna work at the hospital,' he said. 'Nurses, huh?'

'Doctors,' Kat corrected him.

He looked at her skeptically. 'Doctors? You mean, like *real* doctors?'

'Yes, like real doctors,' Paige told him.

He grunted. 'Tell you the truth, if I needed medical attention, I don't think I'd want a woman examining my body.'

'We'll keep that in mind.'

'Where's the television set?' Kat asked. 'I don't see one.'

'If you want one, you'll have to buy it. Enjoy the apartment, ladies—er, doctors.' He chuckled.

They watched him leave.

Kat said, imitating his voice, 'Nurses, eh?' She snorted. 'Male chauvinist. Well, let's pick out our bedrooms.'

'Any one of them is fine with me,' Honey said softly.

They examined the three bedrooms. The master bedroom was larger than the other two.

Kat said, 'Why don't you take it, Paige? You found this place.'

Paige nodded. 'All right.'

They went to their respective rooms and began to unpack. From her suitcase, Paige carefully removed a framed photograph of a man in his early thirties. He was attractive, wearing black-framed glasses that

37

gave him a scholarly look. Paige put the photograph at her bedside, next to a bundle of letters.

Kat and Honey wandered in. 'How about going out and getting some dinner?'

'I'm ready,' Paige said.

Kat saw the photograph. 'Who's that?'

Paige smiled. 'That's the man I'm going to marry. He's a doctor who works for the World Health Organization. His name is Alfred Turner. He's working in Africa right now, but he's coming to San Francisco so we can be together.'

'Lucky you,' Honey said wistfully. 'He looks nice.'

Paige looked at her. 'Are you involved with anyone?'

'No. I'm afraid I don't have much luck with men.'

Kat said, 'Maybe your luck will change at Embarcadero.'

The three of them had dinner at Tarantino's, not far from their apartment building. During dinner they chatted about their backgrounds and lives, but there was a restraint to their conversation, a holding back. They were three strangers, probing, cautiously getting to know one another.

Honey spoke very little. *There's a shyness about her*, Paige thought. *She's vulnerable. Some man in Memphis probably broke her heart.*

Paige looked at Kat. *Self-confident. Great dignity. I like the way she speaks. You can tell she came from a good family.*

Meanwhile, Kat was studying Paige. *A rich girl who never had to work for anything in her life. She's gotten by on her looks.*

Honey was looking at the two of them. *They're so confident, so sure of themselves. They're going to have an easy time of it.*

They were all mistaken.

When they returned to their apartment, Paige was too excited to sleep. She lay in bed, thinking about the future. Outside her window, in the street, there was the sound of a car crash, and then people shouting, and in Paige's mind it dissolved into the memory of African natives yelling and chanting, and guns being fired. She was transported back in time, to the small jungle village in East Africa, caught in the middle of a deadly tribal war.

Paige was terrified. 'They're going to kill us!'

Her father took her in his arms. 'They won't harm us, darling. We're here to help them. They know we're their friends.'

And without warning, the chief of one of the tribes had burst into their hut . . .

Honey lay in bed thinking, *This is sure a long way from Memphis, Tennessee, Betty Lou. I guess I can never go back there. Never again.* She could hear the sheriff's voice saying to her, 'Out of respect for his family, we're going to list the death of the Reverend Douglas Lipton as a "suicide for reasons unknown," but I would suggest that you get the fuck out of this town fast, and stay out . . .'

*   *   *

Kat was staring out the window of her bedroom, listening to the sounds of the city. A voice inside her head whispered, *You made it . . . you made it . . . I showed them all they were wrong. You want to be a doctor? A black woman doctor? And the rejections from medical schools. 'Thank you for sending us your application. Unfortunately our enrollment is complete at this time.'*

'In view of your background, perhaps we might suggest that you would be happier at a smaller university.'

She had top grades, but out of twenty-five schools she had applied to, only one had accepted her. The dean of the school had said, 'In these days, it's nice to see someone who comes from a normal, decent background.'

If he had only known the terrible truth.

2

At five-thirty the following morning, when the new residents checked in, members of the hospital staff were standing by to guide them to their various assignments. Even at that early hour, the bedlam had begun.

The patients had been coming in all night, arriving in ambulances, and police cars, and on foot. The staff called them the 'F and J's'—the flotsam and jetsam that streamed into the emergency rooms, broken and bleeding, victims of shootings and stabbings and automobile accidents, the wounded in flesh and spirit, the homeless and the unwanted, the ebb and flow of humanity that streamed through the dark sewers of every large city.

There was a pervasive feeling of organized chaos, frenetic movements and shrill sounds and dozens of unexpected crises that all had to be attended to at once.

The new residents stood in a protective huddle, getting attuned to their new environment, listening to the arcane sounds around them.

Paige, Kat, and Honey were waiting in the corridor when a senior resident approached them. 'Which one of you is Dr Taft?'

Honey looked up and said, 'I am.'

41

The resident smiled and held out his hand. 'It's an honor to meet you. I've been asked to look out for you. Our chief of staff says that you have the highest medical school grades this hospital has ever seen. We're delighted to have you here.'

Honey smiled, embarrassed. 'Thank you.'

Kat and Paige looked at Honey in astonishment. *I wouldn't have guessed she was that brilliant*, Paige thought.

'You're planning to go into internal medicine, Dr Taft?'

'Yes.'

The resident turned to Kat. 'Dr Hunter?'

'Yes.'

'You're interested in neurosurgery.'

'I am.'

He consulted a list. 'You'll be assigned to Dr Lewis.'

The resident looked over at Paige. 'Dr Taylor?'

'Yes.'

'You're going into cardiac surgery.'

'That's right.'

'Fine. We'll assign you and Dr Hunter to surgical rounds. You can report to the head nurse's office. Margaret Spencer. Down the hall.'

'Thank you.'

Paige looked at the others and took a deep breath. 'Here I go! I wish us all luck!'

Margaret Spencer was more a battleship than a woman, heavyset and stern-looking, with a brusque manner. She was busy behind the nurses' station when Paige approached.

'Excuse me . . .'

Nurse Spencer looked up. 'Yes?'

'I was told to report here. I'm Dr Taylor.'

Nurse Spencer consulted a sheet. 'Just a moment.' She walked through a door and returned a minute later with some scrubs and a white coat.

'Here you are. The scrubs are to wear in the operating theater, and on rounds. And when you're doing rounds you put a white coat over the scrubs.'

'Thanks.'

'Oh. And here.' She reached down and handed Paige a metal tag that read 'Paige Taylor, M.D.' 'Here's your name tag, doctor.'

Paige held it in her hand and looked at it for a long time. *Paige Taylor, M.D.* She felt as though she had been handed the Medal of Honor. All the long hard years of work and study were summed up in those brief words. *Paige Taylor, M.D.*

Nurse Spencer was watching her. 'Are you all right?'

'I'm fine.' Paige smiled. 'I'm just fine, thank you. Where do I . . . ?'

'Doctors' dressing room is down the corridor to the left. You'll be making rounds, so you'll want to change.'

'Thank you.'

Paige walked down the corridor, amazed at the amount of activity around her. The corridor was crowded with doctors, nurses, technicians, and patients, hurrying to various destinations. The insistent chatter of the public address system added to the din.

'Dr Keenan . . . OR Three . . . Dr Keenan . . . OR Three.'

'Dr Talbot . . . Emergency Room One. Stat . . . Dr Talbot . . . Emergency Room One. Stat.'

'Dr Engel . . . Room 212 . . . Dr Engel . . . Room 212.'

Paige approached a door marked DOCTORS' DRESSING ROOM and opened it. Inside there were a dozen male doctors in various stages of undress. Two of them were totally naked. They turned to stare at Paige as the door opened.

'Oh! I . . . I'm sorry,' Paige mumbled, and quickly closed the door. She stood there, uncertain about what to do. A few feet down the corridor, she saw a door marked NURSES' DRESSING ROOM. Paige walked over to it and opened the door. Inside, several nurses were changing into their uniforms.

One of them looked up. 'Hello. Are you one of the new nurses?'

'No,' Paige said tightly. 'I'm not.' She closed the door and walked back to the doctors' dressing room. She stood there a moment, then took a deep breath and entered. The conversation came to a stop.

One of the men said, 'Sorry, honey. This room is for doctors.'

'I'm a doctor,' Paige said.

They turned to look at one another. 'Oh? Well, er . . . welcome.'

'Thank you.' She hesitated a moment, then walked over to an empty locker. The men watched as she put her hospital clothes into the locker. She looked at the men for a moment, then slowly started to unbutton her blouse.

The doctors stood there, not sure what to do. One of them said, 'Maybe we should—er—give the little lady some privacy, gentlemen.'

44

The little lady! 'Thank you,' Paige said. She stood there, waiting, as the doctors finished dressing and left the room. *Am I going to have to go through this every day?* she wondered.

In hospital rounds, there is a traditional formation that never varies. The attending physician is always in the lead, followed by the senior resident, then the other residents, and one or two medical students. The attending physician Paige had been assigned to was Dr William Radnor. Paige and five other residents were gathered in the hallway, waiting to meet him.

In the group was a young Chinese doctor. He held out his hand. 'Tom Chang,' he said. 'I hope you're all as nervous as I am.'

Paige liked him immediately.

A man was approaching the group. 'Good morning,' he said. 'I'm Dr Radnor.' He was soft-spoken, with sparkling blue eyes. Each resident introduced himself.

'This is your first day of rounds. I want you to pay close attention to everything you see and hear, but at the same time, it's important to appear relaxed.'

Paige made a mental note. *Pay close attention, but appear to be relaxed.*

'If the patients see that you're tense, *they're* going to be tense, and they'll probably think they're dying of some disease you aren't telling them about.'

Don't make patients tense.

'Remember, from now on, you're going to be responsible for the lives of other human beings.'

Now responsible for other lives. Oh, my God!

The longer Dr Radnor talked, the more nervous Paige became, and by the time he was finished, her self-confidence had completely vanished. *I'm not ready for this!* she thought. *I don't know what I'm doing. Who ever said I could be a doctor? What if I kill somebody?*

Dr Radnor was going on, 'I will expect detailed notes on each one of your patients—lab work, blood, electrolytes, everything. Is that clear?'

There were murmurs of 'Yes, doctor.'

'There are always thirty to forty surgical patients here at one time. It's your job to make sure that everything is properly organized for them. We'll start the morning rounds now. In the afternoon, we'll make the same rounds again.'

It had all seemed so easy at medical school. Paige thought about the four years she had spent there. There had been one hundred and fifty students, and only fifteen women. She would never forget the first day of Gross Anatomy class. The students had walked into a large white tiled room with twenty tables lined up in rows, each table covered with a yellow sheet. Five students were assigned to each table.

The professor had said, 'All right, pull back the sheets.' And there, in front of Paige, was her first cadaver. She had been afraid that she would faint or be sick, but she felt strangely calm. The cadaver had been preserved, which somehow removed it one step from humanity.

In the beginning the students had been hushed and

respectful in the anatomy laboratory. But, incredibly to Paige, within a week, they were eating sandwiches during the dissections, and making rude jokes. It was a form of self-defense, a denial of their own mortality. They gave the corpses names, and treated them like old friends. Paige tried to force herself to act as casually as the other students, but she found it difficult. She looked at the cadaver she was working on, and thought: *Here was a man with a home and a family. He went to an office every day, and once a year he took a vacation with his wife and children. He probably loved sports and enjoyed movies and plays, and he laughed and cried, and he watched his children grow up and he shared their joys and their sorrows, and he had big, wonderful dreams. I hope they all came true . . .* A bittersweet sadness engulfed her because he was dead and *she* was alive.

In time, even to Paige, the dissections became routine. *Open the chest, examine the ribs, lungs, pericardial sac covering the heart, the veins, arteries, and nerves.*

Much of the first two years of medical school was spent memorizing long lists that the students referred to as the Organ Recital. First the cranial nerves: olfactory, optic, oculomotor, trochlear, trigeminal, abducens, facial, auditory, glossopharyngeal, vagus, spinal, and hypoglossal.

The students used mnemonics to help them remember. The classic one was '*O*n *o*ld *O*lympus's *t*owering *t*ops, *a* *F*rench *a*nd *G*erman *v*ended *s*ome *h*ops.' The modern male version was '*O*h, *o*h, *o*h, *t*o *t*ouch *a*nd *f*eel *a* girl's *v*agina—*s*uch *h*eaven.'

The last two years of medical school were more

interesting, with courses in internal medicine, surgery, pediatrics, and obstetrics, and they worked at the local hospital. *I remember the time . . .* Paige was thinking.

'Dr Taylor . . .' The senior resident was staring at her.

Paige came to with a start. The others were already halfway down the corridor.

'Coming,' she said hastily.

The first stop was at a large, rectangular ward, with rows of beds on both sides of the room, with a small stand next to each bed. Paige had expected to see curtains separating the beds, but here there was no privacy.

The first patient was an elderly man with a sallow complexion. He was sound asleep, breathing heavily. Dr Radnor walked over to the foot of the bed, studied the chart there, then went to the patient's side and gently touched his shoulder. 'Mr Potter?'

The patient opened his eyes. 'Huh?'

'Good morning. I'm Dr Radnor. I'm just checking to see how you're doing. Did you have a comfortable night?'

'It was okay.'

'Do you have any pain?'

'Yeah. My chest hurts.'

'Let me take a look at it.'

When he finished the examination, he said, 'You're doing fine. I'll have the nurse give you something for the pain.'

'Thanks, doctor.'

'We'll be back to see you this afternoon.'

They moved away from the bed. Dr Radnor turned to the residents. 'Always try to ask questions that have a yes or no answer so the patient doesn't tire himself out. And reassure him about his progress. I want you to study his chart and make notes. We'll come back here this afternoon to see how he's doing. Keep a running record of every patient's chief complaint, present illness, past illnesses, family history, and social history. Does he drink, smoke, etc.? When we make the rounds again, I'll expect a report on the progress of each patient.'

They moved on to the bed of the next patient, a man in his forties.

'Good morning, Mr Rawlings.'

'Good morning, doctor.'

'Are you feeling better this morning?'

'Not so good. I was up a lot last night. My stomach's hurting.'

Dr Radnor turned to the senior resident. 'What did the proctoscopy show?'

'No sign of any problem.'

'Give him a barium enema and an upper GI, stat.'

The senior resident made a note.

The resident standing next to Paige whispered in her ear, 'I guess you know what stat stands for. "Shake that ass, tootsie!"'

Dr Radnor heard. '"Stat" comes from the Latin, *statim*. Immediately.'

In the years ahead, Paige was to hear it often.

The next patient was an elderly woman who had had a by-pass operation.

'Good morning, Mrs Turkel.'

'How long are you going to keep me in here?'

'Not very long. The procedure was a success. You'll be going home soon.'

And they moved on to the next patient.

The routine was repeated over and over, and the morning went by swiftly. They saw thirty patients. After each patient, the residents frantically scribbled notes, praying that they would be able to decipher them later.

One patient was a puzzle to Paige. She seemed to be in perfect health.

When they had moved away from her, Paige asked, 'What's her problem, doctor?'

Dr Radnor sighed. 'She has no problem. She's a gomer. And for those of you who forgot what you were taught in medical school, gomer is an acronym for "Get out of my emergency room!" Gomers are people who *enjoy* poor health. That's their hobby. I've admitted her six times in the last year.'

They moved on to the last patient, an old woman on a respirator, who was in a coma.

'She's had a massive heart attack,' Dr Radnor explained to the residents. 'She's been in a coma for six weeks. Her vital signs are failing. There's nothing more we can do for her. We'll pull the plug this afternoon.'

Paige looked at him in shock. 'Pull the plug?'

Dr Radnor said gently, 'The hospital ethics committee made the decision this morning. She's a vegetable. She's eighty-seven years old, and she's brain-dead. It's cruel to keep her alive, and it's breaking her family financially. I'll see you all at rounds this afternoon.'

They watched him walk away. Paige turned to look

at the patient again. She was alive. *In a few hours she will be dead. We'll pull the plug this afternoon.*
That's murder! Paige thought.

3

That afternoon, when the rounds were finished, the new residents gathered in the small upstairs lounge. The room held eight tables, an ancient black-and-white television set, and two vending machines that dispensed stale sandwiches and bitter coffee.

The conversations at each table were almost identical.

One of the residents said, 'Take a look at my throat, will you? Does it look raw to you?'

'I think I have a fever. I feel lousy.'

'My abdomen is swollen and tender. I know I have appendicitis.'

'I've got this crushing pain in my chest. I hope to God I'm not having a heart attack!'

Kat sat down at a table with Paige and Honey. 'How did it go?' she asked.

Honey said, 'I think it went all right.'

They both looked at Paige. 'I was tense, but I was relaxed. I was nervous, but I stayed calm.' She sighed. 'It's been a long day. I'll be glad to get out of here and have some fun tonight.'

'Me, too,' Kat agreed. 'Why don't we have dinner and then go see a movie?'

'Sounds great.'

An orderly approached their table. 'Dr Taylor?'

Paige looked up. 'I'm Dr Taylor.'

'Dr Wallace would like to see you in his office.'

The hospital administrator! *What have I done?* Paige wondered.

The orderly was waiting. 'Dr Taylor . . .'

'I'm coming.' She took a deep breath and got to her feet. 'I'll see you later.'

'This way, doctor.'

Paige followed the orderly into an elevator and rode up to the fifth floor, where Dr Wallace's office was located.

Benjamin Wallace was seated behind his desk. He glanced up as Paige walked in. 'Good afternoon, Dr Taylor.'

'Good afternoon.'

Wallace cleared his throat. 'Well! Your first day and you've already made quite an impression!'

Paige looked at him, puzzled. 'I . . . I don't understand.'

'I hear you had a little problem in the doctors' dressing room this morning.'

'Oh.' *So, that's what this is all about!*

Wallace looked at her and smiled. 'I suppose I'll have to make some arrangements for you and the other girls.'

'We're . . .' *We're not girls*, Paige started to say. 'We would appreciate that.'

'Meanwhile, if you don't want to dress with the nurses . . .'

'I'm not a nurse,' Paige said firmly. 'I'm a doctor.'

'Of course, of course. Well, we'll do something about accommodations for you, doctor.'

'Thank you.'

He handed Paige a sheet of paper. 'Meanwhile, this is your schedule. You'll be on call for the next twenty-four hours, starting at six o'clock.' He looked at his watch. 'That's thirty minutes from now.'

Paige was looking at him in astonishment. Her day had started at five-thirty that morning. *'Twenty-four hours?'*

'Well, thirty-six, actually. Because you'll be starting rounds again in the morning.'

Thirty-six hours! I wonder if I can handle this.

She was soon to find out.

Paige went to look for Kat and Honey.

'I'm going to have to forget about dinner and a movie,' Paige said. 'I'm on a thirty-six-hour call.'

Kat nodded. 'We just got our bad news. I go on it tomorrow, and Honey goes on Wednesday.'

'It won't be so bad,' Paige said cheerfully. 'I understand there's an on-call room to sleep in. I'm going to enjoy this.'

She was wrong.

An orderly was leading Paige down a long corridor.

'Dr Wallace told me that I'll be on call for thirty-six hours,' Paige said. 'Do all the residents work those hours?'

'Only for the first three years,' the orderly assured her.

Great!

'But you'll have plenty of chance to rest, doctor.'

'I will?'

'In here. This is the on-call room.' He opened the door, and Paige stepped inside. The room resembled a monk's cell in some poverty-stricken monastery. It contained nothing but a cot with a lumpy mattress, a cracked washbasin, and a bedside stand with a telephone on it. 'You can sleep here between calls.'

'Thanks.'

The calls began as Paige was in the coffee shop, just starting to have her dinner.

'Dr Taylor . . . ER Three . . . Dr Taylor . . . ER Three.'

And all the time she was pursued by nurses.

'We have a patient with a fractured rib . . .'

'Mr Henegan is complaining of chest pains . . .'

'The patient in Ward Two has a headache. Is it all right to give him an acetaminophen . . . ?'

At midnight, Paige had just managed to fall asleep when she was awakened by the telephone.

'Report to ER One.' It was a knife wound, and by the time Paige had taken care of it, it was one-thirty in the morning. At two-fifteen she was awakened again.

'Dr Taylor . . . Emergency Room Two. Stat.'

Paige said, groggily, 'Right.' *What did he say it meant? Shake that ass, tootsie.* She forced herself up and moved down the corridor to the emergency room. A patient had been brought in with a broken leg. He was screaming with pain.

'Get an X-ray,' Paige ordered. 'And give him Demerol, 50 milligrams.' She put her hand on the patient's arm. 'You're going to be fine. Try to relax.'

Over the PA system, a metallic disembodied voice said, 'Dr Taylor . . . Ward Three. Stat.'

Paige looked at the moaning patient, reluctant to leave him.

The voice came on again, 'Dr Taylor . . . Ward Three. Stat.'

'Coming,' Paige mumbled. She hurried out the door and down the corridor to Ward Three. A patient had vomited, aspirated, and was choking.

'He can't breathe,' the nurse said.

'Suction him,' Paige ordered. As she watched the patient begin to catch his breath, she heard her name again on the PA system. 'Dr Taylor . . . Ward Four. Ward Four.' Paige shook her head and ran down to Ward Four, to a screaming patient with abdominal spasms. Paige gave him a quick examination. 'It could be intestinal dysfunction. Get an ultrasound,' Paige said.

By the time she returned to the patient with the broken leg, the pain reliever had taken effect. She had him moved to the operating room and set the leg. As she was finishing, she heard her name again. 'Dr Taylor, report to Emergency Room Two. Stat.'

'The stomach ulcer in Ward Four is having a pain . . .'

At 3:30 A.M.: 'Dr Taylor, the patient in Room 310 is hemorrhaging . . .'

There was a heart attack in one of the wards, and Paige was nervously listening to the patient's heartbeat when she heard her name called over the PA system: 'Dr Taylor . . . ER Two. Stat . . . Dr Taylor . . . ER Two. Stat.'

I must not panic, Paige thought. *I've got to remain calm and cool.* She panicked. Who was more important, the patient she was examining, or the next patient? 'You stay here,' she said inanely. 'I'll be right back.'

As Paige hurried toward ER Two, she heard her name called again. 'Dr Taylor . . . ER One. Stat . . . Dr Taylor . . . ER One. Stat.'

Oh, my God! Paige thought. She felt as though she were caught up in the middle of some endless terrifying nightmare.

During what was left of the night, Paige was awakened to attend to a case of food poisoning, a broken arm, a hiatal hernia, and a fractured rib. By the time she stumbled back into the on-call room, she was so exhausted that she could hardly move. She crawled onto the little cot and had just started to doze off when the telephone rang.

She reached out for it with her eyes closed. 'H'lo . . .'

'Dr Taylor, we're waiting for you.'

'Wha'?' She lay there, trying to remember where she was.

'Your rounds are starting, doctor.'

'My rounds?' *This is some kind of bad joke*, Paige thought. *It's inhuman. They can't work anyone like this!* But they were waiting for her.

Ten minutes later, Paige was making the rounds again, half asleep. She stumbled against Dr Radnor. 'Excuse me,' she mumbled, 'but I haven't had any sleep . . .'

He patted her on the shoulder sympathetically. 'You'll get used to it.'

When Paige finally got off duty, she slept for fourteen straight hours.

*　　　*　　　*

The intense pressure and punishing hours proved to be too much for some of the residents, and they simply disappeared from the hospital. *That's not going to happen to me*, Paige vowed.

The pressure was unrelenting. At the end of one of Paige's shifts, thirty-six grueling hours, she was so exhausted that she had no idea where she was. She stumbled to the elevator and stood there, her mind numb.

Tom Chang came up to her. 'Are you all right?'

'Fine,' Paige mumbled.

He grinned. 'You look like hell.'

'Thanks. Why do they do this to us?' Paige asked.

Chang shrugged. 'The theory is that it keeps us in touch with our patients. If we go home and leave them, we don't know what's happening to them while we're gone.'

Paige nodded. 'That makes sense.' It made no sense at all. 'How can we take care of them if we're asleep on our feet?'

Chang shrugged again. 'I don't make the rules. It's the way all hospitals operate.' He looked at Paige more closely. 'Are you going to be able to make it home?'

Paige looked at him and said haughtily, 'Of course.'

'Take care.' Chang disappeared down the corridor.

Paige waited for the elevator to arrive. When it finally came, she was standing there, sound asleep.

Two days later, Paige was having breakfast with Kat.

'Do you want to hear a terrible confession?' Paige

58

asked. 'Sometimes when they wake me up at four o'clock in the morning to give somebody an aspirin, and I'm stumbling down the hall, half conscious, and I pass the rooms where all the patients are tucked in and having a good night's sleep, I feel like banging on all the doors and yelling, "Everybody wake up!"'

Kat held out her hand. 'Join the club.'

The patients came in all shapes, sizes, ages, and colors. They were frightened, brave, gentle, arrogant, demanding, considerate. They were human beings in pain.

Most of the doctors were dedicated people. As in any profession, there were good doctors and bad doctors. They were young and old, clumsy and adept, pleasant and nasty. A few of them, at one time or another, made sexual advances to Paige. Some were subtle and some were crude.

'Don't you ever feel lonely at night? I know that I do. I was wondering . . .'

'These hours are murder, aren't they? Do you know what I find gives me energy? Good sex. Why don't we . . . ?'

'My wife is out of town for a few days. I have a cabin near Carmel. This weekend we could . . .'

And the patients.

'So you're my doctor, eh? You know what would cure me . . . ?'

'Come closer to the bed, baby. I want to see if those are real . . .'

Paige gritted her teeth and ignored them all. *When Alfred and I are married, this will stop*. And just the

59

thought of Alfred gave her a glow. He would be returning from Africa soon. *Soon.*

One morning before rounds, Paige and Kat talked about the sexual harassment they were experiencing.

'Most of the doctors behave like perfect gentlemen, but a few of them seem to think we're perks that go with the territory, and that we're there to service them,' Kat said. 'I don't think a week goes by but what one of the doctors hits on me. "Why don't you come over to my place for a drink? I've got some great CDs." Or in the OR, when I'm assisting, the surgeon will brush his arm across my breast. One moron said to me, "You know, whenever I order chicken, I like the dark meat."'

Paige sighed. 'They think they're flattering us by treating us as sex objects. I'd rather they treated us as doctors.'

'A lot of them don't even want us around. They either want to fuck us or they want to fuck us. You know, it's not fair. Women are judged inferior until we prove ourselves, and men are judged superior until they prove what assholes they are.'

'It's the old boys' network,' Paige said. 'If there were more of us, we could start a new girls' network.'

Paige had heard of Arthur Kane. He was the subject of constant gossip around the hospital. His nickname was Dr 007—licensed to kill. His solution to every problem was to operate, and he had a higher rate of operations than any other doctor at the hospital. He also had a higher mortality rate.

He was bald, short, hawk-nosed, with tobacco-stained teeth, and was grossly overweight. Incredibly, he fancied himself a ladies' man. He liked to refer to the new nurses and female residents as 'fresh meat'.

Paige Taylor was fresh meat. He saw her in the upstairs lounge and sat down at her table, uninvited.

'I've been keeping an eye on you.'

Paige looked up, startled. 'I beg your pardon?'

'I'm Dr Kane. My friends call me Arthur.' There was a leer in his voice.

Paige wondered how many friends he had.

'How are you getting along here?'

The question caught Paige off guard. 'I . . . all right, I think.'

He leaned forward. 'This is a big hospital. It's easy to get lost here. Do you know what I mean?'

Paige said warily, 'Not exactly.'

'You're too pretty to be just another face in the crowd. If you want to get somewhere here, you need someone to help you. Someone who knows the ropes.'

The conversation was getting more unpleasant by the minute.

'And you'd like to help me.'

'Right.' He bared his tobacco-stained teeth. 'Why don't we discuss it at dinner?'

'There's nothing to discuss, Dr Kane,' Paige said. 'I'm not interested.'

Arthur Kane watched Paige get up and walk away, and there was a baleful expression on his face.

*   *   *

61

First-year surgical residents were on a two-month rotation schedule, alternating among obstetrics, orthopedics, urology, and surgery.

Paige learned that it was dangerous to go into a training hospital in the summer for any serious illness, because many of the staff doctors were on vacation and the patients were at the mercy of the inexperienced young residents.

Nearly all surgeons liked to have music in the operating room. One of the doctors was nicknamed Mozart and another Axl Rose because of their tastes in music.

For some reason, operations always seemed to make everyone hungry. They constantly discussed food. A surgeon would be in the middle of removing a gangrenous gallbladder from a patient and say, 'I had a great dinner last night at Bardelli's. Best Italian food in all of San Francisco.'

'Have you eaten the crab cakes at the Cypress Club?'

'If you like good beef, try the House of Prime Rib over on Van Ness.'

And meanwhile, a nurse would be mopping up the patient's blood.

When they weren't talking about food, the doctors talked about baseball or football scores.

'Did you see the 49ers play last Sunday? I bet they miss Joe Montana. He always came through for them in the last two minutes of a game.'

And out would come a ruptured appendix.

Kafka, Paige thought. *Kafka would have loved this.*

*　　　*　　　*

At three in the morning when Paige was asleep in the on-call room, she was awakened by the telephone.

A raspy voice said, 'Dr Taylor — Room 419 — a heart attack patient. You'll have to hurry!' The line went dead.

Paige sat on the edge of the bed, fighting sleep, and stumbled to her feet. *You have to hurry!* She went into the corridor, but there was no time to wait for an elevator. She rushed up the stairs and ran down the fourth-floor corridor to Room 419, her heart pounding. She flung open the door and stood there, staring.

Room 419 was a storage room.

Kat Hunter was making her rounds with Dr Richard Hutton. He was in his forties, brusque and fast. He spent no more than two or three minutes with each patient, scanning their charts, then snapping out orders to the surgical residents in a machine-gun, staccato fashion.

'Check her hemoglobin and schedule surgery for tomorrow . . .'

'Keep a close eye on his temperature chart . . .'

'Cross-match four units of blood . . .'

'Remove these stitches . . .'

'Get some chest films . . .'

Kat and the other residents were busily making notes on everything, trying hard to keep up with him.

They approached a patient who had been in the hospital a week and had had a battery of tests for a high fever, with no results.

When they were out in the corridor, Kat asked, 'What's the matter with him?'

'It's a GOK,' a resident said. 'A God only knows. We've done X-rays, CAT scans, MRIs, spinal taps, liver biopsy. Everything. We don't know what's wrong with him.'

They moved into a ward where a young patient, his head bandaged after an operation, was sleeping. As Dr Hutton started to unwrap the head dressing, the patient woke up, startled. 'What . . . what's going on?'

'Sit up,' Dr Hutton said curtly. The young man was trembling.

I'll never treat my patients that way, Kat vowed.

The next patient was a healthy-looking man in his seventies. As soon as Dr Hutton approached the bed, the patient yelled, '*Gonzo!* I'm going to sue you, you dirty son of a bitch.'

'Now, Mr Sparolini . . .'

'Don't Mr Sparolini me! You turned me into a fucking eunuch.'

That's an oxymoron, Kat thought.

'Mr Sparolini, you agreed to have the vasectomy, and—'

'It was my wife's idea. Damn bitch! Just wait till I get home.'

They left him muttering to himself.

'What's his problem?' one of the residents asked.

'His problem is that he's a horny old goat. His young wife has six kids and she doesn't want any more.'

Next was a little girl, ten years old. Dr Hutton looked at her chart. 'We're going to give you a shot to make the bad bugs go away.'

64

A nurse filled a syringe and moved toward the little girl.

'No!' she screamed. 'You're going to hurt me!'

'This won't hurt, baby,' the nurse assured her.

The words were a dark echo in Kat's mind.

This won't hurt, baby . . . It was the voice of her stepfather whispering to her in the scary dark.

'This will feel good. Spread your legs. Come on, you little bitch!' And he had pushed her legs apart and forced his male hardness into her and put his hand over her mouth to keep her from screaming with the pain. She was thirteen years old. After that, his visits became a terrifying nightly ritual. 'You're lucky you got a man like me to teach you how to fuck,' he would tell her. 'Do you know what a Kat is? A little pussy. And I want some.' And he would fall on top of her and grab her, and no amount of crying or pleading would make him stop.

Kat had never known her father. Her mother was a cleaning woman who worked nights at an office building near their tiny apartment in Gary, Indiana. Kat's stepfather was a huge man who had been injured in an accident at a steel mill, and he stayed home most of the time, drinking. At night, when Kat's mother left for work, he would go into Kat's room. 'You say anything to your mother or brother, and I'll kill him,' he told Kat. *I can't let him hurt Mike*, Kat thought. Her brother was five years younger than she, and Kat adored him. She mothered him and protected him and fought his battles for him. He was the only bright spot in Kat's life.

One morning, terrified as Kat was by her step-father's threats, she decided she had to tell her mother what was happening. Her mother would put a stop to it, would protect her.

'Mama, your husband comes to my bed at night when you're away, and forces himself on me.'

Her mother stared at her a moment, then slapped Kat hard across the face.

'Don't you dare make up lies like that, you little slut!'

Kat never discussed it again. The only reason she stayed at home was Mike. *He'd be lost without me*, Kat thought. But the day she learned she was pregnant, she ran away to live with an aunt in Minneapolis. From then, her life completely changed.

'You don't have to tell me what happened,' her Aunt Sophie had said. 'You know that song they sing on *Sesame Street*? "It's Not Easy Being Green"? Well, honey, it's not easy being black, either. You have two choices. You can keep running and hiding and blaming the world for your problems, or you can stand up for yourself and decide to be somebody important.'

'How do I do that?'

'By *knowing* that you're important. First, you get an image in your mind of who you want to be, child, and what you want to be. And then you go to work, *becoming* that person.'

'I'm not going to have his baby,' Kat decided. 'I want an abortion.'

It was arranged quietly, during a weekend, and it was performed by a midwife who was a friend of Kat's aunt. When it was over, Kat thought fiercely,

I'm never going to let a man touch me again. Never!

Minneapolis was a fairyland for Kat. Within a few blocks of almost every home were lakes and streams and rivers. And there were over eight thousand acres of landscaped parks. She went sailing on the city lakes and took boat rides on the Mississippi.

She visited the Great Zoo with Aunt Sophie and spent Sundays at the Valleyfair Amusement Park. She went on the hay rides at Cedar Creek Farm, and watched knights in armor jousting at the Shakopee Renaissance Festival.

Aunt Sophie watched Kat and thought, *The girl has never had a childhood.*

Kat was learning to enjoy herself, but Aunt Sophie sensed that deep inside her niece was a place that no one could reach, a barrier she had set up to keep her from being hurt again.

She made friends at school. But never with boys. Her girlfriends were all dating, but Kat was a loner, and too proud to tell anyone why. She looked up to her aunt, whom she loved very much.

Kat had taken little interest in school, or in reading books, but Aunt Sophie changed all that. Her home was filled with books, and Sophie's excitement about them was contagious.

'There are wonderful worlds in there,' she told the young girl. 'Read, and you'll learn where you came from and where you're going. I've got a feeling that you're going to be famous one day, baby. But you have to get an education first. This is America. You can become anybody you want to be. You may be black and poor, but so were some of our congresswomen, and movie stars, and scientists, and sports legends. One day we're going to have a black president. You can be anything you want to be. It's up to you.'

It was the beginning.

Kat became the top student in her class. She was an avid reader. In the school library one day, she happened to pick up a copy of Sinclair Lewis's *Arrowsmith*, and she was fascinated by the story of the dedicated young doctor. She read Agnes Cooper's *Promises to Keep*, and *Woman Surgeon* by Dr Else Roe, and it opened up a whole new world for her. She discovered that there were people on this earth who devoted themselves to helping others, to saving lives. When Kat came home from school one day, she said to Aunt Sophie, 'I'm going to be a doctor. A famous one.'

4

On Monday morning, three of Paige's patients' charts were missing, and Paige was blamed.

On Wednesday, Paige was awakened at 4:00 A.M. in the on-call room. Sleepily, she picked up the telephone. 'Dr Taylor.'

Silence.

'Hello . . . hello.'

She could hear breathing at the other end of the line. And then there was a click.

Paige lay awake for the rest of the night.

In the morning, Paige said to Kat, 'I'm either becoming paranoid or someone hates me.' She told Kat what had happened.

'Patients sometimes get grudges against doctors,' Kat said. 'Can you think of anyone who . . . ?'

Paige sighed. 'Dozens.'

'I'm sure there's nothing to worry about.'

Paige wished that she could believe it.

In late summer the magic telegram arrived. It was waiting for Paige when she returned to the apartment late at night. It read: 'Arriving San Francisco noon Sunday. Can't wait to see you. Love, Alfred.'

He was finally on his way back to her! Paige read the telegram again and again, her excitement growing each time. *Alfred!* His name conjured up a tumbling kaleidoscope of exciting memories . . .

Paige and Alfred had grown up together. Their fathers were part of a medical cadre of WHO that traveled to Third World countries, fighting exotic and virulent diseases. Paige and her mother accompanied Dr Taylor, who headed the team.

Paige and Alfred had had a fantasy childhood. In India, Paige learned to speak Hindi. At the age of two, she knew that the name for the bamboo hut they lived in was *basha*. Her father was *gorashaib*, a white man, and she was *nani*, a little sister. They addressed Paige's father as *abadhan*, the leader, or *baba*, father.

When Paige's parents were not around, she drank *bhanga*, an intoxicating drink made with hashish leaves, and ate *chapati* with *ghi*.

And then they were on their way to Africa. Off to another adventure!

Paige and Alfred became used to swimming and bathing in rivers that had crocodiles and hippopotamuses. Their pets were baby zebras and cheetahs and snakes. They grew up in windowless round huts made of wattle and daub, with packed dirt floors and conical thatched roofs. *Someday*, Paige vowed to herself, *I'm going to live in a real house, a beautiful cottage with a green lawn and a white picket fence*.

To the doctors and nurses, it was a difficult, frustrating life. But to the two children, it was a constant adventure, living in the land of lions, giraffes, and elephants. They went to primitive cinder-block schoolhouses, and when none was available, they had tutors.

Paige was a bright child, and her mind was a sponge, absorbing everything. Alfred adored her.

'I'm going to marry you one day, Paige,' he said when she was twelve, he fourteen.

'I'm going to marry you, too, Alfred.'

They were two serious children, determined to spend the rest of their lives together.

The doctors from WHO were selfless, dedicated men and women who devoted their lives to their work. They often worked under nearly impossible circumstances. In Africa, they had to compete with *wogesha*—the native medical practitioners whose primitive remedies were passed on from father to son, and often had deadly effects. The Masai's traditional remedy for flesh wounds was *olkilorite*, a mixture of cattle blood, raw meat, and essence of a mysterious root.

The Kikuyu remedy for smallpox was to have children drive out the sickness with sticks.

'You must stop that,' Dr Taylor would tell them. 'It doesn't help.'

'Better than having you stick sharp needles in our skin,' they would reply.

The dispensaries were tables lined up under the trees, for surgery. The doctors saw hundreds of patients a day, and there was always a long line, waiting to see them—lepers, natives with tubercular lungs, whooping cough, smallpox, dysentery.

Paige and Alfred were inseparable. As they grew older, they would walk to the market together, to a village miles away. And they would talk about their plans for the future.

Medicine was a part of Paige's early life. She learned to care for patients, to give shots and dispense medications, and she anticipated ways to help her father.

Paige loved her father. Curt Taylor was the most caring, selfless man she had ever known. He genuinely liked people, dedicating his life to helping those who needed him, and he instilled that passion in Paige. In spite of the long hours he worked, he managed to find time to spend with his daughter. He made the discomfort of the primitive places they lived in fun.

Paige's relationship with her mother was something else. Her mother was a beauty from a wealthy social background. Her cool aloofness kept Paige at a distance. Marrying a doctor who was going to work in far-off exotic places had seemed romantic to her, but the harsh reality had embittered her. She was not a warm, loving woman, and she seemed to Paige always to be complaining.

'Why did we ever have to come to this godforsaken place, Curt?'

'The people here live like animals. We're going to catch some of their awful diseases.'

'Why can't you practice medicine in the United States and make money like other doctors?'

And on and on it went.

The more her mother criticized him, the more Paige adored her father.

When Paige was fifteen years old, her mother disappeared with the owner of a large cocoa plantation in Brazil.

'She's not coming back, is she?' Paige asked.

'No, darling. I'm sorry.'

'I'm glad!' She had not meant to say that. She was hurt that her mother had cared so little for her and her father that she had abandoned them.

The experience made Paige draw even closer to Alfred Turner. They played games together and went on expeditions together, and shared their dreams.

'I'm going to be a doctor, too, when I grow up,' Alfred confided. 'We'll get married, and we'll work together.'

'And we'll have lots of children!'

'Sure. If you like.'

On the night of Paige's sixteenth birthday, their lifelong emotional intimacy exploded into a new dimension. At a little village in East Africa, the doctors had been called away on an emergency, because of an epidemic, and Paige, Alfred, and a cook were the only ones left in camp.

They had had dinner and gone to bed. But in the middle of the night Paige had been awakened in her tent by the faraway thunder of stampeding animals. She lay there, and as the minutes went by and the sound of the stampede came closer, she began to grow afraid. Her breath quickened. There was no telling when her father and the others would return.

She got up. Alfred's tent was only a few feet away. Terrified, Paige got up, raised the flap of the tent, and ran to Alfred's tent.

He was asleep.

'Alfred!'

He sat up, instantly awake. 'Paige? Is anything wrong?'

'I'm frightened. Could I get into bed with you for a while?'

73

'Sure.' They lay there, listening to the animals charging through the brush.

In a few minutes, the sounds began to die away.

Alfred became conscious of Paige's warm body lying next to him.

'Paige, I think you'd better go back to your tent.'

Paige could feel his male hardness pressing against her.

All the physical needs that had been building up within them came boiling to the surface.

'Alfred.'

'Yes?' His voice was husky.

'We're getting married, aren't we?'

'Yes.'

'Then it's all right.'

And the sounds of the jungle around them disappeared, and they began to explore and discover a world no one had ever possessed but themselves. They were the first lovers in the world, and they gloried in the wonderful miracle of it.

At dawn, Paige crept back to her tent and she thought, happily, *I'm a woman now.*

From time to time, Curt Taylor suggested to Paige that she return to the United States to live with his brother in his beautiful home in Deerfield, north of Chicago.

'Why?' Paige would ask.

'So that you can grow up to be a proper young lady.'

'I *am* a proper young lady.'

'Proper young ladies don't tease wild monkeys and try to ride baby zebras.'

Her answer was always the same. 'I won't leave you.'

When Paige was seventeen, the WHO team went to a jungle village in South Africa to fight a typhoid epidemic. Making the situation even more perilous was the fact that shortly after the doctors arrived, war broke out between two local tribes. Curt Taylor was warned to leave.

'I can't, for God's sake. I have patients who will die if I desert them.'

Four days later, the village came under attack. Paige and her father huddled in their little hut, listening to the yelling and the sounds of gunfire outside.

Paige was terrified. 'They're going to kill us!'

Her father had taken her in his arms. 'They won't harm us, darling. We're here to help them. They know we're their friends.'

And he had been right.

The chief of one of the tribes had burst into the hut with some of his warriors. 'Do not worry. We guard you.' And they had.

The fighting and shooting finally stopped, but in the morning Curt Taylor made a decision.

He sent a message to his brother. *Sending Paige out on next plane. Will wire details. Please meet her at airport.*

Paige was furious when she heard the news. She was taken, sobbing wildly, to the dusty little airport where a Piper Cub was waiting to fly her to a town where she could catch a plane to Johannesburg.

'You're sending me away because you want to get rid of me!' she cried.

Her father held her close in his arms. 'I love you more than anything in the world, baby. I'll miss you every minute. But I'll be going back to the States soon, and we'll be together again.'

'Promise?'

'Promise.'

Alfred was there to see Paige off.

'Don't worry,' Alfred told Paige. 'I'll come and get you as soon as I can. Will you wait for me?'

It was a pretty silly question, after all those years.

'Of course I will.'

Three days later, when Paige's plane arrived at O'Hare Airport in Chicago, Paige's Uncle Richard was there to greet her. Paige had never met him. All she knew about him was that he was a very wealthy businessman whose wife had died several years earlier. 'He's the successful one in the family,' Paige's father always said.

Paige's uncle's first words stunned her. 'I'm sorry to tell you this, Paige, but I just received word that your father was killed in a native uprising.'

Her whole world had been shattered in an instant. The ache was so strong that she did not think she could bear it. *I won't let my uncle see me cry*, Paige vowed. *I won't. I never should have left. I'm going back there*.

Driving from the airport, Paige stared out the window, looking at the heavy traffic.

'I hate Chicago.'

76

'Why, Paige?'
'It's a jungle.'

Richard would not permit Paige to return to Africa and her father's funeral, and that infuriated her.

He tried to reason with her. 'Paige, they've already buried your father. There's no point in your going back.'

But there was a point: *Alfred was there.*

A few days after Paige arrived, her uncle sat down with her to discuss her future.

'There's nothing to discuss,' Paige informed him. 'I'm going to be a doctor.'

At twenty-one, when Paige finished college, she applied to ten medical schools and was accepted by all of them. She chose a school in Boston.

It took two days to reach Alfred by telephone in Zaire, where he was working part-time with a WHO unit.

When Paige told him the news, he said, 'That's wonderful, darling. I'm nearly finished with my medical courses. I'll stay with WHO for a while, but in a few years we'll be practicing together.'

Together. The magical word.

'Paige, I'm desperate to see you. If I can get out for a few days, could you meet me in Hawaii?'

There wasn't the slightest hesitation. 'Yes.'

And they had both managed it. Later, Paige could only imagine how difficult it must have been for Alfred to make the long journey, but he never mentioned it.

They spent three incredible days at a small hotel in Hawaii, called Sunny Cove, and it was as though they had never been apart. Paige wanted so much to ask Alfred to go back to Boston with her, but she knew how selfish that would have been. The work that he was doing was far more important.

On their last day together, as they were getting dressed, Paige asked, 'Where will they be sending you, Alfred?'

'Gambia, or maybe Bangladesh.'

To save lives, to help those who so desperately need him. She held him tightly and closed her eyes. She never wanted to let him go.

As though reading her thoughts, he said, 'I'll never let you get away.'

Paige started medical school, and she and Alfred corresponded regularly. No matter in what part of the world he was, Alfred managed to telephone Paige on her birthday and at Christmas. Just before New Year's Eve, when Paige was in her second year of school, Alfred telephoned.

'Paige?'

'Darling! Where are you?'

'I'm in Senegal. I figured out it's only eighty-eight hundred miles from the Sunny Cove hotel.'

It took a minute for it to sink in.

'Do you mean . . . ?'

'Can you meet me in Hawaii for New Year's Eve?'

'Oh, yes! Yes!'

Alfred traveled nearly halfway round the world to meet her, and this time the magic was even stronger. Time had stood still for both of them.

'Next year I'll be in charge of my own cadre at WHO,' Alfred said. 'When you finish school, I want us to get married . . .'

They were able to get together once more, and when they weren't able to meet, their letters spanned time and space.

All those years he had worked as a doctor in Third World countries, like his father and Paige's father, doing the wonderful work that they did. And now, at last, he was coming home to her.

As Paige read Alfred's telegram for the fifth time, she thought, *He's coming to San Francisco!*

Kat and Honey were in their bedrooms, asleep. Paige shook them awake. 'Alfred's coming! He's coming! He'll be here Sunday!'

'Wonderful,' Kat mumbled. 'Why don't you wake me up Sunday? I just got to bed.'

Honey was more responsive. She sat up and said, 'That's great! I'm dying to meet him. How long since you've seen him?'

'Two years,' Paige said, 'but we've always stayed in touch.'

'You're a lucky girl,' Kat sighed. 'Well, we're all awake now. I'll put on some coffee.'

The three of them sat around the kitchen table.

'Why don't we give Alfred a party?' Honey suggested. 'Kind of a "Welcome to the Groom" party.'

'That's a good idea,' Kat agreed.

'We'll make it a real celebration—a cake, balloons—the works!'

'We'll cook dinner for him here,' Honey said.

79

Kat shook her head. 'I've tasted your cooking. Let's send out for food.'

Sunday was four days away, and they spent all their spare time discussing Alfred's arrival. By some miracle, the three of them were off duty on Sunday.

Saturday, Paige managed to get to a beauty salon. She went shopping and splurged on a new dress.

'Do I look all right? Do you think he'll like it?'

'You look sensational!' Honey assured her. 'I hope he deserves you.'

Paige smiled. 'I hope I deserve *him*. You'll love him. He's fantastic!'

On The Sunday, an elaborate lunch they had ordered was laid out on the dining-room table, with a bottle of iced champagne. The women stood around, nervously waiting for Alfred's arrival.

At two o'clock, the doorbell rang, and Paige ran to the door to open it. There was Alfred. A bit tired-looking, a little thinner. But he was her Alfred. Standing next to him was a brunette who appeared to be in her thirties.

'Paige!' Alfred exclaimed.

Paige threw her arms around him. Then she turned to Honey and Kat and said proudly, 'This is Alfred Turner. Alfred, these are my roommates, Honey Taft and Kat Hunter.'

'Pleased to meet you,' Alfred said. He turned to the woman at his side. 'And this is Karen Turner. My wife.'

The three women stood there, frozen.

Paige said slowly, 'Your wife?'

'Yes.' He frowned. 'Didn't . . . didn't you get my letter?'

'Letter?'

'Yes. I sent it several weeks ago.'

'No . . .'

'Oh. I . . . I'm terribly sorry. I explained it all in my . . . but of course, if you didn't get the . . .' His voice trailed off. 'I'm really sorry, Paige. You and I have been apart so long, that I . . . and then I met Karen . . . and you know how it is . . .'

'I know how it is,' Paige said numbly. She turned to Karen and forced a smile. 'I . . . I hope you and Alfred will be very happy.'

'Thank you.'

There was an awkward silence.

Karen said, 'I think we had better go, darling.'

'Yes. I think you had,' Kat said.

Alfred ran his fingers through his hair. 'I'm really sorry, Paige. I . . . well . . . goodbye.'

'Goodbye, Alfred.'

The three women stood there, watching the departing newlyweds.

'That bastard!' Kat said. 'What a lousy thing to do.'

Paige's eyes were brimming with tears. 'I . . . he didn't mean to . . . I mean . . . he must have explained everything in his letter.'

Honey put her arms around Paige. 'There ought to be a law that all men should be castrated.'

'I'll drink to that,' Kat said.

'Excuse me,' Paige said. She hurried to her bedroom and closed the door behind her.

She did not come out for the rest of the day.

5

During the next few months, Paige saw very little of Kat and Honey. They would have a hurried breakfast in the cafeteria and occasionally pass one another in the corridors. They communicated mainly by leaving notes in the apartment.

'Dinner is in the fridge.'

'The microwave is out.'

'Sorry, I didn't have time to clean up.'

'What about the three of us having dinner out Saturday night?'

The impossible hours continued to be a punishment, testing the limits of endurance for all the residents.

Paige welcomed the pressure. It gave her no time to think about Alfred and the wonderful future they had planned together. And yet, she could not get him out of her mind. What he had done filled her with a deep pain that refused to go away. She tortured herself with the futile game of 'what if?'

What if I had stayed with Alfred in Africa?

What if he had come to Chicago with me?

What if he had not met Karen?

What if . . . ?

*   *   *

On a Friday when Paige went into the change room to put on her scrubs, the word 'bitch' had been written on them with a black marker pen.

The following day when Paige went to look for her scut book, it was gone. All her notes had disappeared. *Maybe I misplaced it*, Paige thought.

But she couldn't make herself believe it.

The world outside the hospital ceased to exist. Paige was aware that Iraq was pillaging Kuwait, and that was overshadowed by the needs of a fifteen-year-old patient who was dying of leukemia. The day East and West Germany became united, Paige was busy trying to save the life of a diabetic patient. Margaret Thatcher resigned as prime minister of Great Britain, but more important, the patient in 214 was able to walk again.

What made it bearable were the doctors Paige worked with. With few exceptions, they had dedicated themselves to healing others, relieving pain, and saving lives. Paige watched the miracles they performed every day, and it filled her with a sense of pride.

The greatest stress was working in the ER. The emergency room was constantly overcrowded with people suffering every form of trauma imaginable.

The long hours at the hospital and the pressures placed an enormous strain on the doctors and nurses who worked there. The divorce rate among the doctors was extraordinarily high, and extramarital affairs were common.

Tom Chang was one of those having a problem. He told Paige about it over coffee.

'I can handle the hours,' Chang confided, 'but my wife can't. She complains that she never sees me anymore and that I'm a stranger to our little girl. She's right. I don't know what to do about it.'

'Has your wife visited the hospital?'

'No.'

'Why don't you invite her here for lunch, Tom? Let her see what you're doing here and how important it is.'

Chang brightened. 'That's a good idea. Thanks, Paige. I will. I would like you to meet her. Will you join us for lunch?'

'I'd love to.'

Chang's wife, Sye, turned out to be a lovely young woman with a classic, timeless beauty. Chang showed her around the hospital, and afterward they had lunch in the cafeteria with Paige.

Chang had told Paige that Sye had been born and raised in Hong Kong.

'How do you like San Francisco?' Paige asked.

There was a small silence. 'It's an interesting city,' Sye said politely, 'but I feel as though I am a stranger here. It is too big, too noisy.'

'But I understand Hong Kong is also big and noisy.'

'I come from a small village an hour away from Hong Kong. There, there is no noise and no automobiles, and everyone knows his neighbors.' She looked at her husband. 'Tom and I and our little daughter were very happy there. It is very beautiful on the island of Lamma. It has white beaches and small farms, and nearby is a little fishing village, Sak Kwu Wan. It is so peaceful.'

Her voice was filled with a wistful nostalgia. 'My husband and I were together much of the time, as a family should be. Here, I never see him.'

Paige said, 'Mrs Chang, I know it's difficult for you right now, but in a few years, Tom will be able to set up his own practice, and then his hours will be much easier.'

Tom Chang took his wife's hand. 'You see? Everything will be fine, Sye. You must be patient.'

'I understand,' she said. There was no conviction in her voice.

As they talked, a man walked into the cafeteria, and as he stood at the door, Paige could see only the back of his head. Her heart started to race. He turned around. It was a complete stranger.

Chang was watching Paige. 'Are you all right?'

'Yes,' Paige lied. *I've got to forget him. It's over.* And yet, the memories of all those wonderful years, the fun, the excitement, the love they had for each other . . . *How do I forget all that? I wonder if I could persuade any of the doctors here to do a lobotomy on me.*

Paige ran into Honey in the corridor. Honey was out of breath and looked worried.

'Is everything all right?' Paige asked.

Honey smiled uneasily. 'Yes. Fine.' She hurried on.

Honey had recently been assigned to an attending

85

physician named Charles Isler, who was known around the hospital as a martinet.

On Honey's first day of rounds, he had said, 'I've been looking forward to working with you, Dr Taft. Dr Wallace has told me about your outstanding record at medical school. I understand you're going to practice internal medicine.'

'Yes.'

'Good. So, we'll have you here for three more years.'

They began their rounds.

The first patient was a young Mexican boy. Dr Isler ignored the other residents and turned to Honey. 'I think you'll find this an interesting case, Dr Taft. The patient has all the classic signs and symptoms: anorexia, weight loss, metallic taste, fatigue, anemia, hyperirritability, and unco-ordination. How would you diagnose it?' He smiled expectantly.

Honey looked at him for a moment. 'Well, it could be several things, couldn't it?'

Dr Isler was watching her, puzzled. 'It's a clear-cut case of —'

One of the other residents broke in, 'Lead poisoning?'

'That's right,' Dr Isler said.

Honey smiled. 'Of course. Lead poisoning.'

Dr Isler turned to Honey again. 'How would you treat it?'

Honey said evasively, 'Well, there are several different methods of treatment, aren't there?'

A second resident spoke up. 'If the patient has had long-term exposure, he should be treated as a potential case of encephalopathy.'

Dr Isler nodded. 'Right. That's what we're doing. We're correcting the dehydration and electrolyte disturbances, and giving him chelation therapy.'

He looked at Honey. She nodded in agreement.

The next patient was a man in his eighties. His eyes were red and his eyelids were nearly stuck together.

'We'll have your eyes taken care of in a moment,' Dr Isler assured him. 'How are you feeling?'

'Oh, not too bad for an old man.'

Dr Isler pulled aside the blanket to reveal the patient's swollen knee and ankle. There were lesions on the soles of his feet.

Dr Isler turned to the residents. 'The swelling is caused by arthritis.' He looked at Honey. 'Combined with the lesions and the conjunctivitis, I'm sure you know what the diagnosis is.'

Honey said slowly, 'Well, it could be . . . you know . . .'

'It's Reiter's syndrome,' one of the residents spoke up. 'The cause is unknown. It's usually accompanied by low-grade fever.'

Dr Isler nodded. 'That's right.' He looked at Honey. 'What is the prognosis?'

'The prognosis?'

The resident replied. 'The prognosis is unclear. It can be treated with anti-inflammation drugs.'

'Very good,' Dr Isler said.

They made the rounds of a dozen more patients, and when they were finished, Honey said to Dr Isler, 'Could I see you for a moment alone, Dr Isler?'

'Yes. Come into my office.'

When they were seated in his office, Honey said, 'I know you're disappointed in me.'

'I must admit that I was a little surprised that you —'

Honey interrupted. 'I know, Dr Isler. I didn't close my eyes last night. To tell you the truth, I was so excited about working with you that I . . . I just couldn't sleep.'

He looked at her in surprise. 'Oh. I see. I knew there had to be a reason for . . . I mean, your medical school record was so fantastic. What made you decide to become a doctor?'

Honey looked down for a moment, then said softly, 'I had a younger brother who was injured in an accident. The doctors did everything they could to try to save him . . . but I watched him die. It took a long time, and I felt so helpless. I decided then that I was going to spend my life helping other people get well.' Her eyes welled up with tears.

She's so vulnerable, Isler thought. 'I'm glad we had this little talk.'

Honey looked at him and thought, *He believed me.*

6

Across town, in another part of the city, reporters and TV crews were waiting in the street for Lou Dinetto as he left the courtroom, smiling and waving, the greeting of royalty to the peasants. There were two bodyguards at his side, a tall, thin man known as the Shadow, and a heavyset man called Rhino. Lou Dinetto was, as always, dressed elegantly and expensively, in a gray silk suit with a white shirt, blue tie, and alligator shoes. His clothes had to be carefully tailored to make him look trim, because he was short and stout, with bandy legs. He always had a smile and a ready quip for the press, and they enjoyed quoting him. Dinetto had been indicted and tried three times on charges ranging from arson to racketeering to murder, and each time he had gone free.

Now as he left the courtroom, one of the reporters yelled out, 'Did you know you were going to be acquitted, Mr Dinetto?'

Dinetto laughed. 'Of course I did. I'm an innocent businessman. The government has got nothing better to do than to persecute me. That's one of the reasons our taxes are so high.'

A TV camera was aimed at him. Lou Dinetto stopped to smile into it.

'Mr Dinetto, can you explain why two witnesses

who were scheduled to testify against you in your murder trial failed to appear?'

'Certainly I can explain it,' Dinetto said. 'They were honest citizens who decided not to perjure themselves.'

'The government claims that you're the head of the West Coast mob, and that it was you who arranged for—'

'The only thing I arrange for is where people sit at my restaurant. I want everybody to be comfortable.' He grinned at the milling crowd of reporters. 'By the way, you're all invited to the restaurant tonight for a free dinner and drinks.'

He was moving toward the curb, where a black stretch limousine was waiting for him.

'Mr Dinetto . . .'

'Mr Dinetto . . .'

'Mr Dinetto . . .'

'I'll see you at my restaurant tonight, boys and girls. You all know where it is.'

And Lou Dinetto was in the car, waving and smiling. Rhino closed the door of the limousine and got into the front seat. The Shadow slipped behind the wheel.

'That was great, boss!' Rhino said. 'You sure know how to handle them bums.'

'Where to?' the Shadow asked.

'Home. I can use a hot bath and a good steak.'

The car started off.

'I don't like that question about the witnesses,' Dinetto said. 'You sure they'll never . . . ?'

'Not unless they can talk underwater, boss.'

Dinetto nodded. 'Good.'

The car was speeding along Fillmore Street.

Dinetto said, 'Did you see the look on the DA's face when the judge dismissed . . . ?'

A small dog appeared out of nowhere, directly in front of the limousine. The Shadow swung the wheel hard to avoid hitting it and jammed on the brakes. The car jumped the curb and crashed into a lamppost. Rhino's head flew forward into the windshield.

'What the *fuck* are you doing?' Dinetto screamed. 'You trying to kill me?'

The Shadow was trembling. 'Sorry, boss. A dog ran in front of the car . . .'

'And you decided his life was more important than mine? You stupid asshole!'

Rhino was moaning. He turned around, and Dinetto saw blood pouring from a large cut in his forehead.

'For Christ's sake!' Dinetto screamed. 'Look what you've done!'

'I'm all right,' Rhino mumbled.

'The hell you are!' Dinetto turned to the Shadow. 'Get him to a hospital.'

The Shadow backed the limousine off the curb.

'The Embarcadero is only a couple of blocks down. We'll take him to the emergency ward there.'

'Right, boss.'

Dinetto sank back in his seat. 'A dog,' he said disgustedly. 'Jesus!'

Kat was in the emergency ward when Dinetto, the Shadow, and Rhino walked in. Rhino was bleeding heavily.

Dinetto called out to Kat, 'Hey, you!'

Kat looked up. 'Are you talking to me?'

'Who the hell do you think I'm talking to? This man is bleeding. Get him fixed up right away.'

'There are half a dozen others ahead of him,' Kat said quietly. 'He'll have to wait his turn.'

'He's not waiting for anything,' Dinetto told her. 'You'll take care of him now.'

Kat stepped over to Rhino and examined him. She took a piece of cotton and pressed it against the cut. 'Hold it there. I'll be back.'

'I said to take care of him *now*,' Dinetto snapped.

Kat turned to Dinetto. 'This is an emergency hospital ward. I'm the doctor in charge. So either keep quiet or get out.'

The Shadow said, 'Lady, you don't know who you're talking to. You better do what the man says. This is Mr Lou Dinetto.'

'Now that the introductions are over,' Dinetto said impatiently, 'take care of my man.'

'You have a hearing problem,' Kat said. 'I'll tell you once more. Keep quiet or get out of here. I have work to do.'

Rhino said, 'You can't talk to—'

Dinetto turned to him. 'Shut up!' He looked at Kat again, and his tone changed. 'I would appreciate it if you could get to him as soon as possible.'

'I'll do my best.' Kat sat Rhino down on a cot. 'Lie down. I'll be back in a few minutes.' She looked at Dinetto. 'There are some chairs over there in the corner.'

Dinetto and the Shadow watched her walk to the other end of the ward to take care of the waiting patients.

'Jesus,' the Shadow said. 'She has no idea who you are.'

'I don't think it would make any difference. She's got balls.'

Fifteen minutes later, Kat returned to Rhino and examined him. 'No concussion,' she announced. 'You're lucky. That's a nasty cut.'

Dinetto stood watching as Kat skillfully put stitches in Rhino's forehead.

When Kat was finished, she said, 'That should heal nicely. Come back in five days, and I'll take out the stitches.'

Dinetto walked over and examined Rhino's forehead. 'That's a damn good job.'

'Thanks,' Kat said. 'Now, if you'll excuse me . . .'

'Wait a minute,' Dinetto called. He turned to the Shadow. 'Give her a C-note.'

The Shadow took a hundred-dollar bill out of his pocket. 'Here.'

'The cashier's office is outside.'

'This isn't for the hospital. It's for you.'

'No, thanks.'

Dinetto stared as Kat walked away and began working on another patient.

The Shadow said, 'Maybe it wasn't enough, boss.'

Dinetto shook his head. 'She's an independent broad. I like that.' He was silent for a moment. 'Doc Evans is retiring, right?'

'Yeah.'

'Okay. I want you to find out everything you can about this doctor.'

'What for?'

'Leverage. I think she might come in very handy.'

7

Hospitals are run by nurses. Margaret Spencer, the chief nurse, had worked at Embarcadero County Hospital for twenty years and knew where all the bodies—literally and figuratively—were buried. Nurse Spencer was in charge of the hospital, and doctors who did not recognize it were in trouble. She knew which doctors were on drugs or addicted to alcohol, which doctors were incompetent, and which doctors deserved her support. In her charge were all the student nurses, registered nurses, and operating room nurses. It was Margaret Spencer who decided which of them would be assigned to the various surgeries, and since the nurses ranged from indispensable to incompetent, it paid the doctors to get along with her. She had the power to assign an inept scrub nurse to assist on a complicated kidney removal, or, if she liked the doctor, to send her most competent nurse to help him with a simple tonsillectomy. Among Margaret Spencer's many prejudices was an antipathy to woman doctors and to blacks.

Kat Hunter was a black woman doctor.

Kat was having a hard time. Nothing was overtly said or done, and yet prejudice was at work in ways too subtle to pin down. The nurses she asked for

94

were unavailable, those assigned to her were close to incompetent. Kat found herself frequently being sent to examine male clinic patients with venereal diseases. She accepted the first few cases as routine, but when she was given half a dozen to examine in one day, she became suspicious.

At a lunch break she said to Paige, 'Have you examined many men with venereal disease?'

Paige thought for a moment. 'One last week. An orderly.'

I'm going to have to do something about this, Kat thought.

Nurse Spencer had planned to get rid of Dr Hunter by making her life so miserable that she would be forced to quit, but she had not counted on Kat's dedication or her ability. Little by little, Kat was winning over the people she worked with. She had a natural skill that impressed her fellow workers as well as her patients. But the real breakthrough happened because of what came to be known around the hospital as the famous pig blood caper.

On morning rounds one day, Kat was working with a senior resident named Dundas. They were at the bedside of a patient who was unconscious.

'Mr Levy was in an automobile accident,' Dundas informed the younger residents. 'He's lost a great deal of blood, and he needs an immediate transfusion. The hospital is short of blood right now. This man has a family, and they refuse to donate any blood to him. It's infuriating.'

Kat asked, 'Where is his family?'

'In the visitors' waiting room,' Dr Dundas said.

'Do you mind if I talk to them?' Kat asked.

'It won't do any good. I've already spoken to them. They've made up their minds.'

When the rounds were over, Kat went into the visitors' waiting room. The man's wife and grown son and daughter were there. The son wore a yarmulke and ritual tallis.

'Mrs Levy?' Kat asked the woman.

She stood up. 'How is my husband? Is the doctor going to operate?'

'Yes,' Kat said.

'Well, don't ask us to give any of our blood. It's much too dangerous these days, with AIDS and all.'

'Mrs Levy,' Kat said, 'you can't get AIDS by donating blood. It's not poss —'

'Don't tell me! I read the papers. I know what's what.'

Kat studied her a moment. 'I can see that. Well, it's all right, Mrs Levy. The hospital is short of blood right now, but we've solved the problem.'

'Good.'

'We're going to give your husband pig's blood.'

The mother and son were staring at Kat, shocked. '*What?*'

'Pig's blood,' Kat said cheerfully. 'It probably won't do him any harm.' She turned to leave.

'Wait a minute!' Mrs Levy cried.

Kat stopped. 'Yes?'

'I, uh . . . just give us a minute, will you?'

'Certainly.'

Fifteen minutes later, Kat went up to Dr Dundas. 'You don't have to worry about Mr Levy's family anymore. They're all happy to make a blood donation.'

96

The story became an instant legend around the hospital. Doctors and nurses who had ignored Kat before made a point of speaking to her.

A few days later, Kat went into the private room of Tom Leonard, an ulcer patient. He was eating an enormous lunch that he had had brought in from a nearby delicatessen.

Kat walked up to his bed. 'What are you doing?'

He looked up and smiled. 'Having a decent lunch for a change. Want to join me? There's plenty here.'

Kat rang for a nurse.

'Yes, doctor?'

'Get this food out of here. Mr Leonard is on a strict hospital diet. Didn't you read his chart?'

'Yes, but he insisted on —'

'Remove it, please.'

'Hey! Wait a minute!' Leonard protested. 'I can't eat the pap this hospital is giving me!'

'You'll eat it if you want to get rid of your ulcer.' Kat looked at the nurse. 'Take it out.'

Thirty minutes later, Kat was summoned to the office of the administrator.

'You wanted to see me, Dr Wallace?'

'Yes. Sit down. Tom Leonard is one of your patients, isn't he?'

'That's right. I found him eating a hot pastrami sandwich with pickles and potato salad for lunch today, full of spices and —'

'And you took it away from him.'

'Of course.'

Wallace leaned forward in his chair. 'Doctor, you probably were not aware that Tom Leonard is on

97

the hospital's supervisory board. We want to keep him happy. Do you get my meaning?'

Kat looked at him and said stubbornly, 'No, sir.'

He blinked. 'What?'

'It seems to me that the way to keep Tom Leonard happy is to get him healthy. He's not going to be cured if he tears his stomach apart.'

Benjamin Wallace forced a smile. 'Why don't we let him make that decision?'

Kat stood up. 'Because *I'm* his doctor. Is there anything else?'

'I . . . er . . . no. That's all.'

Kat walked out of the office.

Benjamin Wallace sat there stunned. *Woman doctors!*

Kat was on night duty when she received a call. 'Dr Hunter, I think you had better come up to 320.'

'Right away.'

The patient in Room 320 was Mrs Molloy, a cancer patient in her eighties, with a poor prognosis. As Kat neared the door she heard voices inside, raised in argument. Kat stepped inside the room.

Mrs Molloy was in bed, heavily sedated, but conscious. Her son and two daughters were in the room.

The son was saying, 'I say we split the estate up three ways.'

'No!' one of the daughters said. 'Laurie and I are the ones who have been taking care of Mama. Who's been doing the cooking and cleaning for her? We have! Well, we're entitled to her money and—'

'I'm as much her flesh and blood as you are!' the man yelled.

Mrs Molloy lay in bed, helpless, listening.

Kat was furious. 'Excuse me,' she said.

One of the women glanced at her. 'Come back later, nurse. We're busy.'

Kat said angrily, 'This is my patient. I'm giving you all ten seconds to get out of this room. You can wait in the visitors' waiting room. Now get out before I call security and have you thrown out.'

The man started to say something, but the look in Kat's eyes stopped him. He turned to his sisters and shrugged. 'We can talk outside.'

Kat watched the three of them leave the room. She turned to Mrs Molloy in bed and stroked her head. 'They didn't mean anything by it,' Kat said softly. She sat at the bedside, holding the old woman's hand, and watched her drop off to sleep.

We're all dying, Kat thought. *Forget what Dylan Thomas said. The real trick is to go gentle into that good night.*

Kat was in the middle of treating a patient when an orderly came into the ward. 'There's an urgent call for you at the desk, doctor.'

Kat frowned. 'Thank you.' She turned to the patient, who was in a full body cast, with his legs suspended on a pulley. 'I'll be right back.'

In the corridor, at the nurses' station, Kat picked up the desk telephone. 'Hello?'

'Hi, sis.'

'Mike!' She was excited to hear from him, but her excitement immediately turned to concern. 'Mike, I told you never to call me here. You have the number at the apartment if—'

'Hey, I'm sorry. This couldn't wait. I have a little problem.'

Kat knew what was coming.

'I borrowed some money from a fellow to invest in a business . . .'

Kat didn't bother asking what kind of business. 'And it failed.'

'Yeah. And now he wants his money.'

'How much, Mike?'

'Well, if you could send five thousand . . .'

'*What?*'

The desk nurse was looking at Kat curiously.

Five thousand dollars. Kat lowered her voice. 'I don't have that much. I . . . I can send you half now and the rest in a few weeks. Will that be all right?'

'I guess so. I hate to bother you, sis, but you know how it is.'

Kat knew exactly how it was. Her brother was twenty-two years old and was always involved in mysterious deals. He ran with gangs, and God only knew what they were up to, but Kat felt a deep responsibility toward him. *It's all my fault*, Kat thought. *If I hadn't run away from home and deserted him* . . . 'Stay out of trouble, Mike. I love you.'

'I love you, too, Kat.'

I'll have to get that money, somehow, Kat thought. *Mike's all I have in the world.*

Dr Isler had been looking forward to working with Honey Taft again. He had forgiven her inept performance and, in fact, was flattered that she was in such awe of him. But now, on rounds with her once

100

more, Honey stayed behind the other residents and never volunteered an answer to his questions.

Thirty minutes after rounds, Dr Isler was seated in Benjamin Wallace's office.

'What's the problem?' Wallace asked.

'It's Dr Taft.'

Wallace looked at him in genuine surprise. 'Dr Taft? She has the best recommendations I've ever seen.'

'That's what puzzles me,' Dr Isler said. 'I've been getting reports from some of the other residents. She's misdiagnosing cases and making serious mistakes. I'd like to know what the hell is going on.'

'I don't understand. She went to a fine medical school.'

'Maybe you should give the dean of the school a call,' Dr Isler suggested.

'That's Jim Pearson. He's a good man. I'll call him.'

A few minutes later, Wallace had Jim Pearson on the telephone. They exchanged pleasantries, and then Wallace said, 'I'm calling about Betty Lou Taft.'

There was a brief silence. 'Yes?'

'We seem to be having a few problems with her, Jim. She was admitted here with your wonderful recommendation.'

'Right.'

'In fact, I have your report in front of me. It says she was one of the brightest students you ever had.'

'That's right.'

'And that she was going to be a credit to the medical profession.'

'Yes.'

'Was there any doubt about . . . ?'

'None,' Dr Pearson said firmly. 'None at all. She's probably a little nervous. She's high-strung, but if you just give her a chance, I'm sure she'll be fine.'

'Well, I appreciate your telling me. We'll certainly give her every chance. Thank you.'

'Not at all.' The line went dead.

Jim Pearson sat there, hating himself for what he had done.

But my wife and children come first.

8

Honey Taft had the bad fortune to have been born into a family of overachievers. Her handsome father was the founder and president of a large computer company in Memphis, Tennessee, her lovely mother was a genetic scientist, and Honey's older twin sisters were as attractive, as brainy, and as ambitious as their parents. The Tafts were among the most prominent families in Memphis.

Honey had inconveniently come along when her sisters were six years old.

'Honey was our little accident,' her mother would tell their friends. 'I wanted to have an abortion, but Fred was against it. Now he's sorry.'

Where Honey's sisters were stunning, Honey was plain. Where they were brilliant, Honey was average. Her sisters had started talking at nine months. Honey had not uttered a word until she was almost two.

'We call her "the dummy",' her father would laugh. 'Honey is the ugly duckling of the Taft family. Only I don't think she's going to turn into a swan.'

It was not that Honey was ugly, but neither was she pretty. She was ordinary-looking, with a thin, pinched face, mousy blond hair, and an unenviable figure. What Honey *did* have was an extraordinarily sweet, sunny disposition, a quality not particularly prized in a family of competitive overachievers.

From the earliest time Honey could remember, her greatest desire was to please her parents and sisters and make them love her. It was a futile effort. Her parents were busy with their careers, and her sisters were busy winning beauty contests and scholarships. To add to Honey's misery, she was inordinately shy. Consciously or unconsciously, her family had implanted in her a feeling of deep inferiority.

In high school, Honey was known as the Wall-flower. She attended school dances and parties by herself, and smiled and tried not to show how miserable she was, because she did not want to spoil anyone's fun. She would watch her sisters picked up at the house by the most popular boys at school, and then she would go up to her lonely room to struggle with her homework.

And try not to cry.

On weekends and during the summer holidays, Honey made pocket money by baby-sitting. She loved taking care of children, and the children adored her.

When Honey was not working, she would go off and explore Memphis by herself. She visited Grace-land, where Elvis Presley had lived, and walked down Beale Street, where the blues started. She wandered through the Pink Palace Museum, and the Planetarium, with its roaring, stomping dinosaur. She went to the aquarium.

And Honey was always alone.

She was unaware that her life was about to change drastically.

*   *   *

Honey knew that many of her classmates were having love affairs. They discussed it constantly at school.

'Have you gone to bed with Ricky yet? He's the best . . . !'

'Joe is really into orgasms . . .'

'I was out with Tony last night. I'm exhausted. What an animal! I'm seeing him again tonight . . .'

Honey stood there listening to their conversations and she was filled with a bittersweet envy, and a feeling that she would never know what sex was like. *Who would want me?* Honey wondered.

One Friday night, there was a school prom. Honey had no intention of going, but her father said, 'You know, I'm concerned. Your sisters tell me that you're a wallflower, and that you're not going to the prom because you can't get a date.'

Honey blushed. 'That's not true,' she said. 'I do have a date, and I *am* going.' *Don't let him ask who my date is*, Honey prayed.

He didn't.

Now Honey found herself at the prom, seated in her usual corner, watching the others dancing and having a wonderful time.

And that was when the miracle occurred.

Roger Merton, the captain of the football team and the most popular boy at school, was on the dance floor, having a fight with his girlfriend. He had been drinking.

'You're a no-good, selfish bastard!' she said.

'And you're a dumb bitch!'

'You can go screw yourself.'

'I don't have to screw myself, Sally. I can screw somebody else. Anyone I want to.'

'Go ahead!' She stormed off the dance floor.

Honey could not help but overhear.

Merton saw her looking at him. 'What the hell are you staring at?' He was slurring his words.

'Nothing,' Honey said.

'I'll show the bitch! You think I won't show her?'

'I . . . yes.'

'Damn right. Let's have a li'l drink.'

Honey hesitated. Merton was obviously drunk. 'Well, I don't . . .'

'Great. I have a bottle in the car.'

'I really don't think I . . .'

And he had Honey's arm and was steering her out of the room. She went along because she did not want to make a scene and embarrass him.

Outside, Honey tried to pull away. 'Roger, I don't think this is a good idea. I . . .'

'What the hell are you—chicken?'

'No, I . . .'

'Okay, then. Come on.'

He led her to his car and opened the door. Honey stood there a moment.

'Get in.'

'I can only stay a moment,' Honey said.

She got in the car because she did not want to upset Roger. He climbed in beside her.

'We're going to show that dumb broad, aren't we?' He held out a bottle of bourbon. 'Here.'

Honey had had only one drink of alcohol before

and she had hated it. But she did not want to hurt Roger's feelings. She looked at him and reluctantly took a small sip.

'You're okay,' he said. 'You're new at school, huh?'

Honey was in three of his classes. 'No,' Honey said. 'I . . .'

He leaned over and began to play with her breasts. Startled, Honey pulled away.

'Hey! Come on. Don't you want to please me?' he said.

And that was the magic phrase. Honey wanted to please everybody, and if this was the way to do it . . .

In the uncomfortable backseat of Merton's car, Honey had sex for the first time, and it opened an incredible new world to her. She did not particularly enjoy the sex, but that was not important. The important thing was that Merton enjoyed it. In fact, Honey was amazed by how *much* he enjoyed it. It seemed to make him ecstatic. She had never seen anyone enjoy anything so much. *So this is how to please a man*, Honey thought.

It was an epiphany.

Honey was unable to get the miracle of what had occurred out of her mind. She lay in bed, remembering Merton's hard maleness inside her, thrusting faster and faster, and then his moans, 'Oh, yes, yes . . . Jesus, you're fantastic, Sally . . .'

And Honey had not even minded that. She had pleased the captain of the football team! The most popular boy in school! *And I really didn't even know*

107

what I was doing, Honey thought. *If I truly learned how to please a man . . .*

And that was when Honey had her second epiphany.

The following morning, Honey went to the Pleasure Chest, a porno bookstore on Poplar Street, and bought half a dozen books on eroticism. She smuggled them home and read them in the privacy of her room. She was astounded by what she was reading.

She raced through the pages of *The Perfumed Garden* and the *Kama Sutra*, the *Tibetan Arts of Love*, the *Alchemy of Ecstasy*, and then went back for more. She read the words of Gedun Chopel and the arcane accounts by Kanchinatha.

She studied the exciting photographs of the thirty-seven positions of lovemaking, and she learned the meaning of the Half Moon and the Circle, the Lotus Petal, and the Pieces of Cloud, and the way of churning.

Honey became an expert on the eight types of oral sex, and the paths of the sixteen pleasures, and the ecstasy of the string of marbles. She knew how to teach a man to perform *karuna*, to intensify his pleasure. In theory, at least.

Honey felt she was now ready to put her knowledge into practice.

The *Kama Sutra* had several chapters on aphrodisiacs to arouse a man, but since Honey had no idea where she could obtain *Hedysarum gangeticum*, the *kshirika* plant, or the *Xanthochymus pictorius*, she figured out her own substitutes.

108

When Honey saw Roger Merton in class the following week, she walked up to him and said, 'I really enjoyed the other night. Can we do it again?'

It took him a moment to remember who Honey was. 'Oh. Sure. Why not? My folks are out tonight. Why don't you come by about eight o'clock?'

When Honey arrived at Merton's house that night, she had a small jar of maple syrup with her.

'What's that for?' Merton said.

'I'm going to show you,' Honey said.

She showed him.

The next day, Merton was telling his buddies at school about Honey.

'She's incredible,' he said. 'You wouldn't believe what she can do with a little warm syrup!'

That afternoon, half a dozen boys were asking Honey for dates. From that time on, she started going out every night. The boys were very happy, and that made Honey very happy.

Honey's parents were delighted by their daughter's sudden popularity.

'It took our girl a little while to bloom,' her father said proudly, 'but now she's turned into a real Taft!'

Honey had always had poor grades in mathematics, and she knew she had failed badly on her final test. Her mathematics teacher, Mr Janson, was a bachelor and lived near the school. Honey paid him a visit one evening. He opened the door and looked at her in surprise.

'Honey! What are you doing here?'

'I need your help,' Honey said. 'My father will kill me if I fail your course. I brought some math problems, and I wonder if you would mind going over them with me.'

He hesitated a moment. 'This is unusual, but . . . very well.'

Mr Janson liked Honey. She was not like the other girls in his class. They were raucous and indifferent, while Honey was sensitive and caring, always eager to please. He wished that she had more of an aptitude for mathematics.

Mr Janson sat next to Honey on the couch and began to explain the arcane intricacies of logarithms.

Honey was not interested in logarithms. As Mr Janson talked, Honey moved closer and closer to him. She started breathing on his neck and into his ear, and before he knew what was happening, Mr Janson found that his pants were unzipped.

He was looking at Honey in astonishment. 'What are you doing?'

'I've wanted you since the first time I saw you,' Honey said. She opened her purse and took out a small can of whipped cream.

'What's that?'

'Let me show you . . .'

Honey received an A in math.

It was not only the accessories Honey used that made her so popular. It was the knowledge she had gleaned from all the ancient books on erotica she had read. She delighted her partners with techniques they had never dreamed of, that were thousands of years old, and long forgotten. She brought a new meaning to the word 'ecstasy'.

Honey's grades improved dramatically, and she

was suddenly even more popular than her sisters had been in their high school days. Honey was dined at the Private Eye and the Bombay Bicycle Club, and taken to the Ice Capades at the Memphis Mall. The boys took her skiing at Cedar Cliff and sky diving at Landis Airport.

Honey's years at college were just as successful socially. At dinner one evening, her father said, 'You'll be graduating soon. It's time to think about your future. Do you know what you want to do with your life?'

She answered immediately. 'I want to be a nurse.'

Her father's face reddened. 'You mean a doctor.'

'No, Father. I —'

'You're a Taft. If you want to go into medicine, you'll be a doctor. Is that understood?'

'Yes, Father.'

Honey had meant it when she told her father she wanted to be a nurse. She loved taking care of people, helping them and nurturing them. She was terrified by the idea of becoming a doctor, and being responsible for people's lives, but she knew that she must not disappoint her father. *You're a Taft.*

Honey's college grades were not good enough to get her into medical school, but her father's influence was. He was a heavy contributor to a medical school in Knoxville, Tennessee. He met with Dr Jim Pearson, the dean.

'You're asking for a big favor,' Pearson said, 'but I'll tell you what I'll do. I'll admit Honey on a probationary basis. If at the end of six months we

111

feel she's not qualified to continue, we'll have to let her go.'

'Fair enough. She's going to surprise you.'

He was right.

Honey's father had made arrangements for her to stay in Knoxville with a cousin of his, the Reverend Douglas Lipton.

Douglas Lipton was the minister of the Baptist Church. He was in his sixties, married to a woman ten years older.

The minister was delighted to have Honey in the house.

'She's like a breath of fresh air,' he told his wife.

He had never seen anyone so eager to please.

Honey did fairly well in medical school, but she lacked dedication. She was there only to please her father.

Honey's teachers liked her. There was a genuine niceness about her that made her professors want her to succeed.

Ironically, she was particularly weak in anatomy. During the eighth week, her anatomy teacher sent for her. 'I'm afraid I'm going to have to fail you,' he said unhappily.

I can't fail, Honey thought. *I can't let my father down. What would Boccaccio have advised?*

Honey moved closer to the professor. 'I came to this school because of you. I have heard so much about you.' She moved closer to him. 'I want to be like you.' And closer. 'Being a doctor means everything to me.' And closer. 'Please help me . . .'

One hour later, when Honey left his office, she had the answers to the next examination.

Before Honey was finished with medical school, she had seduced several of her professors. There was a helplessness about her that they were unable to resist. They were all under the impression that it was *they* who were seducing *her*, and they felt guilty about taking advantage of her innocence.

Dr Jim Pearson was the last to succumb to Honey. He was intrigued by all the reports he had heard about her. There were rumors of her extraordinary sexual skills. He sent for Honey one day to discuss her grades. She brought a small box of powdered sugar with her, and before the afternoon was over, Dr Pearson was as hooked as all the others. Honey made him feel young and insatiable. She made him feel that he was a king who had subjugated her and made her his slave.

He tried not to think of his wife and children.

Honey was genuinely fond of the Reverend Douglas Lipton, and it upset her that his wife was a cold, frigid woman who was always criticizing him. Honey felt sorry for the minister. *He doesn't deserve that*, Honey thought. *He needs comforting*.

In the middle of the night, when Mrs Lipton was out of town visiting a sister, Honey walked into the minister's bedroom. She was naked. 'Douglas . . .'

His eyes flew open. 'Honey? Are you all right?'

'No,' she said. 'Can I talk to you?'

'Of course.' He reached for the lamp.

'Don't turn on the light.' She crept into bed beside him.

'What's the matter? Aren't you feeling well?'

'I'm worried.'

'About what?'

'You. You deserve to be loved. I want to make love to you.'

He was wide awake. 'My God!' he said. 'You're just a child. You can't be serious.'

'I am. Your wife's not giving you any love . . .'

'Honey, this is impossible! You'd better get back to your room now, and . . .'

He could feel her naked body pressing against his. 'Honey, we can't do this. I'm . . .'

Her lips were on his, and her body was on top of him, and he was completely swept away. She spent the night in his bed.

At six o'clock in the morning, the door to the bedroom opened and Mrs Lipton walked in. She stood there, staring at the two of them, then walked out without a word.

Two hours later, the Reverend Douglas Lipton committed suicide in his garage.

When Honey heard the news, she was devastated, unable to believe what had happened.

The sheriff arrived at the house and had a talk with Mrs Lipton.

When he was through, he went to find Honey. 'Out of respect for his family, we're going to list the death of the Reverend Douglas Lipton as a "suicide for reasons unknown," but I would suggest that you get the fuck out of this town fast, and stay out.'

Honey had gone to Embarcadero County Hospital in San Francisco.

With a glowing recommendation from Dr Jim Pearson.

9

Time had lost all meaning for Paige. There was no beginning and no end, and the days and nights flowed into one another in a seamless rhythm. The hospital had become her whole life. The outside world was a foreign, faraway planet.

Christmas came and went, and a new year began. In the world outside, US troops liberated Kuwait from Iraq.

There was no word from Alfred. *He'll find out he made a mistake*, Paige thought. *He'll come back to me.*

The early morning crank telephone calls had stopped as suddenly as they had started. Paige was relieved that no new mysterious or threatening incidents had befallen her. It was almost as if they had all been a bad dream . . . except, of course, they hadn't been.

The routine continued to be frantic. There was no time to know patients. They were simply gallbladders and ruptured livers, fractured femurs and broken backs.

The hospital was a jungle filled with mechanical demons—respirators, heart rate monitors, CAT scan equipment, X-ray machines. And each had its own peculiar sound. There were whistles, and buzzers, and the constant chatter on the PA system, and they all blended into a loud, insane cacophony.

The second year of residency was a rite of passage. The residents moved up to more demanding duties and watched the new group come in, feeling a mixture of scorn and arrogance toward them.

'Those poor devils,' Kat said to Paige. 'They have no idea what they're in for.'

'They'll find out soon enough.'

Paige and Honey were becoming worried about Kat. She was losing weight, and seemed depressed. In the middle of conversations, they would find Kat looking off into space, her mind preoccupied. From time to time, she would receive a mysterious phone call, and after each one her depression seemed to worsen.

Paige and Honey sat down to have a talk with her.

'Is everything all right?' Paige asked. 'You know we love you, and if there's a problem, we'd like to help.'

'Thanks. I appreciate it, but there's nothing you can do. It's a money problem.'

Honey looked at her in surprise. 'What do you need money for? We never go anyplace. We haven't any time to buy anything. We —'

'It's not for me. It's for my brother.' Kat had not mentioned her brother before.

'I didn't know you had a brother,' Paige said.

'Does he live in San Francisco?' Honey asked.

Kat was hesitant. 'No. He lives back East. In Detroit. You'll have to meet him one day.'

'We'd like to. What does he do?'

'He's kind of an entrepreneur,' Kat said vaguely. 'He's a little down on his luck right now, but Mike will bounce back. He always does.' *I hope to God I'm right*, Kat thought.

Harry Bowman had transferred from a residency program in Iowa. He was a good-humored, happy-go-lucky fellow who went out of his way to be pleasant to everyone.

One day, he said to Paige, 'I'm giving a little party tomorrow night. If you and Dr Hunter and Dr Taft are free, why don't you come? I think you'll have a good time.'

'Fine,' Paige said. 'What shall we bring?'

Bowman laughed. 'Don't bring anything.'

'Are you sure?' Paige asked. 'A bottle of wine, or . . .'

'Forget it! It's going to be at my little apartment.'

Bowman's little apartment turned out to be a ten-room penthouse, filled with antique furniture.

The three women walked in and stared in amazement.

'My God!' Kat said. 'Where did all this come from?'

'I was smart enough to have a clever father,' Bowman said. 'He left all his money to me.'

'And you're working?' Kat marveled.

Bowman smiled. 'I like being a doctor.'

The buffet consisted of Beluga Malossol caviar, *pâté de campagne*, smoked Scottish salmon, oysters on the half shell, backfin lump crabmeat, *crudités* with a shallot vinaigrette dressing, and Cristal champagne.

Bowman had been right. The three of them did have a wonderful time.

'I can't thank you enough,' Paige told Bowman at the end of the evening when they were leaving.

'Are you free Saturday?' he asked.

'Yes.'

'I have a little motorboat. I'll take you out for a spin.'

'Sounds great.'

At four o'clock in the morning, Kat was awakened out of a deep sleep in the on-call room. 'Dr Hunter, Emergency Room Three . . . Dr Hunter, Emergency Three.'

Kat got out of bed, fighting exhaustion. Rubbing sleep from her eyes, she took the elevator down to the ER.

An orderly greeted her at the door. 'He's over on the gurney in the corner. He's in a lot of pain.'

Kat walked over to him. 'I'm Dr Hunter,' she said sleepily.

He groaned. 'Jesus, doc. You've got to do somethin'. My back is killin' me.'

Kat stifled a yawn. 'How long have you been in pain?'

'About two weeks.'

Kat was looking at him, puzzled. 'Two weeks? Why didn't you come in sooner?'

He tried to move, and winced. 'To tell you the truth, I hate hospitals.'

'Then why are you coming in now?'

He brightened. 'There's a big golf tournament coming up, and if you don't fix my back, I won't be able to enjoy it.'

119

Kat took a deep breath. 'A golf tournament.'

'Yeah.'

She was fighting to control herself. 'I'll tell you what. Go home. Take two aspirins, and if you aren't feeling better in the morning, give me a call.' She turned and stormed out of the room, leaving him gaping after her.

Harry Bowman's little motorboat was a sleek fifty-foot motor cruiser.

'Welcome aboard!' he said as he greeted Paige, Kat, and Honey at the dock.

The women looked at the boat admiringly.

'It's beautiful,' Paige said.

They cruised around the bay for three hours, enjoying the warm, sunny day. It was the first time any of them had relaxed in weeks.

While they were anchored off Angel Island, eating a delicious lunch, Kat said, 'This is the life. Let's not go back to shore.'

'Good thinking,' Honey said.

All in all, it was a heavenly day.

When they returned to the dock, Paige said, 'I can't tell you how much I've enjoyed this.'

'It's been my pleasure.' Bowman patted her arm. 'We'll do it again. Anytime. You three are always welcome.'

What a lovely man, Paige thought.

Honey liked working in obstetrics. It was a ward filled with new life and new hope, in a timeless, joyful ritual.

The first-time mothers were eager and apprehensive. The veterans could not wait to get it over with.

One of the women who was about to deliver said to Honey, 'Thank God! I'll be able to see my toes again.'

If Paige had kept a diary, she would have marked the fifteenth of August as a red-letter day. That was the day Jimmy Ford came into her life.

Jimmy was a hospital orderly, with the brightest smile and the sunniest disposition Paige had ever seen. He was small and thin, and looked seventeen. He was twenty-five, and moved around the hospital corridors like a cheerful tornado. Nothing was too much trouble for him.

He was constantly running errands for everyone. He had absolutely no sense of status and treated doctors, nurses, and janitors alike.

Jimmy Ford loved to tell jokes.

'Did you hear about the patient in a body cast? The fellow in the bed next to him asked him what he did for a living.

'He said, "I was a window washer at the Empire State Building."

'The other fellow said, "When did you quit?"

' "Halfway down." '

And Jimmy would grin and hurry off to help somebody.

He adored Paige. 'I'm going to be a doctor one day. I want to be like you.'

He would bring her little presents — candy bars, and stuffed toys. A joke went with each gift.

'In Houston, a man stopped a pedestrian and asked, "What's the quickest way to the hospital?"

121

The other man said, "Say something bad about Texas."'

The jokes were terrible, but Jimmy made them sound funny.

He would arrive at the hospital the same time as Paige, and he would race up to her on his motorcycle.

'The patient asked, "Will my operation be dangerous?" And the surgeon said, "No. You can't get a dangerous operation for two hundred dollars."'

And he would be gone.

Whenever Paige, Kat, and Honey were free on the same day, they went out exploring San Francisco. They visited the Dutch Mill and the Japanese Tea Garden. They went to Fisherman's Wharf and rode the cable car. They went to see plays at the Curran Theater, and had dinner at the Maharani on Post Street. All the waiters were Indian, and to the astonishment of Kat and Honey, Paige addressed them in Hindi.

'*Hum Hindustani baht bahut ocho bolta hi.*' And from that moment, the restaurant was theirs.

'Where in the world did you learn to talk Indian?' Honey asked.

'Hindi,' Paige said. She hesitated. 'We . . . I lived in India for a while.' It was still so vivid. She and Alfred were at Agra, staring at the Taj Mahal. *Shah Jahan built that in memory of his wife. It took twenty years, Alfred.*

I'm going to build you a Taj Mahal. I don't care how long it takes!

This is Karen Turner. My wife.

She heard her name called, and turned.

'Paige . . .' There was a look of concern on Kat's face. 'Are you all right?'

'Fine. I'm fine.'

The impossible hours continued. Another New Year's Eve came and went, and the second year slid into the third, and nothing had changed. The hospital was untouched by the outside world. The wars and famines and disasters of far-off countries paled by comparison with the life-and-death crises they coped with twenty-four hours a day.

Whenever Kat and Paige met in the hospital corridors, Kat would grin and say, 'Having a good time?'

'When did you sleep last?' Paige asked.

Kat sighed. 'Who can remember?'

They stumbled through the long days and nights, trying to keep up with the incessant, demanding pressure, grabbing sandwiches when they had time, and drinking cold coffee out of paper cups.

The sexual harassment seemed to have become a part of Kat's life. There were the constant innuendos not only from the doctors, but also from patients who tried to get her into bed. They got the same response as the doctors. *There's not a man in the world I'll let touch me.*

And she really believed it.

In the middle of a busy morning, there was another telephone call from Mike.

'Hi, sis.'

And Kat knew what was coming. She had sent him all the money she could spare, but deep down inside, she knew that whatever she sent would never be enough.

'I hate like hell to bother you, Kat. I really do. But I got into a small jam.' His voice sounded strained.

'Mike . . . are you all right?'

'Oh, yeah. It's nothing serious. It's just that I owe somebody who needs his money back right away, and I was wondering . . .'

'I'll see what I can do,' Kat said wearily.

'Thanks. I can always count on you, can't I, sis? I love you.'

'I love you, too, Mike.'

One day, Kat said to Paige and Honey, 'Do you know what we all need?'

'A month's sleep?'

'A vacation. That's where we should be, strolling down the Champs-Elysées, looking in all those expensive shop windows.'

'Right. First-class all the way!' Paige giggled. 'We'll sleep all day and play all night.'

Honey laughed. 'Sounds good.'

'We have some vacation time coming up in a few months,' Paige observed. 'Why don't we make some plans for the three of us to go away somewhere?'

'That's a great idea,' Kat said enthusiastically. 'Saturday, let's stop in at a travel agency.'

They spent the next three days excitedly making plans.

'I'm dying to see London. Maybe we'll run into the queen.'

'Paris is where I want to go. It's supposed to be the most romantic city in the world.'

'I want to ride a gondola in the moonlight in Venice.'

Maybe we'll go to Venice on our honeymoon, Paige, Alfred had said. *Would you like that?*

Oh, yes!

She wondered if Alfred had taken Karen to Venice on their honeymoon.

Saturday morning the three of them stopped in at the Corniche Travel Agency on Powell Street.

The woman behind the counter was polite. 'What kind of trip are you interested in?'

'We'd like to go to Europe—London, Paris, Venice . . .'

'Lovely. We have some economical package tours that—'

'No, no, no.' Paige looked at Honey and grinned. 'First-class.'

'Right. First-class air travel,' Kat chimed in.

'First-class hotels,' Honey added.

'Well, I can recommend the Ritz in London, the Crillon in Paris, the Cipriani in Venice, and—'

Paige said, 'Why don't we just take some brochures with us? We can study them and make up our minds.'

'That will be fine,' the travel agent said.

Paige was looking at a brochure. 'You arrange yacht charters, too?'

'Yes.'

'Good. We may be chartering one.'

'Excellent.' The travel agent collected a handful of brochures and handed them to Paige. 'Whenever you're ready, just let me know and I'll be happy to make your reservations.'

'You'll hear from us,' Honey promised.

When they got outside, Kat laughed and said, 'Nothing like dreaming big, is there?'

'Don't worry,' Paige assured her. 'One day we'll be able to go to all those places.'

10

Seymour Wilson, the chief of medicine at Embarcadero County Hospital, was a frustrated man with an impossible job. There were too many patients, too few doctors and nurses, and too few hours in a day. He felt like the captain of a sinking ship, running around vainly trying to plug up the holes.

At the moment, Dr Wilson's immediate concern was Honey Taft. While some doctors seemed to like her a great deal, reliable residents and nurses kept reporting that Dr Taft was incapable of doing her job.

Wilson finally went to see Ben Wallace. 'I want to get rid of one of our doctors,' he said. 'The residents she makes rounds with tell me she's incompetent.'

Wallace remembered Honey. She was the one who had the extraordinarily high grades and glowing recommendation. 'I don't understand it,' he said. 'There must be some mistake.' He was thoughtful for a moment. 'I'll tell you what we'll do, Seymour. Who's the meanest son of a bitch on your staff?'

'Ted Allison.'

'All right. Tomorrow morning, send Honey Taft out on rounds with Dr Allison. Have him give you a report on her. If he says she's incompetent, I'll get rid of her.'

'Fair enough,' Dr Wilson said. 'Thanks, Ben.'

*   *   *

At lunch, Honey told Paige that she had been assigned to make the rounds with Dr Allison the following morning.

'I know him,' Paige said. 'He has a miserable reputation.'

'That's what I hear,' Honey said thoughtfully.

At that moment, in another part of the hospital, Seymour Wilson was talking to Ted Allison. Allison was a hard-bitten veteran of twenty-five years. He had served as a medical officer in the navy, and he still took pride in 'kicking ass'.

Seymour Wilson was saying, 'I want you to keep a close eye on Dr Taft. If she can't cut it, she's out. Understood?'

'Understood.'

He was looking forward to this. Like Seymour Wilson, Ted Allison despised incompetent doctors. In addition, he had a strong conviction that if women wanted to be in the medical profession, they should be nurses. If it was good enough for Florence Nightingale, it was good enough for the rest of them.

At six o'clock the following morning, the residents gathered in the corridor to begin their rounds. The group consisted of Dr Allison, Tom Benson, who was his chief assistant, and five residents, including Honey Taft.

Now, as Allison looked at Honey, he thought, *Okay, sister, let's see what you've got.* He turned to the group. 'Let's go.'

The first patient in Ward One was a teenage girl lying in bed, covered with heavy blankets. She was asleep when the group approached her.

'All right,' Dr Allison said. 'I want you all to take a look at her chart.'

The residents began to study the patient's chart. Dr Allison turned to Honey. 'This patient has fever, chills, general malaise, and anorexia. She has a temperature, a cough, and pneumonia. What's your diagnosis, Dr Taft?'

Honey stood there, frowning, silent.

'Well?'

'Well,' Honey said thoughtfully, 'I would say she probably has psittacosis—parrot fever.'

Dr Allison was looking at her in surprise. 'What . . . what makes you say that?'

'Her symptoms are typical of psittacosis, and I noticed that she works part-time as a clerk in a pet shop. Psittacosis is transmitted by infected parrots.'

Allison nodded slowly. 'That's . . . that's very good. Do you know what the treatment is?'

'Yes. Tetracycline for ten days, strict bed rest, and plenty of fluids.'

Dr Allison turned to the group, 'Did you all hear that? Dr Taft is absolutely right.'

They moved on to the next patient.

Dr Allison said, 'If you'll examine his chart, you'll find that he has mesothelial tumors, bloody effusion, and fatigue. What's the diagnosis?'

One of the residents said, hopefully, 'It sounds like some form of pneumonia.'

A second resident spoke up, 'It could be cancer.'

Dr Allison turned to Honey. 'What is your diagnosis, doctor?'

Honey looked thoughtful. 'Offhand, I'd say it was fibrous pneumoconiosis, a form of asbestos poisoning. His chart shows that he works in a carpet mill.'

129

Ted Allison could not conceal his admiration. 'Excellent! Excellent! Do you happen to know what the therapy is?'

'Unfortunately, no specific therapy is available yet.'

It became even more impressive. In the next two hours, Honey diagnosed a rare case of Reiter's syndrome, osteitis deformans polycythemia, and malaria.

When the rounds were over, Dr Allison shook Honey's hand. 'I'm not easily impressed, doctor, but I want to tell you that you have a tremendous future!'

Honey blushed. 'Thank you, Dr Allison.'

'And I intend to tell Ben Wallace so,' he said as he walked away.

Tom Benson, Allison's senior assistant, looked at Honey and smiled. 'I'll meet you in half an hour, baby.'

Paige tried to stay out of the way of Dr Arthur Kane — 007. But at every opportunity, Kane asked for Paige to assist him with operations. And each time, he would become more offensive.

'What do you mean, you won't go out with me? You must be getting it from someone else.'

And, 'I may be short, honey, but not everywhere. You know what I mean?'

She came to dread the occasions she had to work with him. Time after time, Paige watched Kane perform unnecessary surgery and take out organs that were healthy.

One day, as Paige and Kane were walking toward

the operating room, Paige asked, 'What are we going to operate on, doctor?'

'His wallet!' He saw the look on Paige's face. 'Just kidding, honey.'

'He should be working in a butcher shop,' Paige later said angrily to Kat. 'He has no right to be operating on people.'

After a particularly inept liver operation, Dr Kane turned to Paige and shook his head. 'Too bad. I don't know if he's going to make it.'

It was all Paige could do to contain her anger. She decided to have a talk with Tom Chang.

'Someone should report Dr Kane,' Paige said. 'He's murdering his patients!'

'Take it easy.'

'I can't! It's not right that they let a man like that operate. It's criminal. He should be brought up before the credentials committee.'

'What good would it do? You'd have to get other doctors to testify against him, and no one would be willing to do that. This is a close community, and we all have to live in it, Paige. It's almost impossible to get one doctor to testify against another. We're all vulnerable and we need each other too much. Calm down. I'll take you out and buy you lunch.'

Paige sighed. 'All right, but it's a lousy system.'

At lunch, Paige asked, 'How are you and Sye doing?'

He took a moment to answer. 'I . . . we're having problems. My work is destroying our marriage. I don't know what to do.'

'I'm sure it will work out,' Paige said.

Chang said fiercely, 'It had better.'

Paige looked up at him.

'I would kill myself if she left me.'

The following morning, Arthur Kane was scheduled to perform a kidney operation. The chief of surgery said to Paige, 'Dr Kane asked for you to assist him in OR Four.'

Paige's mouth was suddenly dry. She hated the thought of being near him.

Paige said, 'Couldn't you get someone else to . . . ?'

'He's waiting for you, doctor.'

Paige sighed. 'Right.'

By the time Paige had scrubbed up, the operation was already in progress.

'Give me a hand here, darling,' Kane said to Paige.

The patient's abdomen had been painted with an iodine solution and an incision had been made in the right upper quadrant of the abdomen, just below the rib cage. *So far, so good*, Paige thought.

'Scalpel!'

The scrub nurse handed Dr Kane a scalpel.

He looked up. 'Put some music on.'

A moment later a CD began to play.

Dr Kane kept cutting. 'Let's have something a little peppier.' He looked over at Paige. 'Start the bovie, sweetheart.'

Sweetheart. Paige gritted her teeth and picked up a bovie — an electric cautery tool. She began to cauterize the arteries to reduce the amount of blood in the abdomen. The operation was going well.

Thank God, Paige thought.

'Sponge.'

The scrub nurse handed Kane a sponge.

'Good. Let's have some suction.' He cut around the kidney until it was exposed. 'There's the little devil,' Dr Kane said. 'More suction.' He lifted up the kidney with forceps. 'Right. Let's sew him back up.'

For once, everything had gone well, yet something was bothering Paige. She took a closer look at the kidney. It looked healthy. She frowned, wondering if . . .

As Dr Kane began sewing up the patient, Paige hurried over to the X-ray in the lighted wall frame. She studied it for a moment and said softly, 'Oh, my God!'

The X-ray had been put up backward. Dr Kane had removed the wrong kidney.

Thirty minutes later, Paige was in Ben Wallace's office.

'He took out a healthy kidney and left in a diseased one!' Paige's voice was trembling. 'The man should be put in jail!'

Benjamin Wallace said soothingly, 'Paige, I agree with you that it's regrettable. But it certainly wasn't intentional. It was a mistake, and—'

'A *mistake*? That patient is going to have to live on dialysis for the rest of his life. Someone should pay for that!'

'Believe me, we're going to have a peer review evaluation.'

Paige knew what that meant: a group of physicians would review what had happened, but it would be done in confidence. The information would be withheld from the public and the patient.

'Dr Wallace . . .'

'You're part of our team, Paige. You've got to be a team player.'

'He has no business working in this hospital. Or any other hospital.'

'You've got to look at the whole picture. If he were removed, there would be bad publicity and the reputation of the hospital would be hurt. We'd probably face a lot of malpractice suits.'

'What about the patients?'

'We'll keep a closer eye on Dr Kane.' He leaned forward in his chair. 'I'm going to give you some advice. When you get into private practice, you're going to need the goodwill of other doctors for referrals. Without that, you'll go nowhere, and if you get the reputation of being a maverick and blowing the whistle on your fellow doctors, you won't get any referrals. I can promise you that.'

Paige rose. 'So you aren't going to do anything?'

'I told you, we're going to do a peer review evaluation.'

'And that's it?'

'That's it.'

'It's not fair,' Paige said. She was in the cafeteria having lunch with Kat and Honey.

Kat shook her head. 'Nobody said life has to be fair.'

Paige looked around the antiseptic white-tiled room. 'This whole place depresses me. Everybody is sick.'

'Or they wouldn't be here,' Kat pointed out.

'Why don't we give a party?' Honey suggested.

'A party? What are you talking about?'

Honey's voice was suddenly filled with enthusiasm. 'We could order up some decent food and liquor, and have a celebration! I think we could all use a little cheering up.'

Paige thought for a second. 'You know,' she said, 'that's not a bad idea. Let's do it!'

'It's a deal. I'll organize things,' Honey told them. 'We'll do it tomorrow after rounds.'

Arthur Kane approached Paige in the corridor. There was ice in his voice. 'You've been a naughty girl. Someone should teach you to keep your mouth shut!' And he walked away.

Paige looked after him in disbelief. *Wallace told him what I said. He shouldn't have done that. 'If you get the reputation of being a maverick and blowing the whistle on your fellow doctors . . .' Would I do it again?* Paige pondered. *Darned right I would!*

News of the forthcoming party spread rapidly. All the residents chipped in. A lavish menu was ordered from Ernie's restaurant, and liquor was delivered from a nearby store. The party was set for five o'clock in the doctors' lounge. The food and drinks arrived at four-thirty. There was a feast: seafood platters with lobster and shrimp, a variety of pâtés, Swedish meatballs, hot pasta, fruit, and desserts. When Paige, Kat, and Honey walked into the lounge at five-fifteen, it was already crowded with eager residents, interns, and nurses, eating and having a wonderful time.

Paige turned to Honey. 'This was a great idea!'

Honey smiled. 'Thank you.'

An announcement came over the loudspeaker. 'Dr Finley and Dr Ketler to the ER. Stat.' And the two doctors, in the middle of downing shrimp, looked at each other, sighed, and hurriedly left the room.

Tom Chang came up to Paige. 'We ought to do this every week,' he said.

'Right. It's —'

The loudspeaker came on again. 'Dr Chang . . . Room 317 . . . Dr Chang . . . Room 317.'

And a minute later, 'Dr Smythe . . . ER Two . . . Dr Smythe to ER Two.'

The loudspeaker never stopped. Within thirty minutes, almost every doctor and nurse had been called away on some emergency. Honey heard her name called, and then Paige's, and Kat's.

'I can't believe what's happening,' Kat said. 'You know how people talk about having a guardian angel? Well, I think the three of us are under the spell of a guardian devil.'

Her words proved to be prophetic.

The next Monday morning, when Paige got off duty and went to get into her car, two of the tires had been slashed. She stared at them in disbelief. *Someone should teach you to keep your mouth shut!*

When she got back to the apartment she said to Kat and Honey, 'Watch out for Arthur Kane. He's crazy.'

11

Kat was awakened by the ring of the telephone. Without opening her eyes, she reached out for it and put the receiver to her ear.

'H'lo?'

'Kat? It's Mike.'

She sat up, her heart suddenly pounding. 'Mike, are you all right?' She heard him laugh.

'Never better, sis. Thanks to you and your friend.'

'My friend?'

'Mr Dinetto.'

'Who?' Kat tried to concentrate, groggy with sleep.

'Mr Dinetto. He really saved my life.'

Kat had no idea what he was talking about. 'Mike . . .'

'You know the fellows I owed money to? Mr Dinetto got them off my back. He's a real gentleman. And he thinks the world of you, Kat.'

Kat had forgotten the incident with Dinetto, but now it suddenly flashed into her mind: *Lady, you don't know who you're talking to. You better do what the man says. This is Mr Lou Dinetto.*

Mike was going on. 'I'm sending you some cash, Kat. Your friend arranged for me to get a job. It pays real good money.'

137

Your friend. Kat was nervous. 'Mike, listen to me. I want you to be careful.'

She heard him laugh again.

'Don't worry about me. Didn't I tell you everything would be coming up roses? Well, I was right.'

'Take care of yourself, Mike. Don't—'

The connection was broken.

Kat was unable to go back to sleep. *Dinetto! How did he find out about Mike, and why is he helping him?*

The following night, when Kat left the hospital, a black limousine was waiting for her at the curb. The Shadow and Rhino were standing beside it.

As Kat started to pass, Rhino said, 'Get in, doctor. Mr Dinetto wants to see you.'

She studied the man for a moment. Rhino was ominous-looking, but it was the Shadow who frightened Kat. There was something deadly about his stillness. Under other circumstances, Kat would never have gotten into the car, but Mike's telephone call had puzzled her. And worried her.

She was driven to a small apartment on the outskirts of the city, and when she arrived, Dinetto was waiting for her.

'Thanks for coming, Dr Hunter,' he said. 'I appreciate it. A friend of mine had a little accident. I want you to take a look at him.'

'What are you doing with Mike?' Kat demanded.

'Nothing,' he said innocently. 'I heard he was in a little trouble, and I got it taken care of.'

'How did . . . how did you find out about him? I mean, that he was my brother and . . .'

Dinetto smiled. 'In my business, we're all friends. We help each other. Mike got mixed up with some bad boys, so I helped him out. You should be grateful.'

'I am,' Kat said. 'I really am.'

'Good! You know the saying "One hand washes the other"?'

Kat shook her head. 'I won't do anything illegal.'

'Illegal?' Dinetto said. He seemed hurt. 'I wouldn't ask you to do anything like that. This friend of mine was in a little accident and he hates hospitals. Would you take a look at him?'

What am I letting myself in for? Kat wondered. 'Very well.'

'He's in the bedroom.'

Dinetto's friend had been badly beaten up. He was lying in bed, unconscious.

'What happened to him?' Kat asked.

Dinetto looked at her and said, 'He fell down a flight of stairs.'

'He should be in a hospital.'

'I told you, he doesn't like hospitals. I can get whatever hospital equipment you need. I had another doctor who took care of my friends, but he had an accident.'

The words sent a chill through Kat. She wanted nothing more than to run out of the place and go home, and never hear Dinetto's name again, but nothing in life was free. *Quid pro quo.* Kat took off her coat and went to work.

12

By the beginning of her fourth year of residency, Paige had assisted in hundreds of operations. They had become second nature to her. She knew the surgery procedures for the gallbladder, spleen, liver, appendix, and, most exciting, the heart. But Paige was frustrated because she was not doing the operations herself. *Whatever happened to 'Watch one, do one, teach one'?* she wondered.

The answer came when George Englund, chief of surgery, sent for her.

'Paige, there's a hernia operation scheduled for tomorrow in OR Three, seven-thirty A.M.'

She made a note. 'Right. Who's doing the operation?'

'You are.'

'Right. I . . .' The words suddenly sank in. '*I* am?'

'Yes. Any problem with that?'

Paige's grin lit up the room. 'No, sir! I . . . thanks!'

'You're ready for it. I think the patient's lucky to have you. His name is Walter Herzog. He's in 314.'

'Herzog. Room 314. Right.'

And Paige was out the door.

Paige had never been so excited. *I'm going to do my first operation! I'm going to hold a human being's life in my hands. What if I'm not ready? What if I make a mistake? Things can go wrong. It's Murphy's Law.* By the time Paige was through arguing with herself, she was in a state of panic.

She went into the cafeteria and sat down to have a cup of black coffee. *It's going to be all right*, she told herself. *I've assisted in dozens of hernia operations. There's nothing to it. He's lucky to have me.* By the time she finished her coffee, she was calm enough to face her first patient.

Walter Herzog was in his sixties, thin, bald, and very nervous. He was in bed, clutching his groin, when Paige walked in, carrying a bouquet of flowers. Herzog looked up.

'Nurse . . . I want to see a doctor.'

Paige walked over to the bed and handed him the flowers. 'I'm the doctor. I'm going to operate on you.'

He looked at the flowers, and looked at her. 'You're *what*?'

'Don't worry,' Paige said reassuringly. 'You're in good hands.' She picked up his chart at the foot of the bed and studied it.

'What does it say?' the man asked anxiously. *Why did she bring me flowers?*

'It says you're going to be just fine.'

He swallowed. 'Are you really going to do the operation?'

'Yes.'

'You seem awfully . . . awfully young.'

Paige patted his arm. 'I haven't lost a patient yet.' She looked around the room. 'Are you comfortable?

Can I get you anything to read? A book or magazine?'

He was listening, nervously. 'No, I'm okay.' *Why was she being so nice to him? Was there something she wasn't telling him?*

'Well, then, I'll see you in the morning,' Paige said cheerfully. She wrote something on a piece of paper and handed it to him. 'Here's my home number. You call me if you need me tonight. I'll stay right by the phone.'

By the time Paige left, Walter Herzog was a nervous wreck.

A few minutes later, Jimmy found Paige in the lounge. He walked up to her with his wide grin. 'Congratulations! I hear you're going to do a procedure.'

Word gets around fast, Paige thought. 'Yes.'

'Whoever he is, he's lucky,' Jimmy said. 'If anything ever happened to me, you're the only one I'd let operate on me.'

'Thanks, Jimmy.'

And, of course, with Jimmy, there was always a joke.

'Did you hear the one about the man who had a strange pain in his ankles? He was too cheap to go to a doctor, so when his friend told him he had exactly the same pain, he said, "You'd better get to a doctor right away. And tell me exactly what he says."

'The next day, he learns his friend is dead. He rushes to a hospital and has five thousand dollars' worth of tests. They can't find anything wrong. He calls his friend's widow, and says, "Was Chester in a lot of pain before he died?"

'"No," she says. "He didn't even see the truck that hit him!"'

And Jimmy was gone.

Paige was too excited to eat dinner. She spent the evening practicing tying surgical knots on table legs and lamps. *I'm going to get a good night's sleep*, Paige decided, *so I'll be nice and fresh in the morning*.

She was awake all night, going over the operation again and again in her mind.

There are three types of hernias: reducible hernia, where it's possible to push the intestines back into the abdomen; irreducible hernia, where adhesions prevent returning the contents to the abdomen; and the most dangerous, strangulated hernia, where the blood flow through the hernia is shut off, damaging the intestines. Walter Herzog's was a reducible hernia.

At six o'clock in the morning, Paige drove to the hospital parking lot. A new red Ferrari was next to her parking space. Idly, Paige wondered who owned it. Whoever it was had to be rich.

At seven o'clock, Paige was helping Walter Herzog change from pajamas to a blue hospital gown. The nurse had already given him a sedative to relax him while they waited for the gurney that would take him to the operating room.

'This is my first operation,' Walter Herzog said.

Mine, too, Paige thought.

The gurney arrived and Walter Herzog was on his way to OR Three. Paige walked down the corridor beside him, and her heart was pounding so loudly that she was afraid he could hear it.

OR Three was one of the larger operating rooms, able to accommodate a heart monitor, a heart-lung machine, and an array of other technical paraphernalia. When Paige walked into the room, the staff were already there, preparing the equipment. There was an attending physician, the anesthesiologist, two residents, a scrub nurse, and two circulating nurses.

The staff were watching her expectantly, eager to see how she would handle her first operation.

Paige walked up to the operating table. Walter Herzog had had his groin shaved and scrubbed with an antiseptic solution. Sterile drapes had been placed around the operating area.

Herzog looked up at Paige and said drowsily, 'You're not going to let me die, are you?'

Paige smiled. 'What? And spoil my perfect record?'

She looked over at the anesthesiologist, who would give the patient an epidural anesthesia, a saddle block. Paige took a deep breath and nodded.

The operation began.

'Scalpel.'

As Paige was about to make the first cut through the skin, the circulating nurse said something.

'What?'

'Would you like some music, doctor?'

It was the first time she had been asked that question. Paige smiled. 'Right. Let's have some Jimmy Buffett.'

The moment Paige made the first incision, her nervousness vanished. It was as though she had done this all her life. Skillfully, she cut through the first layers of fat and muscle, to the site of the hernia. All the while, she was aware of the familiar litany that was echoing through the room.

'Sponge . . .'

'Give me a bovie . . .'

'There it is . . .'

'Looks like we got there just in time . . .'

'Clamp . . .'

'Suction, please . . .'

Paige's mind was totally focused on what she was doing. Locate the hernial sac . . . free it . . . place the contents back into the abdominal cavity . . . tie off the base of the sac . . . cut off the remainder . . . inguinal ring . . . suture it . . .

One hour and twenty minutes after the first incision, the operation was finished.

Paige should have felt drained, but instead she felt wildly exhilarated.

When Walter Herzog had been sewn up, the scrub nurse turned to Paige. 'Dr Taylor . . .'

Paige looked up. 'Yes?'

The nurse grinned. 'That was beautiful, doctor.'

It was Sunday and the three women had the day off.

'What should we do today?' Kat asked.

Paige had an idea. 'It's such a lovely day, why

145

don't we drive out to Tree Park? We can pack a picnic lunch and eat outdoors.'

'That sounds lovely,' Honey said.

'Let's do it!' Kat agreed.

The telephone rang. The three of them stared at it.

'Jesus!' Kat said. 'I thought Lincoln freed us. Don't answer it. It's our day off.'

'We *have* no days off,' Paige reminded her.

Kat walked over to the telephone and picked it up. 'Dr Hunter.' She listened for a moment and handed the telephone to Paige. 'It's for you, Dr Taylor.'

Paige said resignedly, 'Right.' She picked up the receiver. 'Dr Taylor . . . Hello, Tom . . . What? . . . No, I was just going out . . . I see . . . All right. I'll be there in fifteen minutes.' She replaced the receiver. *So much for the picnic*, she thought.

'Is it bad?' Honey asked.

'Yes, we're about to lose a patient. I'll try to be back for dinner tonight.'

When Paige arrived at the hospital, she drove into the doctors' parking lot and parked next to the new bright red Ferrari. *I wonder how many operations it took to pay for that?*

Twenty minutes later, Paige was walking into the visitors' waiting room. A man in a dark suit was seated in a chair, staring out the window.

'Mr Newton?'

He rose to his feet. 'Yes.'

'I'm Dr Taylor. I was just in to see your little

boy. He was brought in suffering abdominal pains.'

'Yes. I'm going to take him home.'

'I'm afraid not. Peter has a ruptured spleen. He needs an immediate transfusion and an operation, or he'll die.'

Mr Newton shook his head. 'We are Jehovah's Witnesses. The Lord will not let him die, and I will not let him be tainted with someone else's blood. It was my wife who brought him here. She will be punished for that.'

'Mr Newton, I don't think you understand how serious the situation is. If we don't operate right away, your son is going to die.'

The man looked at her and smiled. 'You don't know God's ways, do you?'

Paige was angry. 'I may not know a lot about God's ways, but I do know a lot about a ruptured spleen.' She took out a piece of paper. 'He's a minor, so you'll have to sign this consent form for him.' She held it out.

'And if I don't sign it?'

'Why . . . then we can't operate.'

He nodded. 'Do you think your powers are stronger than the Lord's?'

Paige was staring at him. 'You're not going to sign, are you?'

'No. A higher power than yours will help my son. You will see.'

When Paige returned to the ward, six-year-old Peter Newton had lapsed into unconsciousness.

'He's not going to make it,' Chang said. 'He's lost too much blood. What do you want to do?'

Paige made her decision. 'Get him into OR One. Stat.'

Chang looked at her in surprise. 'His father changed his mind?'

Paige nodded. 'Yes. He changed his mind. Let's move it.'

'Good for you! I talked to him for an hour and I couldn't budge him. He said God would take care of it.'

'God is taking care of it,' Paige assured him.

Two hours and four pints of blood later, the operation was successfully completed. All the boy's vital signs were strong.

Paige gently stroked his forehead. 'He's going to be fine.'

An orderly hurried into the operating room. 'Dr Taylor? Dr Wallace wants to see you right away.'

Benjamin Wallace was so angry his voice was cracking. 'How could you do such an outrageous thing? You gave him a blood transfusion and operated without permission? You broke the law!'

'I saved the boy's life!'

Wallace took a deep breath. 'You should have gotten a court order.'

'There was no time,' Paige said. 'Ten minutes more and he would have been dead. God was busy elsewhere.'

Wallace was pacing back and forth. 'What are we going to do now?'

'Get a court order.'

'What for? You've already *done* the operation.'

'I'll backdate the court order one day. No one will ever know the difference.'

Wallace looked at her and began to hyperventilate. 'Jesus!' He mopped his brow. 'This could cost me my job.'

Paige looked at him for a long moment. Then she turned and started toward the door.

'Paige . . . ?'

She stopped. 'Yes?'

'You'll never do anything like this again, will you?'

'Only if I have to,' Paige assured him.

⊃+ +⊂

All hospitals have problems with drug theft. By law, each narcotic that is taken from the dispensary must be signed for, but no matter how controlled the security is, drug addicts almost invariably find a way to circumvent it.

Embarcadero County Hospital was having a major problem. Margaret Spencer went to see Ben Wallace.

'I don't know what to do, doctor. Our fentanyl keeps disappearing.'

Fentanyl is a highly addictive narcotic and anesthetic drug.

'How much is missing?'

'A great deal. If it were just a few bottles, there could be an innocent explanation for it, but it's happening now on a regular basis. More than a dozen bottles a week are disappearing.'

'Do you have any idea who might be taking it?'

'No, sir. I've talked to security. They're at a loss.'

'Who has access to the dispensary?'

'That's the problem. Most of the anesthetists have pretty free access to it, and most of the nurses and surgeons.'

Wallace was thoughtful. 'Thank you for coming to me. I'll take care of it.'

'Thank you, doctor.' Nurse Spencer left.

I don't need this right now, Wallace thought

angrily. A hospital board meeting was coming up, and there were already enough problems to be dealt with. Ben Wallace was well aware of the statistics. More than 10 percent of the doctors in the United States became addicted, at one time or another, to either drugs or alcohol. The easy accessibility of the drugs made them a temptation. It was simple for a doctor to open a cabinet, take out the drug he wanted, and use a tourniquet and syringe to inject it. An addict could need a fix as often as every two hours.

Now it was happening at his hospital. Something had to be done about it before the board meeting. *It would look bad on my record.*

Ben Wallace was not sure whom he could trust to help him find the culprit. He had to be careful. He was certain that neither Dr Taylor nor Dr Hunter was involved, and after a great deal of thought, he decided to use them.

He sent for the two of them. 'I have a favor to ask of you,' he told them. He explained about the missing fentanyl. 'I want you to keep your eyes open. If any of the doctors you work with has to step out of the OR for a moment, in the middle of an operation, or shows any other signs of addiction, I want you to let me know. Look for any changes in personality — depression or mood swings — or tardiness, or missed appointments. I would appreciate it if you would keep this strictly confidential.'

When they left the office, Kat said, 'This is a big hospital. We're going to need Sherlock Holmes.'

'No, we won't,' Paige said unhappily. 'I know who it is.'

*   *   *

Mitch Campbell was one of Paige's favorite doctors. Dr Campbell was a likable gray-haired man in his fifties, always good-humored, and one of the hospital's best surgeons. Paige had noticed lately that he was always a few minutes late for an operation, and that he had developed a noticeable tremor. He used Paige to assist him as often as possible, and he usually let her do a major part of the surgery. In the middle of an operation, his hands would begin to shake and he would hand the scalpel to Paige.

'I'm not feeling well,' he would mumble. 'Would you take over?'

And he would leave the operating room.

Paige had been concerned about what could be wrong with him. Now she knew. She debated what to do. She was aware that if she brought her information to Wallace, Dr Campbell would be fired, or worse, his career would be destroyed. On the other hand, if she did nothing, she would be putting patients' lives in danger. *Perhaps I could talk to him*, Paige thought. *Tell him what I know, and insist that he get treatment.* She discussed it with Kat.

'It's a problem,' Kat agreed. 'He's a nice guy, and a good doctor. If you blow the whistle, he's finished, but if you don't, you have to think about the harm he might do. What do you think will happen if you confront him?'

'He'll probably deny it, Kat. That's the usual pattern.'

'Yeah. It's a tough call.'

*   *   *

152

The following day, Paige had an operation scheduled with Dr Campbell. *I hope I'm wrong*, Paige prayed. *Don't let him be late, and don't let him leave during the operation*.

Campbell was fifteen minutes late, and in the middle of the operation, he said, 'Take over, will you, Paige? I'll be right back.'

I must talk to him, Paige decided. *I can't destroy his career*.

The following morning, as Paige and Honey drove into the doctors' parking lot, Harry Bowman pulled up next to them in the red Ferrari.

'That's a beautiful car,' Honey said. 'How much does one of those cost?'

Bowman laughed. 'If you have to ask, you can't afford it.'

But Paige wasn't listening. She was staring at the car, and thinking about the penthouse, the lavish parties, and the boat. *I was smart enough to have a clever father. He left all his money to me.* And yet Bowman worked at a county hospital. Why?

Ten minutes later, Paige was in the personnel office, talking to Karen, the secretary in charge of records.

'Do me a favor, will you, Karen? Just between us, Harry Bowman has asked me to go out with him and I have a feeling he's married. Would you let me have a peek at his personnel file?'

'Sure. Those horny bastards. They never get enough, do they? You're darn right I'll let you look at his file.' She went over to a cabinet and found what she was looking for. She brought some papers back to Paige.

Paige glanced through them quickly. Dr Harry Bowman's application showed that he had come from a small university in the Midwest and, according to the records, had worked his way through medical school. He was an anesthesiologist.

His father was a barber.

Honey Taft was an enigma to most of the doctors at Embarcadero County Hospital. During the morning rounds, she appeared to be unsure of herself. But on the afternoon rounds, she seemed like a different person. She was surprisingly knowledgeable about each patient, and crisp and efficient in her diagnoses.

One of the senior residents was discussing her with a colleague.

'I'll be damned if I understand it,' he said. 'In the morning, the complaints about Dr Taft keep piling up. She keeps making mistakes. You know the joke about the nurse who gets everything wrong? A doctor is complaining that he told her to give the patient in Room 4 three pills, and she gave the patient in Room 3 four pills, and just as he's talking about her, he sees her chasing a naked patient down the hall, holding a pan of boiling water. The doctor says, "Look at that! I told her to prick his boil!"'

His colleague laughed.

'Well, that's Dr Taft. But in the afternoon she's absolutely brilliant. Her diagnoses are correct, her notes are wonderful, and she's as sharp as hell. She must be taking some kind of miracle pill that only works afternoons.' He scratched his head. 'It beats the hell out of me.'

Dr Nathan Ritter was a pedant, a man who lived and worked by the book. While he lacked the spark of brilliance, he was capable and dedicated, and he expected the same qualities from those who worked with him.

Honey had the misfortune to be assigned to his team.

Their first stop was a ward containing a dozen patients. One of them was just finishing breakfast. Ritter looked at the chart at the foot of the bed. 'Dr Taft, the chart says this is your patient.'

Honey nodded. 'Yes.'

'He's having a bronchoscopy this morning.'

Honey nodded. 'That's right.'

'And you're allowing him to *eat*?' Dr Ritter snapped. '*Before* a bronchoscopy?'

Honey said, 'The poor man hasn't had anything to eat since —'

Nathan Ritter turned to his assistant. 'Postpone the procedure.' He started to say something to Honey, then controlled himself. 'Let's move on.'

The next patient was a Puerto Rican who was coughing badly. Dr Ritter examined him. 'Whose patient is this?'

'Mine,' Honey said.

He frowned. 'His infection should have cleared up before now.' He took a look at the chart. 'You're giving him fifty milligrams of ampicillin four times a day?'

155

'That's right.'

'That's *not* right. It's *wrong*! That's supposed to be *five hundred* milligrams four times a day. You left off a zero.'

'I'm sorry, I . . .'

'No wonder the patient's not getting any better! I want it changed immediately.'

'Yes, doctor.'

When they came to another patient of Honey's, Dr Ritter said impatiently, 'He's scheduled for a colonoscopy. Where is the radiology report?'

'The radiology report? Oh. I'm afraid I forgot to order one.'

Ritter gave Honey a long speculative look.

The morning went downhill from there.

The next patient they saw was moaning tearfully. 'I'm in such pain. What's wrong with me?'

'We don't know,' Honey said.

Dr Ritter glared at her. 'Dr Taft, may I see you outside for a moment?'

In the corridor, he said, 'Never, *never* tell a patient that you don't know. You're the one they're looking to for help! And if you don't know the answer, make one up. Do you understand?'

'It doesn't seem right to . . .'

'I didn't ask you whether it seemed right. Just do as you're told.'

They examined a hiatal hernia, a hepatitis patient, a patient with Alzheimer's disease, and two dozen others. The minute the rounds were over, Dr Ritter went to Benjamin Wallace's office.

'We have a problem,' Ritter said.

'What is it, Nathan?'

'It's one of the residents here. Honey Taft.'

Again! 'What about her?'

'She's a disaster.'

'But she had such a wonderful recommendation.'

'Ben, you'd better get rid of her before the hospital gets in real trouble, before she kills a patient or two.'

Wallace thought about it for a moment, then made his decision. 'Right. She'll be out of here.'

Paige was busy in surgery most of the morning. As soon as she was free, she went to see Dr Wallace, to tell him of her suspicions about Harry Bowman.

'Bowman? Are you sure? I mean . . . I've seen no signs of any addiction.'

'He doesn't use it,' Paige explained. 'He sells it. He's living like a millionaire on a resident's salary.'

Ben Wallace nodded. 'Very well. I'll check it out. Thank you, Paige.'

Wallace sent for Bruce Anderson, head of security. 'We may have identified the drug thief,' Wallace told him. 'I want you to keep a close watch on Dr Harry Bowman.'

'Bowman?' Anderson tried to conceal his surprise. Dr Bowman was constantly giving the guards Cuban cigars and other little gifts. They all loved him.

'If he goes into the dispensary, search him when he comes out.'

'Yes, sir.'

Harry Bowman was headed for the dispensary. He had orders to fill. A *lot* of orders. It had started as a lucky accident. He had been working in a small hospital in Ames, Iowa, struggling to get by on a

157

resident's salary. He had champagne taste and a beer pocketbook, and then Fate had smiled on him.

One of his patients who had been discharged from the hospital telephoned him one morning.

'Doctor, I'm in terrible pain. You have to give me something for it.'

'Do you want to check back in?'

'I don't want to leave the house. Couldn't you bring something here for me?'

Bowman thought about it. 'All right. I'll drop by on my way home.'

When he visited the patient, he brought with him a bottle of fentanyl.

The patient grabbed it. 'That's wonderful!' he said. He pulled out a handful of bills. 'Here.'

Bowman looked at him, surprised. 'You don't have to pay me for that.'

'Are you kidding? This stuff is like gold. I have a lot of friends who will pay you a fortune if you bring them this stuff.'

That was how it had begun. Within two months, Harry Bowman was making more money than he had ever dreamed possible. Unfortunately, the head of the hospital got wind of what was going on. Fearing a public scandal, he told Bowman that if he left quietly, nothing would appear on his record.

I'm glad I left, Bowman thought. *San Francisco has a much bigger market.*

He reached the dispensary. Bruce Anderson was standing outside. Bowman nodded to him. 'Hi, Bruce.'

'Good afternoon, Dr Bowman.'

Five minutes later when Bowman came out of the dispensary, Anderson said, 'Excuse me. I'm going to have to search you.'

Harry Bowman stared at him. 'Search me? What are you talking about, Bruce?'

'I'm sorry, doctor. We have orders to search everyone who uses the dispensary,' Anderson lied.

Bowman was indignant. 'I've never heard of such a thing. I absolutely refuse!'

'Then I'll have to ask you to come along with me to Dr Wallace's office.'

'Fine! He's going to be furious when he hears about this.'

Bowman stormed into Wallace's office. 'What's going on, Ben? This man wanted to search me, for God's sake!'

'And did you refuse to be searched?'

'Absolutely.'

'All right.' Wallace reached for the telephone. 'I'll let the San Francisco police do it, if you prefer.' He began to dial.

Bowman panicked. 'Wait a minute! That's not necessary.' His face suddenly cleared. 'Oh! I know what this is all about!' He reached in his pocket and took out a bottle of fentanyl. 'I was taking these to use for an operation, and . . .'

Wallace said quietly, 'Empty your pockets.'

A look of desperation came over Bowman's face. 'There's no reason to . . .'

'Empty your pockets.'

Two hours later, the San Francisco office of the Drug Enforcement Agency had a signed confession and the names of the people to whom Bowman had been selling drugs.

*   *   *

When Paige heard the news, she went to see Mitch Campbell. He was sitting in an office, resting. His hands were on the desk when Paige walked in, and she could see the tremor in them.

Campbell quickly moved his hands to his lap. 'Hello, Paige. How're you doing?'

'Fine, Mitch. I wanted to talk to you.'

'Sit down.'

She took a seat opposite him. 'How long have you had Parkinson's?'

He turned a shade whiter. 'What?'

'That's it, isn't it? You've been trying to cover it up.'

There was a heavy silence. 'I . . . I . . . yes. But I . . . I can't give up being a doctor. I . . . I just can't give it up. It's my whole life.'

Paige leaned forward and said earnestly, 'You don't have to give up being a doctor, but you shouldn't be operating.'

He looked suddenly old. 'I know. I was going to quit last year.' He smiled wanly. 'I guess I'll have to quit now, won't I? You're going to tell Dr Wallace.'

'No,' Paige said gently. '*You're* going to tell Dr Wallace.'

Paige was having lunch in the cafeteria when Tom Chang joined her.

'I heard what happened,' he said. 'Bowman! Unbelievable. Nice work.'

She shook her head. 'I almost had the wrong man.'

Chang sat there, silent.

'Are you all right, Tom?'

'Do you want the "I'm fine", or do you want the truth?'

'We're friends. I want the truth.'

'My marriage has gone to hell.' His eyes suddenly filled with tears. 'Sye has left. She's gone back home.'

'I'm so sorry.'

'It's not her fault. We didn't have a marriage anymore. She said I'm married to the hospital, and she's right. I'm spending my whole life here, taking care of strangers, instead of being with the people I love.'

'She'll come back. It will work out,' Paige said soothingly.

'No. Not this time.'

'Have you thought about counseling, or . . . ?'

'She refuses.'

'I'm sorry, Tom. If there's anything I . . .' She heard her name on the loudspeaker.

'Dr Taylor, Room 410 . . .'

Paige felt a sudden pang of alarm. 'I have to go,' she said. Room 410. That was Sam Bernstein's room. He was one of her favorite patients, a gentle man in his seventies who had been brought in with inoperable stomach cancer. Many of the patients at the hospital were constantly complaining, but Sam Bernstein was an exception. Paige admired his courage and his dignity. He had a wife and two grown sons who visited him regularly, and Paige had grown fond of them, too.

He had been put on life-support systems with a note, DNR—Do Not Resuscitate—if his heart stopped.

When Paige walked into his room, a nurse was at the bedside. She looked up as Paige entered. 'He's

161

gone, doctor. I didn't start emergency procedures, because . . .' Her voice trailed off.

'You were right not to,' Paige said slowly. 'Thank you.'

'Is there anything I . . . ?'

'No. I'll make the arrangements.' Paige stood by the bedside and looked down at the body of what had been a living, laughing human being, a man who had a family and friends, someone who had spent his life working hard, taking care of the ones he loved. And now . . .

She walked over to the drawer where he kept his possessions. There was an inexpensive watch, a set of keys, fifteen dollars in cash, dentures, and a letter to his wife. All that remained of a man's life.

Paige was unable to shake the feeling of depression that hung over her. 'He was such a dear man. Why . . . ?'

Kat said, 'Paige, you can't let yourself get emotionally involved with your patients. It will tear you apart.'

'I know. You're right, Kat. It's just that . . . it's over so quickly, isn't it? This morning he and I were talking. Tomorrow is his funeral.'

'You're not thinking of going to it?'

'No.'

The funeral took place at the Hills of Eternity Cemetery.

In the Jewish religion, burial must take place as soon as possible following the death, and the service usually takes place the next day.

The body of Sam Bernstein was dressed in a *takhri-*

162

khim, a white robe, and wrapped in a *talit*. The family was gathered around the graveside. The rabbi was intoning, '*Hamakom y'nathaim etkhem b'tokh sh'ar availai tziyon veeyerushalayim.*'

A man standing next to Paige saw the puzzled expression on her face, and he translated for her. '"May the Lord comfort you with all the mourners of Zion and Jerusalem."'

To Paige's astonishment, the members of the family began tearing at the clothes they were wearing as they chanted, '*Baruch ata adonai elohainu melech haolam dayan ha-emet.*'

'What . . . ?'

'That's to show respect,' the man whispered. '"From dust you are and to dust you have returned, but the spirit returns to God who gave it."'

The ceremony was over.

The following morning, Kat ran into Honey in the corridor. Honey looked nervous.

'Anything wrong?' Kat asked.

'Dr Wallace sent for me. He asked me to be in his office at two o'clock.'

'Do you know why?'

'I think I messed up at rounds the other day. Dr Ritter is a monster.'

'He can be,' Kat said. 'But I'm sure everything will be all right.'

'I hope so. I just have a bad feeling.'

Promptly at two o'clock, she arrived at Benjamin Wallace's office, carrying a small jar of honey in her purse. The receptionist was at lunch. Dr Wallace's door was open. 'Come in, Dr Taft,' he called.

Honey walked into his office.

'Close the door behind you, please.'

Honey closed the door.

'Take a seat.'

Honey sat down across from him. She was almost trembling.

Benjamin Wallace had been putting this off as long as he could. He looked across at her and thought, *It's like kicking a puppy. But what has to be done has to be done.* 'I'm afraid I have some unfortunate news for you,' he said.

One hour later, Honey met Kat in the solarium. Honey sank into a chair next to her, smiling.

'Did you see Dr Wallace?' Kat asked.

'Oh, yes. We had a long talk. Did you know that his wife left him last September? They were married for fifteen years. He has two grown children from an earlier marriage, but he hardly ever sees them. The poor darling is so lonely.'

Book Two

14

It was New Year's Eve again, and Paige, Kat and Honey ushered in 1994 at Embarcadero County Hospital. It seemed to them that nothing in their lives had changed except the names of their patients.

As Paige walked through the parking lot, she was reminded of Harry Bowman and his red Ferrari. *How many lives were destroyed by the poison Harry Bowman was selling?* she wondered. Drugs were so seductive. And, in the end, so deadly.

Jimmy Ford showed up with a small bouquet of flowers for Paige.

'What's this for, Jimmy?'

He blushed. 'I just wanted you to have it. Did you know I'm getting married?'

'No! That's wonderful. Who's the lucky girl?'

'Her name is Betsy. She works at a dress shop. We're going to have half a dozen kids. The first girl is going to be named Paige. I hope you don't mind.'

'Mind? I'm flattered.'

He was embarrassed. 'Did you hear the one about the doctor who gave a patient two weeks to live? "I can't pay you right now," the man said. "All right, I'll give you another two weeks."'

And Jimmy was gone.

Paige was worried about Tom Chang. He was having violent mood swings from euphoria to deep depression.

One morning during a talk with Paige, he said, 'Do you realize that most of the people in here would die without us? We have the power to heal their bodies and make them whole again.'

And the next morning: 'We're all kidding ourselves, Paige. Our patients would get better faster without us. We're hypocrites, pretending that we have all the answers. Well, we don't.'

Paige studied him a moment. 'What do you hear from Sye?'

'I talked to her yesterday. She won't come back here. She's going ahead with the divorce.'

Paige put her hand on his arm. 'I'm so sorry, Tom.'

He shrugged. 'Why? It doesn't bother me. Not anymore. I'll find another woman.' He grinned. 'And have another child. You'll see.'

There was something unreal about the conversation.

That night Paige said to Kat, 'I'm worried about Tom Chang. Have you talked to him lately?'

'Yes.'

'Did he seem normal to you?'

'No man seems normal to me,' Kat said.

Paige was still concerned. 'Let's invite him out for dinner tomorrow night.'

'All right.'

168

The next morning when Paige reported to the hospital, she was greeted with the news that a janitor had found Tom Chang's body in a basement equipment room. He had died of an overdose of sleeping pills.

Paige was near hysteria. 'I could have saved him,' she cried. 'All this time he was calling out for help, and I didn't hear him.'

Kat said firmly, 'There's no way you could have helped him, Paige. You were not the problem, and you were not the solution. He didn't want to live without his wife and child. It's as simple as that.'

Paige wiped the tears from her eyes. 'Damn this place!' she said. 'If it weren't for the pressure and the hours, his wife never would have left him.'

'But she did,' Kat said gently. 'It's over.'

Paige had never been to a Chinese funeral before. It was an incredible spectacle. It began at the Green Street Mortuary in Chinatown early in the morning, where a crowd started gathering outside. A parade was assembled, with a large brass marching band, and at the head of the parade, mourners carried a huge blowup of a photograph of Tom Chang.

The march began with the band loudly playing, winding through the streets of San Francisco, with a hearse at the end of the procession. Most of the mourners were on foot, but the more elderly rode in cars.

To Paige, the parade seemed to be moving around the city at random. She was puzzled. 'Where are they going?' she asked one of the mourners.

He bowed slightly and said, 'It is our custom to

169

take the departed past some of the places that have meaning in his life — restaurants where he ate, shops that he used, places he visited . . .'

'I see.'

The parade ended in front of Embarcadero County Hospital.

The mourner turned to Paige and said, 'This is where Tom Chang worked. This is where he found his happiness.'

Wrong, Paige thought. *This is where he lost his happiness.*

Walking down Market Street one morning, Paige saw Alfred Turner. Her heart started pounding. She had not been able to get him out of her mind. He was starting to cross the street as the light was changing. When Paige got to the corner, the light had turned to red. She ignored it and ran out into the street, oblivious to the honking horns and the outraged cries of motorists.

Paige reached the other side and hurried to catch up with him. She grabbed his sleeve. 'Alfred . . .'

The man turned. 'I beg your pardon?'

It was a total stranger.

Now that Paige and Kat were fourth-year residents, they were performing operations on a regular basis.

Kat was working with doctors in neurosurgery, and she never ceased to be amazed at the miracle of the hundred billion complex digital computers called neurons that lived in the skull. The work was exciting.

Kat had enormous respect for most of the doctors she worked with. They were brilliant, skilled surgeons. There were a few doctors who gave her a hard time. They tried to date her, and the more Kat refused to go out with them, the more of a challenge she became.

She heard one doctor mutter, 'Here comes old ironpants.'

She was assisting Dr Kibler at a brain operation. A tiny incision was made in the cortex, and Dr Kibler pushed the rubber cannula into the left lateral ventricle, the cavity in the center of the left half of the brain, while Kat held the incision open with a small retractor. Her entire concentration was focused on what was happening in front of her.

Dr Kibler glanced at her and, as he worked, said, 'Did you hear about the wino who staggered into a bar and said, "Give me a drink, quick!" "I can't do that," the bartender said. "You're already drunk."'

The burr was cutting in deeper.

'"If you don't give me a drink, I'll kill myself."'

Cerebral spinal fluid flowed out of the cannula from the ventricle.

'"I'll tell you what I'll do," the bartender said. "There are three things I want. You do them for me, and I'll give you a bottle."'

As he went on talking, fifteen milliliters of air were injected into the ventricle, and X-rays were taken of the anterior-posterior view and the lateral view.

'"See that football player sitting in the corner? I can't get him out of here. I want you to throw him out. Next, I have a pet crocodile in my office with a bad tooth. He's so mean I can't get a vet to go near

171

him. Lastly, there's a lady doctor from the Department of Health who's trying to close up this place. You fuck her, and you get the bottle."'

A scrub nurse was using suction to reduce the amount of blood in the field.

'The wino throws out the football player, and goes into the office where the crocodile is. He comes out fifteen minutes later, all bloody, and his clothes torn, and he says, "Where's the lady doctor with the bad tooth?"'

Dr Kibler roared with laughter. 'Do you get it? He fucked the crocodile instead of the doctor. It was probably a better experience!'

Kat stood there, furious, wanting to slap him.

When the operation was over, Kat went to the on-call room to try to get over her anger. *I'm not going to let the bastards beat me down. I'm not.*

From time to time, Paige went out with doctors from the hospital, but she refused to get romantically involved with any of them. Alfred Turner had hurt her too deeply, and she was determined never to go through that again.

Most of her days and nights were spent at the hospital. The schedule was grueling, but Paige was doing general surgery and she enjoyed it.

One morning, George Englund, the chief of surgery, sent for her.

'You're starting your specialty this year. Cardiovascular surgery.'

She nodded. 'That's right.'

'Well, I have a treat for you. Have you heard of Dr Barker?'

Paige looked at him in surprise. 'Dr *Lawrence* Barker?'

'Yes.'

'Of course.'

Everyone had heard of Lawrence Barker. He was one of the most famous cardiovascular surgeons in the world.

'Well, he returned last week from Saudi Arabia, where he operated on the king. Dr Barker's an old friend of mine, and he's agreed to give us three days a week here. *Pro bono*.'

'That's fantastic!' Paige exclaimed.

'I'm putting you on his team.'

For a moment, Paige was speechless. 'I . . . I don't know what to say. I'm very grateful.'

'It's a wonderful opportunity for you. You can learn a lot from him.'

'I'm sure I can. Thank you, George. I really appreciate this.'

'You'll start your rounds with him tomorrow morning at six o'clock.'

'I'm looking forward to it.'

'Looking forward to it' was an understatement. It had been Paige's dream to work with someone like Dr Lawrence Barker. *What do I mean, 'someone like Dr Lawrence Barker'? There's only one Dr Lawrence Barker.*

She had never seen a photograph of him, but she could visualize what he looked like. He would be tall and handsome, with silver-gray hair, and slender, sensitive hands. A warm and gentle man. *We'll be working closely together*, Paige thought, *and I'm going to make myself absolutely indispensable. I wonder if he's married?*

That night, Paige had an erotic dream about Dr Barker. They were performing an operation in the nude. In the middle of it, Dr Barker said, 'I want you.' A nurse moved the patient off the operating table and Dr Barker picked Paige up and put her on the table, and made love to her.

When Paige woke up, she was falling off the bed.

At six o'clock the following morning, Paige was nervously waiting in the second-floor corridor with Joel Philips, the senior resident, and five other residents, when a short, sour-faced man stormed toward them. He leaned forward as he walked, as though battling a stiff wind.

He approached the group. 'What the hell are you all standing around for? Let's go!'

It took Paige a moment to regain her composure. She hurried along to catch up with the rest of the group. As they moved along the corridor, Dr Barker snapped, 'You'll have between thirty and thirty-five patients to care for every day. I'll expect you to make detailed notes on each one of them. Clear?'

There were murmurs of 'Yes, sir.'

They had reached the first ward. Dr Barker walked over to the bed of a patient, a man in his forties. Barker's gruff and forbidding manner went through an instant change. He touched the patient gently on the shoulder and smiled. 'Good morning. I'm Dr Barker.'

'Good morning, doctor.'

'How are you feeling this morning?'

'My chest hurts.'

Dr Barker studied the chart at the foot of the bed, then turned to Dr Philips. 'What do his X-rays show?'

'No change. He's healing nicely.'

'Let's do another CBC.'

Dr Philips made a note.

Dr Barker patted the man on the arm and smiled. 'It's looking good. We'll have you out of here in a week.' He turned to the residents and snapped, 'Move it! We have a lot of patients to see.'

My God! Paige thought. *Talk about Dr Jekyll and Mr Hyde!*

The next patient was an obese woman who had had a pacemaker put in. Dr Barker studied her chart. 'Good morning, Mrs Shelby.' His voice was soothing. 'I'm Dr Barker.'

'How long are you going to keep me in this place?'

'Well, you're so charming, I'd like to keep you here forever, but I have a wife.'

Mrs Shelby giggled. 'She's a lucky woman.'

Barker was examining her chart again. 'I'd say you're just about ready to go home.'

'Wonderful.'

'I'll stop by to see you this afternoon.'

Lawrence Barker turned to the residents. 'Move on.'

They obediently trailed behind the doctor to a semiprivate room where a young Guatemalan boy lay in bed, surrounded by his anxious family.

'Good morning,' Dr Barker said warmly. He scanned the patient's chart. 'How are you feeling this morning?'

'I am feeling good, doctor.'

175

Dr Barker turned to Philips. 'Any change in the electrolytes?'

'No, doctor.'

'That's good news.' He patted the boy's arm. 'You hang in there, Juan.'

The mother asked anxiously, 'Is my son going to be all right?'

Dr Barker smiled. 'We're going to do everything we can for him.'

'Thank you, doctor.'

Dr Barker stepped out into the corridor, the others trailing behind him. He stopped. 'The patient has myocardiopathy, irregular fever tremors, headaches, and localized edema. Can any of you geniuses tell me what the most common cause of it is?'

There was a silence. Paige said hesitantly, 'I believe it's congenital . . . hereditary.'

Dr Barker looked at her and nodded encouragingly.

Pleased, Paige went on. 'It skips . . . wait . . .' She was struggling to remember. 'It skips a generation and is passed along by the genes of the mother.' She stopped, flushed, proud of herself.

Dr Barker stared at her a moment. 'Horseshit! It's Chagas' disease. It affects people from Latin American countries.' He looked at Paige with disgust. 'Jesus! Who told you you were a doctor?'

Paige's face was flaming red.

The rest of the rounds was a blur to her. They saw twenty-four patients and it seemed to Paige that Dr Barker spent the morning trying to humiliate her. She was always the one Barker addressed his questions to, testing, probing. When she was right, he never complimented her. When she was wrong, he

176

yelled at her. At one point, when Paige made a mistake, Barker roared, 'I wouldn't let you operate on my dog!'

When the rounds were finally over, Dr Philips, the senior resident, said, 'We'll start rounds again at two o'clock. Get your scut books, make notes on each patient, and don't leave anything out.'

He looked at Paige pityingly, started to say something, then turned away to join Dr Barker.

Paige thought, *I never want to see that bastard again.*

The following night, Paige was on call. She ran from one crisis to the next, frantically trying to stem the tide of disasters that flooded the emergency rooms.

At 1:00 A.M., she finally fell asleep. She did not hear the sound of a siren screaming out its warning as an ambulance roared to a stop in front of the emergency entrance of the hospital. Two paramedics swung open the ambulance door, transferred the unconscious patient from his stretcher to a gurney, and ran it through the entrance doors of ER One.

The staff had been alerted by radiophone. A nurse ran alongside the patient, while a second nurse waited at the top of the ramp. Sixty seconds later, the patient was transferred from the gurney to the examination table.

He was a young man, and he was covered with so much blood that it was difficult to tell what he looked like.

A nurse went to work, cutting his torn clothes off with large shears.

'It looks like everything's broken.'

177

'He's bleeding like a stuck pig.'

'I'm not getting a pulse.'

'Who's on call?'

'Dr Taylor.'

'Get her. If she hurries, he may still be alive.'

Paige was awakened by the ringing of the telephone.

'H'lo . . .'

'We have an emergency in ER One, doctor. I don't think he's going to make it.'

Paige sat up on the cot. 'Right. I'm coming.'

She looked at her wristwatch. 1:30 A.M. She stumbled out of bed and made her way to the elevator.

A minute later, she was walking into ER One. In the middle of the room, on the examining table, was the blood-covered patient.

'What do we have here?' Paige asked.

'Motorcycle accident. He was hit by a bus. He wasn't wearing a helmet.'

Paige moved toward the unconscious figure, and even before she saw his face, she somehow knew.

She was suddenly wide awake. 'Get three IV lines in him!' Paige ordered. 'Get him on oxygen. I want some blood sent down, stat. Call Records to get his blood type.'

The nurse looked at her in surprise. 'You know him?'

'Yes.' She had to force herself to say the words. 'His name is Jimmy Ford.'

Paige ran her fingers over his scalp. 'There's heavy edema. I want a head scan and X-rays. We're going to push the envelope on this one. I want him alive!'

'Yes, doctor.'

Paige spent the next two hours making sure that everything possible was being done for Jimmy Ford. The X-rays showed a fractured skull, a brain contusion, a broken humerus, and multiple lacerations. But everything would have to wait until he was stabilized.

At 3:30 A.M., Paige decided there was nothing more she could do for the present. He was breathing better, and his pulse was stronger. She looked down at the unconscious figure. *We're going to have half a dozen kids. The first girl is going to be named Paige. I hope you don't mind.*

'Call me if there's any change at all,' Paige said.

'Don't worry, doctor,' one of the nurses said. 'We'll take good care of him.'

Paige made her way back to the on-call room. She was exhausted, but she was too concerned about Jimmy to go back to sleep.

The telephone rang again. She barely had the energy to pick it up. 'H'lo.'

'Doctor, you'd better come up to the third floor. Stat. I think one of Dr Barker's patients is having a heart attack.'

'Coming,' Paige said. *One of Dr Barker's patients.* Paige took a deep breath, staggered out of bed, threw cold water on her face, and hurried to the third floor.

A nurse was waiting outside a private room. 'It's Mrs Hearns. It looks like she's having another heart seizure.'

Paige went into the room.

Mrs Hearns was a woman in her fifties. Her face

179

still held the remnants of a onetime beauty, but her body was fat and bloated. She was holding her chest and moaning. 'I'm dying,' she said. 'I'm dying. I can't breathe.'

'You're going to be all right,' Paige said reassuringly. She turned to the nurse. 'Did you do an EKG?'

'She won't let me touch her. She said she's too nervous.'

'We must do an EKG,' Paige told the patient.

'No! I don't want to die. Please don't let me die . . .'

Paige said to the nurse, 'Call Dr Barker. Ask him to get down here right away.'

The nurse hurried off.

Paige put a stethoscope to Mrs Hearns's chest. She listened. The heartbeat seemed normal, but Paige could not afford to take any chances.

'Dr Barker will be here in a few minutes,' she told Mrs Hearns. 'Try to relax.'

'I've never felt this bad. My chest feels so heavy. Please don't leave me.'

'I'm not going to leave you,' Paige promised her.

While she was waiting for Dr Barker to arrive, Paige telephoned the intensive care unit. There was no change in Jimmy Ford's condition. He was still in a coma.

Thirty minutes later, Dr Barker appeared. He had obviously dressed in haste. 'What's going on?' he demanded.

Paige said, 'I think Mrs Hearns is having another heart attack.'

Dr Barker moved over to the bedside. 'Did you do an EKG?'

'She wouldn't let us.'

180

'Pulse?'

'Normal. No fever.'

Dr Barker put a stethoscope against Mrs Hearns's back. 'Take a deep breath.'

She obliged.

'Again.'

Mrs Hearns let out a loud belch. 'Excuse me.' She smiled. 'Oh. That's better.'

He studied her a moment. 'What did you have for dinner, Mrs Hearns?'

'I had a hamburger.'

'Just a hamburger? That's all? One?'

'Two.'

'Anything else?'

'Well, you know . . . onions and french fries.'

'And to drink?'

'A chocolate milk shake.'

Dr Barker looked down at the patient. 'Your heart is fine. It's your appetite we have to worry about.' He turned to Paige. 'What you're seeing here is a case of heartburn. I'd like to see you outside, doctor.'

When they were in the corridor, he roared, 'What the hell did they teach you in medical school? Don't you even know the difference between heartburn and a heart attack?'

'I thought . . .'

'The problem is, you *didn't*! If you ever wake me up again in the middle of the night for a heartburn case, I'll have your ass. You understand that?'

Paige stood there stiffly, her face grim.

'Give her some antacid, *doctor*,' Lawrence Barker said sarcastically, 'and you'll find that she's cured. I'll see you at six o'clock for rounds.'

181

Paige watched him storm out.

When Paige stumbled back to her cot in the on-call room, she thought, *I'm going to kill Lawrence Barker. I'll do it slowly. He'll be very ill. He'll have a dozen tubes in his body. He'll beg me to put him out of his misery, but I won't. I'll let him suffer, and then when he feels better . . . that's when I'll kill him!*

15

Paige was on morning rounds with the Beast, as she
secretly referred to Dr Barker. She had assisted him
in three cardiothoracic surgeries, and in spite of her
bitter feelings toward him, she could not help but
admire his incredible skill. She watched in awe as he
opened up a patient, deftly replaced the old heart
with a donor heart, and sewed him up. The operation
took less than five hours.

Within a few weeks, Paige thought, *that patient will
be able to return to a normal life. No wonder surgeons
think they're gods. They bring the dead back to
life*.

Time after time, Paige watched a heart stop and
turn to an inert piece of flesh. And then the miracle
would occur, and a lifeless organ would begin to
pulsate again and send blood through a body that
had been dying.

One morning, a patient was scheduled for a
procedure to insert an intra-aortic balloon. Paige
was in the operating room assisting Dr Barker.
As they were about to begin, Dr Barker snapped,
'Do it!'

Paige looked at him. 'I beg your pardon?'

'It's a simple procedure. Do you think you can
handle it?' There was contempt in his voice.

'Yes,' Paige said tightly.

'Well, then, get on with it!'

He was infuriating.

Barker watched as Paige expertly inserted a hollow tube into the patient's artery and threaded it up into the heart. It was done flawlessly. Barker stood there, without saying a word.

To hell with him, Paige thought. *Nothing I could ever do would please him.*

Paige injected a radiopaque dye through the tube. They watched the monitor as the dye flowed into the coronary arteries. Images appeared on a fluoroscopy screen and showed the degree of blockage and its location in the artery, while an automatic motion-picture camera recorded the X-rays for a permanent record.

The senior resident looked at Paige and smiled. 'Nice job.'

'Thank you.' Paige turned to Dr Barker.

'Too damned slow,' he growled.

And he walked out.

Paige was grateful for the days that Dr Barker was away from the hospital, working at his private practice. She said to Kat, 'Being away from him for a day is like a week in the country.'

'You really hate him, don't you?'

'He's a brilliant doctor, but he's a miserable human being. Have you ever noticed how some people fit their names? If Dr Barker doesn't stop barking at people, he's going to have a stroke.'

'You should see some of the beauties I have to put up with.' Kat laughed. 'They all think they're

God's gift to pussies. Wouldn't it be great if there were no men in the world!'

Paige looked at her, but said nothing.

Paige and Kat went to check on Jimmy Ford. He was still in a coma. There was nothing they could do.

Kat sighed. 'Dammit. Why does it happen to the good guys?'

'I wish I knew.'

'Do you think he'll make it?'

Paige hesitated. 'We've done everything we can. Now it's up to God.'

'Funny. I thought *we* were God.'

The following day when Paige was in charge of afternoon rounds, Kaplan, a senior resident, stopped her in the corridor. 'This is your lucky day.' He grinned. 'You're getting a new medical school student to take around.'

'Really?'

'Yeah, the IN.'

'IN?'

'Idiot nephew. Dr Wallace's wife has a nephew who wants to be a doctor. They threw him out of his last two schools. We've all had to put up with him. Today it's your turn.'

Paige groaned. 'I don't have time for this. I'm up to my . . .'

'It's not an option. Be a good girl and Dr Wallace will give you brownie points.' Kaplan moved off.

Paige sighed and walked over to where the new residents were waiting to start the rounds. *Where's the IN?* She looked at her watch. He was already three minutes late. *I'll give him one more minute,* Paige decided, *and then to hell with him.* She saw him then, a tall, lean-looking man, hurrying toward her, down the hall.

He walked up to Paige, out of breath, and said, 'Excuse me. Dr Wallace asked me to—'

'You're late,' Paige said curtly.

'I know. I'm sorry. I was held up at—'

'Never mind. What's your name?'

'Jason. Jason Curtis.' He was wearing a sport jacket.

'Where's your white coat?'

'My white coat?'

'Didn't anyone tell you to wear a white coat on rounds?'

He looked flustered. 'No. I'm afraid I . . .'

Paige said irritably, 'Go back to the head nurse's office and tell her to give you a white coat. And you don't have a scut book.'

'No.'

'Idiot nephew' doesn't begin to describe him. 'Meet us in Ward One.'

'Are you sure? I . . .'

'Just do it!' Paige and the others started off, leaving Jason Curtis staring after them.

They were examining their third patient when Jason Curtis came hurrying up. He was wearing a white coat. Paige was saying, '. . . tumors of the heart can be primary, which is rare, or secondary, which is much more common.'

She turned to Curtis. 'Can you name the three types of tumors?'

He stared at her. 'I'm afraid I . . . I can't.'

186

Of course not. 'Epicardial. Myocardial. Endo-cardial.'

He looked at Paige and smiled. 'That's really interesting.'

My God! Paige thought. *Dr Wallace or no Dr Wallace, I'm going to get rid of him fast.*

They moved on to the next patient, and when Paige was through examining him, she took the group into the corridor, out of earshot. 'We're dealing here with a thyroid storm, with fever and extreme tachycardia. It came on after surgery.' She turned to Jason Curtis. 'How would you treat him for that?'

He stood there, thoughtful for a moment. Then he said, 'Gently?'

Paige fought for self-control. 'You're not his mother, you're his doctor! He needs continuous IV fluids to combat dehydration, along with IV iodine and antithyroid drugs and sedatives for convulsions.'

Jason nodded. 'That sounds about right.'

The rounds got no better. When they were over, Paige called Jason Curtis aside. 'Do you mind my being frank with you?'

'No. Not at all,' he said agreeably. 'I'd appreciate it.'

'Look for another profession.'

He stood there, frowning. 'You don't think I'm cut out for this?'

'Quite honestly, no. You don't enjoy this, do you?'

'Not really.'

'Then why did you choose to go into this?'

'To tell you the truth, I was pushed into it.'

'Well, you tell Dr Wallace that he's making a mistake. I think you should find something else to do with your life.'

'I really appreciate your telling me this,' Jason

Curtis said earnestly. 'I wonder if we could discuss this further. If you aren't doing anything for dinner tonight . . . ?'

'We have nothing further to discuss,' Paige said curtly. 'You can tell your uncle . . .'

At that moment Dr Wallace came into view. 'Jason!' he called. 'I've been looking all over for you.' He turned to Paige. 'I see you two have met.'

'Yes, we've met,' Paige said grimly.

'Good. Jason is the architect in charge of designing the new wing we're building.'

Paige stood there, motionless. 'He's . . . *what*?'

'Yes. Didn't he tell you?'

She felt her face getting red. *Didn't anyone tell you to wear a white coat on rounds? Why did you go into this? To tell you the truth, I was pushed into it. By me!*

Paige wanted to crawl into a hole. He had made a complete fool of her. She turned to Jason. 'Why didn't you tell me who you were?'

He was watching her, amused. 'Well, you really didn't give me a chance.'

'She didn't give you a chance to what?' Dr Wallace asked.

'If you'll excuse me . . .' Paige said tightly.

'What about dinner tonight?'

'I don't eat. And I'm busy.' And Paige was gone.

Jason looked after her, admiringly. 'That's quite a woman.'

'She is, isn't she? Shall we go to my office and talk about the new designs?'

'Fine.' But his thoughts were on Paige.

* * *

188

It was July, time for the ritual that took place every twelve months at hospitals all over the United States, as new residents came in to begin their journey toward becoming real doctors.

The nurses had been looking forward to the new crop of residents, staking out claims on the ones they thought would make good lovers or husbands. On this particular day, as the new residents appeared, nearly every female eye was fixed on Dr Ken Mallory.

No one knew why Ken Mallory had transferred from an exclusive private hospital in Washington, DC, to Embarcadero County Hospital in San Francisco. He was a fifth-year resident, and a general surgeon. There were rumors that he had had to leave Washington in a hurry because of an affair with a congressman's wife. There was another rumor that a nurse had committed suicide because of him and he had been asked to leave. The only thing the nurses were sure of was that Ken Mallory was, without doubt, the best-looking man they had ever seen. He had a tall, athletic body, wavy blond hair, and a face that would have looked great on a movie screen.

Mallory blended into the hospital routine as though he had been there forever. He was a charmer, and almost from the beginning, the nurses were fighting for his attention. Night after night, the other doctors would watch Mallory disappear into an empty on-call room with a different nurse. His reputation as a stud was becoming legendary around the hospital.

Paige, Kat, and Honey were discussing him.

'Can you believe all those nurses throwing

themselves at him?' Kat laughed. 'They're actually fighting to be the flavor of the week!'

'You have to admit, he *is* attractive,' Honey pointed out.

Kat shook her head. 'No. I don't.'

One morning, half a dozen residents were in the doctors' dressing room when Mallory walked in.

'We were just talking about you,' one of them said. 'You must be exhausted.'

Mallory grinned. 'It was not a bad night.' He had spent the night with two nurses.

Grundy, one of the residents, said, 'You're making the rest of us look like eunuchs, Ken. Isn't there anyone in this hospital you can't lay?'

Mallory laughed. 'I doubt it.'

Grundy was thoughtful for a moment. 'I'll bet I can name someone.'

'Really? Who's that?'

'One of the senior residents here. Her name is Kat Hunter.'

Mallory nodded. 'The black doll. I've seen her. She's very attractive. What makes you think I can't take her to bed?'

'Because we've all struck out. I don't think she likes men.'

'Or maybe she just hasn't met the right one,' Mallory suggested.

Grundy shook his head. 'No. You wouldn't have a chance.'

It was a challenge. 'I'll bet you're wrong.'

One of the other residents spoke up. 'You mean you're willing to bet on it?'

Mallory smiled. 'Sure. Why not?'

'All right.' The group began to crowd around Mallory. 'I'll bet you five hundred dollars you can't lay her.'

'You're on.'

'I'll bet you three hundred.'

Another one spoke up. 'Let me in on it. I'll bet you six hundred.'

In the end, five thousand dollars was bet.

'What's the time limit?' Mallory asked.

Grundy thought for a moment. 'Let's say thirty days. Is that fair?'

'More than fair. I won't need that much time.'

Grundy said, 'But you have to prove it. She has to admit that she went to bed with you.'

'No problem.' Mallory looked around the group and grinned. 'Suckers!'

Fifteen minutes later, Grundy was in the cafeteria where Kat, Paige, and Honey were having breakfast. He walked over to their table. 'Can I join you ladies—you doctors—for a moment?'

Paige looked up. 'Sure.'

Grundy sat down. He looked at Kat and said apologetically, 'I hate to tell you this, but I'm really mad, and I think it's only fair that you should know . . .'

Kat was looking at him, puzzled. 'Know what?'

Grundy sighed. 'That new senior resident who came in—Ken Mallory?'

'Yes. What about him?'

Grundy said, 'Well, I . . . God, this is embarrassing. He bet some of the doctors five thousand dollars that he could get you into bed in the next thirty days.'

Kat's face was grim. 'He did, did he?'

Grundy said piously, 'I don't blame you for being angry. It made me sick when I heard about it. Well, I just wanted to warn you. He'll be asking you out, and I thought it was only right that you should know why he was doing it.'

'Thanks,' Kat said. 'I appreciate your telling me.'

'It was the least I could do.'

They watched Grundy leave.

In the corridor outside the cafeteria, the other residents were waiting for him.

'How did it go?' they asked.

Grundy laughed. 'Perfect. She's as mad as hell. The son of a bitch is dead meat!'

At the table, Honey was saying, 'I think that's just terrible.'

Kat nodded. 'Someone should give him a dickotomy. They'll be ice skating in hell before I go out with that bastard.'

Paige sat there thinking. After a moment, she said, 'You know something, Kat? It might be interesting if you *did* go out with him.'

Kat looked at her in surprise. *'What?'*

There was a glint in Paige's eye. 'Why not? If he wants to play games, let's help him — only he'll play *our* game.'

Kat leaned forward. 'Go on.'

'He has thirty days, right? When he asks you out, you'll be warm and loving and affectionate. I mean, you'll be absolutely *crazy* about the man. You'll drive him out of his mind. The only thing you *won't* do, bless your heart, is to go to bed with him. We'll teach him a five-thousand-dollar lesson.'

Kat thought of her stepfather. It was a way of getting revenge. 'I like it,' she said.

'You mean you're going to do it?' Honey said.

'I am.'

And Kat had no idea that with those words, she had signed her death warrant.

16

Jason Curtis had been unable to get Paige Taylor out of his mind. He telephoned Ben Wallace's secretary. 'Hi. This is Jason Curtis. I need a home telephone number for Dr Paige Taylor.'

'Certainly, Mr Curtis. Just a moment.' She gave him the number.

Honey answered the telephone. 'Dr Taft.'

'This is Jason Curtis. Is Dr Taylor there?'

'No, she's not. She's on call at the hospital.'

'Oh. That's too bad.'

Honey could hear the disappointment in his voice. 'If it's some kind of emergency, I can . . .'

'No, no.'

'I could take a message for her and have her call you.'

'That will be fine.' Jason gave her his telephone number.

'I'll give her the message.'

'Thank you.'

'Jason Curtis called,' Honey said when Paige returned to the apartment. 'He sounded cute. Here's his number.'

'Burn it.'

'Aren't you going to call him back?'

194

'No. Never.'

'You're still hung up on Alfred, aren't you?'

'Of course not.'

And that was all Honey could get out of her.

Jason waited two days before he called again.

This time Paige answered the telephone. 'Dr Taylor.'

'Hello there!' Jason said. 'This is Dr Curtis.'

'Doctor . . . ?'

'You may not remember me,' Jason said lightly. 'I was on rounds with you the other day, and I asked you to have dinner with me. You said—'

'I said I was busy. I still am. Goodbye, Mr Curtis.' She slammed the receiver down.

'What was that all about?' Honey asked.

'About nothing.'

At six o'clock the following morning, when the residents gathered with Paige for morning rounds, Jason Curtis appeared. He was wearing a white coat.

'I hope I'm not late,' he said cheerfully. 'I had to get a white coat. I know how upset you get when I don't wear one.'

Paige took a deep, angry breath. 'Come in here,' she said. She led Jason into the deserted doctors' dressing room. 'What are you doing here?'

'To tell you the truth, I've been worried about some of the patients we saw the other day,' he said earnestly. 'I came to see if everyone is all right.'

The man was infuriating. 'Why aren't you out building something?'

Jason looked at her and said, quietly, 'I'm trying to.' He pulled out a handful of tickets. 'Look, I don't know what your tastes are, so I got tickets for tonight's Giants game, the theater, the opera, and a concert. Take your choice.'

The man was exasperating. 'Do you always throw your money away like this?'

'Only when I'm in love,' Jason said.

'Wait a min—'

He held the tickets out to her. 'Take your choice.'

Paige reached out and took them all. 'Thank you,' she said sweetly. 'I'll give them to my outpatients. Most of them don't have a chance to go to the theater or opera.'

He smiled. 'Great! I hope they enjoy it. Will you have dinner with me?'

'No.'

'You have to eat, anyway. Won't you change your mind?'

Paige felt a small frisson of guilt about the tickets. 'I'm afraid I wouldn't be very good company. I was on call last night, and . . .'

'We'll make it an early evening. Scout's honor.'

She sighed. 'All right, but . . .'

'Wonderful! Where shall I pick you up?'

'I'll be through here at seven.'

'I'll pick you up here then.' He yawned. 'Now I'm going home and going back to bed. What an ungodly hour to be up! What makes you do it?'

Paige watched him walk away, and she could not help smiling.

*   *   *

At seven o'clock that evening when Jason arrived at the hospital to pick up Paige, the supervising nurse said, 'I think you'll find Dr Taylor in the on-call room.'

'Thanks.' Jason walked down the corridor to the on-call room. The door was closed. He knocked. There was no answer. He knocked again, then opened the door and looked inside. Paige was on the cot, in a deep sleep. Jason walked over to where she lay and stood there for a long time, looking down at her. *I'm going to marry you, lady*, he thought. He tiptoed out of the room and quietly closed the door behind him.

The following morning, Jason was in a meeting when his secretary came in with a small bouquet of flowers. The card read: *I'm sorry. RIP.* Jason laughed. He telephoned Paige at the hospital. 'This is your date calling.'

'I really am sorry about last night,' Paige said. 'I'm embarrassed.'

'Don't be. But I have a question.'

'Yes?'

'Does RIP stand for Rest in Peace or Rip Van Winkle?'

Paige laughed. 'Take your choice.'

'My choice is dinner tonight. Can we try again?'

She hesitated. *I don't want to become involved. You're not still hung up on Alfred, are you?*

'Hello. Are you there?'

'Yes.' *One evening won't do any harm*, Paige decided. 'Yes. We can have dinner.'

'Wonderful.'

*   *   *

As Paige was getting dressed that evening, Kat said, 'It looks like you have a heavy date. Who is it?'

'He's a doctor-architect,' Paige said.

'A *what*?'

Paige told her the story.

'He sounds like fun. Are you interested in him?'

'Not really.'

The evening went by pleasantly. Paige found Jason easy to be with. They talked about everything and nothing, and the time seemed to fly.

'Tell me about you,' Jason said. 'Where did you grow up?'

'You won't believe me.'

'I promise I will.'

'All right. The Congo, India, Burma, Nigeria, Kenya . . .'

'I don't believe you.'

'It's true. My father worked for WHO.'

'Who? I give up. Is this going to be an Abbott and Costello rerun?'

'The World Health Organization. He was a doctor. I spent my childhood traveling to most of the Third World countries with him.'

'That must have been difficult for you.'

'It was exciting. The hardest part was that I was never able to stay long enough to make friends.' *We don't need anyone else, Paige. We'll always have each other . . . This is my wife, Karen.* She shook off the memory. 'I learned a lot of strange languages, and exotic customs.'

'For instance?'

'Well, for instance, I . . .' She thought for a

moment. 'In India they believe in life after death, and that the next life depends on how you behaved in this one. If you were bad, you would come back as an animal. I remember that in one village, we had a dog, and I used to wonder who he used to be and what he did that was bad.'

Jason said, 'He probably barked up the wrong tree.'

Paige smiled. 'And then there was the *gherao*.'

'The *gherao*?'

'It's a very powerful form of punishment. A crowd surrounds a man.' She stopped.

'And?'

'That's it.'

'That's it?'

'They don't say anything or do anything. But he can't move, and he can't get away. He's trapped until he gives in to what they want. It can last for many, many hours. He stays inside the circle, but the crowd keeps changing shifts. I saw a man try to escape the *gherao* once. They beat him to death.'

The memory of it made Paige shudder. The normally friendly people had turned into a screaming frenzied mob. 'Let's get away from here,' Alfred had yelled. He had taken her arm and led her to a quiet side street.

'That's terrible,' Jason said.

'My father moved us away the next day.'

'I wish I could have known your father.'

'He was a wonderful doctor. He would have been a big success on Park Avenue, but he wasn't interested in money. His only interest was in helping people.' *Like Alfred*, she thought.

'What happened to him?'

199

'He was killed in a tribal war.'

'I'm sorry.'

'He loved doing what he did. In the beginning, the natives fought him. They were very superstitious. In the remote Indian villages, everyone has a *jatak*, a horoscope done by the village astrologer, and they live by it.' She smiled. 'I loved having mine done.'

'And did they tell you that you were going to marry a handsome young architect?'

Paige looked at him and said firmly, 'No.' The conversation was getting too personal. 'You're an architect, so you'll appreciate this. I grew up in huts made of wattle, with earthen floors and thatched roofs which mice and bats liked to inhabit. I lived in *tukuls* with grass roofs and no windows. My dream was to live one day in a comfortable two-story house with a veranda and a green lawn and a white picket fence, and . . .' Paige stopped. 'Sorry. I didn't mean to go on like this, but you *did* ask.'

'I'm glad I asked,' Jason said.

Paige looked at her watch. 'I had no idea it was so late.'

'Can we do this again?'

I don't want to lead him on, Paige thought. *Nothing is going to come of this*. She thought of something Kat had said to her. *You're clinging to a ghost. Let go*. She looked at Jason and said, 'Yes.'

Early the following morning, a messenger arrived with a package. Paige opened the door for him.

'I have something for Dr Taylor.'

'I'm Dr Taylor.'

The messenger looked at her in surprise. 'You're a doctor?'

'Yes,' Paige said patiently. 'I'm a doctor. Do you mind?'

He shrugged. 'No, lady. Not at all. Would you sign here, please?'

The package was surprisingly heavy. Curious, Paige carried it to the living-room table and unwrapped it. It was a miniature model of a beautiful white two-story house with a veranda. In front of the house was a little lawn and garden, surrounded by a white picket fence. *He must have stayed up all night, making it*. There was a card that read:

Mine   [ ]
Ours   [ ]
Please check one.

She sat there looking at it for a long time. It was the right house, but it was the wrong man.

What's the matter with me? Paige asked herself. *He's bright and attractive and charming*. But she knew what the matter was. He was not Alfred.

The telephone rang. It was Jason. 'Did you get your house?' he asked.

'It's beautiful!' Paige said. 'Thank you so much.'

'I'd like to build you the real thing. Did you fill in the box?'

'No.'

'I'm a patient man. Are you free for dinner tonight?'

'Yes, but I have to warn you, I'm going to be operating all day, and by this evening I'll be exhausted.'

201

'We'll make it an early evening. By the way, it's going to be at my parents' home.'

Paige hesitated a moment. 'Oh?'

'I've told them all about you.'

'That's fine,' Paige said. Things were moving too quickly. It made her nervous.

When Paige hung up, she thought: *I really shouldn't be doing this. By tonight I'm going to be too tired to do anything but go to sleep.* She was tempted to telephone Jason back and cancel their date. *It's too late to do that now. We'll make it an early evening.*

As Paige was getting dressed that night, Kat said, 'You look exhausted.'

'I am.'

'Why are you going out? You should be going to bed. Or is that redundant?'

'No. Not tonight.'

'Jason again?'

'Yes. I'm going to meet his parents.'

'Ah.' Kat shook her head.

'It's not like that at all,' Paige said. *It's really not.*

Jason's mother and father lived in a charming old house in the Pacific Heights district. Jason's father was an aristocratic-looking man in his seventies. Jason's mother was a warm, down-to-earth woman. They made Paige feel instantly at home.

'Jason has told us so much about you,' Mrs Curtis said. 'He didn't tell us how beautiful you are.'

'Thank you.'

They went into the library, filled with miniature models of buildings that Jason and his father had designed.

'I guess that between us, Jason, his great-grandfather, and I have done a lot of the landscape of San Francisco,' Jason's father said. 'My son is a genius.'

'That's what I keep telling Paige,' Jason said.

Paige laughed. 'I believe it.' Her eyes were getting heavy and she was fighting to stay awake.

Jason was watching her, concerned. 'Let's go in to dinner,' he suggested.

They went into the large dining room. It was oak-paneled, furnished with attractive antiques and portraits on the wall. A maid began serving.

Jason's father said, 'That painting over there is Jason's great-grandfather. All the buildings he designed were destroyed in the earthquake of 1906. It's too bad. They were priceless. I'll show you some photographs of them after dinner if you . . .'

Paige's head had dropped to the table. She was sound asleep.

'I'm glad I didn't serve soup,' Jason's mother said.

Ken Mallory had a problem. As word of the wager about Kat had spread around the hospital, the bets had quickly increased to ten thousand dollars. Mallory had been so confident of his success that he had bet much more than he could afford to pay off.

If I fail, I'm in a hell of a lot of trouble. But I'm not going to fail. Time for the master to go to work.

Kat was having lunch in the cafeteria with Paige and Honey when Mallory approached the table.

203

'Mind if I join you doctors?'

Not ladies, not girls. Doctors. The sensitive type, Kat thought cynically. 'Not at all. Sit down,' she said.

Paige and Honey exchanged a look.

'Well, I have to get going,' Paige said.

'Me, too. See you later.'

Mallory watched Paige and Honey leave.

'Busy morning?' Mallory asked. He made it sound as though he really cared.

'Aren't they all?' Kat gave him a warm, promising smile.

Mallory had planned his strategy carefully. *I'm going to let her know I'm interested in her as a person, not just as a woman. They hate the sex-object thing. Discuss medicine with her. I'll take it slow and easy. I have a whole month to get her in the sack.*

'Did you hear about the postmortem on Mrs Turnball?' Mallory began. 'The woman had a Coca-Cola bottle in her stomach! Can you imagine how . . . ?'

Kat leaned forward. 'Are you doing anything Saturday night, Ken?'

Mallory was caught completely off guard. 'What?'

'I thought you might like to take me out to dinner.'

He found himself almost blushing. *My God!* he thought. *Talk about shooting fish in a barrel! This is no lesbian. The guys said that because they couldn't get into her pants. Well, I'm going to. She's actually asking for it!* He tried to remember with whom he had a date on Saturday. *Sally, the little nurse in OR. She can wait.*

'Nothing important,' Mallory said. 'I'd love to take you to dinner.'

Kat put her hand over his. 'Wonderful,' she said softly. 'I'll really be looking forward to it.'

He grinned. 'So will I.' *You have no idea how much, baby. Ten thousand dollars' worth!*

That afternoon, Kat reported back to Paige and Honey.

'His mouth dropped open!' Kat laughed. 'You should have seen the look on his face! He looked like the cat that swallowed the canary.'

Paige said, 'Remember, you're the Kat. He's the canary.'

'What are you going to do Saturday night?' Honey asked.

'Any suggestions?'

'I have,' Paige answered. 'Here's the plan . . .'

Saturday evening, Kat and Ken Mallory had dinner at Emilio's, a restaurant on the bay. She had dressed carefully for him, in a white cotton dress, off the shoulder.

'You look sensational,' Mallory said. He was careful to strike just the right note. *Appreciative, but not pressing. Admiring, but not suggestive.* Mallory had determined to be at his most charming, but it was not necessary. It quickly became obvious to him that Kat was intent on charming *him*.

Over a drink, she said, 'Everyone talks about what a wonderful doctor you are, Ken.'

'Well,' Mallory said modestly, 'I've had fine training, and I care a lot about my patients. They're very important to me.' His voice was filled with sincerity.

Kat put her hand over his. 'I'm sure they are.

Where are you from? I want to know all about you. The *real* you.'

Jesus! Mallory thought. *That's the line I use.* He could not get over how easy this was going to be. He was an expert on the subject of women. His radar knew all the signals they put out. They could say yes with a look, a smile, a tone of voice. Kat's signals were jamming his radar.

She was leaning close to him, and her voice was husky. 'I want to know everything.'

He talked about himself during dinner, and every time he tried to change the subject and bring it around to Kat, she said, 'No, no. I want to hear more. You've had such a fascinating life!'

She's crazy about me, Mallory decided. He wished now that he had taken more bets. *I might even win tonight*, he thought. And he was sure of it when Kat said, as they were having coffee, 'Would you like to come up to my apartment for a nightcap?'

Bingo! Mallory stroked her arm and said softly, 'I'd love to.' *The guys were all crazy*, Mallory decided. *She's the horniest broad I've ever met*. He had a feeling that he was about to be raped.

Thirty minutes later, they were walking into Kat's apartment.

'Nice,' Mallory said, looking around. 'Very nice. Do you live here alone?'

'No. Dr Taylor and Dr Taft live with me.'

'Oh.' She could hear the note of regret in his voice.

Kat gave him a beguiling smile. 'But they won't be home until much later.'

Mallory grinned. 'Good.'

'Would you like a drink?'

'Love one. Scotch and soda, please.' He watched as Kat walked over to the little bar and mixed two drinks. *She's got great buns*, Mallory thought. *And she's damned good-looking, and I'm getting ten thousand dollars to lay her*. He laughed aloud.

Kat turned. 'What's so funny?'

'Nothing. I was just thinking how lucky I am to be here alone with you.'

'I'm the lucky one,' Kat said warmly. She handed him his drink.

Mallory raised his glass and started to say, 'Here's to . . .'

Kat beat him to it. 'Here's to us!' she said.

He nodded. 'I'll drink to that.'

He started to say, 'How about a little music?' and as he opened his mouth, Kat said, 'Would you like some music?'

'You're a mind reader.'

Kat put on an old Cole Porter standard. She surreptitiously glanced at her watch, then turned to Mallory. 'Do you like to dance?'

Mallory moved closer to her. 'It depends on whom I'm dancing with. I'd love to dance with you.'

Kat moved into his arms, and they began to dance to the slow and dreamy music. He felt Kat's body pressing hard against his, and he could feel himself getting aroused. He held her tighter, and Kat smiled up at him.

Now is the time to go in for the kill, he thought.

'You're lovely, you know,' Mallory said huskily. 'I've wanted you since the first moment I saw you.'

Kat looked into his eyes. 'I've felt the same way

207

about you, Ken.' His lips moved toward hers, and he gave her a warm, passionate kiss.

'Let's go into the bedroom,' Mallory said. There was a sudden urgency in him.

'Oh, yes!'

He took her by the arm and she started leading him toward her bedroom. And at that moment, the front door opened and Paige and Honey walked in.

'Hi, there!' Paige called. She looked at Ken Mallory in surprise. 'Oh, Dr Mallory! I didn't expect to see you here.'

'Well, I . . . I . . .'

'We went out to dinner,' Kat said.

Mallory was filled with a dark rage. He fought to control it. He turned to Kat. 'I should go. It's late and I have a big day tomorrow.'

'Oh. I'm sorry you're leaving,' Kat said. There was a world of promise in her eyes.

Mallory said, 'What about tomorrow night?'

'I'd love to . . .'

'Great!'

'. . . but I can't.'

'Oh. Well, what about Friday?'

Kat frowned. 'Oh, dear. I'm afraid Friday isn't good, either.'

Mallory was getting desperate. 'Saturday?'

Kat smiled. 'Saturday would be lovely.'

He nodded, relieved. 'Good. Saturday it is, then.'

He turned to Paige and Honey. 'Good night.'

'Good night.'

Kat walked Mallory to the door. 'Sweet dreams,' she said softly. 'I'm going to dream about you.'

208

Mallory squeezed her hand. 'I believe in making dreams come true. We'll make up for this Saturday night.'

'I can't wait.'

That night, Kat lay in her bed thinking about Mallory. She hated him. But to her surprise, she had enjoyed the evening. She was sure that Mallory had enjoyed it too, in spite of the fact that he was playing a game. *If only this were real*, Kat thought, *and not a game*. She had no idea how dangerous a game it was.

Maybe it's the weather, Paige thought wearily. It was cold and dreary outside, with a heavy fog that depressed the spirits. Her day had begun at six o'clock in the morning, and it was filled with constant problems. The hospital seemed to be full of gomers, all complaining at once. The nurses were surly and careless. They drew blood from the wrong patients, lost X-rays that were urgently needed, and snapped at the patients. In addition, there was a staff shortage because of a flu epidemic. It was that kind of day.

The only bright spot was the telephone call from Jason Curtis.

'Hello,' he said cheerily. 'Just thought I'd check in and see how all our patients are doing.'

'They're surviving.'

'Any chance of our having lunch?'

Paige laughed. 'What's lunch? If I'm lucky, I'll be able to grab a stale sandwich about four o'clock this afternoon. It's pretty hectic around here.'

'All right. I won't keep you. May I call you again?'

'All right.' *No harm in that.*

'Bye.'

Paige worked until midnight without a moment to rest, and when she was finally relieved, she was almost too tired to move. She briefly debated staying at the hospital and sleeping on the cot in the on-call room, but the thought of her warm, cozy bed at home was too tempting. She changed clothes and lurched her way to the elevator.

Dr Peterson came up to her. 'My God!' he said. 'Where's the cat that dragged you in?'

Paige smiled wearily. 'Do I look that bad?'

'Worse.' Peterson grinned. 'You're going home now?'

Paige nodded.

'You're lucky. I'm just starting.'

The elevator arrived. Paige stood there half asleep.

Peterson said gently, 'Paige?'

She shook herself awake. 'Yes?'

'Are you going to be able to drive home?'

'Sure,' Paige mumbled. 'And when I get there, I'm going to sleep for twenty-four hours straight.'

She walked to the parking lot and got into her car. She sat there drained, too tired to turn on the ignition. *I mustn't go to sleep here. I'll sleep at home.*

Paige drove out of the parking lot and headed toward the apartment. She was unaware of how erratically she was driving until a driver yelled at her, 'Hey, get off the road, you drunken broad!'

She forced herself to concentrate. *I must not fall asleep . . . I must not fall asleep.* She snapped the radio on and turned the volume up loudly. When she reached her apartment building, she sat in the car for a long time before she was able to summon enough strength to go upstairs.

Kat and Honey were in their beds, asleep. Paige looked at the clock at her bedside. *One o'clock.* She

211

stumbled into her bedroom and started to get undressed, but the effort was too much for her. She fell into bed with her clothes on, and in an instant was sound asleep.

She was awakened by the shrill ringing of a telephone that seemed to be coming from some far-off planet. Paige fought to stay asleep, but the ringing was like needles penetrating her brain. She sat up groggily and reached for the phone. 'H'lo?'

'Dr Taylor?'

'Yes.' Her voice was a hoarse mumble.

'Dr Barker wants you in OR Four to assist him, stat.'

Paige cleared her throat. 'There must be some mistake,' she mumbled. 'I just got off duty.'

'OR Four. He's waiting.' The line went dead.

Paige sat on the edge of the bed, numb, her mind clouded by sleep. She looked at the clock on the bedside table. Four-fifteen. Why was Dr Barker asking for her in the middle of the night? There was only one answer. Something had happened to one of her patients.

Paige staggered into the bathroom and threw cold water on her face. She looked in the mirror and thought, *My God! I look about eighty*.

Ten minutes later, Paige was making her way back to the hospital. She was still half asleep when she took the elevator to the fourth floor to OR Four. She went into the dressing room and changed, then scrubbed up and stepped into the operating room.

There were three nurses and a resident assisting Dr Barker.

He looked up as Paige entered and yelled, 'For Christ's sake, you're wearing a hospital gown! Didn't

212

anyone ever inform you that you're supposed to wear *scrubs* in an operating room?'

Paige stood there, stunned, jolted wide awake, her eyes blazing. 'You listen to me,' she said, furiously. 'I'm supposed to be off duty. I came in as a favor to you. I don't —'

'Don't argue with me,' Dr Barker said curtly. 'Get over here and hold this retractor.'

Paige walked over to the operating table and looked down. It was not her patient on the table. It was a stranger. *Barker had no reason to call me. He's trying to force me to quit the hospital. Well, I'll be damned if I will!* She gave him a baleful look, picked up the retractor, and went to work.

The operation was an emergency coronary artery bypass graft. The skin incision had already been made down the center of the chest to the breastbone, which had been split with an electric saw. The heart and major blood vessels were exposed.

Paige inserted the metal retractor between the cut sides of the breastbone, forcing the edges apart. She watched as Dr Barker skillfully opened the pericardial sac, exposing the heart.

He indicated the coronary arteries. 'Here's the problem,' Barker said. 'We're going to do some grafting.'

He had already removed a long strip of vein from one leg. He sewed a piece of it into the main artery coming out of the heart. The other end he attached to one of the coronary arteries, beyond the obstructed area, sending the blood through the vein graft, bypassing the obstruction.

Paige was watching a master at work. *If only he weren't such a bastard!*

The operation took three hours. By the time it was over, Paige was only half conscious. When the incision had been closed, Dr Barker turned to the staff and said, 'I want to thank all of you.' He was not looking at Paige.

Paige stumbled out of the room without a word and went upstairs to the office of Dr Benjamin Wallace.

Wallace was just arriving. 'You look exhausted,' he said. 'You should get some rest.'

Paige took a deep breath to control her anger. 'I want to be transferred to another surgical team.'

Wallace studied her a moment. 'You're assigned to Dr Barker, right?'

'Right.'

'What's the problem?'

'Ask *him*. He hates me. He'll be glad to get rid of me. I'll go with anyone else. Anyone.'

'I'll talk to him,' Wallace said.

'Thank you.'

Paige turned and walked out of the office. *They'd better take me away from him. If I see him again, I'll kill him.*

Paige went home and slept for twelve hours. She woke up with a feeling that something wonderful had happened, and then she remembered. *I don't have to see the Beast anymore!* She drove to the hospital, whistling.

As Paige was walking down the corridor, an orderly came up to her. 'Dr Taylor . . .'

'Yes?'

'Dr Wallace would like to see you in his office.'

'Thank you,' Paige said. She wondered who the new senior surgeon would be. *Anybody will be an improvement*, Paige thought. She walked into Benjamin Wallace's office.

'Well, you look much better now, Paige.'

'Thanks. I feel much better.' And she did. She felt great, filled with an enormous sense of relief.

'I talked to Dr Barker.'

Paige smiled. 'Thank you. I really appreciate it.'

'He won't let you go.'

Paige's smile faded. *What?*

'He said you're assigned to his team and you'll stay there.'

She could not believe what she was hearing. 'But *why*?' She knew why. The sadistic bastard needed a whipping girl, someone to humiliate. 'I'm not going to stand for it.'

Dr Wallace said ruefully, 'I'm afraid you have no choice. Unless you want to leave the hospital. Would you like to think about it?'

Paige did not have to think about it. 'No.' She was not going to let Barker force her to quit. That was his plan. 'No,' she repeated slowly. 'I'll stay.'

'Good. Then that's settled.'

Not by a long shot, Paige thought. *I'm going to find some way to pay him back.*

In the doctors' dressing room, Ken Mallory was getting ready to make his rounds. Dr Grundy and three other doctors walked in.

'There's our man!' Grundy said. 'How are you doing, Ken?'

'Fine,' Mallory said.

Grundy turned to the others. 'He doesn't look like he just got laid, does he?' He turned back to Mallory. 'I hope you have our money ready. I plan to make a down payment on a little car.'

Another doctor joined in. 'I'm buying a whole new wardrobe.'

Mallory shook his head pityingly. 'I wouldn't count on it, suckers. Get ready to pay me off!'

Grundy was studying him. 'What do you mean?'

'If she's a lesbian, I'm a eunuch. She's the horniest broad I ever met. I practically had to hold her off the other night!'

The men were looking at one another, worried.

'But you didn't get her into the sack?'

'The only reason I didn't, my friends, is because we were interrupted on the way to the bedroom. I have a date with her Saturday night, and it's already over but the shouting.' Mallory finished dressing. 'Now, if you gentlemen will excuse me . . .'

An hour later, Grundy stopped Kat in the corridor.

'I've been looking for you,' he said. He looked angry.

'Is something wrong?'

'It's that bastard Mallory. He's so sure of himself that he's telling everyone that he's going to get you into bed by Saturday night.'

'Don't worry,' Kat said grimly. 'He's going to lose.'

When Ken Mallory picked Kat up Saturday night, she had on a low-cut dress that accentuated her voluptuous figure.

216

'You look gorgeous,' he said admiringly.

She put her arms around him. 'I want to look good for you.' She was clinging to him.

God, she really wants it! When Mallory spoke, his voice was husky. 'Look, I have an idea, Kat. Before we go out to dinner, why don't we slip into the bedroom and . . .'

She was stroking his face. 'Oh, darling, I wish we could. Paige is home.' Paige was actually at the hospital, working.

'Oh.'

'But after dinner . . .' She let the suggestion hang in the air.

'Yes?'

'We could go to your place.'

Mallory put his arms around her and kissed her. 'That's a wonderful idea!'

He took her to the Iron Horse, and they had a delicious dinner. In spite of herself, Kat was having a wonderful time. He was charming and amusing, and incredibly attractive. He seemed genuinely interested in knowing everything about her. She knew he was flattering her, but the look in his eye made the compliments seem real.

If I didn't know better . . .

Mallory had hardly tasted his food. All he could think was, *In two hours I will be making ten thousand dollars . . . In one hour, I will be making ten thousand dollars . . . In thirty minutes . . .*

They finished their coffee.

'Are you ready?' Mallory asked.

Kat put her hand over his. 'You have no idea how ready, darling. Let's go.'

They took a taxi to Mallory's apartment. 'I'm

217

absolutely crazy about you,' Mallory murmured. 'I've never known anyone like you.'

And she could hear Grundy's voice: *He's so sure of himself that he says he's going to get you into bed by Saturday night.*

When they arrived at the apartment, Mallory paid the taxi driver and led Kat into the elevator. It seemed to Mallory to take forever to get up to his apartment. He opened the door and said eagerly, 'Here it is.'

Kat stepped inside.

It was an ordinary little bachelor's apartment that desperately needed a woman's touch.

'Oh, it's lovely,' Kat breathed. She turned to Mallory. 'It's *you.*'

He grinned. 'Let me show you *our* room. I'll put some music on.'

As he went over to the tape deck, Kat glanced at her watch. The voice of Barbra Streisand filled the room.

Mallory took her hand. 'Let's go, honey.'

'Wait a minute,' Kat said softly.

He was looking at her, puzzled. 'What for?'

'I just want to enjoy this moment with you. You know, before we . . .'

'Why don't we enjoy it in the bedroom?'

'I'd love a drink.'

'A drink?' He tried to hide his impatience. 'Fine. What would you like?'

'A vodka and tonic, please.'

He smiled. 'I think we can handle that.' He went over to the little bar and hurriedly mixed two drinks.

Kat looked at her watch again.

Mallory returned with the drinks and handed one to Kat. 'Here you are, baby.' He raised his glass. 'To togetherness.'

'To togetherness,' Kat said. She took a sip of the drink. 'Oh, my God!'

He looked at her, startled. 'What's the matter?'

'This is vodka!'

'That's what you asked for.'

'Did I? I'm sorry. I hate vodka!' She stroked his face. 'May I have a scotch and soda?'

'Sure.' He swallowed his impatience and went back to the bar to mix another drink.

Kat glanced at her watch again.

Ken Mallory returned. 'Here you are.'

'Thank you, darling.'

She took two sips of her drink. Mallory took the glass from her and set it on a table. He put his arms around Kat and held her close, and she could feel that he was aroused.

'Now,' Ken said softly, 'let's make history.'

'Oh, yes!' Kat said. 'Yes!'

She let him lead her into the bedroom.

I've done it! Mallory exulted. *I've done it! Here go the walls of Jericho!* He turned to Kat. 'Get undressed, baby.'

'You first, darling. I want to watch you get undressed. It excites me.'

'Oh? Well, sure.'

As Kat stood there watching, Mallory slowly took his clothes off. First his jacket, then his shirt and tie, then his shoes and stockings, and then his trousers. He had the firm figure of an athlete.

'Does this excite you, baby?'

'Oh, yes. Now take off your shorts.'

219

Slowly Mallory let his shorts fall to the floor. He had a turgid erection.

'That's beautiful,' Kat said.

'Now it's your turn.'

'Right.'

And at that moment, Kat's beeper went off.

Mallory was startled. 'What the hell . . . ?'

'They're calling me,' Kat said. 'May I use your telephone?'

'*Now?*'

'Yes. It must be an emergency.'

'*Now?* Can't it wait?'

'Darling, you know the rules.'

'But . . .'

As Mallory watched, Kat walked over to the telephone and dialed a number. 'Dr Hunter.' She listened. 'Really? Of course. I'll be right there.'

Mallory was staring at her, stupefied. 'What's going on?'

'I have to get back to the hospital, angel.'

'*Now?*'

'Yes. One of my patients is dying.'

'Can't he wait until . . . ?'

'I'm sorry. We'll do this another night.'

Ken Mallory stood there, buck naked, watching Kat walk out of his apartment, and as the door closed behind her, he picked up her drink and slammed it into the wall. *Bitch . . bitch . . . bitch . . .*

When Kat got back to the apartment, Paige and Honey were eagerly waiting for her.

'How did it go?' Paige asked. 'Was I on time?'

Kat laughed. 'Your timing was perfect.'

220

She began to describe the evening. When she came to the part about Mallory standing in the bedroom naked, with an erection, they laughed until tears came to their eyes.

Kat was tempted to tell them how enjoyable she really found Ken Mallory, but she felt foolish. After all, he was seeing her only so he could win a bet.

Somehow, Paige seemed to sense how Kat felt. 'Be careful of him, Kat.'

Kat smiled. 'Don't worry. But I will admit that if I didn't know about that bet . . . He's a snake, but he gives good snake oil.'

'When are you going to see him again?' Honey asked.

'I'm going to give him a week to cool off.'

Paige was studying her. 'Him or you?'

Dinetto's black limousine was waiting for Kat outside the hospital. This time, the Shadow was alone. Kat wished that Rhino were there. There was something about the Shadow that petrified her. He never smiled and seldom spoke, but he exuded menace.

'Get in,' he said as Kat approached the car.

'Look,' Kat said indignantly, 'you tell Mr Dinetto that he can't order me around. I don't work for him. Just because I did him a favor once . . .'

'Get in. You can tell him yourself.'

Kat hesitated. It would be easy to walk away and not get involved any further, but how would it affect Mike? Kat got into the car.

* * *

The victim this time had been badly beaten, whipped with a chain. Lou Dinetto was there with him.

Kat took one look at the patient and said, 'You've got to get him to a hospital right away.'

'Kat,' Dinetto said, 'you have to treat him here.'

'Why?' Kat demanded. But she knew the answer, and it terrified her.

18

It was one of those clear days in San Francisco when there was a magic in the air. The night wind had swept away the rainclouds, producing a crisp, sunny Sunday morning.

Jason had arranged to pick up Paige at the apartment. When he arrived, she was surprised at how pleased she was to see him.

'Good morning,' Jason said. 'You look beautiful.'

'Thank you.'

'What would you like to do today?'

Paige said, 'It's your town. You lead, I'll follow.'

'Fair enough.'

'If you don't mind,' Paige said, 'I'd like to make a quick stop at the hospital.'

'I thought this was your day off.'

'It is, but there's a patient I'm concerned about.'

'No problem.' Jason drove her to the hospital.

'I won't be long,' Paige promised as she got out of the car.

'I'll wait for you here.'

Paige went up to the third floor and into Jimmy Ford's room. He was still in a coma, attached to an array of tubes feeding him intravenously.

A nurse was in the room. She looked up as Paige entered. 'Good morning, Dr Taylor.'

'Good morning.' Paige walked over to the boy's bedside. 'Has there been any change?'

'I'm afraid not.'

Paige felt Jimmy's pulse and listened to his heartbeat.

'It's been several weeks now,' the nurse said. 'It doesn't look good, does it?'

'He's going to come out of it,' Paige said firmly. She turned to the unconscious figure on the bed and raised her voice. 'Do you hear me? You're going to get well!' There was no reaction. She closed her eyes a moment and said a silent prayer. 'Have them beep me at once if there's any change.'

'Yes, doctor.'

He's not going to die, Paige thought. *I'm not going to let him die . . .*

Jason got out of the car as Paige approached. 'Is everything all right?'

There was no point in burdening him with her problems. 'Everything's fine,' Paige said.

'Let's play real tourists today,' Jason said. 'There's a state law that all tours have to start at Fisherman's Wharf.'

Paige smiled. 'We mustn't break the law.'

Fisherman's Wharf was like an outdoor carnival. The street entertainers were out in full force. There were mimes, clowns, dancers and musicians. Vendors were selling steaming caldrons of Dungeness crabs and clam chowder with fresh sourdough bread.

224

'There's no place like this in the world,' Jason said warmly.

Paige was touched by his enthusiasm. She had seen Fisherman's Wharf before and most of the other tourist sites of San Francisco, but she did not want to spoil his fun.

'Have you ridden a cable car yet?' Jason asked.

'No.' *Not since last week.*

'You haven't lived! Come along.'

They walked to Powell Street and boarded a cable car. As they started up the steep grade, Jason said, 'This was known as Hallidie's Folly. He built it in 1873.'

'And I'll bet they said it wouldn't last!'

Jason laughed. 'That's right. When I was going to high school, I used to work weekends as a tour guide.'

'I'm sure you were good.'

'The best. Would you like to hear some of my spiel?'

'I'd love to.'

Jason adopted the nasal tone of a tour guide. 'Ladies and gentlemen, for your information, the oldest street in San Francisco is Grant Avenue, the longest is Mission Street—seven and a half miles long—the widest is Van Ness Avenue at one hundred twenty-five feet, and you'll be surprised to know that the narrowest, DeForest Street, is only four and a half feet. That's right, ladies and gentlemen, four and a half feet. The steepest street we can offer you is Filbert Street, with a thirty-one and a half percent grade.' He looked at Paige and grinned. 'I'm surprised that I still remember all that.'

When they alit from the cable car, Paige looked up at Jason and smiled. 'What's next?'

'We're going to take a carriage ride.'

Ten minutes later, they were seated in a horse-drawn carriage that took them from Fisherman's Wharf to Ghirardelli Square to North Beach. Jason pointed out the places of interest along the way, and Paige was surprised at how much she was enjoying herself. *Don't let yourself get carried away.*

They went up to Coit Tower for a view of the city. As they ascended, Jason asked, 'Are you hungry?'

The fresh air had made Paige very hungry. 'Yes.'

'Good. I'm going to take you to one of the best Chinese restaurants in the world — Tommy Toy's.'

Paige had heard the hospital staff speak of it.

The meal turned out to be a banquet. They started with lobster pot stickers with chili sauce, and hot and sour soup with seafood. That was followed by filet of chicken with snow peas and pecans, veal filet with Szechuan sauce, and four-flavored fried rice. For dessert, they had a peach mousse. The food was wonderful.

'Do you come here often?' Paige asked.

'As often as I can.'

There was a boyish quality about Jason that Paige found very attractive.

'Tell me,' Paige said, 'did you always want to be an architect?'

'I had no choice.' Jason grinned. 'My first toys were Erector sets. It's exciting to dream about something and then watch that dream become concrete

226

and bricks and stone, and soar up into the sky and become a part of the city you live in.'

I'm going to build you a Taj Mahal. I don't care how long it takes!

'I'm one of the lucky ones, Paige, spending my life doing what I love to do. Who was it who said, "Most people live lives of quiet desperation"?'

Sounds like a lot of my patients, Paige thought.

'There's nothing else I would want to do, or any other place I would want to live. This is a fabulous city.' His voice was filled with excitement. 'It has everything anyone could want. I never get tired of it.'

Paige studied him for a moment, enjoying his enthusiasm. 'You've never been married?'

Jason shrugged. 'Once. We were both too young. It didn't work out.'

'I'm sorry.'

'No need to be. She's married to a very wealthy meat packer. Have you been married?'

I'm going to be a doctor, too, when I grow up. We'll get married, and we'll work together.

'No.'

They took a bay cruise under the Golden Gate and Bay Bridge. Jason assumed his tour guide's voice again. 'And there, ladies and gentlemen, is the storied Alcatraz, former home of some of the world's most infamous criminals — Machine Gun Kelly, Al Capone, and Robert Stroud, known as the Birdman! "Alcatraz" means pelican in Spanish. It was originally called Isla de los Alcatraces, after the birds that were its only inhabitants. Do you know why they had hot showers every day for the prisoners here?'

'No.'

'So that they wouldn't get used to the cold bay water when they were trying to escape.'

'Is that true?' Paige asked.

'Have I ever lied to you?'

It was late afternoon when Jason said, 'Have you ever been to Noe Valley?'

Paige shook her head. 'No.'

'I'd like to show it to you. It used to be farms and streams. Now it's filled with brightly colored Victorian homes and gardens. The houses are very old, because it was about the only area spared in the 1906 earthquake.'

'It sounds lovely.'

Jason hesitated. 'My home is there. Would you like to see it?' He saw Paige's reaction. 'Paige, I'm in love with you.'

'We hardly know each other. How could you . . . ?'

'I knew it from the moment you said, "Don't you know you're supposed to wear a white coat on rounds?" That's when I fell in love with you.'

'Jason . . .'

'I'm a firm believer in love at first sight. My grandfather saw my grandmother riding a bicycle in the park and he followed her, and they got married three months later. They were together for fifty years, until he died. My father saw my mother crossing a street, and he knew she was going to be his wife. They've been married for forty-five years. You see, it runs in the family. I want to marry you.'

It was the moment of truth.

Paige looked at Jason and thought, *He's the first man I've been attracted to since Alfred. He's adorable and bright and genuine. He's everything a woman could want in a man. What's the matter with me? I'm holding on to a ghost.* Yet deep inside her, she still had the overpowering feeling that one day Alfred was going to come back to her.

She looked at Jason and made her decision. 'Jason . . .'

And at that moment, Paige's beeper went off.

'Paige . . .'

'I have to get to a telephone.' Two minutes later, she was talking to the hospital.

Jason watched Paige's face turn pale.

She was shouting into the telephone, 'No! Absolutely not! Tell them I'll be right there.' She slammed the phone down.

'What is it?' Jason asked.

She turned to him, and her eyes were filled with tears. 'It's Jimmy Ford, my patient. They're going to take him off the respirator. They're going to let him die.'

When Paige reached Jimmy Ford's room, there were three people there beside the comatose figure in bed: George Englund, Benjamin Wallace, and a lawyer, Silvester Damone.

'What's going on here?' Paige demanded.

Benjamin Wallace said, 'At the hospital ethics committee meeting this morning, it was decided that Jimmy Ford's condition is hopeless. We've decided to remove —'

'No!' Paige said. 'You can't! I'm his doctor. I say

229

he has a chance to come out of it! We're *not* going to let him die.'

Silvester Damone spoke up. 'It's not your decision to make, doctor.'

Paige looked at him defiantly. 'Who are you?'

'I'm the family's attorney.' He pulled out a document and handed it to Paige. 'This is Jimmy Ford's living will. It specifically states that if he has a life-threatening trauma, he's not to be kept alive by mechanical means.'

'But I've been monitoring his condition,' Paige pleaded. 'He's been stabilized for weeks. He could come out of the coma any moment.'

'Can you guarantee that?' Damone asked.

'No, but . . .'

'Then you'll have to do as you're ordered, doctor.'

Paige looked down at the figure of Jimmy. 'No! You have to wait a little longer.'

The lawyer said smoothly, 'Doctor, I'm sure it benefits the hospital to keep patients here as long as possible, but the family cannot afford the medical expenses any longer. I'm ordering you now to take him off the respirator.'

'Just another day or two,' Paige said desperately, 'and I'm sure . . .'

'No,' Damone said firmly. 'Today.'

George Englund turned to Paige. 'I'm sorry, but I'm afraid we have no choice.'

'Thank you, doctor,' the lawyer said. 'I'll leave it to you to handle it. I'll notify the family that it will be taken care of immediately, so they can begin to make the funeral arrangements.' He turned to Benjamin Wallace. 'Thank you for your cooperation. Good day.'

They watched him walk out of the room.

'We can't do this to Jimmy!' Paige said.

Dr Wallace cleared his throat. 'Paige . . .'

'What if we got him out of here and hid him in another room? There must be something we haven't thought of. Something . . .'

Benjamin Wallace said, 'This isn't a request. It's an order.' He turned to George Englund. 'Do you want to . . . ?'

'No!' Paige said. 'I'll . . . I'll do it.'

'Very well.'

'If you don't mind, I'd like to be alone with him.'

George Englund squeezed her arm. 'I'm sorry, Paige.'

'I know.'

Paige watched the two men leave the room.

She was alone with the unconscious boy. She looked at the respirator that was keeping him alive and the IVs that were feeding his body. It would be so simple to turn the respirator off, to snuff out a life. But he had had so many wonderful dreams, such high hopes.

I'm going to be a doctor one day. I want to be like you.

Did you know I'm getting married? . . . Her name is Betsy . . . We're going to have half a dozen kids. The first girl is going to be named Paige.

He had so very much to live for.

Paige stood there looking down at him, tears blurring the room. 'Damn you!' she said. 'You're a quitter!' She was sobbing now. 'What happened to those dreams of yours? I thought you wanted to become a doctor! Answer me! Do you hear me? Open your eyes!' She looked down at the pale figure.

There was no reaction. 'I'm sorry,' Paige said. 'I'm so sorry.' She leaned down to kiss him on the cheek, and as she slowly straightened up, she was looking into his open eyes.

'Jimmy! *Jimmy!*'

He blinked and closed his eyes again. Paige squeezed his hand. She leaned forward and said through her sobs, 'Jimmy, did you hear the one about the patient who was being fed intravenously? He asked the doctor for an extra bottle. He was having a guest for lunch.'

Honey was happier than she had ever been in her life. She had a warm relationship with patients that few of the other doctors had. She genuinely cared about them. She worked in geriatrics, in pediatrics, and in various other wards, and Dr Wallace saw to it that she was given assignments that kept her out of harm's way. He wanted to make sure that she stayed at the hospital and was available to him.

Honey envied the nurses. They were able to nurture their patients without worrying about major medical decisions. *I never wanted to be a doctor*, Honey thought. *I always wanted to be a nurse.*

There are no nurses in the Taft family.

In the afternoon when Honey left the hospital, she would go shopping at the Bay Company, and Streetlight Records, and buy gifts for the children in pediatric care.

'I love children,' she told Kat.

'Are you planning to have a large family?'

'Someday,' Honey said wistfully. 'I have to find their father first.'

One of Honey's favorite patients in the geriatric ward was Daniel McGuire, a cheerful man in his nineties who was suffering from a diseased liver condition. He had been a gambler in his youth, and he liked to make bets with Honey.

'I'll bet you fifty cents the orderly is late with my breakfast.'

'I'll bet you a dollar it's going to rain this afternoon.'

'I'll bet you the Giants win.'

Honey always took his bets.

'I'll bet you ten to one I beat this thing,' he said.

'This time I'm not going to bet you,' Honey told him. 'I'm on your side.'

He took her hand. 'I know you are.' He grinned. 'If I were a few months younger . . .'

Honey laughed. 'Never mind. I like older men.'

One morning a letter came for him at the hospital. Honey took it to him in his room.

'Read it to me, would you?' His eyesight had faded.

'Of course,' Honey said. She opened the envelope, looked at it a moment, and let out a cry. 'You've won the lottery! Fifty thousand dollars! Congratulations!'

'How about that?' He yelled. 'I always knew I'd win the lottery one day! Give me a hug.'

Honey leaned down and hugged him.

'You know something, Honey? I'm the luckiest man in the world.'

When Honey came back to visit him that afternoon, he had passed away. He had lost the most important bet of all.

Honey was in the doctors' lounge when Dr Stevens walked in. 'Is there a Virgo here?'

One of the doctors laughed. 'If you mean a virgin, I doubt it.'

'A *Virgo*,' Stevens repeated. 'I need a Virgo.'

'I'm a Virgo,' Honey said. 'What's the problem?'

He walked up to her. 'The problem is that I have a goddam maniac on my hands. She won't let anyone near her but a Virgo.'

Honey got up. 'I'll go see her.'

'Thanks. Her name is Frances Gordon.'

Frances Gordon had just had a hip replacement. The moment Honey walked into the room, the woman looked up and said, 'You're a Virgo. Born on the cusp, right?'

Honey smiled. 'That's right.'

'Those Aquarians and Leos don't know what the hell they're doin'. They treat patients like they're meat.'

'The doctors here are very good,' Honey protested. 'They —'

'Ha! Most of them are in it for the money.' She looked at Honey more closely. 'You're different.'

Honey scanned the chart at the foot of the bed, a surprised look on her face.

'What's the matter? What are you lookin' at?'

Honey blinked. 'It says here that your occupation is a . . . a psychic.'

Frances Gordon nodded. 'That's right. Don't you believe in psychics?'

Honey shook her head. 'I'm afraid not.'

'That's too bad. Sit down a minute.'

Honey took a chair.

'Let me hold your hand.'

235

Honey shook her head. 'I really don't . . .'

'C'mon, give me your hand.'

Reluctantly, Honey let her take her hand.

Frances Gordon held it for a moment, and closed her eyes. When she opened them, she said, 'You've had a difficult life, haven't you?'

Everyone has had a difficult life, Honey thought. *Next she'll be telling me that I'll be taking a trip across the water.*

'You've used a lot of men, haven't you?'

Honey felt herself stiffen.

'There's been some kind of change in you — just recently — hasn't there?'

Honey could not wait to get out of the room. The woman was making her nervous. She started to pull away.

'You're going to fall in love.'

Honey said, 'I'm afraid I really have to . . .'

'He's an artist.'

'I don't know any artists.'

'You will.' Frances Gordon let go of her hand. 'Come back and see me,' she commanded.

'Sure.'

Honey fled.

Honey stopped in to visit Mrs Owens, a new patient, a thin woman who appeared to be in her late forties. Her chart noted that she was twenty-eight. She had a broken nose and two black eyes, and her face was puffy and bruised.

Honey walked up to the bed. 'I'm Dr Taft.'

The woman looked at her with dull, expressionless eyes. She remained silent.

236

'What happened to you?'

'I fell down some stairs.' When she opened her mouth, she revealed a gap where two front teeth were missing.

Honey glanced at the chart. 'It says here that you have two broken ribs and a fractured pelvis.'

'Yeah. It was a bad fall.'

'How did you get the black eyes?'

'When I fell.'

'Are you married?'

'Yeah.'

'Any children?'

'Two.'

'What does your husband do?'

'Let's leave my husband out of this, okay?'

'I'm afraid it's not okay,' Honey said. 'Is he the one who beat you up?'

'No one beat me up.'

'I'm going to have to file a police report.'

Mrs Owens was suddenly panicky. 'No! Please don't!'

'Why not?'

'He'll kill me! You don't know him!'

'Has he beaten you up before?'

'Yes, but he . . . he doesn't mean anything by it. He gets drunk and loses his temper.'

'Why haven't you left him?'

Mrs Owens shrugged, and the movement caused her pain. 'The kids and I have nowhere to go.'

Honey was listening, furious. 'You don't have to take this, you know. There are shelters and agencies that will take care of you and protect you and the children.'

The woman shook her head in despair. 'I have no

237

money. I lost my job as a secretary when he started . . .' She could not go on.

Honey squeezed her hand. 'You're going to be fine. I'll see that you're taken care of.'

Five minutes later Honey marched into Dr Wallace's office. He was delighted to see her. He wondered what she had brought with her this time. At various times, she had used warm honey, hot water, melted chocolate, and — his favorite — maple syrup. Her ingenuity was boundless.

'Lock the door, baby.'

'I can't stay, Ben. I have to get back.'

She told him about her patient.

'You'll have to file a police report,' Wallace said. 'It's the law.'

'The law hasn't protected her before. Look, all she wants to do is get away from her husband. She worked as a secretary. Didn't you say you needed a new file clerk?'

'Well, yes, but . . . wait a minute!'

'Thanks,' Honey said. 'We'll get her on her feet, and find her a place to live, and she'll have a new job!'

Wallace sighed. 'I'll see what I can do.'

'I knew you would,' Honey said.

The next morning, Honey went back to see Mrs Owens.

'How are you feeling today?' Honey asked.

'Better, thanks. When can I go home? My husband doesn't like it when — '

'Your husband is not going to bother you anymore,' Honey said firmly. 'You'll stay here until we

238

find a place for you and the children to live, and when you're well enough, you're going to have a job here at the hospital.'

Mrs Owens stared at her unbelievingly. 'Do . . . do you mean that?'

'Absolutely. You'll have your own apartment with your children. You won't have to put up with the kind of horror you've been living through, and you'll have a decent, respectable job.'

Mrs Owens clutched Honey's hand. 'I don't know how to thank you,' she sobbed. 'You don't know what it has been like.'

'I can imagine,' Honey said. 'You're going to be fine.'

The woman nodded, too choked up to speak.

The following day when Honey returned to see Mrs Owens, the room was empty.

'Where is she?' Honey asked.

'Oh,' the nurse said, 'she left this morning with her husband.'

Her name was on the PA system again. 'Dr Taft . . . Room 215 . . . Dr Taft . . . Room 215.'

In the corridor Honey ran into Kat. 'How's your day going?' Kat asked.

'You wouldn't believe it!' Honey told her.

Dr Ritter was waiting for her in Room 215. In bed was an Indian man in his late twenties.

Dr Ritter said, 'This is your patient?'

'Yes.'

'It says here that he speaks no English. Right?'

'Yes.'

He showed her the chart. 'And this is your writing? Vomiting, cramps, thirst, dehydration . . .'

'That's right,' Honey said.

'. . . absence of peripheral pulse . . .'

'Yes.'

'And what was your diagnosis?'

'Stomach flu.'

'Did you take a stool sample?'

'No. What for?'

'Because your patient has cholera, that's what for!' He was screaming. 'We're going to have to close down the fucking hospital!'

20

'*Cholera?* Are you telling me this hospital has a patient with *cholera?*' Benjamin Wallace yelled.

'I'm afraid so.'

'Are you absolutely *sure?*'

'No question,' Dr Ritter said. 'His stool is swarming with vibrios. He has low arterial pH, with hypotension, tachycardia, and cyanosis.'

By law, all cases of cholera and other infectious diseases must immediately be reported to the state health board and to the Center for Disease Control in Atlanta.

'We're going to have to report it, Ben.'

'They'll close us down!' Wallace stood up and began to pace. 'We can't afford that. I'll be goddamned if I'm going to put every patient in this hospital under quarantine.' He stopped pacing for a moment. 'Does the patient know what he has?'

'No. He doesn't speak English. He's from India.'

'Who has had contact with him?'

'Two nurses and Dr Taft.'

'And Dr Taft diagnosed it as stomach flu?'

'Right. I suppose you're going to dismiss her.'

'Well, no,' Wallace said. 'Anyone can make a mistake. Let's not be hasty. Does the patient's chart read stomach flu?'

'Yes.'

Wallace made his decision. 'Let's leave it that way.

241

Here's what I want you to do. Start intravenous rehydration—use lactated Ringer's solution. Also give him tetracycline. If we can restore his blood volume and fluid immediately, he could be close to normal in a few hours.'

'We aren't going to report this?' Dr Ritter asked.

Wallace looked him in the eye. 'Report a case of stomach flu?'

'What about the nurses and Dr Taft?'

'Give them tetracycline, too. What's the patient's name?'

'Hari Singh.'

'Put him in quarantine for forty-eight hours. He'll either be cured by then or dead.'

Honey was in a panic. She went to find Paige.

'I need your help.'

'What's the problem?'

Honey told her. 'I wish you would talk to him. He doesn't speak English, and you speak Indian.'

'Hindi.'

'Whatever. Will you talk to him?'

'Of course.'

Ten minutes later, Paige was talking to Hari Singh.

'Aap ki tabyat kaisi hai?'

'Karab hai.'

'Aap jald acha ko hum kardenge.'

'Bhagwan aap ki soney ga.'

'Aap ka ilaj hum jalb shuroo kardenge.'

'Shukria.'

'Dost kiss liay hain?'

*   *   *

242

Paige took Honey outside in the corridor.

'What did he say?'

'He said he feels terrible. I told him he's going to get well. He said to tell it to God. I told him we're going to start treatment immediately. He said he's grateful.'

'So am I.'

'What are friends for?'

Cholera is a disease that can cause death within twenty-four hours from dehydration, or that can be cured within a few hours.

Five hours after his treatment began, Hari Singh was nearly back to normal.

Paige stopped in to see Jimmy Ford.

His face lit up when he saw her. 'Hi.' His voice was weak, but he had improved miraculously.

'How are you feeling?' Paige asked.

'Great. Did you hear about the doctor who said to his patient, "The best thing you can do is give up smoking, stop drinking, and cut down on your sex life"? The patient said, "I don't deserve the best. What's the second best?"'

And Paige knew Jimmy Ford was going to get well.

Ken Mallory was getting off duty and was on his way to meet Kat when he heard his name being paged. He hesitated, debating whether or not simply to slip out. His name was paged once more. Reluctantly, he picked up a telephone. 'Dr Mallory.'

'Doctor, could you come to ER Two, please? We have a patient here who—'

'Sorry,' Mallory said, 'I just checked out. Find someone else.'

'There's no one else available who can handle this. It's a bleeding ulcer, and the patient's condition is critical. I'm afraid we're going to lose him if . . .'

Damn! 'All right. I'll be right there.' *I'll have to call Kat and tell her I'll be late.*

The patient in the emergency room was a man in his sixties. He was semiconscious, ghost-pale, perspiring, and breathing hard, obviously in enormous pain. Mallory took one look at him and said, 'Get him into an OR, stat!'

Fifteen minutes later, Mallory had the patient on an operating table. The anesthesiologist was monitoring his blood pressure. 'It's dropping fast.'

'Pump some more blood into him.'

Ken Mallory began the operation, working against time. It took only a moment to cut through the skin, and after that, the layer of fat, the fascia, the muscle, and finally the smooth, translucent peritoneum, the lining of the abdomen. Blood was pouring into the stomach.

'Bovie!' Mallory said. 'Get me four units of blood from the blood bank.' He began to cauterize the bleeding vessels.

The operation took four hours, and when it was over, Mallory was exhausted. He looked down at the patient and said, 'He's going to live.'

One of the nurses gave Mallory a warm smile. 'It's a good thing you were here, Dr Mallory.'

He looked over at her. She was young and pretty and obviously open to an invitation. *I'll get to you later, baby*, Mallory thought. He turned to a junior resident. 'Close him up and get him into the recovery room. I'll check on him in the morning.'

Mallory debated whether to telephone Kat, but it was midnight. He sent her two dozen roses.

When Mallory checked in at 6:00 A.M., he stopped by the recovery room to see his new patient.

'He's awake,' the nurse said.

Mallory walked over to the bed. 'I'm Dr Mallory. How do you feel?'

'When I think of the alternative, I feel fine,' the patient said weakly. 'They tell me you saved my life. This was the damnedest thing. I was in the car on my way to a dinner party, and I got this sudden pain and I guess I blacked out. Fortunately, we were only a block away from the hospital, and they brought me to the emergency room here.'

'You were lucky. You lost a lot of blood.'

'They told me that in another ten minutes, I would have been gone. I want to thank you, doctor.'

Mallory shrugged. 'I was just doing my job.'

The patient was studying him carefully. 'I'm Alex Harrison.'

The name meant nothing to Mallory. 'Glad to know you, Mr Harrison.' He was checking Harrison's pulse. 'Are you in any pain now?'

'A bit, but I guess they have me pretty well doped up.'

'The anesthetic will wear off,' Mallory assured him. 'So will the pain. You're going to be fine.'

'How long will I have to be in the hospital?'

'We should have you out of here in a few days.'

245

A clerk from the business office came in, carrying some hospital forms. 'Mr Harrison, for our records, the hospital needs to know whether you have medical coverage.'

'You mean you want to know if I can pay my bill.'

'Well, I wouldn't put it like that, sir.'

'You might check with the San Francisco Fidelity Bank,' he said dryly. 'I own it.'

In the afternoon, when Mallory stopped by to see Alex Harrison, there was an attractive woman with him. She was in her early thirties, blond and trim, and elegant-looking. She was wearing an Adolfo dress that Mallory figured must have cost more than his monthly salary.

'Ah! Here's our hero,' Alex Harrison said. 'It's Dr Mallory, isn't it?'

'Yes. Ken Mallory.'

'Dr Mallory, this is my daughter, Lauren.'

She held out a slim, manicured hand. 'Father tells me you saved his life.'

He smiled. 'That's what doctors are for.'

Lauren was looking over him approvingly. 'Not all doctors.'

It was obvious to Mallory that these two did not belong in a county hospital. He said to Alex Harrison, 'You're coming along fine, but perhaps you'd feel more comfortable if you called your own doctor.'

Alex Harrison shook his head. 'That won't be necessary. He didn't save my life. You did. Do you like it here?'

It was a strange question. 'It's interesting, yes. Why?'

Harrison sat up in bed. 'Well, I was just thinking. A good-looking fellow as capable as you are could have a damned bright future. I don't think you have much of a future in a place like this.'

'Well, I . . .'

'Maybe it was fate that brought me here.'

Lauren spoke up. 'I think what my father is trying to say is that he would like to show you his appreciation.'

'Lauren is right. You and I should have a serious talk when I get out of here. I'd like you to come up to the house for dinner.'

Mallory looked at Lauren and said slowly, 'I'd like that.'

And it changed his life.

Ken Mallory was having a surprisingly difficult time getting together with Kat.

'How's Monday night, Kat?'

'Wonderful.'

'Good. I'll pick you up at —'

'Wait! I just remembered. A cousin from New York is coming to town for the night.'

'Well, Tuesday?'

'I'm on call Tuesday.'

'What about Wednesday?'

'I promised Paige and Honey that we'd do something together Wednesday.'

Mallory was getting desperate. His time was running out too fast.

'Thursday?'

'Thursday is fine.'

'Great. Shall I pick you up?'

'No. Why don't we meet at Chez Panisse?'

'Very well. Eight o'clock?'

'Perfect.'

Mallory waited at the restaurant until nine o'clock and then telephoned Kat. There was no answer. He waited another half hour. *Maybe she misunderstood*, he thought. *She wouldn't deliberately break a date with me.*

The following morning, he saw Kat at the hospital. She ran up to him.

'Oh, Ken, I'm so sorry! It was the silliest thing. I decided to take a little nap before our date. I fell asleep and when I woke up it was the middle of the night. Poor darling. Did you wait for me long?'

'No, no. It's all right.' *The stupid woman!* He moved closer to her. 'I want to finish what we started, baby. I go crazy when I think about you.'

'Me, too,' Kat said. 'I can't wait.'

'Maybe next weekend we can . . .'

'Oh, dear. I'm busy over the weekend.'

And so it went.

The clock was running.

Kat was reporting events to Paige when her beeper went off.

'Excuse me.' Kat picked up a telephone. 'Dr Hunter.' She listened a moment. 'Thanks. I'll be right there.' She replaced the receiver. 'I have to go. Emergency.'

Paige sighed. 'What else is new?'

Kat strode down the corridor and took an elevator

down to the emergency room. Inside were two dozen cots, all of them occupied. Kat thought of it as the suffering room, filled day and night with victims of automobile accidents, gunshots or knife wounds, and twisted limbs. A kaleidoscope of broken lives. To Kat it was a small corner of hell.

An orderly hurried up to her. 'Dr Hunter . . .'

'What have we got?' Kat asked. They were moving toward a cot at the far end of the room.

'He's unconscious. It looks as though someone beat him up. His face and head are battered, he has a broken nose, a dislocated shoulder blade, at least two different fractures to his right arm, and . . .'

'Why did you call me?'

'The paramedics think there's a head injury. There could be brain damage.'

They had reached the cot where the victim lay. His face was caked with blood, swollen and bruised. He was wearing alligator shoes and . . . Kat's heart skipped a beat. She leaned forward and took a closer look. It was Lou Dinetto.

Kat ran skillful fingers over his scalp and examined his eyes. There was a definite concussion.

She hurried over to a telephone and dialed. 'This is Dr Hunter. I want a head CAT scan done. The patient's name is Dinetto. Lou Dinetto. Send down a gurney, stat.'

Kat replaced the receiver and turned her attention back to Dinetto. She said to the orderly, 'Stay with him. When the gurney arrives, take him to the third floor. I'll be waiting.'

Thirty minutes later on the third floor, Kat was studying the CAT scan she had ordered. 'He has some brain hemorrhaging, he has a high fever, and he's in shock. I want him stabilized for twenty-four hours. I'll decide then when we'll operate.'

Kat wondered whether what had happened to Dinetto might affect Mike.

And how.

Paige stopped by to see Jimmy. He was feeling much better.

'Did you hear about the flasher in the garment district? He walked up to a little old lady and opened up his raincoat. She studied him a moment and said, "You call *that* a lining?"'

Kat was having dinner with Mallory at an intimate little restaurant near the bay. Seated across from Mallory, studying him, Kat felt guilty. *I should never have started this*, she thought. *I know what he is, and yet I'm having a wonderful time. Damn the man! But I can't stop our plan now.*

They had finished their coffee.

Kat leaned forward. 'Can we go to your place, Ken?'

'You bet!' *Finally*, Mallory thought.

Kat shifted in her chair uncomfortably and frowned. 'Uh, oh!'

'Are you all right?' Mallory asked.

'I don't know. Would you excuse me for a moment?'

'Certainly.' He watched her get up and head for the ladies' room.

When she returned, she said, 'It's bad timing, darling. I'm so sorry. You'd better get me home.'

He stared at her, trying to conceal his frustration. The damned fates were conspiring against him.

'Right,' Mallory said curtly. He was ready to explode.

He was going to lose a precious five days.

Five minutes after Kat returned to the apartment, the front doorbell rang. Kat smiled to herself. Mallory had found an excuse to come back, and she hated herself for being so pleased. She walked over to the door and opened it.

'Ken . . .'

Rhino and the Shadow were standing there. Kat felt a sudden sense of fear. The two men pushed past her into the apartment.

Rhino spoke. 'You doin' the operation on Mr Dinetto?'

Kat's throat was dry. 'Yes.'

'We don't want anything to happen to him.'

'Neither do I,' Kat said. 'Now, if you'll excuse me. I'm tired and—'

'Is there a chance he'll die?' the Shadow asked.

Kat hesitated 'In brain surgery there's always a risk of—'

'You better not let it happen.'

'Believe me, I—'

'Don't let it happen.' He looked at Rhino. 'Let's go.'

Kat watched them start to leave.

At the door, the Shadow turned and said, 'Say hello to Mike for us.'

Kat was suddenly very still. 'Is . . . is this some kind of threat?'

'We don't threaten people, doc. We're telling you. If Mr Dinetto dies, you and your fucking family are gonna be wiped out.'

In the doctors' dressing room, half a dozen doctors were waiting for Ken Mallory to appear.

When he walked in, Grundy said, 'Hail the conquering hero! We want to hear all the lurid details.' He grinned. 'But the catch is, buddy, we want to hear them from *her*.'

'I ran into a little bad luck.' Mallory smiled. '*But* you can all start getting your money ready.'

Kat and Paige were getting into scrubs.

'Have you ever done a procedure on a doctor?' Kat asked.

'No.'

'You're lucky. They're the worst patients in the world. They know too much.'

'Who are you operating on?'

'Dr Mervyn "Don't Hurt Me" Franklin.'

'Good luck.'

'I'll need it.'

Dr Mervyn Franklin was a man in his sixties, thin, bald, and irascible.

When Kat walked into his room, he snapped, 'It's about time you got here. Did the damned electrolyte reports come back?'

'Yes,' Kat said. 'They're normal.'

'Who says so? I don't trust the damn lab. Half the time they don't know what they're doing. And make sure there's no mix-up on the blood transfusion.'

'I'll make sure,' Kat said patiently.

'Who's doing the operation?'

'Dr Jurgenson and I. Dr Franklin, I promise you, there's nothing for you to worry about.'

'Whose brain are they operating on, yours or mine? All operations are risky. You know why? Because half of the damned surgeons are in the wrong profession. They should have been butchers.'

'Dr Jurgenson is very capable.'

'I know he is, or I wouldn't let him touch me. Who's the anesthesiologist?'

'I believe it's Dr Miller.'

'That quack? I don't want him. Get me someone else.'

'Dr Franklin . . .'

'Get me someone else. See if Haliburton is available.'

'All right.'

'And get me the names of the nurses in the OR. I want to check them out.'

Kat looked him in the eye. 'Would you prefer to do the operation yourself?'

'What?' He stared at her a moment, then smiled sheepishly. 'I guess not.'

Kat said gently, 'Then why don't you let us handle it?'

'Okay. You know something? I like you.'

'I like you, too. Did the nurse give you a sedative?'

'Yes.'

'All right. We'll be ready in a few minutes. Is there anything I can do for you?'

'Yeah. Teach my stupid nurse where my veins are located.'

In OR Four, the brain surgery on Dr Mervyn Franklin was going perfectly. He had complained every step of the way from his room to the operating theater.

'Now mind you,' he said, 'minimal anesthetic. The brain has no feeling, so once you get in there, you won't need much.'

'I'm aware of that,' Kat said patiently.

'And see that the temperature is kept down to forty degrees. That's maximum.'

'Right.'

'Let's have some fast music on during the operation. Keep you all on your toes.'

'Right.'

'And make sure you have a top scrub nurse in there.'

'Right.'

And on and on it went.

When the opening in Dr Franklin's skull was drilled, Kat said, 'I see the clot. It doesn't look too bad.' She went to work.

Three hours later as they were beginning to close the incision, George Englund, the chief of surgery, came into the operating room and went up to Kat.

'Kat, are you almost through here?'

'We're just wrapping it up.'

'Let Dr Jurgenson take over. We need you fast. There's an emergency.'

Kat nodded. 'Coming.' She turned to Jurgenson. 'Will you finish up here?'

'No problem.'

Kat walked out with George Englund. 'What's happening?'

'You were scheduled to do an operation later, but your patient has started to hemorrhage. They're taking him to OR Three now. It doesn't look as though he's going to make it. You'll have to operate right away.'

'Who—?'

'A Mr Dinetto.'

Kat looked at him aghast. '*Dinetto?*' *If Mr Dinetto dies, you and your fucking family are gonna be wiped out.*

Kat hurried down the corridor that led to OR Three. Approaching her were Rhino and the Shadow.

'What's going on?' Rhino demanded.

Kat's mouth was so dry that it was difficult to speak. 'Mr Dinetto started hemorrhaging. We must operate right away.'

The Shadow grabbed her arm. 'Then do it! But remember what we told you. Keep him alive.'

Kat pulled away and hurried into the operating room.

Dr Vance was doing the operation with Kat. He was a good surgeon. Kat began the ritual scrub: a half minute on each arm first, then a half minute on each hand. She repeated it and then scrubbed her nails.

Dr Vance stepped in beside her and started his scrub. 'How are you feeling?'

'Fine,' Kat lied.

Lou Dinetto was wheeled semiconscious into the operating room on a gurney, and carefully transferred to the operating table. His shaven head was scrubbed and painted with Merthiolate solution that gleamed a bright orange under the operating lights. He was as pale as death.

The team was in place: Dr Vance, another resident, an anesthesiologist, two scrub nurses, and a circulating nurse. Kat checked to make sure that everything they might require was there. She glanced at the wall monitors—oxygen saturation, carbon dioxide, temperature, muscle stimulators, precordial stethoscope, EKG, automatic blood pressure, and disconnect alarms. Everything was in order.

The anesthesiologist strapped a blood pressure cuff on Dinetto's right arm, then placed a rubber mask over the patient's face. 'All right, now. Breathe deeply. Take three big breaths.'

Dinetto was asleep before the third breath.

The procedure began.

Kat was reporting aloud. 'There's an area of damage in the middle of the brain, caused by a clot that's broken off the aorta valve. It's blocking a small blood vessel on the right side of the brain and extending slightly into the left half.' She probed deeper. 'It's at the lower edge of the aqueduct of Sylvius. Scalpel.'

A tiny burr hole about the size of a dime was made

257

by an electric drill to expose the dura mater. Next, Kat cut open the dura to expose a segment of the cerebral cortex that lay underneath. 'Forceps!'

The scrub nurse handed her the electric forceps.

The incision was held open by a small retractor which maintained itself in place.

'There's a hell of a lot of bleeding,' Vance said.

Kat picked up the bovie and started to cauterize the bleeders. 'We're going to control it.'

Dr Vance started suction on soft cotton patties that were placed on the dura. The oozing veins on the surface of the dura were identified and coagulated.

'It looks good,' Vance said. 'He's going to make it.'

Kat breathed a sigh of relief.

And at that instant, Lou Dinetto stiffened and his body went into spasm. The anesthesiologist called out, 'Blood pressure's dropping!'

Kat said, 'Get some more blood into him!'

They were all looking at the monitor. The curve was rapidly flattening out. There were two quick heartbeats followed by ventricular fibrillation.

'Shock him!' Kat snapped. She quickly attached the electric pads to his body and turned on the machine.

Dinetto's chest heaved up once and then fell.

'Inject him with epinephrine! Quick!'

'No heartbeat!' the anesthesiologist called out a moment later.

Kat tried again, raising the dial.

Once again, there was a quick convulsive movement.

'No heartbeat!' the anesthesiologist cried. 'Asystole. No rhythm at all.'

Desperately, Kat tried one last time. The body rose higher this time, then fell again. Nothing.

'He's dead,' Dr Vance said.

22

Code Red is an alert that immediately brings all-out medical assistance to try to save the life of a patient. When Lou Dinetto's heart stopped in the middle of his operation, the operating room Code Red team rushed to give aid.

Over the public address system Kat could hear, 'Code Red, OR Three . . . Code Red . . .' *Red rhymes with dead.*

Kat was in a panic. She applied the electroshock again. It was not only his life she was trying to save — it was Mike's and her own. Dinetto's body leaped into the air, then fell back, inert.

'Try once more!' Dr Vance urged.

We don't threaten people, doc. We're telling you. If Mr Dinetto dies, you and your fucking family are gonna be wiped out.

Kat turned on the switch and applied the machine to Dinetto's chest again. Once more his body rose a few inches into the air and then fell back.

'Again!'

It's not going to happen, Kat thought despairingly. *I'm going to die with him.*

The operating room was suddenly filled with doctors and nurses.

'What are you waiting for?' someone asked.

Kat took a deep breath and pressed down once

again. For an instant, nothing happened. Then a faint blip appeared on the monitor. It faltered a moment, then appeared again and faltered, and then began to grow stronger and stronger, until it became a steady, stabilized rhythm.

Kat stared at it unbelievingly.

There was a cheer from the crowded room. 'He's going to make it!' someone yelled.

'Jesus, that was close!'

They have no idea how close, Kat thought.

Two hours later, Lou Dinetto was off the table and on a gurney, on his way back to intensive care. Kat was at his side. Rhino and the Shadow were waiting in the corridor.

'The operation was successful,' Kat said. 'He's going to be fine.'

Ken Mallory was in deep trouble. It was the last day to make good on his bet. The problem had been growing so gradually that he had hardly been aware of it. From almost the first night, he had been positive that he would have no trouble getting Kat into bed. *Trouble? She's eager for it!* Now his time was up, and he was facing disaster.

Mallory thought about all the things that had gone wrong—Kat's roommates coming in just as she was about to go to bed with him, the difficulty of getting together for a date, Kat's being called away by her beeper and leaving him standing naked, her cousin coming to town, her oversleeping, her period. He stopped suddenly and thought, *Wait a minute! They couldn't have all been coincidences!* Kat was doing this to him deliberately! She had somehow gotten wind of the bet, and had decided to make a fool of

261

him, to play a joke on him, a joke that was going to cost him ten thousand dollars that he didn't have. *The bitch!* He was no closer to winning than he had been at the beginning. She had deliberately led him on. *How the hell did I let myself get into this?* He knew there was no way he could come up with the money.

When Mallory walked into the doctors' dressing room, they were waiting for him.

'Payoff day!' Grundy sang out.

Mallory forced a smile. 'I have until midnight, right? Believe me, she's ready, fellows.'

There was a snicker. 'Sure. We'll believe you when we hear it from the lady herself. Just have the cash ready in the morning.'

Mallory laughed. 'You'd better have *yours* ready!'

He *had* to find a way. And suddenly he had the answer.

Ken Mallory found Kat in the lounge. He sat down opposite her. 'I hear you saved a patient's life.'

'And my own.'

'What?'

'Nothing.'

'How would you like to save my life?'

Kat looked at him quizzically.

'Have dinner with me tonight.'

'I'm too tired, Ken.' She was weary of the game she was playing with him. *I've had enough*, Kat thought. *It's time to stop. It's over. I've fallen into my own trap.* She wished he were a different kind of man. If only he had been honest with her. *I really could have cared for him*, Kat thought.

There was no way Mallory was going to let Kat get away. 'We'll make it an early night,' he coaxed. 'You have to have dinner somewhere.'

Reluctantly, Kat nodded. She knew it was going to be the last time. She was going to tell him she knew about the bet. She was going to end the game. 'All right.'

Honey finished her shift at 4:00 P.M. She looked at her watch and decided that she had just enough time to do some quick shopping. She went to the Candelier to buy some candles for the apartment, then to the San Francisco Tea and Coffee Company so there would be some drinkable coffee for breakfast, and on to Chris Kelly for linens.

Loaded down with packages, Honey headed for the apartment. *I'll fix myself some dinner at home*, Honey decided. She knew that Kat had a date with Mallory, and that Paige was on call.

Fumbling with her packages, Honey entered the apartment and closed the door behind her. She switched on the light. A huge black man was coming out of the bathroom, dripping blood on the white carpet. He was pointing a gun at her.

'Make one sound, and I'll blow your fucking head off!'

Honey screamed.

23

Mallory was seated across from Kat at Schroeder's restaurant on Front Street.

What was going to happen when he couldn't pay the ten thousand dollars? Word would spread quickly around the hospital, and he would become known as a welcher, a sick joke.

Kat was chatting about one of her patients, and Mallory was looking into her eyes, not hearing a word she said. He had more important things on his mind.

Dinner was almost over, and the waiter was serving coffee. Kat looked at her watch. 'I have an early call, Ken. I think we'd better go.'

He sat there, staring down at the table. 'Kat . . .' He looked up. 'There's something I have to tell you.'

'Yes?'

'I have a confession to make.' He took a deep breath. 'This isn't easy for me.'

She watched him, puzzled. 'What is it?'

'I'm embarrassed to tell you.' He was fumbling for words. 'I . . . I made a stupid bet with some of the doctors that . . . that I could take you to bed.'

Kat was staring at him. 'You . . .'

'Please don't say anything yet. I'm so ashamed of what I did. It started out as a kind of joke, but the joke is on me. Something happened that I didn't count on. I fell in love with you.'

'Ken . . .'

'I've never been in love before, Kat. I've known a lot of women, but never felt anything like this. I haven't been able to stop thinking about you.' He took a shaky breath. 'I want to marry you.'

Kat's mind was spinning. Everything was being turned topsy-turvy. 'I . . . I don't know what to . . .'

'You're the only woman I've ever proposed to. Please say yes. Will you marry me, Kat?'

So he had really meant all the lovely things he had said to her! Her heart was pounding. It was like a wonderful dream suddenly come true. All she had wanted from him was honesty. And now he was being honest with her. All this time he had been feeling guilty about what he had done. He was not like other men. He was genuine, and sensitive.

When Kat looked at him, her eyes were glowing. 'Yes, Ken. Oh, yes!'

His grin lit up the room. 'Kat . . .' He leaned over and kissed her. 'I'm so sorry about that stupid bet.' He shook his head in self-derision. 'Ten thousand dollars. We could have used that money for our honeymoon. But it's worth losing it to have you.'

Kat was thinking, *Ten thousand dollars*.

'I was such a fool.'

'When is your deadline up?'

'At midnight tonight, but that's not important anymore. The important thing is us. That we're going to be married. We —'

'Ken?'

'Yes, darling?'

'Let's go to your place.' There was a mischievous

265

glint in Kat's eyes. 'You still have time to win your bet.'

Kat was a tigress in bed.

My God! This was worth waiting for, Mallory thought. All the feelings that Kat had kept bottled up over the years suddenly exploded. She was the most passionate woman Ken Mallory had ever known. At the end of two hours, he was exhausted. He held Kat in his arms. 'You're incredible,' he said.

She lifted herself up on her elbows and looked down at him. 'So are you, darling. I'm so happy.'

Mallory grinned. 'So am I.' *Ten thousand dollars' worth!* he thought. *And great sex.*

'Promise me it will always be like this, Ken.'

'I promise,' Mallory said in his sincerest voice.

Kat looked at her watch. 'I'd better get dressed.'

'Can't you spend the night here?'

'No, I'm riding to the hospital with Paige in the morning.' She gave him a warm kiss. 'Don't worry. We'll have all our iives to spend together.'

He watched her get dressed.

'I can't wait to collect on that bet. It will buy us a great honeymoon.' He frowned. 'But what if the boys don't believe me? They aren't going to take my word for it.'

Kat was thoughtful for a moment. Finally, she said, 'Don't worry. I'll let them know.'

Mallory grinned. 'Come on back to bed.'

24

The black man with the gun pointed at Honey screamed, 'I told you to shut up!'

'I . . . I'm sorry,' Honey said. She was trembling. 'Wh . . . what do you want?'

He was pressing his hand against his side, trying to stop the flow of blood. 'I want my sister.'

Honey looked at him, puzzled. He was obviously insane. 'Your sister?'

'Kat.' His voice was becoming faint.

'Oh, my God! You're Mike!'

'Yeah.'

The gun dropped, and he slipped to the floor. Honey rushed to him. Blood was pouring out from what looked like a gunshot wound.

'Lie still,' Honey said. She hurried into the bathroom and gathered up some peroxide and a large bath towel. She returned to Mike. 'This is going to hurt,' she warned.

He lay there, too weak to move.

She poured peroxide into the wound and pressed the towel against his side. He bit down on his hand to keep from screaming.

'I'm going to call an ambulance and get you to the hospital,' Honey said.

He grabbed her arm. 'No! No hospitals. No police.' His voice was getting weaker. 'Where's Kat?'

'I don't know,' Honey said helplessly. She knew Kat was out somewhere with Mallory, but she had no idea where. 'Let me call a friend of mine.'

'Paige?' he asked.

Honey nodded. 'Yes.' *So Kat told him about the two of us.*

It took the hospital ten minutes to reach Paige.

'You'd better come home,' Honey said.

'I'm on call, Honey. I'm in the middle of—'

'Kat's brother is here.'

'Oh, well, tell him—'

'He's been shot.'

'He *what*?'

'He's been shot!'

'I'll send the paramedics over and—'

'He says no hospitals and no police. I don't know what to do.'

'How bad is it?'

'Pretty bad.'

There was a pause. 'I'll find someone to cover for me. I'll be there in half an hour.'

Honey replaced the receiver and turned to Mike. 'Paige is coming.'

Two hours later, on her way back to the apartment, Kat was filled with a glorious sense of well-being. She had been nervous about making love, afraid that she would hate it after the terrible experience she had had, but instead, Ken Mallory had turned it into something wonderful. He had unlocked emotions in her that she had never known existed.

Smiling to herself at the thought of how they had outwitted the doctors at the last moment and won the bet, Kat opened the door to the apartment and stood there in shock. Paige and Honey were kneeling beside Mike. He was lying on the floor, a pillow under his head, a towel pressed against his side, his clothes soaked with blood.

Paige and Honey looked up as Kat entered.

'Mike! My God!' She rushed over to Mike and knelt beside him. 'What happened?'

'Hi, sis.' His voice was barely a whisper.

'He's been shot,' Paige said. 'He's hemorrhaging.'

'Let's get him to the hospital,' Kat said.

Mike shook his head. 'No,' he whispered. 'You're a doctor. Fix me up.'

Kat looked over at Paige.

'I've stopped as much of the bleeding as I can, but the bullet is still inside him. We don't have the instruments here to —'

'He's still losing blood,' Kat said. She cradled Mike's head in her arms. 'Listen to me, Mike. If you don't get help, you're going to die.'

'You . . . can't . . . report . . . this . . . I don't want any police.'

Kat asked quietly, 'What are you involved in, Mike?'

'Nothing. I was in a . . . a business deal . . . and it went sour . . . and this guy got mad and shot me.'

It was the kind of story Kat had been listening to for years. Lies. All lies. She had known that then, and she knew it now, but she had tried to keep the truth from herself.

Mike held on to her arm. 'Will you help me, sis?'

'Yes. I'm going to help you, Mike.' Kat leaned down and kissed him on the cheek. Then she rose and went to the telephone. She picked up the receiver and dialed the emergency room at the hospital. 'This is Dr Hunter,' she said in an unsteady voice. 'I need an ambulance right away . . .'

At the hospital, Kat asked Paige to perform the operation to remove the bullet.

'He's lost a lot of blood,' Paige said. She turned to the assisting surgeon. 'Give him another unit.'

It was dawn when the operation was finished. The surgery was successful.

When it was over, Paige called Kat aside. 'How do you want me to report this?' she asked. 'I could list it as an accident, or . . .'

'No,' Kat said. Her voice was filled with pain. 'I should have done this a long time ago. I want you to report it as a gunshot wound.'

Mallory was waiting for Kat outside the operating theater.

'Kat! I heard about your brother and . . .'

Kat nodded wearily.

'I'm so sorry. Is he going to be all right?'

Kat looked at Mallory and said, 'Yes. For the first time in his life, Mike is going to be all right.'

Mallory squeezed Kat's hand. 'I just want you to know how wonderful last night was. You were a miracle. Oh. That reminds me. The doctors I bet with are in the lounge waiting, but I suppose with all that has happened, you wouldn't want to go in and . . .'

'Why not?'

She took his arm and the two of them walked

into the lounge. The doctors watched them as they approached.

Grundy said, 'Hi, Kat. We need to have your word on something. Dr Mallory claims that you and he spent the night together, and it was great.'

'It was better than great,' Kat said. 'It was *fantastic*!' She kissed Mallory on the cheek. 'I'll see you later, lover.'

The men sat there, gaping, as Kat walked away.

In their dressing room, Kat said to Paige and Honey, 'In all the excitement, I haven't had a chance to tell you the news.'

'What news?' Paige asked.

'Ken asked me to marry him.'

There were looks of disbelief on their faces.

'You're joking!' Paige said.

'No. He proposed to me last night. I accepted.'

'But you can't marry him!' Honey exclaimed. 'You know what he's like. I mean, he tried to get you to go to bed on a bet!'

'He succeeded.' Kat grinned.

Paige looked at her. 'I'm confused.'

Kat said, 'We were wrong about him. Completely wrong. Ken told me about that bet himself. All this time, it's been bothering his conscience. Don't you see what happened? I went out with him to punish him, and he went out with me to win some money, and we ended up falling in love with each other. Oh, I can't tell you how happy I am!'

Honey and Paige looked at each other. 'When are you getting married?' Honey asked.

'We haven't discussed it yet, but I'm sure it will

271

be soon. I want you two to be my bridesmaids.'

'You can count on it,' Paige said. 'We'll be there.' But there was a nagging doubt in the back of her mind. She yawned. 'It's been a long night. I'm going home and get some sleep.'

'I'll stay here with Mike,' Kat said. 'When he wakes up, the police want to talk to him.' She took their hands in hers. 'Thank you for being such good friends.'

On the way home, Paige thought about what had happened that night. She knew how much Kat loved her brother. It had taken a lot of courage to turn him over to the police. *I should have done this a long time ago*.

The telephone was ringing as Paige walked into the apartment. She hurried to pick it up.

It was Jason. 'Hi! I just called to tell you how much I miss you. What's going on in your life?'

Paige was tempted to tell him, to share it with somebody, but it was too personal. It belonged to Kat.

'Nothing,' Paige said. 'Everything is fine.'

'Good. Are you free for dinner tonight?'

Paige was aware that it was more than an invitation to dinner. *If I see him any more, I'm going to get involved*, she thought. She knew that it was one of the most important decisions of her life.

She took a deep breath. 'Jason . . .' The doorbell rang. 'Hold it a minute, will you, Jason?'

Paige put the telephone down and went to the door and opened it.

Alfred Turner was standing there.

Paige stood there, frozen.

Alfred smiled. 'May I come in?'

She was flustered. 'Of . . . of course. I'm s . . . sorry.' She watched Alfred walk into the living room, and she was filled with conflicting emotions. She was happy and excited and angry at the same time. *Why am I going on like this?* Paige thought. *He probably dropped by to say hello.*

Alfred turned to her. 'I've left Karen.'

The words were a shock.

Alfred moved closer to her. 'I made a big mistake, Paige. I never should have let you go. Never.'

'Alfred . . .' Paige suddenly remembered. 'Excuse me.'

She hurried to the telephone and picked it up. 'Jason?'

'Yes, Paige. About tonight, we could—'

'I . . . I can't see you.'

'Oh. If tonight is bad, what about tomorrow night?'

'I . . . I'm not sure.'

He sensed the tension in her voice. 'Is anything wrong?'

'No. Everything is fine. I'll call you tomorrow and explain.'

'All right.' He sounded puzzled.

Paige replaced the receiver.

'I've missed you, Paige,' Alfred said. 'Have you missed me?'

No. I just follow strangers on the street and call them Alfred. 'Yes,' Paige admitted.

'Good. We belong together, you know. We always have.'

Have we? Is that why you married Karen? Do you think you can walk in and out of my life anytime you please?

Alfred was standing close to her. 'Haven't we?'

Paige looked at him and said, 'I don't know.' It was all too sudden.

Alfred took her hand in his. 'Of course you do.'

'What happened with Karen?'

Alfred shrugged. 'Karen was a mistake. I kept thinking about you and all the great times we had. We were always good for each other.'

She was watching him, wary, guarded. 'Alfred . . .'

'I'm here to stay, Paige. When I say "here", I don't exactly mean that. We're going to New York.'

'New York?'

'Yes. I'll tell you all about it. I could use a cup of coffee.'

'Of course. I'll make a fresh pot. It will just take a few minutes.'

Alfred followed her into the kitchen, where Paige began to prepare the coffee. She was trying to get her thoughts in order. She had wanted Alfred back so desperately, and now that he was here . . .

Alfred was saying, 'I've learned a lot in the last few years, Paige. I've grown up.'

'Oh?'

274

'Yes. You know I've been working with WHO all these years.'

'I know.'

'Those countries haven't changed any since we were kids. In fact, some of them are worse. There's more disease down there, more poverty . . .'

'But you were there, helping,' Paige said.

'Yes, and I suddenly woke up.'

'Woke up?'

'I realized I was throwing my life away. I was down there, living in misery, working twenty-four hours a day, helping those ignorant savages, when I could have been making a bundle of money over here.'

Paige was listening in disbelief.

'I met a doctor who has a practice on Park Avenue in New York. Do you know how much he makes a year? Over five hundred thousand dollars! Did you hear me? Five hundred thousand a year!'

Paige was staring at him.

'I said to myself, "Where has that kind of money been all of my life?" He offered me a position as an associate,' Alfred said proudly, 'and I'm going in with him. That's why you and I are going to New York.'

Paige stood there, numbed by what she was hearing.

'I'll be able to afford a penthouse apartment for us, and to get you pretty dresses, and all the things I've always promised you.' He was grinning. 'Well, are you surprised?'

Paige's mouth was dry. 'I . . . I don't know what to say, Alfred.'

He laughed. 'Of course you don't. Five hundred

275

thousand dollars a year is enough to make anyone speechless.'

'I wasn't thinking of the money,' Paige said slowly.

'No?'

She was studying him, as though seeing him for the first time. 'Alfred, when you were working for WHO, didn't you feel you were helping people?'

He shrugged. 'Nothing can help those people. And who the hell really cares? Would you believe that Karen wanted me to stay down there in Bangladesh? I told her no way, so she went back.' He took Paige's hand. 'So here I am . . . You're a little quiet. I guess you're overwhelmed by all this, huh?'

Paige thought of her father. *He would have been a big success on Park Avenue, but he wasn't interested in money. His only interest was in helping people.*

'I've already divorced Karen, so we can get married right away.' He patted her hand. 'What do you think of the idea of living in New York?'

Paige took a deep breath. 'Alfred . . .'

There was an expectant smile on his face. 'Yes?'

'Get out.'

The smile slowly faded. 'What?'

Paige rose. 'I want you to get out of here.'

He was confused. 'Where do you want me to go?'

'I won't tell you,' Paige said. 'It would hurt your feelings.'

After Alfred had gone, Paige sat lost in thought. Kat had been right. She had been clinging to a ghost. *Helping those ignorant savages, when I could have*

276

*been making a bundle over here . . . Five hundred
thousand a year!*

And that's what I've been hanging on to, Paige
thought wonderingly. She should have felt depressed, but instead she was filled with a feeling of
elation. She suddenly felt free. She knew now what
she wanted.

She walked over to the telephone and dialed
Jason's number.

'Hello.'

'Jason, it's Paige. Remember telling me about
your house in Noe Valley?'

'Yes . . .'

'I'd love to see it. Are you free tonight?'

Jason said quietly, 'Do you want to tell me what's
going on, Paige? I'm very confused.'

'*I'm* the one who's confused. I thought I was in
love with a man I knew a long time ago, but he's not
the same man. I know what I want now.'

'Yes?'

'I want to see your house.'

Noe Valley belonged to another century. It was a
colorful oasis in the heart of one of the most cosmo-
politan cities in the world.

Jason's house was a reflection of him—comfortable, neat, and charming. He escorted Paige through
the house. 'This is the living room, the kitchen, the
guest bathroom, the study . . .' He looked at her and
said, 'The bedroom is upstairs. Would you like to
see it?'

Paige said quietly, 'Very much.'

They went up the stairs into the bedroom. Paige's

heart was pounding wildly. But what was happening seemed inevitable. *I should have known from the beginning*, she thought.

Paige never knew who made the first move, but somehow they were in each other's arms and Jason's lips were on hers, and it seemed the most natural thing in the world. They started to undress each other, and there was a fierce urgency in both of them. And then they were in bed, and he was making love to her.

'God,' he whispered. 'I love you.'

'I know,' Paige teased. 'Ever since I told you to put on the white coat.'

After they made love, Paige said, 'I'd like to spend the night here.'

Jason smiled. 'You won't hate me in the morning?'

'I promise.'

Paige spent the night with Jason, talking . . . making love . . . talking. In the morning, she cooked breakfast for him.

Jason watched her, and said, 'I don't know how I got so lucky, but thank you.'

'I'm the lucky one,' Paige told him.

'You know something? I never got an answer to my proposal.'

'You'll have an answer this afternoon.'

That afternoon, a messenger arrived at Jason's office, with an envelope. Inside was the card that Jason had sent with the model house.

Mine [ ]
Ours [x]
Please check one.

Lou Dinetto was ready to check out of the hospital. Kat went to his room to say goodbye. Rhino and the Shadow were there.

As Kat walked in, Dinetto turned to them and said, 'Get lost.'

Kat watched them leave the room.

Dinetto looked at Kat and said, 'I owe you one.'

'You don't owe me anything.'

'Is that what you think my life is worth? I hear you're getting married.'

'That's right.'

'To a doctor.'

'Yes.'

'Well, tell him to take good care of you, or he'll have to answer to me.'

'I'll tell him.'

There was a small pause. 'I'm sorry about Mike.'

'He'll be all right,' Kat said. 'I had a long talk with him. He'll be fine.'

'Good.' Dinetto held out a bulky manila envelope. 'A little wedding present for you.'

Kat shook her head. 'No. Thank you.'

'But . . .'

'Take care of yourself.'

'You, too. You know something? You're a real stand-up broad. I'm going to tell you something I

want you to remember. If you ever need a favor —
anything — you come to me. You hear me?'

'I hear you.'

She knew that he meant it. And she knew that she
would never go to him.

During the weeks that followed, Paige and Jason
spoke on the phone three and four times a day, and
were together every time Paige was not on night call.

The hospital was busier than ever. Paige had been
on a thirty-six-hour shift that had been filled with
emergencies. She had just gone to sleep in the on-call
room when she was awakened by the urgent shrill
of the telephone.

She fumbled the phone to her ear. 'H'lo?'

'Dr Taylor, will you come to Room 422, stat?'

Paige tried to clear her mind. *Room 422. One of
Dr Barker's patients. Lance Kelly.* He had just had
a mitral valve replaced. *Something must have gone
wrong.* Paige stumbled off the cot and walked out
into the deserted corridor. She decided not to wait
for the elevator. She ran up the stairs. *Maybe it's
just a nervous nurse. If it's serious, I'll call Dr Barker,*
she thought.

She walked into Room 422 and stood in the doorway, staring. The patient was fighting for breath and
moaning. The nurse turned to Paige in obvious relief.
'I didn't know what to do, doctor. I . . .'

Paige hurried to the bedside. 'You're going to
be fine,' she said reassuringly. She took his wrist
between two fingers. His pulse was jumping wildly.
The mitral valve was malfunctioning.

'Let's sedate him,' Paige ordered.

280

The nurse handed Paige a syringe, and Paige injected it into a vein. Paige turned to the nurse. 'Tell the head nurse to get an operating team together, stat. And send for Dr Barker!'

Fifteen minutes later, Kelly was on the operating table. The team consisted of two scrub nurses, a circulating nurse, and two residents. A television monitor was perched high in a corner of the room to display the heart rate, EKG, and blood pressure.

The anesthesiologist walked in, and Paige felt like cursing. Most of the anesthesiologists at the hospital were skilled doctors, but Herman Koch was an exception. Paige had worked with him before and tried to avoid him as much as possible. She did not trust him. Now she had no choice.

Paige watched him secure a tube to the patient's throat, while she unfolded a paper drape with a clear window and placed it over the patient's chest.

'Put a line into the jugular vein,' Paige said.

Koch nodded. 'Right.'

One of the residents asked, 'What's the problem here?'

'Dr Barker replaced the mitral valve yesterday. I think it's ruptured.' Paige looked over at Dr Koch. 'Is he out?'

Koch nodded. 'Sleeping like he's in bed at home.'

I wish you were, Paige thought. 'What are you using?'

'Propofol.'

She nodded. 'All right.'

She watched Kelly being connected to the heart-lung machine so she could perform a cardiopulmonary bypass. Paige studied the monitors on the wall. Pulse 140 . . . blood oxygen saturation 92

281

percent . . . blood pressure 80 over 60. 'Let's go,' she said.

One of the residents put on music.

Paige stepped up to the operating table under eleven hundred watts of hot white light and turned to the scrub nurse. 'Scalpel, please . . .'

The operation began.

Paige removed all the sternal wires from the operation the day before. She then cut from the base of the neck to the lower end of the sternum, while one of the residents blotted away the blood with gauze pads.

She carefully went through the layers of fat and muscle, and in front of her was the erratically beating heart. 'There's the problem,' Paige said. 'The atrium is perforated. Blood is collecting around the heart and compressing it.' Paige was looking at the monitor on the wall. The pump pressure had dropped dangerously.

'Increase the flow,' Paige ordered.

The door to the operating room opened and Lawrence Barker stepped in. He stood to one side, watching what was happening.

Paige said, 'Dr Barker. Do you want to . . . ?'

'It's your operation.'

Paige took a quick look at what Koch was doing. 'Be careful. You'll overanesthetize him, dammit! Slow it down!'

'But I . . .'

'He's in V-tach! His pressure is dropping!'

'What do you want me to do?' Koch asked helplessly.

He should know, Paige thought angrily. 'Give him lidocaine and epinephrine! *Now!*' She was yelling.

282

'Right.'

Paige watched as Koch picked up a syringe and injected it into the patient's IV.

A resident looked at the monitor and called out, 'Blood pressure is falling.'

Paige was working frantically to stop the flow of blood. She looked up at Koch. 'Too much flow! I told you to . . .'

The noise of the heartbeat on the monitor suddenly became chaotic.

'My God! Something's gone wrong!'

'Give me the defibrillator!' Paige yelled.

The circulating nurse reached for the defibrillator on the crash cart, opened two sterile paddles, and plugged them in. She turned the buttons up to charge them and ten seconds later handed them to Paige.

She took the paddles and positioned them directly over Kelly's heart. Kelly's body jumped, then fell back.

Paige tried again, *willing* him to come back to life, willing him to breathe again. Nothing. The heart lay still, a dead, useless organ.

Paige was in a fury. Her part of the operation had been successful. Koch had overanesthetized the patient.

As Paige was applying the defibrillator to Lance Kelly's body for the third futile time, Dr Barker stepped up to the operating table and turned to Paige.

'You killed him.'

Jason was in the middle of a design meeting when his secretary said, 'Dr Taylor is on the phone for you. Shall I tell her you'll call back?'

'No. I'll take it.' Jason picked up the phone. 'Paige?'

'Jason . . . I need you!' She was sobbing.

'What happened?'

'Can you come to the apartment?'

'Of course. I'll be right there.' He stood up. 'The meeting is over. We'll pick it up in the morning.'

Half an hour later, Jason was at the apartment. Paige opened the door and threw her arms around him. Her eyes were red from crying.

'What happened?' Jason asked.

'It's awful! Dr Barker told me I . . . I killed a patient, and honestly, it . . . it wasn't my fault!' Her voice broke. 'I can't take any more of his . . .'

'Paige,' Jason said gently, 'you've told me how mean he always is. That's the man's character.'

Paige shook her head. 'It's more than that. He's been trying to force me out since the day I started working with him. Jason, if he were a bad doctor and didn't think I was any good, I wouldn't mind so much, but the man is brilliant. I have to respect his opinion. I just don't think I'm good enough.'

'Nonsense,' Jason said angrily. 'Of course you are. Everyone I talk to says you're a wonderful doctor.'

'Not Lawrence Barker.'

'Forget Barker.'

'I'm going to,' Paige said. 'I'm quitting the hospital.'

Jason took her in his arms. 'Paige, I know you love the profession too much to give it up.'

'I won't give it up. I just never want to see that hospital again.'

Jason took out a handkerchief and dried Paige's tears.

'I'm sorry to bother you with all of this,' Paige said.

'That's what husbands-to-be are for, isn't it?'

She managed a smile. 'I like the sound of that. All right.' Paige took a deep breath. 'I feel better now. Thanks for talking to me. I telephoned Dr Wallace and told him I was quitting. I'm going over to the hospital to see him now.'

'I'll see you at dinner tonight.'

Paige walked through the corridors of the hospital, knowing that she was seeing them for the last time. There were the familiar noises and the people hurrying up and down the corridors. It had become more of a home to her than she'd realized. She thought of Jimmy and Chang, and all the wonderful doctors she had worked with. Darling Jason going on rounds with her in his white coat. She passed the cafeteria where she and Honey and Kat had had a hundred breakfasts, and the lounge, where they had tried to have a party. The corridors and rooms were full of so many memories. *I'm going to miss it*, Paige thought, *but I refuse to work under the same roof as that monster*.

She went up to Dr Wallace's office. He was waiting for her.

'Well, I must say, your telephone call surprised me, Paige! Have you definitely made up your mind?'

'Yes.'

Benjamin Wallace sighed. 'Very well. Before you go, Dr Barker would like to see you.'

'I want to see him.' All of Paige's pent-up anger boiled to the surface.

'He's in the lab. Well . . . good luck.'

'Thanks.' Paige headed for the lab.

Dr Barker was examining some slides under a microscope when Paige entered. He looked up. 'I'm told you've decided to quit the hospital.'

'That's right. You finally got your wish.'

'And what was that?' Barker asked.

'You've wanted me out of here from the first moment you saw me. Well, you've won. I can't fight you anymore. When you told me I killed your patient, I . . .' Paige's voice broke. 'I . . . I think you're a sadistic, cold-hearted son of a bitch, and I hate you.'

'Sit down,' Dr Barker said.

'No. I have nothing more to say.'

'Well, I have. Who the hell do you think you . . . ?'

He suddenly stopped and began to gasp.

As Paige watched in horror, he clutched his chest and toppled over in his chair, his face twisted to one side in a horrible rictus.

Paige was at his side instantly. 'Dr Barker!' She

grabbed the telephone and shouted into it, 'Code Red! Code Red!'

Dr Peterson said, 'He's suffered a massive stroke. It's too early to tell whether he's going to come out of it.'

It's my fault, Paige thought. *I wanted him dead.* She felt miserable.

She went back to see Ben Wallace. 'I'm sorry about what happened,' Paige said. 'He was a good doctor.'

'Yes. It's regrettable. Very . . .' Wallace studied her a moment. 'Paige, if Dr Barker can't practice here anymore, would you consider staying on?'

Paige hesitated. 'Yes. Of course.'

28

His chart read, 'John Cronin, white male, age 70. Diagnosis: Cardiac tumor.'

Paige had not yet met John Cronin. He was scheduled to have heart surgery. She walked into his room, a nurse and staff doctor at her side. She smiled warmly and said, 'Good morning, Mr Cronin.'

They had just extubated him, and there were the marks of adhesive tape around his mouth. IV bottles hung overhead, and the tubing had been inserted in his left arm.

Cronin looked over at Paige. 'Who the hell are you?'

'I'm Dr Taylor. I'm going to examine you and—'

'Like hell you are! Keep your fucking hands off me. Why didn't they send in a *real* doctor?'

Paige's smile died. 'I'm a cardiovascular surgeon. I'm going to do everything I can to get you well again.'

'*You're* going to operate on my heart?'

'That's right. I . . .'

John Cronin looked at the staff doctor and said, 'For Christ's sakes, is this the best this hospital can do?'

'I assure you, Dr Taylor is thoroughly qualified,' the staff doctor said.

'So is my ass.'

Paige said stiffly, 'Would you rather bring in your own surgeon?'

'I don't have one. I can't afford those high-priced quacks. You doctors are all alike. All you're interested in is money. You don't give a damn about people. We're just pieces of meat to you, aren't we?'

Paige was fighting to control her temper. 'I know you're upset right now, but—'

'Upset? Just because you're going to cut my heart out?' He was screaming. 'I know I'll die on the operating table. You're going to kill me, and I hope they get you for murder!'

'That's enough!' Paige said.

He was grinning at her maliciously. 'It wouldn't look good on your record if I died, would it, doctor? Maybe I *will* let you operate on me.'

Paige found that she was hyperventilating. She turned to the nurse. 'I want an EKG and a chemistry panel.' She took one last look at John Cronin, then turned and left the room.

When Paige returned an hour later with the reports on the tests, John Cronin looked up. 'Oh, the bitch is back.'

Paige operated on John Cronin at six o'clock the following morning.

The moment she opened him up, she knew that there was no hope. The major problem was not the heart. Cronin's organs showed signs of melanoma.

A resident said, 'Oh, my God! What are we going to do?'

'We're going to pray that he doesn't have to live with this too long.'

When Paige stepped out of the operating room into the corridor, she found a woman and two men waiting for her. The woman was in her late thirties. She had bright red hair and too much makeup, and she wore a heavy, cheap perfume. She had on a tight dress that accentuated a voluptuous figure. The men were in their forties, and both had red hair. To Paige, they looked like a circus troupe.

The woman said to Paige, 'You Dr Taylor?'

'Yes.'

'I'm Mrs Cronin. These are my brothers. How's my husband?'

Paige hesitated. She said carefully, 'The operation went as well as could be expected.'

'Oh, thank God!' Mrs Cronin said melodramatically, dabbing at her eyes with a lace handkerchief. 'I'd die if anything happened to John!'

Paige felt as if she were watching an actress in a bad play.

'Can I see my darling now?'

'Not yet, Mrs Cronin. He's in the recovery room. I suggest that you come back tomorrow.'

'We'll be back.' She turned to the men. 'Come along, fellas.'

Paige watched as they walked away. *Poor John Cronin*, she thought.

Paige was given the report the next morning. The cancer had metastasized throughout Cronin's body. It was too late for radiation treatment.

The oncologist said to Paige, 'There's nothing to do but try to keep him comfortable. He's going to be in a hell of a lot of pain.'

'How much time does he have?'

'A week or two at the most.'

Paige went to visit John Cronin in intensive care. He was asleep. He was no longer a bitter, vitriolic man, but a human being, fighting desperately for his life. He was on a respirator, and being fed intravenously. Paige sat down at his bedside, watching him. He looked tired and defeated. *He's one of the unlucky ones*, Paige thought. *Even with all the modern medical miracles, there's nothing we can do to save him*. Paige touched his arm gently. After a while, she left.

Later that afternoon, Paige stopped by to see John Cronin again. He was off the respirator now. When he opened his eyes and saw Paige, he said drowsily, 'The operation's over, huh?'

Paige smiled reassuringly. 'Yes. I just came by to make sure that you're comfortable.'

'Comfortable?' he snorted. 'What the hell do you care?'

Paige said, 'Please. Let's not fight.'

Cronin lay there, silently studying her. 'The other doctor told me you did a good job.'

Paige said nothing.

'I have cancer, don't I?'

'Yes.'

'How bad is it?'

The question posed a dilemma that all surgeons

291

were faced with sooner or later. Paige said, 'It's pretty bad.'

There was a long silence. 'What about radiation or chemotherapy?'

'I'm sorry. It would make you feel worse, and it wouldn't help.'

'I see. Well . . . I've had a good life.'

'I'm sure you have.'

'You may not think so, looking at me now, but I've had a lot of women.'

'I believe it.'

'Yeah. Women . . . thick steaks . . . good cigars . . . You married?'

'No.'

'You ought to be. Everyone should be married. I've been married. Twice. First, for thirty-five years. She was a wonderful lady. She died of a heart attack.'

'I'm sorry.'

'It's okay.' He sighed. 'Then I got sucked into marrying a bimbo. Her and her two hungry brothers. It's my fault for being so horny, I guess. Her red hair turned me on. She's some piece of work.'

'I'm sure she . . .'

'No offense, but do you know why I'm in this cockamamie hospital? My wife put me here. She didn't want to waste money on me for a private hospital. This way there'll be more to leave to her and her brothers.' He looked up at Paige. 'How much time *do* I have left?'

'Do you want it straight?'

'No . . . yes.'

'A week or two.'

'Jesus! The pain is going to get worse, isn't it?'

292

'I'll try to keep you as comfortable as possible, Mr Cronin.'

'Call me John.'

'John.'

'Life is a bitch, isn't it?'

'You said you've had a good life.'

'I did. It's kinda funny, knowing it's about over. Where do you think we go?'

'I don't know.'

He forced a smile. 'I'll let you know when I get there.'

'Some medication is on the way. Can I do anything to make you more comfortable?'

'Yeah. Come back and talk to me tonight.'

It was Paige's night off, and she was exhausted. 'I'll come back.'

That night when Paige went back to see John Cronin, he was awake.

'How are you feeling?'

He winced. 'Terrible. I was never very good about pain. I guess I've got a low threshold.'

'I understand.'

'You met Hazel, huh?'

'Hazel?'

'My wife. The bimbo. She and her brothers were here to see me. They said they talked to you.'

'Yes.'

'She's something, ain't she? I sure got myself into a bundle of trouble there. They can't wait for me to kick the bucket.'

'Don't say that.'

'It's true. The only reason Hazel married me was

293

for my money. To tell you the truth, I didn't mind that so much. I really had a good time with her in bed, but then she and her brothers started to get greedy. They always wanted more.'

The two of them sat there in a comfortable silence.

'Did I tell you I used to travel a lot?'

'No.'

'Yeah. I've been to Sweden . . . Denmark . . . Germany. Have you been to Europe?'

She thought about the day at the travel agency. *I'm dying to see London. Paris is where I want to go. I want to ride a gondola in the moonlight in Venice.* 'No. I haven't.'

'You ought to go.'

'Maybe one day I will.'

'I guess you don't make much money working at a hospital like this, huh?'

'I make enough.'

He nodded to himself. 'Yeah. You have to go to Europe. Do me a favor. Go to Paris . . . stay at the Crillon, have dinner at Maxim's, order a big, thick steak and a bottle of champagne, and when you eat that steak and drink that champagne, I want you to think of me. Will you do that?'

Paige said slowly, 'I'll do that one day.'

John Cronin was studying her. 'Good. I'm tired now. Will you come back tomorrow and talk to me again?'

'I'll come back,' Paige said.

John Cronin slept.

Ken Mallory was a great believer in Lady Luck, and after meeting the Harrisons, he believed even more firmly that she was on his side. The odds against a man as wealthy as Alex Harrison being brought to Embarcadero County Hospital were enormous. *And I'm the one who saved his life, and he wants to show his gratitude*, Mallory thought gleefully.

He had asked a friend of his about the Harrisons.

'Rich doesn't even begin to cover it,' his friend had said. 'He's a millionaire a dozen times over. And he has a great-looking daughter. She's been married three or four times. The last time to a count.'

'Have you ever met the Harrisons?'

'No. They don't mingle with the *hoi polloi*.'

On a Saturday morning, Alex Harrison telephoned Ken Mallory. 'Ken, do you think I'll be in shape to give a dinner party a week from now?'

'If you don't overdo it, I don't see why not,' Mallory said.

Alex Harrison smiled. 'Fine. You're the guest of honor.'

Mallory felt a sudden thrill. *The old man really meant what he said.* 'Well . . . thank you.'

'Lauren and I will expect you at seven-thirty next Saturday night.' He gave Mallory an address on Nob Hill.

'I'll be there,' Mallory said. *Will I ever!*

Mallory had promised to take Kat to the theater that evening, but it would be easy to cancel. He had collected his winnings, and he enjoyed having sex with her. Several times a week they had managed to get together in one of the empty on-call rooms, or a deserted hospital room, or at her apartment or his. *Her fires were banked a long time*, Mallory thought happily, *but when the explosion came — wow! Well, one of these days, it will be time to say arrivederci.*

On the day he was to have dinner with the Harrisons, Mallory telephoned Kat. 'Bad news, baby.'

'What's the matter, darling?'

'One of the doctors is sick and they've asked me to cover for him. I'm afraid I'm going to have to break our date.'

She did not want to let him know how disappointed she was, how much she needed to be with him. Kat said lightly, 'Oh well, that's the doctor business, isn't it?'

'Yeah. I'll make it up to you.'

'You don't have to make anything up to me,' she said warmly. 'I love you.'

'I love you, too.'

'Ken, when are we going to talk about us?'

'What do you mean?' He knew exactly what she meant. A commitment. They were all alike. *They use their pussies for bait, hoping to hook a sucker into spending his life with them.* Well, he was too smart for that. When the time came, he would regretfully bow out, as he had done a dozen times before.

Kat was saying, 'Don't you think we should set a date, Ken? I have a lot of plans to make.'

'Oh, sure. We'll do that.'

'I thought maybe June. What do you think?'

You don't want to know what I think. If I play my cards right, there's going to be a wedding, but it won't be with you. 'We'll talk about it, baby. I really have to go now.'

The Harrisons' home was a mansion out of a motion picture, situated on acres of manicured grounds. The house itself seemed to go on forever. There were two dozen guests, and in the huge drawing room a small orchestra was playing. When Mallory walked in, Lauren hurried over to greet him. She was wearing a silky clinging gown. She squeezed Mallory's hand. 'Welcome, guest of honor. I'm so glad you're here.'

'So am I. How is your father?'

'Very much alive, thanks to you. You're quite a hero in this house.'

Mallory smiled modestly. 'I only did my job.'

'I suppose that's what God says every day.' She took his hand and began introducing him to the other guests.

The guest list was blue-ribbon. The governor of California was there, the French ambassador, a justice of the Supreme Court, and a dozen assorted politicians, artists, and business tycoons. Mallory could feel the power in the room, and it thrilled him. *This is where I belong*, he thought. *Right here, with these people.*

The dinner was delicious and elegantly served. At the end of the evening, when the guests started to leave, Harrison said to Mallory, 'Don't rush off, Ken. I'd like to talk to you.'

297

'I'd be delighted.'

Harrison, Lauren, and Mallory sat in the library. Harrison was seated in a chair next to his daughter.

'When I told you at the hospital that I thought you had a great future before you, I meant it.'

'I really appreciate your confidence, sir.'

'You should be in private practice.'

Mallory laughed self-deprecatingly. 'I'm afraid it's not that easy, Mr Harrison. It takes a long time to build up a practice, and I'm . . .'

'Ordinarily, yes. But you're not an ordinary man.'

'I don't understand.'

'After you finish your residency, Father wants to set you up in your own practice,' Lauren said.

For a moment, Mallory was speechless. It was too easy. He felt as though he were living in some kind of wonderful dream. 'I . . . I don't know what to say.'

'I have a lot of very wealthy friends. I've already spoken to some of them about you. I can promise you that you'll be swamped the minute you put up your shingle.'

'Father, lawyers put up shingles,' Lauren said.

'Whatever. In any case, I'd like to finance you. Are you interested?'

Mallory was finding it difficult to breathe. 'Very much so. But I . . . I don't know when I would be able to repay you.'

'You don't understand. I'm repaying *you*. You won't owe me anything.'

Lauren was looking at Mallory, her eyes warm. 'Please say yes.'

'I'd be stupid to say no, wouldn't I?'

298

'That's right,' Lauren said softly. 'And I'm sure you're not stupid.'

On his way home, Ken Mallory was in a state of euphoria. *This is as good as it gets*, he thought. But he was wrong. It got better.

Lauren telephoned him. 'I hope you don't mind mixing business with pleasure.'

He smiled to himself. 'Not at all. What did you have in mind?'

'There's a charity ball next Saturday night. Would you like to take me?'

Oh, baby, I'm going to take you all right. 'I'd love to.' He was on duty Saturday night, but he would call in sick and they would have to find someone to take his place.

Mallory was a man who believed in planning ahead, and what was happening to him now went beyond his wildest dreams.

Within a few days he was swept up in Lauren's social circle, and life took on a dizzying pace. He would be out with Lauren dancing half the night, and stumble through his days at the hospital. There were mounting complaints about his work, but he didn't care. *I'll be out of here soon*, he told himself.

The thought of getting away from the dreary county hospital and having his own practice was exciting enough, but Lauren was the bonus that Lady Luck had given him.

Kat was becoming a nuisance. Mallory had to keep finding pretexts to avoid seeing her. When she would press him, he would say, 'Darling, I'm crazy about you . . . of course I want to marry you, but right now, I . . .' and he would go into a litany of excuses.

It was Lauren who suggested that the two of them spend the weekend at the family lodge at Big Sur. Mallory was elated. *Everything is coming up roses*, he thought. *I'm going to own the whole damned world!*

The lodge was spread across pine-covered hills, an enormous structure built of wood and tile and stone, overlooking the Pacific Ocean. It had a master bedroom, eight guest bedrooms, a spacious living room with a stone fireplace, an indoor swimming pool, and a large hot tub. Everything smelled of old money.

When they walked in, Lauren turned to Mallory and said, 'I let the servants go for the weekend.'

Mallory grinned. 'Good thinking.' He put his arms around Lauren and said softly, 'I'm wild about you.'

'Show me,' Lauren said.

They spent the day in bed, and Lauren was almost as insatiable as Kat.

'You're wearing me out!' Mallory laughed.

'Good. I don't want you to be able to make love to anyone else.' She sat up in bed. 'There *is* no one else, is there, Ken?'

'Absolutely not,' Mallory said sincerely. 'There's no one in the world for me but you. I'm in love with you, Lauren.' Now was the time to take the plunge, to wrap his whole future up in one neat package. It would be one thing to be a successful doctor in private practice. It would be something else to be Alex Harrison's son-in-law. 'I want to marry you.'

He held his breath, waiting for her answer.

'Oh, yes, darling,' Lauren said. 'Yes.'

At the apartment, Kat was frantically trying to reach Mallory. She telephoned the hospital.

'I'm sorry, Dr Hunter, Dr Mallory is not on call, and doesn't answer his page.'

'Didn't he leave word where he could be reached?'

'We have no record of it.'

Kat replaced the receiver and turned to Paige. 'Something's happened to him, I know it. He would have called me by now.'

'Kat, there could be a hundred reasons why you haven't heard from him. Perhaps he had to go out of town suddenly, or . . .'

'You're right. I'm sure there's some good excuse.' Kat looked at the phone and *willed* it to ring.

When Mallory returned to San Francisco, he telephoned Kat at the hospital.

'Dr Hunter is off duty,' the receptionist told him.

'Thank you.' Mallory called the apartment. Kat was there.

'Hi, baby!'

'Ken! Where have you been? I've been worried about you. I tried everywhere to reach —'

'I had a family emergency,' he said smoothly. 'I'm sorry. I didn't have a chance to call you. I had to go out of town. May I come over?'

'You know you may. I'm so glad you're all right. I —'

'Half an hour.' He replaced the receiver and

thought happily, *'The time has come,'* the Walrus said, *'To talk of many things.'* Kat, baby, it was great fun, but it was just one of those things.

When Mallory arrived at the apartment, Kat threw her arms around him. 'I've missed you!' She could not tell him how desperately worried she had been. Men hated that kind of thing. She stood back. 'Darling, you look absolutely exhausted.'

Mallory sighed. 'I've been up for the last twenty-four hours.' *That part is true*, he thought.

Kat hugged him. 'Poor baby. Can I fix something for you?'

'No, I'm fine. All I really need is a good night's sleep. Let's sit down, Kat. We have to have a talk.' He sat on the couch next to her.

'Is anything wrong?' Kat asked.

Mallory took a deep breath. 'Kat, I've been thinking a lot about us lately.'

She smiled. 'So have I. I have news for you—'

'No, wait. Let me finish. Kat, I think we're rushing into things too fast. I . . . I think I proposed too hastily.'

She paled. 'What . . . what are you saying?'

'I'm saying that I think we should postpone everything.'

She felt as though the room were closing in on her. She was finding it difficult to breathe. 'Ken, we can't postpone anything. I'm having your baby.'

302

Paige got home at midnight, drained. It had been an exhausting day. There had been no time for lunch, and dinner had consisted of a sandwich between operations. She fell into her bed and was asleep instantly. She was awakened by the ringing of the telephone. Groggily, she reached for the instrument and automatically glanced at the bedside clock. It was three in the morning. 'H'lo?'

'Dr Taylor? I'm sorry to disturb you, but one of your patients is insisting on seeing you right away.'

Paige's throat was so dry she could hardly talk. 'I'm off duty,' she mumbled. 'Can't you get someone . . . ?'

'He won't talk to anyone else. He says he needs *you*.'

'Who is it?'

'John Cronin.'

She sat up straighter. 'What's happened?'

'I don't know. He refuses to speak with anyone but you.'

'All right,' she said wearily. 'I'm on my way.'

Thirty minutes later, Paige arrived at the hospital. She went directly to John Cronin's room. He was lying in bed, awake. Tubes were protruding from his nostrils and his arms.

'Thanks for coming.' His voice was weak and hoarse.

Paige sat down in a chair next to the bed. She smiled. 'That's all right, John. I had nothing to do, anyway, but sleep. What can I do for you that no one else here at this great big hospital couldn't have done?'

'I want you to talk to me.'

Paige groaned. 'At this hour? I thought it was some kind of emergency.'

'It is. I want to leave.'

She shook her head. 'That's impossible. You can't go home now. You couldn't get the kind of treatment —'

He interrupted her. 'I don't want to go home. I want to leave.'

She looked at him and said slowly, 'What are you saying?'

'You know what I'm saying. The medication isn't working anymore. I can't stand this pain. I want out.'

Paige leaned over and took his hand. 'John, I can't do that. Let me give you some —'

'No. I'm tired, Paige. I want to go wherever it is I'm going, but I don't want to hang around here like this. Not anymore.'

'John . . .'

'How much time do I have left? A few more days? I told you, I'm not good about pain. I'm lying here like a trapped animal, filled with all these goddam tubes. My body is being eaten away inside. This isn't living — it's dying. For God's sake, help me!'

He was racked by a sudden spasm of pain. When he spoke again, his voice was even weaker. 'Help me . . . please . . .'

Paige knew what she had to do. She had to report John Cronin's request to Dr Benjamin Wallace. He would pass it on to the administration committee. They would assemble a panel of doctors to assess Cronin's condition, and then make a decision. After that, it would have to be approved by . . .

'Paige . . . it's *my* life. Let me do with it as I like.'

She looked over at the helpless figure locked in his pain.

'I'm begging you . . .'

She took his hand and held it for a long time. When she spoke, she said, 'All right, John. I'll do it.'

He managed a trace of a smile. 'I knew I could count on you.'

Paige leaned over and kissed him on the forehead. 'Close your eyes and go to sleep.'

'Good night, Paige.'

'Good night, John.'

John Cronin sighed and closed his eyes, a beatific smile on his face.

Paige sat there watching him, thinking about what she was about to do. She remembered how horrified she had been on her first day of rounds with Dr Radnor. *She's been in a coma for six weeks. Her vital signs are failing. There's nothing more we can do for her. We'll pull the plug this afternoon.* Was it wrong to release a fellow human being from his misery?

Slowly, as though she were moving under water, Paige rose and walked to a cabinet in the corner, where a bottle of insulin was kept for emergency use. She removed the bottle and stood there, staring at it. Then she uncapped the bottle. She filled a syringe with the insulin and walked back to John Cronin's

305

bedside. There was still time to go back. *I'm lying here like a trapped animal . . . This isn't living — it's dying. For God's sake, help me!*

Paige leaned forward and slowly injected the insulin into the IV attached to Cronin's arm.

'Sleep well,' Paige whispered. She was unaware that she was sobbing.

Paige drove home and stayed awake the rest of the night, thinking about what she had done.

At six o'clock in the morning, she received a telephone call from one of the residents at the hospital.

'I'm sorry to give you bad news, Dr Taylor. Your patient John Cronin died of cardiac arrest early this morning.'

The staff doctor in charge that morning was Dr Arthur Kane.

31

The one other time Ken Mallory had gone to an opera, he had fallen asleep. On this night he was watching *Rigoletto* at the San Francisco Opera House and enjoying every minute of it. He was seated in a box with Lauren Harrison and her father. In the lobby of the opera house during intermission, Alex Harrison had introduced him to a large number of friends.

'This is my future son-in-law and a brilliant doctor, Ken Mallory.'

Being Alex Harrison's son-in-law was enough to *make* him a brilliant doctor.

After the performance, the Harrisons and Mallory went to the Fairmont Hotel for supper in the elegant main dining room. Mallory enjoyed the deferential greeting that the maître d' gave to Alex Harrison as he led them to their booth. *From now on, I'll be able to afford places like this*, Mallory thought, *and everyone is going to know who I am*.

After they had ordered, Lauren said, 'Darling, I think we should have a party to announce our engagement.'

'That's a good idea!' her father said. 'We'll make it a big one. What do you say, Ken?'

A warning bell sounded in Mallory's mind. An

engagement party would mean publicity. *I'll have to set Kat straight first. A little money should take care of that.* Mallory cursed the stupid bet he had made. For a mere ten thousand dollars, his whole shining future might now be in jeopardy. He could just imagine what would happen if he tried to explain Kat to the Harrisons.

By the way, I forgot to mention that I'm already engaged to a doctor at the hospital. She's black . . .

Or: *Do you want to hear something funny? I bet the boys at the hospital ten thousand dollars I could fuck this black doctor . . .*

Or: *I already have one wedding planned . . .*

No, he thought, *I'll have to find a way to buy Kat off.*

They were looking at Mallory expectantly.

Mallory smiled. 'A party sounds like a wonderful idea.'

Lauren said enthusiastically, 'Good. I'll get things started. You men have no idea what it takes to give a party.'

Alex Harrison turned to Mallory. 'I've already started the ball rolling for you, Ken.'

'Sir?'

'Gary Gitlin, the head of North Shore Hospital, is an old golf buddy of mine. I talked to him about you, and he doesn't think there will be any problem about having you affiliated with his hospital. That's quite prestigious, you know. And at the same time, I'll get you set up in your own practice.'

Mallory listened, filled with a sense of euphoria. 'That's wonderful.'

'Of course it will take a few years to build up a really lucrative practice, but I think you should be able to make two or three hundred thousand dollars the first year or two.'

Two or three hundred thousand! My God! Mallory thought. *He makes it sound like peanuts.* 'That . . . that would be very nice, sir.'

Alex Harrison smiled. 'Ken, since I'm going to be your father-in-law, let's get off this "sir" business. Call me Alex.'

'Right, Alex.'

'You know, I've never been a June bride,' Lauren said. 'Is June all right with you, darling?'

He could hear Kat's voice saying: *Don't you think we should set a date? I thought maybe June.*

Mallory took Lauren's hand in his. 'That sounds great.' *That will give me plenty of time to handle Kat,* Mallory decided. He smiled to himself. *I'll offer her some of the money I won getting her into bed.*

'We have a yacht in the south of France,' Alex Harrison was saying. 'Would you two like to honeymoon on the French Riviera? You can fly over in our Gulfstream.'

A yacht. The French Riviera. It was like a fantasy come true. Mallory looked at Lauren. 'I'd honeymoon anywhere with Lauren.'

Alex Harrison nodded. 'Well, it looks like everything is settled.' He smiled at his daughter. 'I'm going to miss you, baby.'

'You're not losing me, Father. You're gaining a doctor!'

Alex Harrison nodded. 'And a damn good one. I can never thank you enough for saving my life, Ken.'

Lauren stroked Mallory's hand. 'I'll thank him for you.'

'Ken, why don't we have lunch next week?' Alex

Harrison said. 'We'll pick out some decent office space for you, maybe in the Post Building, and I'll make a date for you to see Gary Gitlin. A lot of my friends are dying to meet you.'

'I think you might rephrase that, Father,' Lauren suggested. She turned to Ken. 'I've been talking to *my* friends about you and they're eager to meet you, too, only I'm not going to let them.'

'I'm not interested in anyone but you,' Mallory said warmly.

When they got into their chauffeur-driven Rolls-Royce, Lauren asked, 'Where can we drop you, darling?'

'The hospital. I've got to check on a few patients.' He had no intention of seeing any patients. Kat was on duty at the hospital.

Lauren stroked his cheek. 'My poor baby. You work much too hard.'

Mallory sighed. 'It doesn't matter. As long as I'm helping people.'

Mallory went quickly to the doctors' dressing room and changed out of his dinner jacket.

He found Kat in the geriatric ward.

'Hi, Kat.'

She was in an angry mood. 'We had a date last night, Ken.'

'I know. I'm sorry. I wasn't able to make it, and—'

'That's the third time in the last week. What's going on?'

She was becoming a boring nag. 'Kat, I have to talk to you. Is there an empty room around here?'

She thought for a moment. 'A patient checked out of 315. Let's go in there.'

They started down the corridor. A nurse walked up to them. 'Oh, Dr Mallory! Dr Peterson has been looking for you. He —'

'Tell him I'm busy.' He took Kat by the arm and led her to the elevator.

When they arrived at the third floor, they walked silently down the corridor and went into Room 315. Mallory closed the door behind them. He was hyperventilating. His whole golden future depended on the next few minutes.

He took Kat's hand in his. It was time to be sincere. 'Kat, you know I'm crazy about you. I've never felt about anyone the way I feel about you. But, honey, the idea of having a baby right now . . . well . . . can't you see how wrong it would be? I mean . . . we're both working day and night, we aren't making enough money to . . .'

'But we can manage,' Kat said. 'I love you, Ken, and I —'

'Wait. All I'm asking is that we put everything off for a little while. Let me finish my term at the hospital and get started in private practice somewhere. Maybe we'll go back East. In a few years we'll be able to afford to get married and have a baby.'

'*In a few years?* But I told you, I'm pregnant.'

'I know, darling, but it's been what, now . . . two months? There's still plenty of time to abort it.'

Kat looked at him, shocked. 'No! I won't abort it. I want us to get married right away. Now.'

We have a yacht in the south of France. Would you

two like to honeymoon on the French Riviera? You can fly over in our Gulfstream.

'I've already told Paige and Honey that we're getting married. They're going to be my bridesmaids. And I told them about the baby.'

Mallory felt a cold chill go through him. Things were getting out of hand. If the Harrisons got wind of this, he would be finished. 'You shouldn't have done that.'

'Why not?'

Mallory forced a smile. 'I want to keep our private lives private.' *I'll get you set up in your own practice . . . You should be able to make two or three hundred thousand dollars the first year or two.* 'Kat, I'm going to ask you this for the last time. Will you have an abortion?' He was *willing* her to say yes, trying to keep the desperation out of his voice.

'No.'

'Kat . . .'

'I can't, Ken. I told you how I felt about the abortion I had as a girl. I swore I could never live through such a thing again. Don't ask me again.'

And it was at that moment that Ken Mallory realized he could not take a chance. He had no choice. He was going to have to kill her.

32

Honey looked forward every day to seeing the patient in Room 306. His name was Sean Reilly, and he was a good-looking Irishman, with black hair and black sparkling eyes. Honey guessed that he was in his early forties.

When Honey first met him on her rounds, she had looked at his chart and said, 'I see you're here for a cholecystectomy.'

'I thought they were going to remove my gall-bladder.'

Honey smiled. 'Same thing.'

Sean fixed his black eyes on her. 'They can cut out anything they want except my heart. That belongs to you.'

Honey laughed. 'Flattery will get you everywhere.'

'I hope so, darlin'.'

When Honey had a few minutes to spare, she would drop by and chat with Sean. He was charming and amusing.

'It's worth bein' operated on just to have you around, little darlin'.'

'You aren't nervous about the operation, are you?' she asked.

'Not if you're going to operate, love.'

'I'm not a surgeon. I'm an internist.'

'Are internists allowed to have dinner with their patients?'

'No. There's a rule against it.'

'Do internists ever break rules?'

'Never.' Honey was smiling.

'I think you're beautiful,' Sean said.

No one had ever told Honey that before. She found herself blushing. 'Thank you.'

'You're like the fresh mornin' dew in the fields of Killarney.'

'Have you ever been to Ireland?' Honey asked.

He laughed. 'No, but I promise you we'll go there together one day. You'll see.'

It was ridiculous Irish blarney, and yet . . .

That afternoon when Honey went in to see Sean, she said, 'How are you feeling?'

'The better for seeing you. Have you thought about our dinner date?'

'No,' Honey said. She was lying.

'I was hoping after my operation, I could take you out. You're not engaged, or married, or anything silly like that, are you?'

Honey smiled. 'Nothing silly like that.'

'Good! Neither am I. Who would have me?'

A lot of women, Honey thought.

'If you like home cooking, I happen to be a great cook.'

'We'll see.'

When Honey went to Sean's room the following morning, he said, 'I have a little present for you.' He handed her a sheet of drawing paper. On it was a softened, idealized sketch of Honey.

'I love it!' Honey said. 'You're a wonderful artist!' And she suddenly remembered the psychic's words:

You're going to fall in love. He's an artist. She was looking at Sean strangely.

'Is anything wrong?'

'No,' Honey said slowly. 'No.'

Five minutes later, Honey walked into Frances Gordon's room. The psychic was constantly being readmitted for a series of tests.

'Here comes the Virgo!'

Honey said, 'Do you remember telling me that I was going to fall in love with someone — an artist?'

'Yes.'

'Well, I . . . I think I've met him.'

Frances Gordon smiled. 'See? The stars never lie.'

'Could . . . could you tell me a little about him? About us?'

'There are some tarot cards in that drawer over there. Could you give them to me, please?'

As Honey handed her the cards, she thought, *This is ridiculous! I don't believe in this!*

Frances Gordon was laying out the cards. She kept nodding to herself, and nodding and smiling, and suddenly she stopped. Her face went pale. 'Oh, my God!' She looked up at Honey.

'What . . . what's the matter?' Honey asked.

'This artist. You say you've already met him?'

'I think so. Yes.'

Frances Gordon's voice was filled with sadness. 'The poor man.' She looked up at Honey. 'I'm sorry . . . I'm so sorry.'

* * *

Sean Reilly was scheduled to have his operation the following morning.

8:15 A.M. Dr William Radnor was in OR Two, preparing for the operation.

8:25 A.M. A truck containing a week's supply of bags of blood pulled up at the emergency entrance to Embarcadero County Hospital. The driver carried the bags to the blood bank in the basement. Eric Foster, the resident doctor on duty, was sharing coffee and a danish with a pretty young nurse, Andrea.

'Where do you want these?' the driver asked.

'Just set them down there.' Foster pointed to a corner.

'Right.' The driver put the bags down and pulled out a form. 'I need your John Hancock.'

'Okay.' Foster signed the form. 'Thanks.'

'No sweat.' The driver left.

Foster turned to Andrea. 'Where were we?'

'You were telling me how adorable I am.'

'Right. If you weren't married, I'd really go after you,' the resident said. 'Do you ever fool around?'

'No. My husband is a boxer.'

'Oh. Do you have a sister?'

'As a matter of fact, I do.'

'Is she as pretty as you are?'

'Prettier.'

'What's her name?'

'Marilyn.'

'Why don't we double-date one night?'

As they chatted, the fax machine began to click. Foster ignored it.

8:45 A.M. Dr Radnor began the operation on Sean Reilly. The beginning went smoothly. The operating room functioned like a well-oiled machine, run by capable people doing their jobs.

9:05 A.M. Dr Radnor reached the cystic duct. A textbook operation up until then. As he started to excise the gallbladder, his hand slipped and the scalpel nicked an artery. Blood began to pour out.

'Jesus!' He tried to stop the flow.

The anesthesiologist called out, 'His blood pressure just dropped to 95. He's going into shock!'

Radnor turned to the circulating nurse. 'Get some more blood up here, stat!'

'Right away, doctor.'

9:06 A.M. The telephone rang in the blood bank.

'Don't go away,' Foster told Andrea. He walked past the fax machine, which had stopped clicking, and picked up the telephone. 'Blood supply.'

'We need four units of Type O in OR Two, stat.'

'Right.' Foster replaced the receiver and went to the corner where the new blood had been deposited. He pulled out four bags and placed them on the top shelf of the metal cart used for such emergencies. He double-checked the bags. 'Type O,' he said aloud. He rang for an orderly.

'What's going on?' Andrea asked.

317

Foster looked at the schedule in front of him. 'It looks like one of the patients is giving Dr Radnor a bad time.'

9:10 A.M. The orderly came into the blood bank. 'What have we got?'

'Take this to OR Two. They're waiting for it.'

He watched the orderly wheel out the cart, then turned to Andrea. 'Tell me about your sister.'

'She's married, too.'

'Aw . . .'

Andrea smiled. 'But she fools around.'

'Does she really?'

'I'm only kidding. I have to go back to work, Eric. Thanks for the coffee and danish.'

'Anytime.' He watched her leave and thought, *What a great ass!*

9.12 A.M. The orderly was waiting for an elevator to take him to the second floor.

9.13 A.M. Dr Radnor was doing his best to minimize the catastrophe. 'Where's the damned blood?'

9:15 A.M. The orderly pushed at the door to OR Two and the circulating nurse opened it.

'Thanks,' she said. She carried the bags into the room. 'It's here, doctor.'

'Start pumping it into him. Fast!'

*   *   *

318

In the blood bank, Eric Foster finished his coffee, thinking about Andrea. *All the good-looking ones are married.*

As he started toward his desk, he passed the fax machine. He pulled out the fax. It read:

Recall Warning Alert #687, June 25: Red Blood Cells, Fresh Frozen Plasma. Units CB83711, CB800007. Community Blood Bank of California, Arizona, Washington, Oregon. Blood products testing repeatedly reactive for Antibody HIV Type 1 were distributed.

He stared at it a moment, then walked over to his desk and picked up the invoice he had signed for the bags of blood that had just been delivered. He looked at the number on the invoice. The number on the warning was identical.

'Oh, my God!' he said. He grabbed the telephone. 'Get me OR Two, fast!'

A nurse answered.

'This is the blood bank. I just sent up four units of Type O. Don't use it! I'm sending up some fresh blood immediately.'

The nurse said, 'Sorry, it's too late.'

Dr Radnor broke the news to Sean Reilly.

'It was a mistake,' Radnor said. 'A terrible mistake. I would give anything if it had not happened.'

Sean was staring at him, in shock. 'My God! I'm going to die.'

'We won't know whether you're HIV-positive for six or eight weeks. And even if you are, that does

319

not necessarily mean you will get AIDS. We're going to do everything we can for you.'

'What the hell can you do for me that you haven't already done?' Sean said bitterly. 'I'm a dead man.'

When Honey heard the news, she was devastated. She remembered Frances Gordon's words. *The poor man.*

Sean Reilly was asleep when Honey walked into his room. She sat at his bedside for a long time, watching him.

He opened his eyes and saw Honey. 'I dreamed that I was dreaming, and that I wasn't going to die.'

'Sean . . .'

'Did you come to visit the corpse?'

'Please don't talk that way.'

'How could this happen?' he cried.

'Someone made a mistake, Sean.'

'God, I don't want to die of AIDS!'

'Some people who get HIV may never get AIDS. The Irish are lucky.'

'I wish I could believe you.'

She took his hand in hers. 'You've got to.'

'I'm not a praying man,' Sean said, 'but I sure as hell am going to start now.'

'I'll pray with you,' Honey said.

He smiled wryly. 'I guess we can forget about that dinner, huh?'

'Oh, no. You don't get out of it that easily. I'm looking forward to it.'

He studied her a moment. 'You really mean that, don't you?'

'You bet I do! No matter what happens. Remember, you promised to take me to Ireland.'

33

'Are you all right, Ken?' Lauren asked. 'You seem tense, darling.'

They were alone in the huge Harrison library. A maid and a butler had served a six-course dinner, and during dinner he and Alex Harrison—*Call me Alex*—had chatted about Mallory's brilliant future.

'Why are you tense?'

Because this pregnant black bitch expects me to marry her. Because any minute word is going to leak out about our engagement and she'll hear about it and blow the whistle. Because my whole future could be destroyed.

He took Lauren's hand in his. 'I guess I'm working too hard. My patients aren't just patients to me, Lauren. They're people in trouble, and I can't help worrying about them.'

She stroked his face. 'That's one of the things I love about you, Ken. You're so caring.'

'I guess I was brought up that way.'

'Oh, I forgot to tell you. The society editor of the *Chronicle* and a photographer are coming here Monday to do an interview.'

It was like a blow to the pit of his stomach.

'Is there any chance you could be here with me, darling? They want a picture of you.'

'I . . . I wish I could, but I have a busy day scheduled at the hospital.' His mind was racing. 'Lauren, do you think it's a good idea to do an interview now? I mean, shouldn't we wait until . . . ?'

Lauren laughed. 'You don't know the press, darling. They're like bloodhounds. No, it's much better to get it over with now.'

Monday!

The following morning, Mallory tracked down Kat in a utility room. She looked tired and haggard. She had no makeup on and her hair was uncurled. *Lauren would never let herself go like that*, Mallory thought.

'Hi, honey!'

Kat did not answer.

Mallory took her in his arms. 'I've been thinking a lot about us, Kat. I didn't sleep at all last night. There's no one else for me. You were right, and I was wrong. I guess the news came as kind of a shock to me. I want you to have our baby.' He watched the sudden glow on Kat's face.

'Do you really mean that, Ken?'

'You bet I do.'

She put her arms around him. 'Thank God! Oh, darling. I was so worried. I don't know what I would do without you.'

'You don't have to worry about that. From now on, everything is going to be wonderful.' *You'll never know how wonderful.* 'Look, I have Sunday night off. Are you free?'

She grasped his hand. 'I'll make myself free.'

'Great! We'll have a nice quiet dinner and then

we'll go back to your place for a nightcap. Do you think you can get rid of Paige and Honey? I want us to be alone.'

Kat smiled. 'No problem. You don't know how happy you've made me. Did I ever tell you how much I love you?'

'I love you, too. I'll show you how much Sunday night.'

          •

Thinking it over, Mallory decided it was a foolproof plan. He had worked it out to the smallest detail. There was no way Kat's death could ever be blamed on him.

It was too risky to get what he needed from the hospital pharmacy because security had been tightened after the Bowman affair. Instead, early Sunday morning, Mallory went looking for a pharmacy far away from the neighborhood where he lived. Most of them were closed on Sunday, and he went to half a dozen before he found one that was open.

The pharmacist behind the counter said, 'Morning. Can I help you?'

'Yes. I'm going to see a patient in this area, and I want to take a prescription to him.' He pulled out his prescription pad and wrote on it.

The pharmacist smiled. 'Not many doctors make house calls these days.'

'I know. It's a pity, isn't it? People just don't care anymore.' He handed the slip of paper to the pharmacist.

The pharmacist looked at it and nodded. 'This will only take a few minutes.'

'Thank you.'
Step one.

That afternoon, Mallory made a stop at the hospital. He was there no more than ten minutes, and when he left, he was carrying a small package.
Step two.

Mallory had arranged to meet Kat at Trader Vic's for dinner, and he was waiting for her when she arrived. He watched her walking toward the table and thought, *It's the Last Supper, bitch.*

He rose and gave her a warm smile. 'Hello, doll. You look beautiful.' And he had to admit that she did. She looked sensational. *She could have been a model. And she's great in bed. All she lacks*, Ken thought, *is about twenty million dollars, give or take a few million.*

Kat was aware again of how the other women in the restaurant were eyeing Ken, envying her. But he only had eyes for her. He was the old Ken, warm and attentive.

'How was your day?' he asked.

She sighed. 'Busy. Three operations in the morning and two this afternoon.' She leaned forward. 'I know it's too early, but I swear I could feel the baby kicking when I was getting dressed.'

Mallory smiled. 'Maybe it wants to get out.'

'We should do an ultrasound test and find out if it's a boy or a girl. Then I can start buying clothes for it.'

'Great idea.'

'Ken, can we set a wedding date? I'd like to have our wedding as soon as possible.'

'No problem,' Mallory said easily. 'We can apply for a license next week.'

'That's wonderful!' She had a sudden thought. 'Maybe we could get a few days off and go somewhere on our honeymoon. Somewhere not too far away—up to Oregon or Washington.'

Wrong, baby. I'll be honeymooning in June, on my yacht on the French Riviera.

'That sounds great. I'll talk to Wallace.'

Kat squeezed his hand. 'Thank you,' she said huskily. 'I'm going to make you the best wife in the whole world.'

'I'm sure of it.' Mallory smiled. 'Now eat your vegetables. We want the baby to be healthy, don't we?'

They left the restaurant at 9:00 P.M. As they approached Kat's apartment building, Mallory said, 'Are you sure Paige and Honey won't be home?'

'I made sure,' Kat said. 'Paige is at the hospital, on call, and I told Honey you and I wanted to be alone here.'

Shit!

She saw the expression on his face. 'Is anything wrong?'

'No, baby. I told you, I just like our private times to be private.' *I'll have to be careful*, he thought. *Very careful.* 'Let's hurry.'

His impatience warmed Kat.

*   *   *

Inside the apartment, Mallory said, 'Let's go into the bedroom.'

Kat grinned. 'That sounds like a great idea.'

Mallory watched Kat undress, and he thought, *She still has a great figure. A baby would ruin it.*

'Aren't you going to get undressed, Ken?'

'Of course.' He remembered the time she had gotten him to undress and then walked out on him. Well, now she was going to pay for that.

He took his clothes off slowly. *Can I perform?* he wondered. He was almost trembling with nervousness. *What I'm going to do is her fault. Not mine. I gave her a chance to back out and she was too stupid to take it.*

He slipped into bed beside her and felt her warm body against his. They began to stroke each other, and he felt himself getting aroused. He entered her and she began to moan.

'Oh, darling . . . it feels so wonderful . . .' She began to move faster and faster. 'Yes . . . yes . . . oh, my God! . . . Don't stop . . .' And her body began to jerk spasmodically, and she shuddered and then lay still in his arms.

She turned to him anxiously. 'Did you . . . ?'

'Of course,' Mallory lied. He was much too tense. 'How about a drink?'

'No. I shouldn't. The baby . . .'

'But this is a celebration, honey. One little drink isn't going to hurt.'

Kat hesitated. 'All right. A small one.' Kat started to get up.

Mallory stopped her. 'No, no. You stay in bed, Mama. You have to get used to being pampered.'

Kat watched Mallory as he walked into the living

327

room and she thought, *I'm the luckiest woman in the world!*

Mallory walked over to the little bar and poured scotch into two glasses. He glanced toward the bedroom to make sure he could not be seen, then went over to the couch, where he had placed his jacket. He took a small bottle from his pocket and poured the contents into Kat's drink. He returned to the bar and stirred Kat's drink and smelled it. There was no odor. He took the two glasses back to the bedroom, and handed Kat her drink.

'Let's drink a toast to our baby,' Kat said.

'Right. To our baby.'

Ken watched as Kat took a swallow of her drink.

'We'll find a nice apartment somewhere,' Kat said dreamily. 'I'll fix up a nursery. We're going to spoil our child rotten, aren't we?' She took another sip.

Mallory nodded. 'Absolutely.' He was watching her closely. 'How do you feel?'

'Wonderful. I've been so worried about us, darling, but I'm not, not anymore.'

'That's good,' Mallory said. 'You have nothing to worry about.'

Kat's eyes were getting heavy. 'No,' she said. 'There's nothing to worry about.' Her words were beginning to slur. 'Ken, I feel funny.' She was beginning to sway.

'You should never have gotten pregnant.'

She was staring up at him stupidly. 'What?'

'You spoiled everything, Kat.'

'Spoiled . . . ?' She was having trouble concentrating.

'You got in my way.'

'Wha'?'

328

'No one gets in my way.'

'Ken, I feel dizzy.'

He stood there, watching her.

'Ken . . . help me, Ken . . .' Her head fell back onto the pillow.

Mallory looked at his watch again. There was plenty of time.

34

━━━━◦┼ ┼◦━━━━

It was Honey who arrived at the apartment first and stumbled across Kat's mutilated body, lying in a pool of blood on the floor of the bathroom, obscenely sprawled against the cold white tiles. A bloodstained curette lay beside her. She had hemorrhaged from her womb.

Honey stood there in shock. 'Oh, my God!' Her voice was a strangled whisper. She knelt beside the body and placed a trembling finger against the carotid artery. There was no pulse. Honey hurried back into the living room, picked up the telephone and dialed 911.

A male voice said, 'Nine-one-one Emergency.'

Honey stood there paralyzed, unable to speak.

'Nine-one-one Emergency . . . Hello . . . ?'

'H . . . help! I . . . there's . . .' She was choking over her words. 'Sh . . . she's dead.'

'Who is dead, miss?'

'Kat.'

'Your cat is dead?'

'*No!*' Honey screamed. '*Kat's* dead. Get someone over here right away.'

'Lady . . .'

Honey slammed down the receiver. With shaking fingers, she dialed the hospital. 'Dr T . . . Taylor.' Her voice was an agonized whisper.

'One moment, please.'

Honey gripped the telephone and waited two minutes before she heard Paige's voice. 'Dr Taylor.'

'Paige! You . . . you've got to come home right away!'

'Honey? What's happened?'

'Kat's . . . dead.'

'*What?*' Paige's voice was filled with disbelief. 'How?'

'It . . . it looks like she tried to abort herself.'

'Oh, my God! All right. I'll be there as soon as I can.'

By the time Paige arrived at the apartment, there were two policemen, a detective, and a medical examiner there. Honey was in her bedroom, heavily sedated. The medical examiner was leaning over Kat's naked body. The detective looked up as Paige entered the bloody bathroom.

'Who are you?'

Paige was staring at the lifeless body. Her face was pale. 'I'm Dr Taylor. I live here.'

'Maybe *you* can help me. I'm Inspector Burns. I was trying to talk to the other lady who lives here. She's hysterical. The doctor gave her a sedative.'

Paige looked away from the awful sight on the floor. 'What . . . what do you want to know?'

'She lived here?'

'Yes.'

I'm going to have Ken's baby. How good can it get?

'It looks like she tried to get rid of the kid, and messed it up,' the detective said.

331

Paige stood there, her mind spinning. When she spoke, she said, 'I don't believe it.'

Inspector Burns studied her a moment. 'Why don't you believe it, doctor?'

'She wanted that baby.' She was beginning to think clearly again. 'The father didn't want it.'

'The father?'

'Dr Ken Mallory. He works at Embarcadero County Hospital. He didn't want to marry her. Look, Kat is — *was* — ' it was so painful to say *was* — 'a doctor. If she had wanted to have an abortion, there's no way she would try to do it herself in a bathroom.' Paige shook her head. 'There's something wrong.'

The medical examiner rose from beside the body. 'Maybe she tried it herself because she didn't want anyone else to know about the baby.'

'That's not true. She told us about it.'

Inspector Burns was watching Paige. 'Was she alone here this evening?'

'No. She had a date with Dr Mallory.'

Ken Mallory was in bed, carefully going over the events of the evening. He replayed every step of the way, making sure there were no loose ends. *Perfect*, he decided. He lay in bed, wondering why it was taking the police so long, and even as he was thinking it, the doorbell rang. Mallory let it ring three times, then got up, put on a robe over his pajamas, and went into the living room.

He stood in front of the door. 'Who's there?' He sounded sleepy.

A voice said, 'Dr Mallory?'

'Yes.'

'Inspector Burns. San Francisco Police Department.'

'Police Department?' There was just the right note of surprise in his voice. Mallory opened the door.

The man standing in the hall showed his badge. 'May I come in?'

'Yes. What's this all about?'

'Do you know a Dr Hunter?'

'Of course I do.' A look of alarm crossed his face. 'Has something happened to Kat?'

'Were you with her earlier this evening?'

'Yes. My God! Tell me what's happened! Is she all right?'

'I'm afraid I have some bad news. Dr Hunter is dead.'

'*Dead*? I can't believe it. *How?*'

'Apparently she tried to perform an abortion on herself and it went wrong.'

'Oh, my God!' Mallory said. He sank into a chair. 'It's my fault.'

The inspector was watching him closely. 'Your fault?'

'Yes. I . . . Dr Hunter and I were going to be married. I told her I didn't think it was a good idea for her to have a baby now. I wanted to wait, and she agreed. I suggested she go to the hospital and have them take care of it, but she must have decided to . . . I . . . I can't believe it.'

'What time did you leave, Dr Hunter?'

'It must have been about ten o'clock. I dropped her off at her apartment and left.'

'You didn't go into the apartment?'

'No.'

'Did Dr Hunter talk about what she planned to do?'

'You mean about the . . . ? No. Not a word.'

Inspector Burns pulled out a card. 'If you think of anything else that might be helpful, doctor, I'd appreciate it if you gave me a call.'

'Certainly. I . . . you have no idea what a shock this is.'

Paige and Honey stayed up all night, talking about what had happened to Kat, going over it and over it, in shocked disbelief.

At nine o'clock, Inspector Burns came by.

'Good morning. I wanted to tell you that I spoke to Dr Mallory last night.'

'And?'

'He said they went out to dinner, and then he dropped her off and went home.'

'He's lying,' Paige said. She was thinking. 'Wait! Did they find any traces of semen in Kat's body?'

'Yes, as a matter of fact.'

'Well, then,' Paige said excitedly, 'that *proves* he's lying. He did take her to bed and—'

'I went to talk to him about that this morning. He says they had sex *before* they went out to dinner.'

'Oh.' She would not give up. 'His fingerprints will be on the curette he used to kill her.' Her voice was eager. 'Did you find fingerprints?'

'Yes, doctor,' he said patiently. 'They were hers.'

'That's imp—Wait! Then he wore gloves, and when he was finished, he put her prints on the curette. How does that sound?'

'Like someone's been watching too many *Murder, She Wrote* television programs.'

'You don't believe Kat was murdered, do you?'

'I'm afraid I don't.'

'Have they done an autopsy?'

'Yes.'

'And?'

'The medical examiner is listing it as an accidental death. Dr Mallory told me she decided not to have the baby, so apparently she —'

'Went into the bathroom and butchered herself?' Paige interrupted. 'For God's sakes, inspector! She was a doctor, a surgeon! There's no way in the world she would have done that to herself.'

Inspector Burns said thoughtfully, 'You think Mallory persuaded her to have an abortion, and tried to help her, and then left when it went wrong?'

Paige shook her head. 'No. It couldn't have happened that way. Kat would never have agreed. He deliberately murdered her.' She was thinking out loud. 'Kat was strong. She would have had to be unconscious for him to . . . to do what he did.'

'The autopsy showed no signs of any blows or anything that would have caused her to become unconscious. No bruises on her throat . . .'

'Were there any traces of sleeping pills or . . . ?'

'Nothing.' He saw the expression on Paige's face. 'This doesn't look to me like a murder. I think Dr Hunter made an error in judgement, and . . . I'm sorry.'

She watched him start toward the door. 'Wait!' Paige said, 'You have a motive.'

He turned. 'Not really. Mallory says she agreed to have the abortion. That doesn't leave us much, does it?'

'It leaves you with a murder,' Paige said stubbornly.

'Doctor, what we *don't* have is any evidence. It's his word against the victim's and she's dead. I'm really sorry.'

Paige watched him leave.

I'm not going to let Ken Mallory get away with it, she thought despairingly.

Jason came by to see Paige. 'I heard what happened,' he said. 'I can't believe it! How could she have done that to herself?'

'She didn't,' Paige said. 'She was murdered.' She told Jason about her conversation with Inspector Burns. 'The police aren't going to do anything about it. They think it was an accident. Jason, it's my fault that Kat is dead.'

'Your fault?'

'I'm the one who persuaded her to go out with Mallory in the first place. She didn't want to. It started out as a silly joke, and then she . . . she fell in love with him. Oh, Jason!'

'You can't blame yourself for that,' he said firmly.

Paige looked around in despair. 'I can't live in this apartment anymore. I have to get out of here.'

Jason took her in his arms. 'Let's get married right away.'

'It's too soon. I mean, Kat isn't even . . .'

'I know. We'll wait a week or two.'

'All right.'

'I love you, Paige.'

'I love you, too, darling. Isn't it stupid! I feel guilty because Kat and I both fell in love, and she's dead and I'm alive.'

The photograph appeared on the front page of the *San Francisco Chronicle* on Tuesday. It showed a smiling Ken Mallory with his arm around Lauren Harrison. The caption read: 'Heiress to Wed Doctor.'

Paige stared at it in disbelief. Kat had been dead for only two days, and Ken Mallory was announcing his engagement to another woman! All the time he had been promising to marry Kat, he had been planning to marry someone else. *That's why he killed Kat. To get her out of the way!*

Paige picked up the telephone and dialed police headquarters.

'Inspector Burns, please.'

A moment later, she was talking to the inspector.

'This is Dr Taylor.'

'Yes, doctor.'

'Have you seen the photograph in this morning's *Chronicle*?'

'Yes.'

'Well, there's your motive!' Paige exclaimed. 'Ken Mallory had to shut Kat up before Lauren Harrison found out about her. You've got to arrest Mallory.' She was almost yelling into the telephone.

'Wait a minute. Calm down, doctor. We may have a motive, but I told you, we don't have a shred of evidence. You said yourself that Dr Hunter would have had to be unconscious before Mallory could perform an abortion on her. After I spoke to you, I talked to our forensic pathologist again. There was no sign of any kind of blow that could have caused unconsciousness.'

'Then he must have given her a sedative,' Paige said stubbornly. 'Probably chloral hydrate. It's fast-acting and—'

Inspector Burns said patiently, 'Doctor, there was no trace of chloral hydrate in her body. I'm sorry— I really am—but we can't arrest a man because he's going to get married. Was there anything else?'

Everything else. 'No,' Paige said. She slammed down the receiver and sat there thinking. *Mallory has to have given Kat some kind of drug. The easiest place for him to have gotten it would be the hospital pharmacy.*

Fifteen minutes later, Paige was on her way to Embarcadero County Hospital.

Pete Samuels, the chief pharmacist, was behind the counter. 'Good morning, Dr Taylor. How can I help you?'

'I believe Dr Mallory came by a few days ago and picked up some medication. He told me the name of it, but I can't remember what it was.'

Samuels frowned. 'I don't remember Dr Mallory coming by here for at least a month.'

'Are you sure?'

Samuels nodded. 'Positive. I would have remembered. We always talk football.'

Paige's heart sank. 'Thank you.'

He must have written a prescription at some other

pharmacy. Paige knew that the law required that all prescriptions for narcotics be made out in triplicate—one copy for the patient, one to be sent to the Bureau of Controlled Substances, and the third for the pharmacy's files.

Somewhere, Paige thought, *Ken Mallory had a prescription filled. There are probably two or three hundred pharmacies in San Francisco*. There was no way she could track down the prescription. It was likely that Mallory had gotten it just before he murdered Kat. That would have been on Saturday or Sunday. *If it was Sunday, I might have a chance*, Paige thought. *Very few pharmacies are open on Sunday. That narrows it down*.

She went upstairs to the office where the assignment sheets were kept and looked up the roster for Saturday. Dr Ken Mallory had been on call all day, so the chances were that he had had the presciption filled on Sunday. How many pharmacies were open on Sunday in San Francisco?

Paige picked up the telephone and called the state pharmaceutical board.

'This is Dr Taylor,' Paige said. 'Last Sunday, a friend of mine left a prescription at a pharmacy. She asked me to pick it up for her, but I can't remember the name of the pharmacy. I wonder if you could help me.'

'Well, I don't see how, doctor. If you don't know . . .'

'Most drugstores are closed on Sunday, aren't they?'

'Yes, but . . .'

'I'd appreciate it if you could give me a list of those that were open.'

There was a pause. 'Well, if it's important . . .'

'It's very important,' Paige assured her.

'Hold on, please.'

There were thirty-six stores on the list, spread all over the city. It would have been simple if she could have gone to the police for help, but Inspector Burns did not believe her. *Honey and I are going to have to do this ourselves*, Paige thought. She explained to Honey what she had in mind.

'It's a real long shot, isn't it?' Honey said. 'You don't even know if he filled the prescription on Sunday.'

'It's the only shot we have.' *That Kat has.* 'I'll check out the ones in Richmond, the Marina, North Beach, Upper Market, Mission, and Potrero, and you check out the Excelsior, Ingleside, Lake Merced, Western Addition, and Sunset areas.'

'All right.'

At the first pharmacy Paige went into, she showed her identification and said, 'A colleague of mine, Dr Ken Mallory, was in here Sunday for a prescription. He's out of town, and he asked me to get a refill, but I can't remember the name of it. Would you mind looking it up, please?'

'Dr Ken Mallory? Just a moment.' He came back a few minutes later. 'Sorry, we didn't fill any prescriptions Sunday for a Dr Mallory.'

'Thank you.'

Paige got the same response at the next four pharmacies.

340

Honey was having no better luck.

'We have thousands of prescriptions here, you know.'

'I know, but this was last Sunday.'

'Well, we have no prescriptions here from a Dr Mallory. Sorry.'

The two of them spent the day going from pharmacy to pharmacy. They were both getting discouraged. It was not until late afternoon, just before closing time, that Paige found what she was looking for in a small pharmacy in the Potrero district.

The pharmacist said, 'Oh, yes, here we are. Dr Ken Mallory. I remember him. He was on his way to make a house call on a patient. I was impressed, because not many doctors do that these days.'

No resident ever makes house calls. 'What's the prescription for?'

Paige found she was holding her breath.

'Chloral hydrate.'

Paige was almost trembling with excitement. 'You're sure?'

'It says so right here.'

'What was the patient's name?'

He looked at the copy of the prescription. 'Spyros Levathes.'

'Would you mind giving me a copy of that prescription?' Paige asked.

'Not at all, doctor.'

One hour later, Paige was in Inspector Burns's office. She laid the prescription on his desk.

'Here's your proof,' Paige said. 'On Sunday, Dr Mallory went to a pharmacy miles away from where

341

he lives, and had this prescription for chloral hydrate filled. He put the chloral hydrate in Kat's drink, and when she was unconscious, he butchered her to make it look like an accident.'

'There's only one problem with that, Dr Taylor. There *was* no chloral hydrate in her body.'

'There has to be. Your pathologist made a mistake. Ask him to check again.'

He was losing his patience. 'Doctor . . .'

'Please! I know I'm right.'

'You're wasting everybody's time.'

Paige sat across from him, her eyes fixed on his face.

He sighed. 'All right. I'll call him again. Maybe he *did* make a mistake.'

Jason picked Paige up for dinner. 'We're having dinner at my house,' he said. 'There's something I want you to see.'

During the drive there, Paige brought Jason up to date on what was happening.

'They'll find the chloral hydrate in her body,' Paige said. 'And Ken Mallory will get what's coming to him.'

'I'm so sorry about all this, Paige.'

'I know.' She pressed his hand against her cheek. 'Thank God for you.'

The car pulled up in front of Jason's home.

Paige looked out of the window and she gasped. Around the green lawn in front of the house was a new white picket fence.

* * *

She was alone in the dark apartment. Ken Mallory used the key that Kat had given him and moved quietly toward the bedroom. Paige heard his footsteps coming toward her, but before she could move, he had leaped at her, his hands tight around her throat.

'You bitch! You're trying to destroy me. Well, you aren't going to snoop around anymore.' He began squeezing harder. 'I outsmarted all of you, didn't I?' His fingers squeezed tighter. 'No one can ever prove I killed Kat.'

She tried to scream, but it was impossible to breathe. She struggled free, and was suddenly awake. She was alone in her room. Paige sat up in bed trembling.

She stayed awake the rest of the night, waiting for Inspector Burns's phone call. It came at 10:00 A.M.

'Dr Taylor?'

'Yes.' She was holding her breath.

'I just got the *third* report from the forensic pathologist.'

'And?' Her heart was pounding.

'There was no trace of chloral hydrate or any other sedative in Dr Hunter's body. None.'

That was impossible! There had to be. There was no sign of any blow or anything that would have caused her to become unconscious. No bruises on her throat. It didn't make sense. Kat had to have been unconscious when Mallory killed her. The forensic pathologist was wrong.

Paige decided to go talk to him herself.

* * *

Dr Dolan was in an irritable mood. 'I don't like to be questioned like this,' he said. 'I've checked it three times. I told Inspector Burns that there was no trace of chloral hydrate in any of her organs, and there wasn't.'

'But . . .'

'Is there anything else, doctor?'

Paige looked at him helplessly. Her last hope was gone. Ken Mallory was going to get away with murder. 'I . . . I guess not. If you didn't find any chemicals in her body, then I don't . . .'

'I didn't say I didn't find *any* chemicals.'

She looked at him a moment. 'You found something?'

'Just a trace of trichloroethylene.'

She frowned. 'What would that do?'

He shrugged. 'Nothing. It's an analgesic drug. It wouldn't put anyone to sleep.'

'I see.'

'Sorry I can't help you.'

Paige nodded. 'Thank you.'

She walked down the long, antiseptic corridor of the morgue, depressed, feeling that she was missing something. She had been so sure Kat had been put to sleep with chloral hydrate.

All he found was a trace of trichloroethylene. It wouldn't put anyone to sleep. But why would trichloroethylene be in Kat's body? Kat had not been taking any medications. Paige stopped in the middle of the corridor, her mind working furiously.

When Paige arrived at the hospital, she went directly to the medical library on the fifth floor. It took her less than a minute to find trichloroethylene. The description read: *A colorless, clear, volatile liquid with a specific gravity of 1.47 at 59 degrees F. It is a halogenated hydrocarbon, having the chemical formula CCl_2, $CHCl$.*

And there, on the last line, she found what she was looking for. *When chloral hydrate is metabolized, it produces trichloroethylene as a by-product.*

35

'Inspector, Dr Taylor is here to see you.'

'Again?' He was tempted to turn her away. She was obsessed with the half-baked theory she had. He was going to have to put a stop to it. 'Send her in.'

When Paige walked into his office, Inspector Burns said, 'Look, doctor, I think this has gone far enough. Dr Dolan called to complain about—'

'I know how Ken Mallory did it!' Her voice was charged with excitement. 'There was trichloroethylene in Kat's body.'

He nodded. 'Dr Dolan told me that. But he said it couldn't have made her unconscious. He—'

'Chloral hydrate turns into trichloroethylene!' Paige said triumphantly. 'Mallory lied when he said he didn't go back into the apartment with Kat. He put chloral hydrate in her drink. It has no taste when you mix it with alcohol, and it only takes a few minutes for it to work. Then when she was unconscious, he killed her and made it look like a bungled abortion.'

'Doctor, if you'll forgive my saying so, that's a hell of a lot of speculation.'

'No, it isn't. He wrote the prescription for a patient named Spyros Levathes, but he never gave it to him.'

'How do you know that?'

'Because he *couldn't* have. I checked on Spyros Levathes. He has erythropoietic porphyria.'

'What's that?'

'It's a genetic metabolic disorder. It causes photo-sensitivity and lesions, hypertension, tachycardia, and a few other unpleasant symptoms. It's the result of a defective gene.'

'I still don't understand.'

'Dr Mallory didn't give his patient chloral hydrate because it would have killed him! Chloral hydrate is contra-indicated for porphyria. It would have caused immediate convulsive seizures.'

For the first time, Inspector Burns was impressed. 'You've really done your homework, haven't you?'

Paige pressed on. 'Why would Ken Mallory go to a remote pharmacy and fill a prescription for a patient he knew he couldn't *give* it to? You've *got* to arrest him.'

His fingers were drumming on his desk. 'It's not that simple.'

'You've got to . . .'

Inspector Burns raised a hand. 'All right. I'll tell you what I'll do. I'll talk to the district attorney's office and see whether they think we have a case.'

Paige knew she had gone as far as she could. 'Thank you, inspector.'

'I'll get back to you.'

After Paige Taylor left, Inspector Burns sat there thinking about their conversation. There was no hard evidence against Dr Mallory, only the suspicions of a persistent woman. He reviewed the few facts that he had. Dr Mallory had been engaged to Kat Hunter. Two days after she died, he was engaged to Alex

Harrison's daughter. Interesting, but not against the law.

Mallory had said that he dropped Dr Hunter off at her front door and did not go into the apartment. Semen was found in her body, but he had a plausible explanation for that.

Then there was the matter of the chloral hydrate. Mallory had written a prescription for a drug that could have killed his patient. Was he guilty of murder? Not guilty?

Burns buzzed his secretary on the intercom. 'Barbara, get me an appointment with the district attorney this afternoon.'

There were four men in the office when Paige walked in: the district attorney, his assistant, a man named Warren, and Inspector Burns.

'Thank you for stopping by, Dr Taylor,' the district attorney said. 'Inspector Burns has been telling me of your interest in the death of Dr Hunter. I can appreciate that. Dr Hunter was your roommate, and you want to see justice done.'

So they're going to arrest Ken Mallory after all!

'Yes,' Paige said. 'There's no doubt about it. Dr Mallory killed her. When you arrest him, he—'

'I'm afraid we can't do that.'

Paige looked at him blankly. 'What?'

'We can't arrest Dr Mallory.'

'But why?'

'We have no case.'

'Of course you have!' Paige exclaimed. 'The trichloroethylene proves that—'

348

'Doctor, in a court of justice, ignorance of the law is no excuse. But ignorance in medicine *is*.'

'I don't understand.'

'It's simple. It means that Dr Mallory could claim he made a mistake, that he didn't know what effect chloral hydrate would have on a patient with porphyria. No one could prove he was lying. It might prove that he's a lousy doctor, but it wouldn't prove that he's guilty of murder.'

Paige looked at him in frustration. 'You're going to let him get away with this?'

He studied her a moment. 'I'll tell you what I'm prepared to do. I've discussed this with Inspector Burns. With your permission, we're going to send someone to your apartment to pick up the glasses in the bar. If we find any traces of chloral hydrate, we'll take the next step.'

'What if he rinsed them out?'

Inspector Burns said dryly, 'I don't imagine he took the time to use a detergent. If he just rinsed out the glasses, we'll find what we're looking for.'

Two hours later, Inspector Burns was on the phone with Paige.

'We did a chemical analysis of all the glasses in the bar, doctor,' Burns said.

Paige steeled herself for disappointment.

'We found one with traces of chloral hydrate.'

Paige closed her eyes in a silent prayer of thanks.

'And there were fingerprints on that glass. We're going to check them against Dr Mallory's prints.'

Paige felt a surge of excitement.

The inspector went on, 'When he killed her—

if he did kill her—he was wearing gloves, so his fingerprints wouldn't be on the curette. But he couldn't very well have served her a drink while he wore gloves, and he might not have worn them when he put the glass back on the shelf after rinsing it out.'

'No,' Paige said. 'He couldn't, could he?'

'I have to admit that in the beginning, I didn't believe your theory was going anywhere. I think now maybe Dr Mallory could be our man. But proving it is going to be another matter.' He continued, 'The district attorney is right. It would be a tricky business to bring Mallory to trial. He can still say that the prescription was for his patient. There's no law against making a medical mistake. I don't see how we—'

'Wait a minute!' Paige said excitedly. 'I think I know how!'

Ken Mallory was listening to Lauren on the telephone. 'Father and I found some office space that you're going to adore, darling! It's a beautiful suite in the 490 Post Building. I'm going to hire a receptionist for you, someone not too pretty.'

Mallory laughed. 'You don't have to worry about that, baby. There isn't anyone in the world for me but you.'

'I'm dying for you to come see it. Can you get away now?'

'I'm off in a couple of hours.'

'Wonderful! Why don't you pick me up at the house?'

'All right. I'll be there.' Mallory replaced the telephone. *It doesn't get any better than this*, he thought. *There is a God, and She loves me.*

He heard his name called over the PA system, 'Dr Mallory . . . Room 430 . . . Dr Mallory . . . Room 430.' He sat there daydreaming, thinking about the golden future that lay ahead of him. *A beautiful suite in the 490 Post Building, filled with rich old ladies, eager to throw their money at him.* He heard his name called again. 'Dr Mallory . . . Room 430.' He sighed and got to his feet. *I'll be out of this goddam madhouse soon*, he thought. He headed toward Room 430.

A resident was waiting for him in the corridor, outside the room. 'I'm afraid we have a problem here,' he said. 'This is one of Dr Peterson's patients, but Dr Peterson isn't here. I'm having an argument with one of the other doctors.'

They stepped inside. There were three people in the room — a man in bed, a male nurse, and a doctor Mallory had not met before.

The resident said, 'This is Dr Edwards. We need your advice, Dr Mallory.'

'What's the problem?'

The resident explained. 'This patient is suffering from erythropoietic porphyria, and Dr Edwards insists on giving him a sedative.'

'I don't see any problem with that.'

'Thank you,' Dr Edwards said. 'The man hasn't slept in forty-eight hours. I've prescribed chloral hydrate for him so he can get some rest and . . .'

Mallory was looking at him in astonishment. 'Are you out of your mind? That could kill him! He'd have a convulsive seizure, tachycardia, and he'd probably die. Where in hell did you study medicine?'

351

The man looked at Mallory and said quietly, 'I didn't.' He flashed a badge. 'I'm with the San Francisco Police Department, Homicide.' He turned to the man in bed. 'Did you get that?'

The man pulled out a tape recorder from under the pillow. 'I got it.'

Mallory was looking from one to the other, frowning. 'I don't understand. What is this? What's going on?'

The inspector turned to Mallory. 'Dr Mallory, you're under arrest for the murder of Dr Kate Hunter.'

36

The headline in the *San Francisco Chronicle* read, DOCTOR ARRESTED IN LOVE TRIANGLE. The story beneath it went on at length to detail the lurid facts of the case.

Mallory read the newspaper in his cell. He slammed it down.

His cellmate said, 'Looks like they got you cold, pal.'

'Don't you believe it,' Mallory said confidently. 'I've got connections, and they're going to get me the best goddam lawyer in the world. I'll be out of here in twenty-four hours. All I have to do is make one phone call.'

The Harrisons were reading the newspaper at breakfast.

'My God!' Lauren said. 'Ken! I can't believe it!'

A butler approached the breakfast table. 'Excuse me, Miss Harrison. Dr Mallory is on the telephone for you. I believe he's calling from jail.'

'I'll take it.' Lauren started to get up from the table.

'You'll stay here and finish your breakfast,' Alex

Harrison said firmly. He turned to the butler. 'We don't know any Dr Mallory.'

Paige read the newspaper as she was getting dressed. Mallory was going to be punished for the terrible thing he had done, but it gave Paige no satisfaction. Nothing they did to him could ever bring Kat back.

The doorbell rang, and Paige went to answer it. A stranger stood there. He was wearing a dark suit and carried a briefcase.

'Dr Taylor?'

'Yes . . .'

'My name is Roderick Pelham. I'm an attorney with Rothman and Rothman. May I come in?'

Paige studied him, puzzled. 'Yes.'

He entered the apartment.

'What did you want to see me about?'

She watched him open the briefcase and take out some papers.

'You are aware, of course, that you are the principal beneficiary of John Cronin's will?'

Paige looked at him blankly. 'What are you talking about? There must be some mistake.'

'Oh, there's no mistake. Mr Cronin has left you the sum of one million dollars.'

Paige sank into a chair, overwhelmed, remembering.

You have to go to Europe. Do me a favor. Go to Paris . . . stay at the Crillon, have dinner at Maxim's, order a big, thick steak and a bottle of champagne, and when you eat that steak and drink that champagne, I want you to think of me.

354

'If you'll just sign here, we'll take care of all the necessary paperwork.'

Paige looked up. 'I . . . I don't know what to say. I . . . he had a family.'

'According to the terms of his will, they get only the remainder of his estate, not a large amount.'

'I can't accept this,' Paige told him.

Pelham looked at her in surprise. 'Why not?'

She had no answer. John Cronin had wanted her to have this money. 'I don't know. It . . . it seems unethical, somehow. He was my patient.'

'Well, I'll leave the check here with you. You can decide what you want to do with it. Just sign here.'

Paige signed the paper in a daze.

'Goodbye, doctor.'

She watched him leave and sat there thinking of John Cronin.

The news of Paige's inheritance was the talk of the hospital. Somehow, Paige had hoped it could be kept quiet. She still had not made up her mind about what to do with the money. *It doesn't belong to me*, she thought. *He had a family.*

Paige was not emotionally ready to go back to work, but her patients had to be taken care of. An operation was scheduled for that morning. Arthur Kane was waiting for Paige in the corridor. They had not spoken to each other since the incident of the reversed X-rays. Although Paige had no proof it was Kane, the tire-slashing episode had scared her.

'Hello, Paige. Let's let bygones be bygones. What do you say?'

Paige shrugged. 'Fine.'

'Wasn't that a terrible thing about Ken Mallory?' he asked.

'Yes,' Paige said.

Kane was looking at her slyly. 'Can you imagine a doctor deliberately killing a human being? It's horrible, isn't it?'

'Yes.'

'By the way,' he said, 'congratulations. I hear that you're a millionairess.'

'I can't see . . .'

'I have tickets for the theater tonight, Paige. I thought that the two of us could go.'

'Thanks,' Paige said. 'I'm engaged to someone.'

'Then I suggest you get unengaged.'

She looked at him, surprised. 'I beg your pardon?'

Kane moved closer to her. 'I ordered an autopsy on John Cronin.'

Paige found her heart beginning to beat faster. 'Yes?'

'He didn't die of heart failure. Someone gave him an overdose of insulin. I guess that particular someone never figured on an autopsy.'

Paige's mouth was suddenly dry.

'You were with him when he died, weren't you?'

She hesitated. 'Yes.'

'I'm the only one who knows that, and I'm the only one who has the report.' He patted her arm. 'And my lips are sealed. Now, about those tickets tonight . . .'

Paige pulled away from him. 'No!'

'Are you sure you know what you're doing?'

She took a deep breath. 'Yes. Now, if you'll excuse me . . .' And she walked away. Kane looked after her, and his face hardened. He turned and headed toward Dr Benjamin Wallace's office.

The telephone awakened her at 1:00 A.M. at her apartment.

'You have been a naughty girl again.'

It was the same raspy voice disguised in a breathy whisper, but this time Paige recognized it. *My God*, she thought, *I was right to be scared*.

The following morning, when Paige arrived at the hospital, two men were waiting for her.

'Dr Paige Taylor?'

'Yes.'

'You'll have to come with us. You're under arrest for the murder of John Cronin.'

37

It was the final day of Paige's trial. Alan Penn, the defense attorney, was making his summation to the jury.

'Ladies and gentlemen, you have heard a lot of testimony about Dr Taylor's competence or incompetence. Well, Judge Young will instruct you that's not what this trial is about. I'm sure that for every doctor who did not approve of her work, we could produce a dozen doctors who did. But that is not the issue.

'Paige Taylor is on trial for the death of John Cronin. She has admitted helping him die. She did so because he was in great pain, and he asked her to do so. That is euthanasia, and it's being accepted more and more throughout the world. In the past year, the California Supreme Court has upheld the right of a mentally competent adult to refuse or demand the withdrawal of medical treatment of any form. It is the individual who must live or die with the course of treatment chosen or rejected.'

He looked into the faces of the jurors. 'Euthanasia is a crime of compassion, of mercy, and I daresay it takes place in some form or another in hospitals all over the world. The prosecuting attorney is asking for a death sentence. Don't let him confuse the issue. There has never been a death sentence for eutha-

358

nasia. Sixty-three percent of Americans believe euthanasia should be legal, and in eighteen states in this country, it *is* legal. The question is, do we have the right to compel helpless patients to live in pain, to force them to stay alive and suffer? The question has become complicated because of the great strides we've made in medical technology. We've turned the care of patients over to machines. Machines have no mercy. If a horse breaks a leg, we put it out of its misery by shooting it. With a human being, we condemn him or her to a half life that is hell.

'Dr Taylor didn't decide when John Cronin would die. John Cronin decided. Make no mistake about it, what Dr Taylor did was an act of mercy. She has taken full responsibility for that. But you can rest assured that she knew nothing about the money that was left to her. What she did, she did in a spirit of compassion. John Cronin was a man with a failing heart and an untreatable, fatal cancer that had spread through his body, causing him agony. Just ask yourself one question. Under those circumstances, would you like to go on living? Thank you.' He turned, walked back to the table, and sat next to Paige.

Gus Venable rose and stood before the jury. '*Compassion? Mercy?*' He looked over at Paige, shook his head, then turned back to the jury. 'Ladies and gentlemen, I have been practicing law in courtrooms for more than twenty years, and I must tell you that in all those years, I have never—never—seen a more clear-cut case of cold-blooded, deliberate murder for profit.'

359

Paige was hanging on every word, tense and pale.

'The defense talked about euthanasia. Did Dr Taylor do what she did out of a feeling of compassion? I don't think so. Dr Taylor and others have testified that Mr Cronin had only a few more days to live. Why didn't she let him live those few days? Perhaps it was because Dr Taylor was afraid Mrs Cronin might learn about her husband changing his will, and put a stop to it.

'It's a most remarkable coincidence that immediately after Mr Cronin changed his will and left Dr Taylor the sum of one million dollars, she gave him an overdose of insulin and murdered him.

'Again and again, the defendant has convicted herself with her own words. She said that she was on friendly terms with John Cronin, that he liked and respected her. But you have heard witnesses testify that he hated Dr Paige, that he called her "that bitch" and told her "to keep her fucking hands off him".'

Gus Venable glanced at the defendant again. There was a look of despair on Paige's face. He turned back to the jury. 'An attorney has testified that Dr Taylor said, about the million dollars that was left to her, "It's unethical. He was my patient." But she grabbed the money. She needed it. She had a drawerful of travel brochures at home — Paris, London, the Riviera. And bear in mind that she didn't go to the travel agency *after* she got the money. Oh, no. She planned those trips earlier. All she needed was the money and the opportunity, and John Cronin supplied both. A helpless, dying man she could control. She had at her mercy a man who she admitted was in enormous pain — agony, in fact, according to her own admission. When you're in that kind of pain, you can imagine how difficult it must be to think clearly. We don't know *how* Dr Taylor persuaded John Cronin to change his will, to cut out the family he loved and to make her his main beneficiary. What we *do* know is that he summoned her to his bedside on that fatal night. What did they talk about? Could he have offered her a million dollars to put him out of his misery? It's a possibility we must face. In either case, it was cold-blooded murder.

'Ladies and gentlemen, during this trial, do you know who was the most damaging witness of all?' He pointed a dramatic finger at Paige. 'The defendant herself! You've heard her testify that she never violated the sacred Hippocratic oath that she took, but she lied. We've heard testimony that she gave an illegal blood transfusion and then falsified the record. She said that she never killed a patient except John Cronin, but we've heard testimony that Dr Barker, a physician respected by everybody, accused her of killing his patient.

'Unfortunately, ladies and gentlemen, Lawrence Barker suffered a stroke and can't be here with us today to testify against the defendant. But let me remind you of Dr Barker's opinion of the defendant. This is Dr Peterson, testifying about a patient Dr Taylor was operating on.'

He read from the transcript.

'"Dr Barker came into the operating room during the operation?"

'"Yes." And did Dr Barker say anything?'

'Answer: "He turned to Dr Taylor and said, 'You killed him.'"

'This is from Nurse Berry. "Tell me some specific

things you heard Dr Barker say to Dr Taylor."

'Answer: "He said she was incompetent . . . Another time he said he wouldn't let her operate on his dog."'

Gus Venable looked up. 'Either there is some kind of conspiracy going on, where all these reputable doctors and nurses are lying about the defendant, or Dr Taylor is a liar. Not *just* a liar, but a pathological . . .'

The rear door of the courtroom had opened and an aide hurried in. He paused in the doorway a moment, trying to make a decision. Then he moved down the aisle toward Gus Venable.

'Sir . . .'

Gus Venable turned, furious. 'Can't you see I'm . . . ?'

The aide whispered in his ear.

Gus Venable looked at him, stunned. '*What? That's wonderful!*'

Judge Young leaned forward, her voice ominously quiet. 'Forgive me for interrupting you two, but what exactly do you think you're doing?'

Gus Venable turned to the judge excitedly. 'Your honor, I've just been informed that Dr Lawrence Barker is outside this courtroom. He's in a wheel-chair, but he's able to testify. I'd like to call him to the stand.'

There was a loud buzz in the courtroom.

Alan Penn was on his feet. 'Objection!' he yelled. 'The prosecuting attorney is in the middle of his summation. There's no precedent for calling a new witness at this late hour. I —'

Judge Young slammed her gavel down. 'Would counsel please approach the bench.'

362

Penn and Venable moved up to the bench.

'This is highly irregular, your honor. I object . . .'

Judge Young said, 'You're right about its being irregular, Mr Penn, but you're wrong about its being without precedent. I can cite a dozen cases around the country where material witnesses were allowed to testify under special circumstances. In fact, if you're so interested in precedent, you might look up a case that took place in this courtroom five years ago. I happened to be the judge.'

Alan Penn swallowed. 'Does this mean you're going to allow him to testify?'

Judge Young was thoughtful. 'Since Dr Barker is a material witness to this case, and was physically unable to testify earlier, in the interest of justice, I'm going to rule that he be allowed to take the stand.'

'Exception! There is no proof that the witness is competent to testify. I demand a battery of psychiatrists —'

'Mr Penn, in this courtroom, we don't demand. We request.' She turned to Gus Venable. 'You may bring in your witness.'

Alan Penn stood there, deflated. *It's all over*, he thought. *Our case is down the drain*.

Gus Venable turned to his aide. 'Bring Dr Barker in.'

The door opened slowly, and Dr Lawrence Barker entered the courtroom. He was in a wheelchair. His head was tilted, and one side of his face was drawn up in a slight rictus.

Everyone watched the pale and fragile figure being wheeled to the front of the courtroom. As he moved past Paige, he looked over at her.

There was no friendliness in his eyes, and Paige remembered his last words: *Who the hell do you think you . . . ?*

When Lawrence Barker was in front of the bench, Judge Young leaned forward and said gently, 'Dr Barker, are you able to testify here today?'

When Barker spoke, his words were slurred. 'I am, your honor.'

'Are you fully aware of what is going on in this courtroom?'

'Yes, your honor.' He looked over to where Paige was seated. 'That woman is being tried for the murder of a patient.'

Paige winced. *That woman!*

Judge Young made her decision. She turned to the bailiff. 'Would you swear the witness in, please?'

When Dr Barker had been sworn in, Judge Young said, 'You may stay in the chair, Dr Barker. The prosecutor will proceed, and I will allow the defense to cross-examine.'

Gus Venable smiled. 'Thank you, your honor.' He strolled over to the wheelchair. 'We won't keep you very long, doctor, and the court deeply appreciates your coming in to testify under these trying circumstances. Are you familiar with any of the testimony that has been given here over the past month?'

Dr Barker nodded. 'I've been following it on television and in the newspapers, and it made me sick to my stomach.'

Paige buried her head in her hands.

It was all Gus Venable could do to hide his feeling of triumph. 'I'm sure a lot of us feel the same way, doctor,' the prosecutor said piously.

'I came here because I want to see justice done.'

364

Venable smiled. 'Exactly. So do we.'

Lawrence Barker took a deep breath, and when he spoke, his voice was filled with outrage. 'Then how the hell could you bring Dr Taylor to trial?'

Venable thought he had misunderstood him. 'I beg your pardon?'

'This trial is a farce!'

Paige and Alan Penn exchanged a stunned look.

Gus Venable turned pale. 'Dr Barker . . .'

'Don't interrupt me,' Barker snapped. 'You've used the testimony of a lot of biased, jealous people to attack a brilliant surgeon. She —'

'Just a minute!' Venable was beginning to panic. 'Isn't it true that you criticized Dr Taylor's ability so severely that she was finally ready to quit Embarcadero Hospital?'

'Yes.'

Gus Venable was starting to feel better. 'Well, then,' he said patronizingly, 'how can you say that Paige Taylor is a brilliant doctor?'

'Because it happens to be the truth.' Barker turned to look at Paige, and when he spoke again, he was talking to her as though they were the only two people in the courtroom: 'Some people are born to be doctors. You were one of those rare ones. I knew from the beginning how capable you were. I was hard on you — maybe too hard — because you were good. I was tough on you because I wanted you to be tougher on yourself. I wanted you to be perfect, because in our profession, there's no room for error. None.'

Paige was staring at him, mesmerized, her mind spinning. It was all happening too fast.

The courtroom was hushed.

'I wasn't about to let you quit.'

Gus Venable could feel his victory slipping away. His prize witness had become his worst nightmare. 'Dr Barker—it has been testified that you accused Dr Taylor of killing your patient Lance Kelly. How . . . ?'

'I told her that because she was the surgeon in charge. It was her ultimate responsibility. In fact, the anesthetist caused Mr Kelly's death.'

By now the court was in an uproar.

Paige sat there stunned.

Dr Barker went on speaking slowly, with an effort. 'And as for John Cronin leaving her that money, Dr Taylor knew nothing about it. I talked to Mr Cronin myself. He told me that he was going to leave Dr Taylor that money because he hated his family, and he said he was going to ask Dr Taylor to release him from his misery. I agreed.'

There was an uproar from the spectators. Gus Venable was standing there, a look of total bewilderment on his face.

Alan Penn leaped to his feet. 'Your honor, I move for a dismissal!'

Judge Young was slamming her gavel down. 'Quiet!' she yelled. She looked at the two attorneys. 'Into my chambers.'

Judge Young, Alan Penn, and Gus Venable were seated in Judge Young's chambers.

Gus Venable was in a state of shock. 'I . . . I don't know what to say. He's obviously a sick man, your honor. He's confused. I want a battery of psychiatrists to examine him and—'

366

'You can't have it both ways, Gus. It looks like your case just went up in smoke. Let's save you any further embarrassment, shall we? I'm going to grant a dismissal on the murder charge. Any objection?'

There was a long silence. Finally, Venable nodded. 'I guess not.'

Judge Young said, 'Good decision. I'm going to give you some advice. Never, *never* call a witness unless you know what he's going to say.'

The court was in session again. Judge Young said, 'Ladies and gentlemen of the jury, thank you for your time and your patience. The court is going to grant a dismissal on all charges. The defendant is free.'

Paige turned to blow Jason a kiss, then hurried over to where Dr Barker was seated. She slid down to her knees and hugged him.

'I don't know how to thank you,' she whispered.

'You never should have gotten into this mess in the first place,' he growled. 'Damned fool thing to do. Let's get out of here and go somewhere where we can talk.'

Judge Young heard. She stood up and said, 'You may use my chambers if you like. That's the least we can do for you.'

Paige, Jason, and Dr Barker were in the judge's chambers, alone.

Dr Barker said, 'Sorry they wouldn't let me come here to help you sooner. You know what goddam doctors are like.'

Paige was near tears. 'I can't tell you how much I . . .'

'Then don't!' he said gruffly.

Paige was studying him, suddenly remembering something. 'When did you speak to John Cronin?'

'*What?*'

'You heard me. When did you speak to John Cronin?'

'*When?*'

She said slowly, 'You never even *met* John Cronin. You didn't know him.'

There was the trace of a smile on Barker's lips. 'No. But I know you.'

Paige leaned over and threw her arms around him.

'Don't get sloppy,' he growled. He looked over at Jason. 'She gets sloppy sometimes. You'd better take good care of her, or you'll have to answer to me.'

Jason said, 'Don't worry, sir. I will.'

Paige and Jason were married the following day. Dr Barker was their best man.

EPILOGUE

Paige Curtis went into private practice and is affiliated with the prestigious North Shore Hospital. Paige used the million dollars John Cronin left her to set up a medical foundation in her father's name in Africa.

Lawrence Barker shares an office with Paige, as a surgical consultant.

Arthur Kane had his license revoked by the Medical Board of California.

Jimmy Ford fully recovered and married Betsy. They named their first daughter Paige.

Honey Taft moved to Ireland with Sean Reilly, and works as a nurse in Dublin.

Sean Reilly is a successful artist, and shows no symptoms of AIDS, as yet.

Mike Hunter was sentenced to state prison for armed robbery and is still serving time.

Alfred Turner joined a practice on Park Avenue and is enormously successful.

Benjamin Wallace was fired as administrator of Embarcadero County Hospital.

Lauren Harrison married her tennis pro.

Lou Dinetto was sentenced to fifteen years in the penitentiary for tax evasion.

Ken Mallory was sentenced to life imprisonment.

One week after Dinetto arrived at the penitentiary, Mallory was found stabbed to death in his cell.

The Embarcadero Hospital is still there, awaiting the next earthquake.

TELL ME
YOUR DREAMS

This is a work of fiction based on actual cases

Book One

Chapter One

Someone was following her. She had read about stalkers, but they belonged in a different, violent world. She had no idea who it could be, who would want to harm her. She was trying desperately hard not to panic, but lately her sleep had been filled with unberable nightmares, and she had awakened each morning with a feeling of impending doom. *Perhaps it's all in my imagination*, Ashley Patterson thought. *I'm working too hard. I need a vacation.*

She turned to study herself in her bedroom mirror. She was looking at the image of a woman in her late twenties, neatly dressed, with patrician features, a slim figure and intelligent, anxious brown eyes. There was a quiet elegance about her, a subtle attractiveness. Her dark hair fell softly to her shoulders. *I hate my looks*, Ashley thought. *I'm too thin. I must start eating more.* She walked into the kitchen and began to fix breakfast, forcing her mind to forget about the frightening thing that was happening, and concentrating on preparing a fluffy omelette. She turned on the coffeemaker and put a slice of bread in the toaster. Ten minutes later, everything was ready. Ashley placed the dishes on the table and sat down. She picked up a fork, stared at the food for a moment, then shook her head in despair. Fear had taken away her appetite.

This can't go on, she thought angrily. *Whoever he is, I won't let him do this to me. I won't.*

Ashley glanced at her watch. It was time to leave for work. She looked around the familiar apartment, as though seeking some kind of reassurance from it. It was an attractively furnished third-floor apartment on Via Camino Court, with a living room, bedroom and den, bathroom, kitchen and guest powder room. She had lived here in Cupertino, California, for three years. Until two weeks ago, Ashley had thought of it as a comfortable nest, a haven. Now it had turned into a fortress, a place where no one could get in to harm her. Ashley walked to the front door and examined the lock. *I'll have a dead bolt put in,* she thought. *Tomorrow.* She turned off all the lights, checked to make sure the door was firmly locked behind her and took the elevator to the basement garage.

The garage was deserted. Her car was twenty feet from the elevator. She looked around carefully, then ran to the car, slid inside and locked the doors, her heart pounding. She headed downtown, under a sky the color of malice, dark and foreboding. The weather report had said rain. *But it's not going to rain,* Ashley thought. *The sun is going to come out. I'll make a deal with you, God. If it doesn't rain, it means that everything is all right, that I've been imagining things.*

Ten minutes later, Ashley Patterson was driving through down-town Cupertino. She was still awed by the miracle of what this once sleepy little corner of Santa Clara Valley had become. Located fifty miles south of San Francisco, it was where the computer revolution had started, and it had been appropriately nicknamed Silicon Valley.

Ashley was employed at Global Computer Graphics Corporation, a successful, fast-growing young company with two hundred employees.

As Ashley turned the car onto Silverado Street, she had

4

the uneasy feeling that *he* was behind her, following her. *But who? And why?* She looked into her rearview mirror. Everything seemed normal.

Every instinct told her otherwise.

Ahead of Ashley was the sprawling, modern-looking building that housed Global Computer Graphics. She turned into the parking lot, showed the guard her identification and pulled into her parking space. She felt safe here.

As she got out of the car, it began to rain.

At nine o'clock in the morning, Global Computer Graphics was already humming with activity. There were eighty modular cubicles, occupied by computer whizzes, all young, busily building Web sites, creating logos for new companies, doing artwork for record and book publishing companies and composing illustrations for magazines. The work floor was divided into several divisions: administration, sales, marketing and technical support. The atmosphere was casual. The employees walked around in jeans, tank tops and sweaters.

As Ashley headed toward her desk, her supervisor, Shane Miller, approached her. 'Morning, Ashley.'

Shane Miller was in his early thirties, a burly, earnest man with a pleasant personality. In the beginning, he had tried to persuade Ashley to go to bed with him, but he had finally given up, and they had become good friends.

He handed Ashley a copy of the latest *Time* magazine. 'Seen this?'

Ashley looked at the cover. It featured a picture of a distinguished-looking man in his fifties, with silver hair. The caption read 'Dr Steven Patterson, Father of Mini Heart Surgery.'

'I've seen it.'

'How does it feel to have a famous father?'

Ashley smiled. 'Wonderful.'

'He's a great man.'

'I'll tell him you said so. We're having lunch.'

'Good. By the way . . .' Shane Miller showed Ashley a photograph of a movie star who was going to be used in an ad for a client. 'We have a little problem here. Desiree has gained about ten pounds, and it shows. Look at those dark circles under her eyes. And even with makeup, her skin is splotchy. Do you think you can help this?'

Ashley studied the picture. 'I can fix her eyes by applying the blur filter. I could try to thin her face by using the distort tool, but – No. That would probably end up making her look odd.' She studied the picture again. 'I'll have to airbrush or use the clone tool in some areas.'

'Thanks. Are we on for Saturday night?'

'Yes.'

Shane Miller nodded toward the photograph. 'There's no hurry on this. They want it last month.'

Ashley smiled. 'What else is new?'

She went to work. Ashley was an expert in advertising and graphic design, creating layouts with text and images.

Half an hour later, as Ashley was working on the photograph, she sensed someone watching her. She looked up. It was Dennis Tibble.

'Morning, honey.'

His voice grated on her nerves. Tibble was the company's computer genius. He was known around the plant as 'The Fixer.' Whenever a computer crashed, Tibble was sent for. He was in his early thirties, thin and bald with an unpleasant, arrogant attitude. He had an obsessive personality, and the word around the plant was that he was fixated on Ashley.

6

'Need any help?'

'No, thank you.'

'Hey, what about us having a little dinner Saturday night?'

'Thank you. I'm busy.'

'Going out with the boss again?'

Ashley turned to look at him, angry. 'Look, it's none of your—'

'I don't know what you see in him, anyway. He's a nerd, cubed. I can give you a better time.' He winked. 'You know what I mean?'

Ashley was trying to control her temper. 'I have work to do, Dennis.'

Tibble leaned close to her and whispered, 'There's something you're going to learn about me, honey. I don't give up. Ever.'

She watched him walk away, and wondered: *Could he be the one?*

At 12:30, Ashley put her computer in suspend mode and headed for Margherita di Roma, where she was joining her father for lunch.

She sat at a corner table in the crowded restaurant, watching her father come toward her. She had to admit that he was handsome. People were turning to stare at him as he walked to Ashley's table. *'How does it feel to have a famous father?'*

Years earlier, Dr Steven Patterson had pioneered a breakthrough in minimally invasive heart surgery. He was constantly invited to lecture at major hospitals around the world. Ashley's mother had died when Ashley was twelve, and she had no one but her father.

'Sorry I'm late, Ashley.' He leaned over and kissed her on the cheek.

'That's all right. I just got here.'

He sat down. 'Have you seen *Time* magazine?'

'Yes. Shane showed it to me.'

He frowned. 'Shane? Your boss?'

'He's not my boss. He's – he's one of the supervisors.'

'It's never good to mix business with pleasure, Ashley. You're seeing him socially, aren't you? That's a mistake.'

'Father, we're just good—'

A waiter came up to the table. 'Would you like to see a menu?'

Dr Patterson turned to him and snapped, 'Can't you see we're in the middle of a conversation? Go away until you're sent for.'

'I – I'm sorry.' The waiter turned and hurried off.

Ashley cringed with embarrassment. She had forgotten how savage her father's temper was. He had once punched an intern during an operation for making an error in judgment. Ashley remembered the screaming arguments between her mother and father when she was a little girl. They had terrified her. Her parents had always fought about the same thing, but try as she might, Ashley could not remember what it was. She had blocked it from her mind.

Her father went on, as though there had been no interruption. 'Where were we? Oh, yes. Going out with Shane Miller is a mistake. A big mistake.'

And his words brought back another terrible memory.

She could hear her father's voice saying, 'Going out with Jim Cleary is a mistake. A big mistake . . .'

Ashley had just turned eighteen and was living in Bedford, Pennsylvania, where she was born. Jim Cleary was the most popular boy in Bedford Area High School. He was

8

on the football team, was handsome and amusing and had a killer smile. It seemed to Ashley that every girl in school wanted to sleep with him. *And most of them probably have,* she had thought, wryly. When Jim Cleary started asking Ashley out, she was determined not to go to bed with him. She was sure he was interested in her only for sex, but as time went on, she changed her mind. She liked being with him, and he seemed to genuinely enjoy her company.

That winter, the senior class went for a weekend skiing trip in the mountains. Jim Cleary loved to ski.

'We'll have a great time,' he assured Ashley.

'I'm not going.'

He looked at her in astonishment. 'Why?'

'I hate cold weather. Even with gloves, my fingers get numb.'

'But it will be fun to—'

'I'm not going.'

And he had stayed in Bedford to be with her.

They shared the same interests and had the same ideals, and they always had a wonderful time together.

When Jim Cleary had said to Ashley, 'Someone asked me this morning if you're my girlfriend. What shall I tell him?' Ashley had smiled and said, 'Tell him yes.'

Dr Patterson was worried. 'You're seeing too much of that Cleary boy.'

'Father, he's very decent, and I love him.'

'How can you love him? He's a goddamned *football* player. I'm not going to let you marry a football player. He's not good enough for you, Ashley.'

He had said that about every boy she had gone out with.

Her father kept making disparaging remarks about Jim Cleary, but the explosion occurred on the night of the high school graduation. Jim Cleary was taking Ashley to an evening graduation party. When he came to pick her up, she was sobbing.

'What's the matter? What's happened?'

'My – my father told me he's taking me away to London. He's registered me in – in a college there.'

Jim Cleary looked at her, stunned. 'He's doing this because of us, isn't he?'

Ashley nodded, miserable.

'When do you leave?'

'Tomorrow.'

'No! Ashley, for God's sake, don't let him do this to us. Listen to me. I want to marry you. My uncle offered me a really good job in Chicago with his advertising agency. We'll run away. Meet me tomorrow morning at the railroad station. There's a train leaving for Chicago at seven A.M. Will you come with me?'

She looked at him a long moment and said softly, 'Yes.'

Thinking about it later, Ashley could not remember what the graduation party was like. She and Jim had spent the entire evening excitedly discussing their plans.

'Why don't we fly to Chicago?' Ashley asked.

'Because we would have to give our names to the airline. If we go by train, nobody will know where we've gone.'

As they were leaving the party, Jim Cleary asked softly, 'Would you like to stop off at my place? My folks are out of town for the weekend.'

Ashley hesitated, torn. 'Jim . . . we've waited this long. A few more days won't matter.'

'You're right.' He grinned. 'I may be the only man on this continent marrying a virgin.'

* * *

10

When Jim Cleary brought Ashley home from the party, Dr Patterson was waiting, in a rage. 'Do you have any idea how late it is?'

'I'm sorry, sir. The party—'

'Don't give me any of your goddamn excuses, Cleary. Who the hell do you think you're fooling?'

'I'm not—'

'From now on, you keep your goddamned hands off my daughter, do you understand?'

'Father—'

'You keep out of this.' He was screaming now. 'Cleary, I want you to get the hell out of here and stay out.'

'Sir, your daughter and I—'

'Jim—'

'Get up to your room.'

'Sir—'

'If I ever see you around here again, I'll break every bone in your body.'

Ashley had never seen him so furious. It had ended with everyone yelling. When it was over, Jim was gone and Ashley was in tears.

I'm not going to let my father do this to me, Ashley thought, determinedly. *He's trying to ruin my life*. She sat on her bed for a long time. *Jim is my future. I want to be with him. I don't belong here anymore*. She rose and began to pack an overnight bag. Thirty minutes later, Ashley slipped out the back door and started toward Jim Cleary's home, a dozen blocks away. *I'll stay with him tonight, and we'll take the morning train to Chicago*. But as she got nearer to his house, Ashley thought, No. *This is wrong. I don't want to spoil everything. I'll meet him at the station*.

And she turned and headed back home.

*   *   *

11

Ashley was up the rest of that night thinking about her life with Jim and how wonderful it was going to be. At 5:30, she picked up her suitcase and moved silently past the closed door of her father's bedroom. She crept out of the house and took a bus to the railroad station. When she reached the station, Jim had not arrived. She was early. The train was not due for another hour. Ashley sat on a bench eagerly waiting. She thought about her father awakening and finding her gone. He would be furious.

But I can't let him live my life. One day he'll really get to know Jim, and he'll see how lucky I am. 6:30 ... 6:40 ... 6:45 ... 6:50 ... There was still no sign of Jim. Ashley was beginning to panic. What could have happened? She decided to telephone him. There was no answer. 6:55 ... *He'll be coming at any moment.* She heard the train whistle in the distance, and she looked at her watch. 6:59. The train was pulling into the station. She rose to her feet and looked around frantically. *Something terrible has happened to him. He's had an accident. He's in the hospital.* A few minutes later, Ashley stood there watching the train to Chicago pull out of the station, taking all her dreams with it. She waited another half hour and tried to telephone Jim again. When there was still no answer, she slowly headed home, desolate.

At noon, Ashley and her father were on a plane to London ...

She had attended a college in London for two years, and when Ashley decided she wanted to be involved in working with computers, she applied for the prestigious MEI Wang Scholarship for Women in Engineering at the University of California at Santa Cruz. She had been accepted, and three years later, she was recruited by the Global Computer Graphics Corporation.

In the beginning, Ashley had written half a dozen letters to Jim Cleary, but she had torn them all up. His actions and his silence had told her only too clearly how he felt about her.

Her father's voice jarred Ashley back to the present.

'You're a million miles away. What are you thinking about?'

Ashley studied her father across the table. 'Nothing.'

Dr Patterson signaled the waiter, smiled at him genially and said, 'We're ready to look at menus now.'

It was only when Ashley was on her way back to the office that she remembered she had forgotten to congratulate her father on his cover of *Time* magazine.

When Ashley walked up to her desk, Dennis Tibble was waiting for her.

'I hear you had lunch with your father.'

He's an eavesdropping little creep. He makes it his business to know everything that's going on here. 'Yes, I did.'

'That can't have been much fun.' He lowered his voice. 'Why don't you ever have lunch with me?'

'Dennis . . . I've told you before. I'm not interested.'

He grinned. 'You will be. Just wait.'

There was something eerie about him, something scary. She wondered again whether he could be the one who . . . She shook her head. *No.* She had to forget about it, move on.

On her way home, Ashley stopped and parked her car in front of the Apple Tree Book House. Before she went in, she studied the reflection in the storefront mirror to see if there was anyone behind her whom she recognized. No one. She went inside the store.

A young male clerk walked up to her. 'May I help you?'

'Yes. I – Do you have a book on stalkers?'

He was looking at her strangely. *'Stalkers?'*

Ashley felt like an idiot. She said quickly, 'Yes. I also want a book on – er – gardening and – and animals of Africa.'

'Stalkers and gardening and animals of Africa?'

'That's right,' she said firmly.

Who knows? Maybe someday I'll have a garden and I'll take a trip to Africa.

When Ashley returned to the car, it began to rain again. As she drove, the rain beat against the windshield, fracturing space and turning the streets ahead into surreal pointillistic paintings. She turned on the windshield wipers. They began to sweep across the window, hissing, 'He's gonna get you . . . gonna get you . . . gonna get you . . .' Hastily, Ashley turned them off. *No*, she thought. *They're saying, 'No one's there, no one's there, no one's there.'*

She turned the windshield wipers on again. 'He's gonna get you . . . gonna get you . . . gonna get you . . .'

Ashley parked her car in the garage and pressed the button for the elevator. Two minutes later, she was heading for her apartment. She reached the front door, put the key in the lock, opened the door and froze.

Every light in the apartment had been turned on.

Chapter Two

All around the mulberry bush,
The monkey chased the weasel.
The monkey thought 'twas all in fun,
Pop! goes the weasel.'

Toni Prescott knew exactly why she liked to sing that silly song. Her mum had hated it. *'Stop singing that stupid song. Do you hear me? You have no voice, anyway.'*

'Yes, Mother.' And Toni would sing it again and again, under her breath. That had been long ago, but the memory of defying her mother still gave her a glow.

Toni Prescott hated working at Global Computer Graphics. She was twenty-two years old, impish, vivacious, and daring. She was half smoldering, half firecracker. Her face was puckishly heart shaped, her eyes were a mischievous brown, her figure alluring. She had been born in London and she spoke with a delightful British accent. She was athletic and loved sports, particularly winter sports: skiing and bobsledding and ice-skating.

Going to college in London, Toni had dressed conservatively during the day, but at night, she had donned miniskirts and disco gear and made the swinging rounds. She had spent her evenings and nights at the Electric Ballroom on

15

Camden High Street, and at Subterania and the Leopard Lounge, mixing with the trendy West End crowd. She had a beautiful voice, sultry and sensuous, and at some of the clubs, she would go to the piano and play and sing, and the patrons would cheer her. That was when she felt most alive.

The routine inside the clubs would always follow the same pattern:

'Do you know you're a fantastic singer, Toni?'

'Ta.'

'Can I buy you a drink?'

She smiled. 'A Pimm's would be lovely.'

'My pleasure.'

And it would end the same way. Her date would lean close to her and whisper in her ear, 'Why don't we go up to my flat and have a shag?'

'Buzz off.' And Toni would be out of there. She would lie in her bed at night, thinking about how stupid men were and how bloody easy it was to control them. The poor sods did not know it, but they *wanted* to be controlled. They *needed* to be controlled.

And then came the move from London to Cupertino. In the beginning, it had been a disaster. Toni hated Cupertino and she loathed working at Global Computer Graphics. She was bored with hearing about plug-ins and dpi's and halftones and grids. She desperately missed the exciting nightlife of London. There were a few nightspots in the Cupertino area, and Toni frequented those: San Jose Live or P.J. Mulligan's or Hollywood Junction. She wore tight-fitting miniskirts and tube tops with open-toed shoes having five-inch heels or platform shoes with thick cork soles. She used a lot of makeup – thick, dark eyeliner, false eyelashes, colored eye shadow and bright lipstick. It was as though she were trying to hide her beauty.

Some weekends, Toni would drive up to San Francisco, where the real action was. She haunted the restaurants and clubs that had music bars. She would visit Harry Denton's and One Market restaurant and the California Café, and during the evening, while the musicians took their break, Toni would go to the piano and play and sing. The customers loved it. When Toni tried to pay her dinner bills, the owners would say, 'No, this is on the house. You're wonderful. Please come back again.'

Did you hear that, Mother? 'You're wonderful. Please come back again.'

On a Saturday night, Toni was having dinner in the French Room at the Cliff Hotel. The musicians had finished their set and left the bandstand. The maître d' looked at Toni and nodded invitingly.

Toni rose and walked across the room to the piano. She sat down and began to play and sing an early Cole Porter number. When she was finished, there was enthusiastic applause. She sang two more songs and returned to her table.

A bald, middle-aged man came up to her. 'Excuse me. May I join you for a moment?'

Toni started to say no, when he added, 'I'm Norman Zimmerman. I'm producing a road company of *The King and I*. I'd like to talk to you about it.'

Toni had just read a glowing article about him. He was a theatrical genius.

He sat down. 'You have a remarkable talent, young lady. You're wasting your time fooling around in places like this. You should be on Broadway.'

Broadway. Did you hear that, Mother?

'I'd like to audition you for—'

'I'm sorry. I can't.'

He looked at her in surprise. 'This could open a lot of doors for you. I mean it. I don't think you know how talented you are.'

'I have a job.'

'Doing what, may I ask?'

'I work at a computer company.'

'I'll tell you what. I'll start by paying you double whatever you're getting now and—'

Toni said, 'I appreciate it, but I . . . I can't.'

Zimmerman sat back in his chair. 'You're not interested in show business?'

'I'm very interested.'

'Then what's the problem?'

Toni hesitated, then said carefully, 'I'd probably have to leave in the middle of the tour.'

'Because of your husband or—?'

'I'm not married.'

'I don't understand. You said you're interested in show business. This is the perfect showcase for you to—'

'I'm sorry. I can't explain.'

If I did explain, he wouldn't understand, Toni thought miserably. *No one would. It's the unholy curse I have to live with. Forever.*

A few months after Toni started working at Global Computer Graphics, she learned about the Internet, the worldwide open door to meeting men.

She was having dinner at the Duke of Edinburgh with Kathy Healy, a friend who worked for a rival computer company. The restaurant was an authentic pub from England

18

that had been torn down, packed in containers and shipped to California. Toni would go there for Cockney fish and chips, prime ribs with Yorkshire pudding, bangers and mash and English sherry trifle. *One foot on the ground*, she would say. *I have to remember my roots*.

Toni looked up at Kathy. 'I want you to do me a favor.'

'Name it.'

'I want you to help me with the Internet, luv. Tell me how to use it.'

'Toni, the only computer I have access to is at work, and it's against company policy to—'

'Sod company policy. You know how to use the Internet, don't you?'

'Yes.'

Toni patted Kathy Healy's hand and smiled. 'Great.'

The following evening, Toni went to Kathy Healy's office, and Kathy introduced Toni to the world of the Internet. After clicking on the Internet icon, Kathy entered her password and waited a moment to connect, then double clicked another icon and entered a chat room. Toni sat in amazement, watching rapid, typed conversations taking place among people all over the globe.

'I've got to have that!' Toni said. 'I'll get a computer for my flat. Would you be an angel and set me up on the Internet?'

'Sure. It's easy. All you do is click your mouse into the URL field, the uniform resource locator, and—'

'Like the song says, "Don't tell me, show me."'

The next night, Toni was on the Internet, and from that time on, her life changed. She was no longer bored. The Internet became a magic carpet that flew her all over the world. When Toni got home from work, she would immediately turn on her computer and go on-line to explore various chat rooms that were available.

It was so simple. She accessed the Internet, pressed a key and a window opened on the screen, split into an upper portion and a lower portion. Toni typed in 'Hello. Is anyone there?'

The lower portion of the screen flashed the words 'Bob. I'm here. I'm waiting for you.'

She was ready to meet the world.

There was Hans in Holland:

'Tell me about yourself, Hans.'

'I'm a DJ in Amsterdam at a great club. I'm into hip-hop, rave, world beat. You name it.'

Toni typed in her reply. 'Sounds great. I love to dance. I can go all night long. I live in a horrible little town that has nothing to offer except a few disco nights.'

'Sounds sad.'

'It bloody well is.'

'Why don't you let me cheer you up? What are the chances of our meeting?'

'Ta ta.' She exited the chat room.

There was Paul, in South Africa:

'I've been waiting for you to check back in, Toni.'

'I'm here. I'm dying to know all about you, Paul.'

'I'm thirty-two. I'm a doctor at a hospital in Johannesburg. I—'

Toni angrily signed off. *A doctor!* Terrible memories came flooding through her. She closed her eyes a moment, her heart pounding. She took several deep breaths. *No more tonight,* she thought, shakily. She went to bed.

The following evening, Toni was back on the Internet. On-line was Sean from Dublin:

'Toni . . . That's a pretty name.'

'Thank you, Sean.'

'Have you ever been to Ireland?'

'No.'

'You'd love it. It's the land of leprechauns. Tell me what you look like, Toni. I'll bet you're beautiful.'

'You're right. I'm beautiful, I'm exciting and I'm single. What do you do, Sean?'

'I'm a bartender. I—'

Toni ended the chat session.

Every night was different. There was a polo player in Argentina, an automobile salesman in Japan, a department store clerk in Chicago, a television technician in New York. The Internet was a fascinating game, and Toni enjoyed it to the fullest. She could go as far as she wanted and yet know that she was safe because she was anonymous.

And then one night, in an on-line chat room, she met Jean Claude Parent.

'*Bon soir*. I am happy to meet you, Toni.'

'Nice to meet you, Jean Claude. Where are you?'

'In Quebec City.'

'I've never been to Quebec. Would I like it?' Toni expected to see the word *yes* on the screen.

Instead, Jean Claude typed, 'I do not know. It depends on what kind of person you are.'

Toni found his answer intriguing. 'Really? What kind of person would I have to be to enjoy Quebec?'

'Quebec is like the early North American frontier. It is very French. Quebecois are independent. We do not like to take orders from anyone.'

Toni typed in, 'Neither do I.'

21

'Then you would enjoy it. It is a beautiful city, surrounded by mountains and lovely lakes, a paradise for hunting and fishing.'

Looking at the typed words appearing on her screen, Toni could almost feel Jean Claude's enthusiasm. 'It sounds great. Tell me about yourself.'

'*Moi?* There is not much to tell. I am thirty-eight years old, unmarried. I just ended a relationship, and I would like to settle down with the right woman. *Et vous?* Are you married?'

Toni typed back, 'No. I'm looking for someone, too. What do you do?'

'I own a little jewelry store. I hope you will come and visit it one day.'

'Is that an invitation?'

'*Mais oui.* Yes.'

Toni typed in, 'It sounds interesting.' And she meant it. *Maybe I'll find a way to go there*, Toni thought. *Maybe he's the person who can save me.*

Toni communicated with Jean Claude Parent almost every night. He had scanned in a picture of himself, and Toni found herself looking at a very attractive, intelligent-looking man.

When Jean Claude saw the photograph of Toni that she scanned in, he wrote, 'You are beautiful, *ma chérie*. I knew you would be. Please come to visit me.'

'I will.'

'Soon.'

'Ta ta.' Toni signed off.

On the work floor the next morning, Toni heard Shane Miller talking to Ashley Patterson and thought, *What the hell does he see in her? She's a right git.* To Toni, Ashley

22

was a frustrated, spinsterish Miss Goody Two-shoes. *She doesn't bloody know how to have any fun*, Toni thought. Toni disapproved of everything about her. Ashley was a stick-in-the-mud who liked to stay home at night and read a book or watch the History Channel or CNN. She had no interest in sports. *Boring!* She had never entered a chat room. Meeting strangers through a computer was something Ashley would never do, *the cold fish. She doesn't know what she's missing*, Toni thought. *Without the on-line chat room, I never would have met Jean Claude.*

Toni thought about how much her mother would have hated the Internet. But then her mother had hated everything. She had only two means of communicating: screaming or whining. Toni could never please her. *'Can't you ever do anything right, you stupid child?'* Well, her mother had yelled at her once too often. Toni thought about the terrible accident in which her mother had died. Toni could still hear her screams for help. The memory of it made Toni smile.

> *'A penny for a spool of thread,*
> *A penny for a needle.*
> *That's the way the money goes,*
> *Pop! goes the weasel.'*

23

Chapter Three

In another place, at another time, Alette Peters could have been a successful artist. As far back as she could remember, her senses were tuned to the nuances of color. She could see colors, smell colors and hear colors.

Her father's voice was blue and sometimes red.

Her mother's voice was dark brown.

Her teacher's voice was yellow.

The grocer's voice was purple.

The sound of the wind in the trees was green.

The sound of running water was gray.

Alette Peters was twenty years old. She could be plain-looking, attractive or stunningly beautiful, depending on her mood or how she was feeling about herself. But she was never simply pretty. Part of her charm was that she was completely unaware of her looks. She was shy and soft-spoken, with a gentleness that was almost an anachronism.

Alette had been born in Rome, and she had a musical Italian accent. She loved everything about Rome. She had stood at the top of the Spanish Steps and looked over the city and felt that it was hers. When she gazed at the ancient temples and the giant Colosseum, she knew she belonged to that era. She had strolled in the Piazza Navona, listened to the music of the waters in the Fountain of the Four Rivers and walked the Piazza Venezia, with its wedding cake monument to Victor Emanuel II. She had spent endless hours at St Peter's Basilica, the Vatican Museum and the Borghese Gallery, enjoying the timeless works of Raphael and Fra Bartolommeo and Andrea del Sarto and Pontormo. Their talent both transfixed her and frustrated her. She wished she had been born in the sixteenth century and had known them. They were more real to Alette than the passers-by on the streets. She wanted desperately to be an artist.

She could hear her mother's dark brown voice: *'You're wasting paper and paint. You have no talent.'*

The move to California had been unsettling at first. Alette had been concerned as to how she would adjust, but Cupertino had turned out to be a pleasant surprise. She enjoyed the privacy that the small town afforded, and she liked working for Global Computer Graphics Corporation. There were no major art galleries in Cupertino, but on weekends, Alette would drive to San Francisco to visit the galleries there.

'Why are you interested in that stuff?' Toni Prescott would ask her. 'Come on to P.J. Mulligans with me and have some fun.'

'Don't you care about art?'

Toni laughed. 'Sure. What's his last name?'

There was only one cloud hanging over Alette Peter's life. She was manic-depressive. She suffered from anomie, a feeling of alienation from others. Her mood swings always caught her unaware, and in an instant, she could go from a blissful euphoria to a desperate misery. She had no control over her emotions.

Toni was the only one with whom Alette would discuss her problems. Toni had a solution for everything, and it was usually: 'Let's go and have some fun!'

Toni's favorite subject was Ashley Patterson. She was watching Shane Miller talking to Ashley.

'Look at that tight-assed bitch,' Toni said contemptuously. 'She's the ice queen.'

Alette nodded. 'She's very serious. Someone should teach her how to laugh.'

Toni snorted. 'Someone should teach her how to fuck.'

One night a week, Alette would go to the mission for the homeless in San Francisco and help serve dinner. There was one little old woman in particular who looked forward to Alette's visits. She was in a wheelchair, and Alette would help her to a table and bring her hot food.

The woman said gratefully, 'Dear, if I had a daughter, I'd want her to be exactly like you.'

Alette squeezed her hand. 'That's such a great compliment. Thank you.' And her inner voice said, *If you had a daughter, she'd look like a pig like you.* And Alette was horrified by her thoughts. It was as though someone else inside her was saying those words. It happened constantly.

She was out shopping with Betty Hardy, a woman who was a member of Alette's church. They stopped in front of a department store. Betty was admiring a dress in the window. 'Isn't that beautiful?'

'Lovely,' Alette said. *That's the ugliest dress I've ever seen. Perfect for you.*

One evening, Alette had dinner with Ronald, a sexton at the church. 'I really enjoy being with you, Alette. Let's do this more often.'

She smiled shyly. 'I'd like that.' And she thought, *Non*

faccia, lo stupido. Maybe in another lifetime, creep. And again she was horrified. *What's wrong with me?* And she had no answer.

The smallest slights, whether intended or not, drove Alette into a rage. Driving to work one morning, a car cut in front of her. She gritted her teeth and thought, *I'll kill you, you bastard.* The man waved apologetically, and Alette smiled sweetly. But the rage was still there.

When the black cloud descended, Alette would imagine people on the street having heart attacks or being struck by automobiles or being mugged and killed. She would play the scenes out in her mind, and they were vividly real. Moments later, she would be filled with shame.

On her good days, Alette was a completely different person. She was genuinely kind and sympathetic and enjoyed helping people. The only thing that spoiled her happiness was the knowledge that the darkness would come down on her again, and she would be lost in it.

Every Sunday morning, Alette went to church. The church had volunteer programs to feed the homeless, to teach after-school art lessons and to tutor students. Alette would lead children's Sunday school classes and help in the nursery. She volunteered for all of the charitable activities and devoted as much time as she could to them. She particularly enjoyed giving painting classes for the young.

One Sunday, the church had a fair for a fund-raiser, and Alette brought in some of her own paintings for the church to sell. The pastor, Frank Selvaggio, looked at them in amazement.

'These are – These are brilliant! You should be selling them at a gallery.'

Alette blushed. 'No, not really. I just do them for fun.'

The fair was crowded. The churchgoers had brought their friends and families, and game booths as well as arts-and-crafts booths had been set up for their enjoyment. There were beautifully decorated cakes, incredible handmade quilts, homemade jams in beautiful jars, carved wooden toys. People were going from booth to booth, sampling the sweets, buying things they would have no use for the next day.

'But it's in the name of charity,' Alette heard one woman explain to her husband.

Alette looked at the paintings that she had placed around the booth, most of them landscapes in bright, vivid colors that leaped from the canvas. She was filled with misgivings. *'You're wasting good money on paint, child.'*

A man came up to the booth. 'Hi, there. Did you paint these?'

His voice was a deep blue.

No, stupid. Michelangelo dropped by and painted them.

'You're very talented.'

'Thank you.' *What do you know about talent?*

A young couple stopped at Alette's booth. 'Look at those colors! I have to have that one. You're really good.'

And all afternoon people came to her booth to buy her paintings and to tell her how much talent she had. And Alette wanted to believe them, but each time the black curtain came down and she thought, *They're all being cheated.*

An art dealer came by. 'These are really lovely. You should merchandise your talent.'

'I'm just an amateur,' Alette insisted. And she refused to discuss it any further.

At the end of the day, Alette had sold every one of her paintings. She gathered the money that people had paid her, put it in an envelope and handed it to Pastor Frank Selvaggio.

He took it and said, 'Thank you, Alette. You have a great gift, bringing so much beauty into people's lives.'

Did you hear that, Mother?

When Alette was in San Francisco, she spent hours visiting the Museum of Modern Art, and she haunted the De Young Museum to study their collection of American art.

Several young artists were copying some of the paintings on the museum's walls. One young man in particular caught Alette's eye. He was in his late twenties, slim and blond, with a strong, intelligent face. He was copying Georgia O'Keeffe's *Petunias*, and his work was remarkably good. The artist noticed Alette watching him. 'Hi.'

His voice was a warm yellow.

'Hello,' Alette said shyly.

The artist nodded toward the painting he was working on. 'What do you think?'

'*Bellissimo.* I think it's wonderful.' And she waited for her inner voice to say, *For a stupid amateur.* But it didn't happen. She was surprised. 'It's really wonderful.'

He smiled. 'Thank you. My name is Richard, Richard Melton.'

'Alette Peters.'

'Do you come here often?' Richard asked.

'*Sì.* As often as I can. I don't live in San Francisco.'

'Where do you live?'

'In Cupertino.' *Not – 'It's none of your damn business' or 'Wouldn't you like to know?' but – 'In Cupertino.' What is happening to me?*

'That's a nice little town.'

'I like it.' *Not* – *'What the hell makes you think it's a nice little town?'* or *'What do you know about nice little towns?'* but – *'I like it.'*

He was finished with the painting. 'I'm hungry. Can I buy you lunch? Café De Young has pretty good food.'

Alette hesitated only a moment. *'Va bene.* I'd like that.' *Not* – *'You look stupid'* or *'I don't have lunch with strangers,'* but – *'I'd like that.'* It was a new, exhilarating experience for Alette.

The lunch was extremely enjoyable and not once did negative thoughts come into Alette's mind. They talked about some of the great artists, and Alette told Richard about growing up in Rome.

'I've never been to Rome,' he said. 'Maybe one day.'

And Alette thought, *It would be fun to go to Rome with you.*

As they were finishing their lunch, Richard saw his roommate across the room and called him over to the table. 'Gary, I didn't know you were going to be here. I'd like you to meet someone. This is Alette Peters. Gary King.'

Gary was in his late twenties, with bright blue eyes and hair down to his shoulders.

'It's nice to meet you, Gary.'

'Gary's been my best friend since high school, Alette.'

'Yeah. I have ten years of dirt on Richard, so if you're looking for any good stories—'

'Gary, don't you have somewhere to go?'

'Right.' He turned to Alette. 'But don't forget my offer. I'll see you two around.'

They watched Gary leave. Richard said, 'Alette . . .'

31

'Yes?'

'May I see you again?'

'I would like that.' *Very much.*

Monday morning, Alette told Toni about her experience. 'Don't get involved with an artist,' Toni warned. 'You'll be living on the fruit he paints. Are you going to see him again?'

Alette smiled. 'Yes. I think he likes me. And I like him. I really like him.'

It started as a small disagreement and ended up as a ferocious argument. Pastor Frank was retiring after forty years of service. He had been a very good and caring pastor, and the congregation was sorry to see him leave. There were secret meetings held to decide what to give him as a going-away present. A watch . . . money . . . a vacation . . . a painting . . . He loved art.

'Why don't we have someone do a portrait of him, with the church in the background?' They turned to Alette. 'Will you do it?'

'Of course,' she said happily.

Walter Manning was one of the senior members of the church and one of its biggest contributors. He was a very successful businessman, but he seemed to resent everyone else's success. He said, 'My daughter is a fine painter. Perhaps she should do it.'

Someone suggested, 'Why not have them both do it, and we'll vote on which one to give Pastor Frank?'

Alette went to work. The painting took her five days, and it was a masterpiece, glowing with the compassion and goodness of her subject. The following Sunday, the group met to look at the paintings. There were exclamations of appreciation over Alette's painting.

'It's so real, he could almost walk off the canvas . . .'

'Oh, he's going to love that . . .'

'That should be in a museum, Alette . . .'

Walter Manning unwrapped the canvas painted by his daughter. It was a competent painting, but it lacked the fire of Alette's portrait.

'That's very nice,' one of the members of the congregation said tactfully, 'but I think Alette's is—'

'I agree . . .'

'Alette's portrait is the one . . .'

Walter Manning spoke up. 'This has to be a unanimous decision. My daughter's a professional artist' – he looked at Alette – 'not a dilettante. She did this as a favor. We can't turn her down.'

'But, Walter—'

'No, sir. This has to be unanimous. We're either giving him my daughter's painting or we don't give him anything at all.'

Alette said, 'I like her painting very much. Let's give it to the pastor.'

Walter Manning smiled smugly and said, 'He's going to be very pleased with this.'

On his way home that evening, Walter Manning was killed by a hit-and-run driver.

When Alette heard the news, she was stunned.

Chapter Four

Ashley Patterson was taking a hurried shower, late for work, when she heard the sound. A door opening? Closing? She turned off the shower, listening, her heart pounding. *Silence.* She stood there a moment, her body glistening with drops of water, then hurriedly dried herself and cautiously stepped into the bedroom. Everything appeared to be normal. *It's my stupid imagination again. I've got to get dressed.* She walked over to her lingerie drawer, opened it and stared down at it, unbelievingly. Someone had gone through her undergarments. Her bras and pantyhose were all piled together. She always kept them neatly separated.

Ashley suddenly felt sick to her stomach. Had he unzipped his pants, picked up her pantyhose and rubbed them against himself? Had he fantasized about raping her? Raping her and murdering her? She was finding it difficult to breathe. *I should go to the police, but they would laugh at me.*

You want us to investigate this because you think someone got into your lingerie drawer?

Someone has been following me.

Have you seen who it is?

No.

Has anyone threatened you?

No.

Do you know why anyone would want to harm you?

No.

It's no use, Ashley thought despairingly. *I can't go to the police. Those are the questions they would ask me, and I would look like a fool.*

She dressed as quickly as she could, suddenly eager to escape from the apartment. *I'll have to move. I'll go somewhere where he can't find me.*

But even as she thought it, she had the feeling that it was going to be impossible. *He knows where I live, he knows where I work. And what do I know about him? Nothing.*

She refused to keep a gun in the apartment because she hated violence. *But I need some protection now,* Ashley thought. She went into the kitchen, picked up a steak knife, carried it to her bedroom and put it in the dresser drawer next to her bed.

It's possible that I mixed my lingerie up myself. That's probably what happened. Or is it wishful thinking?

There was an envelope in her mailbox in the downstairs entrance hall. The return address read 'Bedford Area High School, Bedford, Pennsylvania.'

Ashley read the invitation twice.

Ten-Year Class Reunion!

Rich man, poor man, beggar man, thief. Have you often wondered how your classmates have fared during the last ten years? Here's your chance to find out. The weekend of June 15th we're going to have a spectacular get-together. Food, drinks, a great orchestra and dancing. Join the fun.

Just mail the enclosed acceptance card so we'll know you're coming. Everyone looks forward to seeing you.

Driving to work, Ashley thought about the invitation. *'Everyone looks forward to seeing you.' Everyone except Jim Cleary,* she thought bitterly.

'I want to marry you. My uncle offered me a really good job in Chicago with his advertising agency . . . There's a train leaving for Chicago at seven A.M. Will you come with me?'

And she remembered the pain of desperately waiting at the station for Jim, believing in him, trusting him. He had changed his mind, and he had not been man enough to come and tell her. Instead, he had left her sitting in a train station, alone. *Forget the invitation. I'm not going.*

Ashley had lunch with Shane Miller at TGI Friday's. They sat in a booth, eating in silence.

'You seem preoccupied,' Shane said.

'Sorry.' Ashley hesitated a moment. She was tempted to tell him about the lingerie, but it would sound stupid. *Someone got into your drawers?* Instead, she said, 'I got an invitation to my ten-year high school reunion.'

'Are you going?'

'Certainly not.' It came out stronger than Ashley had intended.

Shane Miller looked at her curiously. 'Why not? Those things can be fun.'

Would Jim Cleary be there? Would he have a wife and children? What would he say to her? 'Sorry I wasn't able to meet you at the train station. Sorry I lied to you about marrying you?'

'I'm not going.'

But Ashley was unable to get the invitation out of her mind. *It would be nice to see some of my old classmates,* she thought. There were a few she had been close to. One in particular was Florence Schiffer. *I wonder what's become of*

37

her? And she wondered whether the town of Bedford had changed.

Ashley Patterson had grown up in Bedford, Pennsylvania, a small town two hours east of Pittsburgh, deep in the Allegheny Mountains. Her father had been head of the Memorial Hospital of Bedford County, one of the top one hundred hospitals in the country.

Bedford had been a wonderful town to grow up in. There were parks for picnics, rivers to fish in and social events that went on all year. Ashley enjoyed visiting Big Valley, where there was an Amish colony. It was a common sight to see horses pulling Amish buggies with different colored tops, colors that depended on the degree of orthodoxy of the owners.

There were Mystery Village evenings and live theater and the Great Pumpkin Festival. Ashley smiled at the thought of the good times she had had there. *Maybe I will go back,* she thought. *Jim Cleary won't have the nerve to show up.*

Ashley told Shane Miller of her decision. 'It's a week from Friday,' she said. 'I'll be back Sunday night.'

'Great. Let me know what time you're getting back. I'll pick you up at the airport.'

'Thank you, Shane.'

When Ashley returned from lunch, she walked into her work cubicle and turned her computer on. To her surprise, a sudden hail of pixels began rolling down the screen, creating an image. She stared at it, bewildered. The dots were forming a picture of her. As Ashley watched, horrified, a hand holding a butcher knife appeared at the top of the screen. The hand was racing toward her image, ready to plunge the knife into her chest.

Ashley screamed, 'No!'

She snapped off the monitor and jumped to her feet.

Shane Miller had hurried to her side. 'Ashley! What is it?'

She was trembling. 'On the . . . the screen—'

Shane turned on the computer. A picture of a kitten chasing a ball of yarn across a green lawn appeared.

Shane turned to look at Ashley, bewildered. 'What—?'

'It's – it's gone,' she whispered.

'What's gone?'

She shook her head. 'Nothing. I – I've been under a lot of stress lately, Shane. I'm sorry.'

'Why don't you go have a talk with Dr Speakman?'

Ashley had seen Dr Speakman before. He was the company psychologist hired to counsel stressed-out computer whizzes. He was not a medical doctor, but he was intelligent and understanding, and it was helpful to be able to talk to someone.

'I'll go,' Ashley said.

Dr Ben Speakman was in his fifties, a patriarch at the fountain of youth. His office was a quiet oasis at the far end of the building, relaxed and comfortable.

'I had a terrible dream last night,' Ashley said. She closed her eyes, reliving it. 'I was running. I was in a huge garden filled with flowers . . . They had weird, ugly faces . . . They were screaming at me . . . I couldn't hear what they were saying. I just kept running toward something . . . I don't know what . . .' She stopped and opened her eyes.

'Could you have been running *away* from something? Was something chasing you?'

'I don't know. I – I think I'm being followed, Dr Speakman. It sounds crazy, but – I think someone wants to kill me.'

He studied her a moment. 'Who would want to kill you?'

'I – I have no idea.'

'Have you *seen* anyone following you?'

'No.'

'You live alone, don't you?'

'Yes.'

'Are you seeing anyone? I mean romantically?'

'No. Not right now.'

'So it's been a while since you – I mean sometimes when a woman doesn't have a man in her life – well, a kind of physical tension can build up . . .'

What he's trying to tell me is that I need a good – She could not bring herself to say the word. She could hear her father yelling at her, '*Don't ever say that word again. People will think you're a little slut. Nice people don't say fuck. Where do you pick up that kind of language?*'

'I think you've just been working too hard, Ashley. I don't believe you have anything to worry about. It's probably just tension. Take it a little easier for a while. Get more rest.'

'I'll try.'

Shane Miller was waiting for her. 'What did Dr Speakman say?'

Ashley managed a smile. 'He says I'm fine. I've just been working too hard.'

'Well, we'll have to do something about that,' Shane said. 'For openers, why don't you take the rest of the day off?' His voice was filled with concern.

'Thanks.' She looked at him and smiled. He was a dear man. A good friend.

40

He can't be the one, Ashley thought. *He can't.*

During the following week, Ashley could think of nothing but the reunion. *I wonder if my going is a mistake? What if Jim Cleary does show up? Does he have any idea how much he hurt me? Does he care? Will he even remember me?*

The night before Ashley was to leave for Bedford, she was unable to sleep. She was tempted to cancel her flight. *I'm being silly*, she thought. *The past is the past.*

When Ashley picked up her ticket at the airport, she examined it and said, 'I'm afraid there's been some mistake. I'm flying tourist. This is a first-class ticket.'

'Yes. You changed it.'

She stared at the clerk. 'I what?'

'You telephoned and said to change it to a first-class ticket.' He showed Ashley a slip of paper. 'Is this your credit card number?'

She looked at it and said slowly, 'Yes . . .'

She had not made that phone call.

Ashley arrived in Bedford early and checked in at the Bedford Springs Resort. The reunion festivities did not start until six o'clock that evening, so she decided to explore the town. She hailed a taxi in front of the hotel.

'Where to, miss?'

'Let's just drive around.'

Hometowns were supposed to look smaller when a native returned years later, but to Ashley, Bedford looked larger than she had remembered. The taxi drove up and down familiar streets, passing the offices of the *Bedford Gazette* and television station WKYE and a dozen familiar restaurants and art galleries. The Baker's Loaf of Bedford was still there and Clara's Place, the Fort Bedford Museum and Old Bedford Village. They passed the Memorial Hospital, a graceful three-story brick building with a portico. It was there that her father had become famous.

She recalled again the terrible, screaming fights between her mother and father. They had always been about the same thing. *About what?* She could not remember.

At five o'clock, Ashley returned to her hotel room. She changed clothes three times before finally deciding on what she was going to wear. She settled on a simple, flattering black dress.

When Ashley entered the festively decorated gymnasium of Bedford Area High School, she found herself surrounded by 120 vaguely familiar-looking strangers. Some of her former classmates were completely unrecognizable, others had changed little. Ashley was looking for one person: Jim Cleary. *Would he have changed much? Would he have his wife with him?* People were approaching Ashley.

'Ashley, it's Trent Waterson. You look great!'

'Thanks. So do you, Trent.'

'I want you to meet my wife . . .'

'Ashley, it *is* you, isn't it?'

'Yes. Er—'

'Art. Art Davies. Remember me?'

'Of course.' He was badly dressed and looked ill at ease.

'How is everything going, Art?'

'Well, you know I wanted to become an engineer, but it didn't work out.'

'I'm sorry.'

'Yeah. Anyway, I became a mechanic.'

*   *   *

'Ashley! It's Lenny Holland. For God's sake, you look beautiful!'

'Thank you, Lenny.' He had gained weight and was wearing a large diamond ring on his little finger.

'I'm in real estate now, doing great. Did you ever get married?'

Ashley hesitated. 'No.'

'Remember Nicki Brandt? We got married. We have twins.'

'Congratulations.'

It was amazing how much people could change in ten years. They were fatter and thinner . . . prosperous and downtrodden. They were married and divorced . . . parents and parentless . . .

As the evening wore on, there was dining and music and dancing. Ashley made conversation with her former classmates and caught up on their lives, but her mind was on Jim Cleary. There was still no sign of him. *He won't come*, she decided. *He knows I might be here and he's afraid to face me.*

An attractive-looking woman was approaching. 'Ashley! I was *hoping* I'd see you.' It was Florence Schiffer. Ashley was genuinely glad to see her. Florence had been one of her closest friends. The two of them found a table in the corner, where they could talk.

'You look great, Florence,' Ashley said.

'So do you. Sorry I'm so late. The baby wasn't feeling well. Since I last saw you, I've gotten married and divorced. I'm going out with Mr Wonderful now. What about you? After the graduation party, you disappeared. I tried to find you, but you'd left town.'

'I went to London,' Ashley said. 'My father enrolled me

43

in a college over there. We left here the morning after our graduation.'

'I tried every way I could think of to reach you. The detectives thought I might know where you were. They were looking for you because you and Jim Cleary were going together.'

Ashley said slowly, 'The *detectives*?'

'Yes. The ones investigating the murder.'

Ashley felt the blood drain from her face. 'What . . . murder?'

Florence was staring at her. 'My God! You don't know?'

'*Know what?*' Ashley demanded fiercely. 'What are you talking about?'

'The day after the graduation party, Jim's parents came back and found his body. He had been stabbed to death and . . . castrated.'

The room started to spin. Ashley held on to the edge of the table. Florence grabbed her arm.

'I'm – I'm sorry, Ashley. I thought you would have read about it, but of course . . . you had left for London.'

Ashley squeezed her eyes tightly shut. She saw herself sneaking out of the house that night, heading toward Jim Cleary's house. But she had turned and gone back home to wait for him in the morning. *If only I had gone to him,* Ashley thought miserably, *he would still be alive. And all these years I've hated him. Oh, my God. Who could have killed him? Who—?*

She could hear her father's voice, *'You keep your god-damned hands off my daughter, do you understand? . . . If I ever see you around here again, I'll break every bone in your body.'*

She got to her feet. 'You'll have to excuse me, Florence. I – I'm not feeling very well.'

And Ashley fled.

The detectives. They must have gotten in touch with her father. *Why didn't he tell me?*

She took the first plane back to California. It was early in the morning before she could fall asleep. She had a nightmare. A figure standing in the dark was stabbing Jim and screaming at him. The figure stepped into the light.

It was her father.

Chapter Five

The next few months were misery for Ashley. The image of Jim Cleary's bloody, mutilated body kept going through her mind. She thought of seeing Dr Speakman again, but she knew she dare not discuss this with anyone. She felt guilty even *thinking* that her father might have done such a terrible thing. She pushed the thought away and tried to concentrate on her work. It was impossible. She looked down in dismay at a logo she had just botched.

Shane Miller was watching her, concerned. 'Are you all right, Ashley?'

She forced a smile. 'I'm fine.'

'I really am sorry about your friend.' She had told him about Jim.

'I'll – I'll get over it.'

'What about dinner tonight?'

'Thanks, Shane. I – I'm not up to it just yet. Next week.'

'Right. If there's anything I can do—'

'I appreciate it. There's nothing anyone can do.'

Toni said to Alette, 'Miss Tight Ass has a problem. Well, she can get stuffed.'

'I feel *dispiace* – sorry for her. She is troubled.'

'Sod her. We all have our problems, don't we, luv?'

As Ashley was leaving on a Friday afternoon before a

47

holiday weekend, Dennis Tibble stopped her. 'Hey, babe. I need a favor.'

'I'm sorry, Dennis, I—'

'Come on. Lighten up!' He took Ashley's arm. 'I need some advice from a woman's point of view.'

'Dennis, I'm not in the—'

'I've fallen in love with somebody, and I want to marry her, but there are problems. Will you help me?'

Ashley hesitated. She did not like Dennis Tibble, but she could see no harm in trying to help him. 'Can this wait until tomorrow?'

'I need to talk to you now. It's really urgent.'

Ashley took a deep breath. 'All right.'

'Can we go to your apartment?'

She shook her head. 'No.' She would never be able to make him leave.

'Will you stop by my place?'

Ashley hesitated. 'Very well.' *That way I can leave when I want to. If I can help him get the woman he's in love with, maybe he'll leave me alone.*

Toni said to Alette, 'God! Goody Two-shoes is going to the twerp's apartment. Can you believe she could be that stupid? Where's her sodding brains?'

'She's just trying to help him. There's nothing wrong with—'

'Oh, come on, Alette. When are you going to grow up? The man wants to bonk her.'

'Non va. Non si fa così.'

'I couldn't have said it better myself.'

Dennis Tibble's apartment was furnished in neo-nightmare. Posters of old horror movies hung from the walls, next to pinups of naked models and wild animals feeding. Tiny erotic wood carvings were spread out on tables.

It's the apartment of a madman, Ashley thought. She could not wait to get out of there.

'Hey, I'm glad you could come, baby. I really appreciate this. If—'

'I can't stay long, Dennis.' Ashley warned him. 'Tell me about this woman you're in love with.'

'She's really something.' He held out a cigarette. 'Cigarette?'

'I don't smoke.' She watched him light up.

'How about a drink?'

'I don't drink.'

He grinned. 'You don't smoke, you don't drink. That leaves an interesting activity, doesn't it?'

She said to him sharply, 'Dennis, if you don't—'

'Only kidding.' He walked over to the bar and poured some wine. 'Have a little wine. That can't hurt you.' He handed her the glass.

She took a sip of wine. 'Tell me about Miss Right.'

Dennis Tibble sat down on the couch next to Ashley. 'I've never met anybody like her. She's sexy like you and—'

'Stop it or I'll leave.'

'Hey, that was meant as a compliment. Anyway, she's crazy about me, but her mother and father are very social, and they hate me.'

Ashley made no comment.

'So the thing is, if I push it, she'll marry me, but she'll alienate her family. She's really close to them, and if I marry her, they'll sure as hell disown her. Then one day, she'll probably blame me. Do you see the problem?'

Ashley took another sip of wine. 'Yes. I . . .'

After that, time seemed to vanish in a mist.

* * *

She awakened slowly, knowing that something was terribly wrong. She felt as though she had been drugged. It was an enormous effort merely to open her eyes. Ashley looked around the room and began to panic. She was lying in a bed, naked, in a cheap hotel room. She managed to sit up, and her head started to pound. She had no idea where she was or how she had gotten there. There was a room service menu on the nightstand, and she reached over and picked it up. *The Chicago Loop Hotel.* She read it again, stunned. *What am I doing in Chicago? How long have I been here? The visit to Dennis Tibble's apartment had been on Friday. What day is this?* With growing alarm, she picked up the telephone.

'May I help you?'

It was difficult for Ashley to speak. 'What – what day is this?'

'Today is the seventeenth of—'

'No. I mean what *day* of the week is this?'

'Oh. Today is Monday. Can I—'

Ashley replaced the receiver in a daze. *Monday.* She had lost two days and two nights. She sat up at the edge of the bed, trying to remember. She had gone to Dennis Tibble's apartment . . . She had had a glass of wine . . . After that, everything was a blank.

He had put something in her glass of wine that had made her temporarily lose her memory. She had read about incidents where a drug like that had been used. It was called the 'date rape drug.' That was what he had given her. The talk about wanting her advice had been a ruse. *And like a fool, I fell for it.* She had no recollection of going to the airport, flying to Chicago or checking into this seedy hotel room with Tibble. And worse – no recollection of what had happened in this room.

I've got to get out of here, Ashley thought desperately. She felt unclean, as though every inch of her body had been violated. What had he done to her? Trying not to think about it, she got out of bed, walked into the tiny bathroom and stepped into the shower. She let the stream of hot water pound against her body, trying to wash away whatever terrible, dirty things had happened to her. What if he had gotten her pregnant? The thought of having his child was sickening. Ashley got out of the shower, dried herself and walked over to the closet. Her clothes were missing. The only things inside the closet were a black leather miniskirt, a cheap-looking tube top and a pair of spiked high-heeled shoes. She was repelled by the thought of putting on the clothes, but she had no choice. She dressed quickly and glanced in the mirror. She looked like a prostitute.

Ashley examined her purse. Only forty dollars. Her checkbook and credit card were still there. *Thank God!*

She went out into the corridor. It was empty. She took the elevator down to the seedy-looking lobby and walked over to the checkout desk, where she handed the elderly cashier her credit card.

'Leavin' us already?' He leered. 'Well, you had a good time, huh?'

Ashley stared at him, wondering what he meant and afraid to find out. She was tempted to ask him when Dennis Tibble had checked out, but she decided it was better not to bring it up.

The cashier was putting her credit card through a machine. He frowned and put it through again. Finally, he said, 'I'm sorry. This card won't go through. You've exceeded your limit.'

Ashley's mouth dropped open. 'That's impossible! There's some mistake!'

51

The clerk shrugged. 'Do you have another credit card?'

'No. I – I don't. Will you take a personal check?'

He was eyeing her outfit disapprovingly. 'I guess so, if you have some ID.'

'I need to make a telephone call . . .'

'Telephone booth in the corner.'

'San Francisco Memorial Hospital . . .'

'Dr Steven Patterson.'

'One moment, please . . .'

'Dr Patterson's office.'

'Sarah? This is Ashley. I need to speak to my father.'

'I'm sorry, Miss Patterson. He's in the operating room and—'

Ashley's grip tightened ont he telephone. 'Do you know how long he'll be there?'

'It's hard to say. I know he has another surgery scheduled after—'

Ashley found herself fighting hysteria. 'I need to talk to him. It's urgent. Can you get word to him, please? As soon as he gets a chance, have him call me.' She looked at the telephone number in the booth and gave it to her father's receptionist. 'I'll wait here until he calls.'

'I'll be sure to tell him.'

She sat in the lobby for almost an hour, willing the telephone to ring. People passing by stared at her or ogled her, and she felt naked in the tawdry outfit she was wearing. When the phone finally rang, it startled her.

She hurried back into the phone booth. 'Hello . . .'

'Ashley?' It was her father's voice.

'Oh, Father, I—'

'What's wrong?'

52

'I'm in Chicago and—'

'What are you doing in Chicago?'

'I can't go into it now. I need an airline ticket to San Jose. I don't have any money with me. Can you help me?'

'Of course. Hold on.' Three minutes later, her father came back on the line. 'There's an American Airlines plane leaving O'Hare at ten-forty A.M., Flight 407. There will be a ticket waiting for you at the check-in counter. I'll pick you up at the airport in San Jose and—'

'No!' She could not let him see her like this. 'I'll – I'll go to my apartment to change.'

'All right. I'll come down and meet you for dinner. You can tell me all about it then.'

'Thank you, Father. Thank you.'

On the plane going home, Ashley thought about the unforgivable thing Dennis Tibble had done to her. *I'm going to have to go to the police,* she decided. *I can't let him get away with this. How many other women has he done this to?*

When Ashley got back to her apartment, she felt as though she had returned to a sanctuary. She could not wait to get out of the tacky outfit she was wearing. She stripped it off as quickly as she could. She felt as though she needed another shower before she met her father. She started to walk over to her closet and stopped. In front of her, on the dressing table, was a burned cigarette butt.

They were seated at a corner table in a restaurant at The Oaks. Ashley's father was studying her, concerned. 'What were you doing in Chicago?'

'I – I don't know.'

He looked at her, puzzled. 'You don't know?'

Ashley hesitated, trying to make up her mind whether to tell him what had happened. Perhaps he could give her some advice.

She said carefully, 'Dennis Tibble asked me up to his apartment to help him with a problem . . .'

'Dennis Tibble? That *snake*?' Long ago, Ashley had introduced her father to the people she worked with. 'How could you have anything to do with him?'

Ashley knew instantly that she had made a mistake. Her father had always overreacted to any problems she had. Especially when it involved a man.

'If I ever see you around here again, Cleary. I'll break every bone in your body.'

'It's not important,' Ashley said.

'I want to hear it.'

Ashley sat still for a moment, filled with a sense of foreboding. 'Well, I had a drink at Dennis's apartment and . . .'

As she talked, she watched her father's face grow grim. There was a look in his eyes that frightened her. She tried to cut the story short.

'No,' her father insisted. 'I want to hear it all . . .'

Ashley lay in bed that night, too drained to sleep, her thoughts chaotic. *If what Dennis did to me becomes public, it will be humiliating. Everyone at work will know what happened. But I can't let him do this to anyone else. I have to tell the police.*

People had tried to warn her that Dennis was obsessed with her, but she had ignored them. Now, looking back on it, she could see all the signs: Dennis had hated to see anyone else talking to her; he was constantly begging her for dates; he was always eavesdropping . . .

At least I know who the stalker is, Ashley thought.

* * *

At 8:30 in the morning, as Ashley was getting ready to leave for work, the telephone rang. She picked it up. 'Hello.'

'Ashley, it's Shane. Have you heard the news?'

'What news?'

'It's on television. They just found Dennis Tibble's body.'

For an instant the earth seemed to shift. 'Oh, my God! What happened?'

'According to the sheriff's office, somebody stabbed him to death and then castrated him.'

Chapter Six

Deputy Sam Blake had earned his position in the Cupertino Sheriff's Office the hard way: He had married the sheriff's sister, Serena Dowling, a virago with a tongue sharp enough to fell the forests of Oregon. Sam Blake was the only man Serena had ever met who was able to handle her. He was a short, gentle, mild-mannered person with the patience of a saint. No matter how outrageous Serena's behavior, he would wait until she had calmed down and then have a quiet talk with her.

Blake had joined the sheriff's department because Sheriff Matt Dowling was his best friend. They had gone to school together and grown up together. Blake enjoyed police work and was exceedingly good at it. He had a keen, inquiring intelligence and a stubborn tenacity. The combination made him the best detective on the force.

Earlier that morning, Sam Blake and Sheriff Dowling were having coffee together.

Sheriff Dowling said, 'I hear my sister gave you a bad time last night. We got half a dozen calls from the neighbors complaining about the noise. Serena's a champion screamer, all right.'

Sam shrugged. 'I finally got her calmed down, Matt.'

'Thank God she's not living with me anymore, Sam. I don't know what gets into her. Her temper tantrums—'

Their conversation was interrupted. 'Sheriff, we just got a 911. There's been a murder over on Sunnyvale Avenue.'

Sheriff Dowling looked at Sam Blake.

Blake nodded. 'I'll catch it.'

Fifteen minutes later, Deputy Blake was walking into Dennis Tibble's apartment. A patrolman in the living room was talking to the building superintendent.

'Where's the body?' Blake asked.

The patrolman nodded toward the bedroom. 'In there, sir.' He looked pale.

Blake walked to the bedroom and stopped, in shock. A man's naked body was sprawled across the bed, and Blake's first impression was that the room was soaked in blood. As he stepped closer to the bed, he saw where the blood had come from. The ragged edge of a broken bottle had punctured the victim's back, over and over again, and there were shards of glass in his body. The victim's testicles had been slashed off.

Looking at it, Blake felt a pain in his groin. 'How the hell could a human being do a thing like this?' he said aloud. There was no sign of the weapon, but they would make a thorough search.

Deputy Blake went back into the living room to talk to the building superintendent. 'Did you know the deceased?'

'Yes, sir. This is his apartment.'

'What's his name?'

'Tibble. Dennis Tibble.'

Deputy Blake made a note. 'How long had he lived here?'

'Almost three years.'

'What can you tell me about him?'

'Not too much, sir. Tibble kept pretty much to himself,

always paid his rent on time. Once in a while he'd have a woman in here. I think they were mostly pros.'

'Do you know where he worked?'

'Oh, yes. Global Computer Graphics Corporation. He was one of them computer nerds.'

Deputy Blake made another note. 'Who found the body?'

'One of the maids. Maria. Yesterday was a holiday, so she didn't come in until this morning—'

'I want to talk to her.'

'Yes, sir. I'll get her.'

Maria was a dark-looking Brazilian woman in her forties, nervous and frightened.

'You discovered the body, Maria?'

'I didn't do it. I swear to you.' She was on the verge of hysteria. 'Do I need a lawyer?'

'No. You don't need a lawyer. Just tell me what happened.'

'Nothing happened. I mean – I walked in here this morning to clean, the way I always do. I – I thought he was gone. He's always out of here by seven in the morning. I tidied up the living room and—'

Damn! 'Maria, do you remember what the room looked like before you tidied up?'

'What do you mean?'

'Did you move anything? Take anything out of here?'

'Well, yes. There was a broken wine bottle on the floor. It was all sticky. I—'

'What did you do with it?' he asked excitedly.

'I put it in the garbage compactor and ground it up.'

'What else did you do?'

'Well, I cleaned out the ashtray and—'

'Were there any cigarette butts in it?'

She stopped to remember. 'One. I put it in the trash basket in the kitchen.'

'Let's take a look at it.' He followed her to the kitchen, and she pointed to a wastebasket. Inside was a cigarette butt with lipstick on it. Carefully, Deputy Blake scooped it up in a coin envelope.

He led her back to the living room. 'Maria, do you know if anything is missing from the apartment? Does it look as if any valuables are gone?'

She looked around. 'I don't think so. Mr Tibble, he liked to collect those little statues. He spent a lot of money on them. It looks like they're all here.'

So the motive was not robbery. Drugs? Revenge? A love affair gone wrong?

'What did you do after you tidied up here, Maria?'

'I vacuumed in here, the way I always do. And then—' Her voice faltered. 'I walked into the bedroom and . . . I saw him.' She looked at Deputy Blake. 'I swear I didn't do it.'

The coroner and his assistants arrived in a coroner's wagon, with a body bag.

Three hours later, Deputy Sam Blake was back in the sheriff's office.

'What have you got, Sam?'

'Not much.' Deputy Blake sat down across from Sheriff Dowling. 'Dennis Tibble worked over at Global. He was apparently some kind of genius.'

'But not genius enough to keep himself from getting killed.'

'He wasn't just killed, Matt. He was slaughtered. You should have seen what someone did to his body. It has to be some kind of maniac.'

'Nothing to go on?'

'We aren't sure what the murder weapon is, we're waiting for results from the lab, but it may be a broken wine bottle. The maid threw it in the compactor. It looks like there's a fingerprint on one of the pieces of glass in his back. I talked to the neighbors. No help there. No one saw anyone coming in or out of his apartment. No unusual noises. Apparently, Tibble stuck pretty much to himself. He wasn't the neighborly type. One thing. Tibble had sex before he died. We have vaginal traces, pubic hairs, other trace evidence and a cigarette stub with lipstick. We'll test for DNA.'

'The newspapers are going to have a good time with this one, Sam. I can see the headlines now – MANIAC STRIKES SILICON VALLEY.' Sheriff Dowling sighed. 'Let's knock this off as fast as we can.'

'I'm on my way over to Global Computer Graphics now.'

It had taken Ashley an hour to decide whether she should go into the office. She was torn. *One look at me, and everyone will know that something is wrong. But if I don't show up, they'll want to know why. The police will probably be there asking questions. If they question me, I'll have to tell them the truth. They won't believe me. They'll blame me for killing Dennis Tibble. And if they do believe me, and if I tell them my father knew what he did to me, they'll blame him.*

She thought of Jim Cleary's murder. She could hear Florence's voice: *'Jim's parents came back and found his body. He had been stabbed to death and castrated.'*

Ashley squeezed her eyes shut tightly. *My God, what's happening? What's happening?*

Deputy Sam Blake walked onto the work floor where groups of somber employees stood around, talking quietly.

Blake could imagine what the subject of conversation was. Ashley watched him apprehensively as he headed toward Shane Miller's office.

Shane rose to greet him. 'Deputy Blake?'

'Yes.' The two men shook hands.

'Sit down, Deputy.'

Sam Blake took a seat. 'I understand Dennis Tibble was an employee here?'

'That's right. One of the best. It's a terrible tragedy.'

'He worked here about three years?'

'Yes. He was our genius. There wasn't anything he couldn't do with a computer.'

'What can you tell me about his social life?'

Shane Miller shook his head. 'Not much, I'm afraid. Tibble was kind of a loner.'

'Do you have any idea if he was into drugs?'

'Dennis? Hell, no. He was a health nut.'

'Did he gamble? Could he have owed someone a lot of money?'

'No. He made a damned good salary, but I think he was pretty tight with a buck.'

'What about women? Did he have a girlfriend?'

'Women weren't very attracted to Tibble.' He thought for a moment. 'Lately, though, he was going around telling people there was someone he was thinking of marrying.'

'Did he happen to mention her name?'

Miller shook his head. 'No. Not to me, anyway.'

'Would you mind if I talked to some of your employees?'

'Not at all. Go ahead. I have to tell you, they're all pretty shaken up.'

They would be more shaken up if they could have seen his body, Blake thought.

The two men walked out onto the work floor.

Shane Miller raised his voice. 'May I have your attention, please? This is Deputy Blake. He'd like to ask a few questions.'

The employees had stopped what they were doing and were listening.

Deputy Blake said, 'I'm sure that all of you have heard what happened to Mr Tibble. We need your help in finding out who killed him. Do any of you know of any enemies he had? Anyone who hated him enough to want to murder him?' There was a silence. Blake went on. 'There was a woman he was interested in marrying. Did he discuss her with any of you?'

Ashley was finding it difficult to breathe. Now was the time to speak up. Now was the time to tell the deputy what Tibble had done to her. But Ashley remembered the look on her father's face when she had told him about it. They would blame him for the murder.

Her father could never kill anyone.

He was a doctor.

He was a surgeon.

Dennis Tibble had been castrated.

Deputy Blake was saying, '. . . and none of you saw him after he left here on Friday?'

Toni Prescott thought, *Go ahead. Tell him, Miss Goody Two-shoes. Tell him you went to his apartment. Why don't you speak up?*

Deputy Blake stood there a moment, trying to hide his disappointment. 'Well, if any of you remembers anything that might be helpful, I'd appreciate it if you'd give me a call. Mr Miller has my number. Thank you.'

They watched as he moved toward the exit with Shane.

Ashley felt faint with relief.

Deputy Blake turned to Shane. 'Was there anyone here he was particularly close to?'

'No, not really,' Shane said. 'I don't think Dennis was close to anybody. He was very attracted to one of our computer operators, but he never got anywhere with her.'

Deputy Blake stopped. 'Is she here now?'

'Yes, but—'

'I'd like to talk to her.'

'All right. You can use my office.' They walked back into the room, and Ashley saw them coming. They were headed straight for her cubicle. She could feel her face redden.

'Ashley, Deputy Blake would like to talk to you.'

So he knew! He was going to ask her about her visit to Tibble's apartment. *I've got to be careful,* Ashley thought.

The deputy was looking at her. 'Do you mind, Miss Patterson?'

She found her voice. 'No, not at all.' She followed him into Shane Miller's office.

'Sit down.' They both took chairs. 'I understand that Dennis Tibble was fond of you?'

'I – I suppose . . .' *Careful.* 'Yes.'

'Did you go out with him?'

Going to his apartment would not be the same as going out with him. 'No.'

'Did he talk to you about this woman he wanted to marry?'

She was getting in deeper and deeper. Could he be taping this? Maybe he already knew she had been in Tibble's apartment. They could have found her fingerprints. Now was the time to tell the deputy what Tibble had done to her. *But if I do,* Ashley thought in despair, *it will lead to my father, and they'll connect that to Jim Cleary's murder.* Did they know about that, too? But the police department in Bedford

64

would have no reason to notify the police department in Cupertino. Or would they?

Deputy Blake was watching her, waiting for an answer. 'Miss Patterson?'

'What? Oh, I'm sorry. This has got me so upset . . .'

'I understand. Did Tibble ever mention this woman he wanted to marry?'

'Yes . . . but he never told me her name.' That, at least, was true.

'Have you ever been to Tibble's apartment?'

Ashley took a deep breath. If she said no, the questioning would probably end. But if they had found her fingerprints . . . 'Yes.'

'You have been to his apartment?'

'Yes.'

He was looking at her more closely now. 'You said you'd never been out with him.'

Ashley's mind was racing now. 'That's right. Not on a date, no. I went to bring him some papers he had forgotten.'

'When was this?'

She felt trapped. 'It was . . . it was about a week ago.'

'And that's the only time you've been to his place?'

'That's right.'

Now if they had her fingerprints, she would be in the clear.

Deputy Blake sat there, studying her, and she felt guilty. She wanted to tell him the truth. Maybe some burglar had broken in and killed him – the same burglar who had killed Jim Cleary ten years earlier and three thousand miles away. If you believed in coincidences. If you believed in Santa Claus. If you believed in the tooth fairy.

Damn you, Father.

Deputy Blake said, 'This is a terrible crime. There doesn't seem to be any motive. But you know, in all the years I've been on the force, I've never seen a crime without a motive.' There was no response. 'Do *you* know if Dennis Tibble was into drugs?'

'I'm sure he wasn't.'

'So what do we have? It wasn't drugs. He wasn't robbed. He didn't owe anybody money. That kind of leaves a romantic situation, doesn't it? Someone who was jealous of him.'

Or a father who wanted to protect his daughter.

'I'm as puzzled as you are, Deputy.'

He stared at her for a moment and his eyes seemed to say, 'I don't believe you, lady.'

Deputy Blake got to his feet. He took out a card and handed it to Ashley. 'If there's anything you can think of, I'd appreciate your giving me a call.'

'I'll be happy to.'

'Good day.'

She watched him leave. *It's over. Father's in the clear.*

When Ashley returned to her apartment that evening, there was a message on the answering machine: 'You got me real hot last night, baby. I'm talking blue balls. But you'll take care of me tonight, though, the way you promised. Same time, same place.'

Ashley stood there, listening in disbelief. *I'm going crazy,* she thought. *This has nothing to do with Father. Someone else must be behind all this. But who? And why?*

Five days later, Ashley received a statement from the credit card company. Three items caught her attention:

A bill from the Mod Dress Shop for $450.

A bill from the Circus Club for $300.

A bill from Louie's Restaurant for $250.

She had never heard of the dress shop, the club or the restaurant.

Chapter Seven

Ashley Patterson followed the investigation of Dennis Tibble's murder in the newspapers and on television every day. The police appeared to have reached a dead end.

It's over, Ashley thought. *There's nothing more to worry about.*

That evening, Deputy Sam Blake appeared at her apartment. Ashley looked at him, her mouth suddenly dry.

'I hope I'm not bothering you,' Deputy Blake said. 'I was on my way home, and I just thought I'd drop in for a minute.'

Ashley swallowed. 'No. Come in.'

Deputy Blake walked into the apartment. 'Nice place you have here.'

'Thank you.'

'I'll bet Dennis Tibble didn't like this kind of furniture.'

Ashley's heart began to pound. 'I don't know. He's never been in this apartment.'

'Oh. I thought he might have, you know.'

'No, I don't know, Deputy. I told you, I never dated him.'

'Right. May I sit down?'

'Please.'

'You see, I'm having a big problem with this case, Miss Patterson. It doesn't fit into any pattern. Like I said, there's always a motive. I've talked to some of the people over

69

at Global Computer Graphics, and no one seems to have known Tibble very well. He kept pretty much to himself.'

Ashley listened, waiting for the blow to fall.

'In fact, from what they tell me, you're the only one he was really interested in.'

Had he found out something, or was he on a fishing expedition?

Ashley said carefully, 'He was interested in me, Deputy, but I was not interested in him. I made that quite clear to him.'

He nodded. 'Well, I think it was nice of you to deliver those papers to his apartment.'

Ashley almost said, 'What papers?' and then suddenly remembered. 'It – it was no trouble. It was on my way.'

'Right. Someone must have hated Tibble a lot to do what they did.'

Ashley sat there tense, saying nothing.

'Do you know what I hate?' Deputy Blake said. 'Unsolved murders. They always leave me frustrated. Because when a murder goes unsolved, I don't think it means that the criminals were that smart. I think it means that the police weren't smart enough. Well, so far, I've been lucky. I've solved all the crimes that have come my way.' He got to his feet. 'I don't intend to give up on this one. If you can think of anything that will be helpful, you'll call me, won't you, Miss Patterson?'

'Yes, of course.'

Ashley watched him leave, and she thought, *Did he come here as a warning? Does he know more than he's telling me?*

Toni was more absorbed than ever in the Internet. She enjoyed her chats with Jean Claude the most, but that did not stop her from having other chat-room correspondents.

At every chance, she sat in front of her computer, and the typed messages flew back and forth, spilling onto the computer screen.

'Toni? Where have you been? I've been in the chat room waiting for you.'

'I'm worth waiting for, luv. Tell me about yourself. What do you do?'

'I work at a pharmacy. I can be good to you. Do you do drugs?'

'Sod off.'

'Is that you, Toni?'

'The answer to your dreams. Is it Mark?'

'Yes.'

'You haven't been on the Internet lately.'

'I've been busy. I'd like to meet you, Toni.'

'Tell me, Mark, what do you do?'

'I'm a librarian.'

'Isn't that exciting! All those books and everything . . .'

'When can we meet?'

'Why don't you ask Nostradamus?'

'Hello, Toni. My name is Wendy.'

'Hello, Wendy.'

'You sound like fun.'

'I enjoy life.'

'Maybe I can help you enjoy it more.'

'What did you have in mind?'

'Well, I hope you're not one of those narrow-minded people who are afraid to experiment and try exciting new things. I'd like to show you a good time.'

'Thanks, Wendy. You don't have the equipment I need.'

* * *

71

And then, Jean Claude Parent came back on.

'*Bonne nuit. Comment ça va?* How are you?'

'I'm great. How about you?'

'I have missed you. I wish very much to meet you in person.'

'I want to meet you, too. Thanks for sending me your photograph. You're a good-looking bloke.'

'And you are beautiful. I think it is very important for us to get to know each other. Is your company coming to Quebec for the computer convention?'

'What? Not that I know of. When is it?'

'In three weeks. Many big companies will be coming. I hope you will be here.'

'I hope so, too.'

'Can we meet in the chat room tomorrow at the same time?'

'Of course. Until tomorrow.'

'*À demain.*'

The following morning, Shane Miller walked up to Ashley. 'Ashley, have you heard about the big computer convention coming up in Quebec City?'

She nodded. 'Yes. It sounds interesting.'

'I was just debating whether we should send a contingent up there.'

'All the companies are going,' Ashley said. 'Symantec, Microsoft, Apple. Quebec City is putting on a big show for them. A trip like that could be kind of a Christmas bonus.'

Shane Miller smiled at her enthusiasm. 'Let me check it out.'

The following morning, Shane Miller called Ashley into his office.

'How would you like to spend Christmas in Quebec City?'

'We're going? That's great,' Ashley said, enthusiastically. In the past, she had spent the Christmas holidays with her father, but this year she had dreaded the prospect.

'You'd better take plenty of warm clothes.'

'Don't worry. I will. I'm really looking forward to this, Shane.'

Toni was in the Internet chat room. 'Jean Claude, the company is sending a group of us to Quebec City!'

'*Formidable!* I am so pleased. When will you arrive?'

'In two weeks. There will be fifteen of us.'

'*Merveilleux!* I feel as though something very important is going to happen.'

'So do I.' *Something very important.*

Ashley anxiously watched the news every night, but there were still no new developments in the Dennis Tibble murder. She began to relax. If the police could not connect her with the case, there was no way they could find a connection to her father. Half a dozen times she steeled herself to ask him about it, but each time she backed off. What if he were innocent? Could he ever forgive her for accusing him of being a murderer? *And if he is guilty, I don't want to know*, Ashley thought. *I couldn't bear it. And if he has done those terrible things, in his mind, he would have done them to protect me. At least I won't have to face him this Christmas.*

Ashley telephoned her father in San Francisco. She said, without preamble, 'I'm not going to be able to spend Christmas with you this year, Father. My company is sending me to a convention in Canada.'

There was a long silence. 'That's bad timing, Ashley. You and I have always spent Christmas together.'

'I can't help—'

'You're all I have, you know.'

'Yes, Father, and . . . you're all I have.'

'That's what's important.'

Important enough to kill for?

'Where is this convention?'

'In Quebec City. It's—'

'Ah. Lovely place. I haven't been there in years. I'll tell you what I'll do. I haven't anything scheduled at the hospital around that time. I'll fly up, and we'll have a Christmas dinner together.'

Ashley said quickly, 'I don't think it's—'

'You just make a reservation for me at whatever hotel you're staying at. We don't want to break tradition, do we?'

She hesitated and said slowly, 'No, Father.'

How can I face him?

Alette was excited. She said to Toni, 'I've never been to Quebec City. Do they have museums there?'

'Of course they have museums there,' Toni told her. 'They have everything. A lot of winter sports. Skiing, skating . . .'

Alette shuddered. 'I hate cold weather. No sports for me. Even with gloves, my fingers get numb. I will stick to the museums . . .'

On the twenty-first of December, the group from Global Computer Graphics arrived at the Jean-Lesage International Airport in Sainte-Foy and were driven to the storied Château Frontenac in Quebec City. It was below zero outside, and the streets were blanketed with snow.

Jean Claude had given Toni his home telephone number. She called as soon as she checked into her room. 'I hope I'm not calling too late.'

'*Mais non!* I cannot believe you are here. When may I see you?'

'Well, we're all going to the convention center tomorrow morning, but I could slip away and have lunch with you.'

'*Bon!* There is a restaurant, Le Paris-Brest, on the Grande Allée Est. Can you meet me there at one o'clock?'

'I'll be there.'

The Centre des Congrès de Quebec on René Lévesque Boulevard is a four-story, glass-and-steel, state-of-the-art building that can accommodate thousands of conventioneers. At nine o'clock in the morning, the vast halls were crowded with computer experts from all over the world, exchanging information on up-to-the-minute developments. They filled multimedia rooms, exhibit halls and video-conferencing centers. There were half a dozen seminars going on simultaneously. Toni was bored. *All talk and no action*, she thought. At 12:45, she slipped out of the convention hall and took a taxi to the restaurant.

Jean Claude was waiting for her. He took her hand and said warmly, 'Toni, I am so pleased you could come.'

'So am I.'

'I will try to make certain that your time here is very agreeable,' Jean Claude told her. 'This is a beautiful city to explore.'

Toni looked at him and smiled. 'I know I'm going to enjoy it.'

'I would like to spend as much time with you as I can.'

'Can you take the time off? What about the jewelry store?'

Jean Claude smiled. 'It will have to manage without me.'

The maître d' brought menus.

Jean Claude said to Toni, 'Would you like to try some of our French-Canadian dishes?'

'Fine.'

'Then please let me order for you.' He said to the maître d', '*Nous voudrions le Brome Lake Duckling.*' He explained to Toni, 'It is a local dish, duckling cooked in calvados and stuffed with apples.'

'Sounds delicious.'

And it was.

During luncheon, they filled each other in on their pasts.

'So. You've never been married?' Toni asked.

'No. And you?'

'No.'

'You have not found the right man.'

Oh, God, wouldn't it be wonderful if it were that simple. 'No.'

They talked of Quebec City and what there was to do there.

'Do you ski?'

Toni nodded. 'I love it.'

'Ah, *bon, moi aussi*. And there is snowmobiling, ice-skating, wonderful shopping . . .'

There was something almost boyish about his enthusiasm. Toni had never felt more comfortable with anyone.

Shane Miller arranged it so his group attended the convention mornings and had their afternoons free.

'I don't know what to do here,' Alette complained to Toni. 'It's freezing. What are you going to do?'

'Everything.' Toni grinned.

'*A più tardi.*'

Toni and Jean Claude had lunch together every day, and every afternoon, Jean Claude took Toni on a tour. She had never seen any place like Quebec City. It was like finding a turn-of-the-century picturesque French village in North America. The ancient streets had colorful names like Break Neck Stairs and Below the Fort and Sailor's Leap. It was a Currier & Ives city, framed in snow.

They visited La Citadelle, with its walls protecting Old Quebec, and they watched the traditional changing of the guard inside the walls of the fort. They explored the shopping streets, Saint Jean, Cartier, Côte de la Fabrique, and wandered through the Quartier Petit Champlain.

'This is the oldest commercial district in North America,' Jean Claude told her.

'It's super.'

Everywhere they went, there were sparkling Christmas trees, nativity scenes and music for the enjoyment of the strollers.

Jean Claude took Toni snowmobiling in the countryside. As they raced down a narrow slope, he called out, 'Are you having a good time?'

Toni sensed that it was not an idle question. She nodded and said softly, 'I'm having a wonderful time.'

Alette spent her time at museums. She visited the Basilica of Notre-Dame and the Good Shepherd Chapel and the Augustine Museum, but she had no interest in anything else that Quebec City offered. There were dozens of gourmet restaurants, but when she was not dining at the hotel, she ate at Le Commensal, a vegetarian cafeteria.

From time to time, Alette thought about her artist friend, Richard Melton, in San Francisco, and wondered what he was doing and if he would remember her.

Ashley was dreading Christmas. She was tempted to call her father and tell him not to come. *But what excuse can I give? You're a murderer. I don't want to see you?*

And each day Christmas was coming closer.

'I would like to show you my jewelry store,' Jean Claude told Toni. 'Would you care to see it?'

Toni nodded. 'Love to.'

Parent Jewelers was located in the heart of Quebec City, on rue Notre-Dame. When she walked in the door, Toni was stunned. On the Internet, Jean Claude had said, *'I have a little jewelry store.'* It was a very large store, tastefully done. Half a dozen clerks were busy with customers.

Toni looked around and said, 'It's – it's smashing.'

He smiled. *'Merci.* I would like to give you a *cadeau* – a gift, for Christmas.'

'No. That isn't necessary. I—'

'Please do not deprive me of the pleasure.' Jean Claude led Toni to a showcase filled with rings. 'Tell me what you like.'

Toni shook her head. 'Those are much too expensive. I couldn't—'

'Please.'

Toni studied him a moment, then nodded. 'All right.' She examined the showcase again. In the center was a large emerald ring set with diamonds.

Jean Claude saw her looking at it. 'Do you like the emerald ring?'

'It's lovely, but it's much too—'

'It is yours.' Jean Claude took out a small key, unlocked the case and pulled out the ring.

'No, Jean Claude—'

'*Pour moi.*' He slipped it on Toni's finger. It was a perfect fit.

'*Voilà!* It is a sign.'

Toni squeezed his hand. 'I – I don't know what to say.'

'I cannot tell you how much pleasure this gives me. There is a wonderful restaurant here called Pavillon. Would you like to have dinner there tonight?'

'Anywhere you say.'

'I will call for you at eight o'clock.'

At six o'clock that night, Ashley's father telephoned. 'I'm afraid I'm going to have to disappoint you, Ashley. I won't be able to be there for Christmas. An important patient of mine in South America has had a stroke. I'm flying to Argentina tonight.'

'I'm – I'm sorry, Father,' Ashley said. She tried to sound convincing.

'We'll make up for it, won't we, darling?'

'Yes, Father. Have a good flight.'

Toni was looking forward to dinner with Jean Claude. It was going to be a lovely evening. As she dressed, she sang softly to herself.

> '*Up and down the city road,*
> *In and out of the Eagle,*
> *That's the way the money goes,*
> *Pop! goes the weasel.*'

I think Jean Claude is in love with me, Mother.

79

Pavillon is located in the cavernous Gare du Palais, Quebec City's old railroad station. It is a large restaurant with a long bar at the entrance and rows of tables spreading toward the back. At eleven o'clock each night, a dozen tables are moved to the side to create a dance floor, and a disc jockey takes over with a variety of tapes ranging from reggae to jazz to blues.

Toni and Jean Claude arrived at nine, and they were warmly greeted at the door by the owner.

'Monsieur Parent. How nice to see you.'

'Thank you, André. This is Miss Toni Prescott. Mr Nicholas.'

'A pleasure, Miss Prescott. Your table is ready.'

'The food is excellent here,' Jean Claude assured Toni, when they were seated. 'Let us start with champagne.'

They ordered paillard de veau and torpille and salad and a bottle of Valpolicella.

Toni kept studying the emerald ring Jean Claude had given her. 'It's so beautiful!' she exclaimed.

Jean Claude leaned across the table. *'Tu aussi.* I cannot tell you how happy I am that we have finally met.'

'I am, too,' Toni said softly.

The music began. Jean Claude looked at Toni. 'Would you like to dance?'

'I'd love to.'

Dancing was one of Toni's passions, and when she got out on the dance floor, she forgot everything else. *She was a little girl dancing with her father, and her mother said, 'The child is clumsy.'*

Jean Claude was holding her close. 'You're a wonderful dancer.'

'Thank you.' *Do you hear that, Mother?*

Toni thought, *I wish this could go on forever.*

80

On the way back to the hotel, Jean Claude said, '*Chérie,* would you like to stop at my house and have a nightcap?'

Toni hesitated. 'Not tonight, Jean Claude.'

'Tomorrow, *peut-être*?'

She squeezed his hand. 'Tomorrow.'

At 3:00 A.M., Police Officer René Picard was in a squad car cruising down Grande Allée in the Quartier Montcalm when he noticed that the front door of a two-story redbrick house was wide open. He pulled over to the curb and stepped out to investigate. He walked to the front door and called, '*Bon soir. Y a-t-il, quelqu'un?*'

There was no answer. He stepped into the foyer and moved toward the large drawing room. '*C'est la police. Y a-t-il, quelqu'un?*'

There was no response. The house was unnaturally quiet. Unbuttoning his gun holster, Officer Picard began to go through the downstairs room, calling out as he moved from room to room. The only response was an eerie silence. He returned to the foyer. There was a graceful staircase leading to the floor above. 'Allo!' Nothing.

Officer Picard started up the stairs. When he got to the top of the stairs, his gun was in his hand. He called out again, then started down the long hallway. Ahead, a bedroom door was ajar. He walked over to it, opened it wide and turned pale. '*Mon Dieu!*'

At five o'clock that morning, in the gray stone and yellow brick building on Story Boulevard, where Centrale de Police is located, Inspector Paul Cayer was asking, 'What do we have?'

81

Officer Guy Fontaine replied, 'The victim's name is Jean Claude Parent. He was stabbed at least a dozen times, and his body was castrated. The coroner says that the murder took place in the last three or four hours. We found a restaurant receipt from Pavillon in Parent's jacket pocket. He had dinner there earlier in the evening. We got the owner of the restaurant out of bed.'

'Yes?'

'Monsieur Parent was at Pavillon with a woman named Toni Prescott, a brunette, very attractive, with an English accent. The manager of Monsieur Parent's jewelry store said that earlier that day, Monsieur Parent had brought a woman answering that description into the store and introduced her as Toni Prescott. He gave her an expensive emerald ring. We also believe that Monsieur Parent had sex with someone before he died, and that the murder weapon was a steel-blade letter opener. There were fingerprints on it. We sent them on to our lab and to the FBI. We are waiting to hear.'

'Have you picked up Toni Prescott?'

'*Non.*'

'And why not?'

'We cannot find her. We have checked all the local hotels. We have checked our files and the files of the FBI. She has no birth certificate, no social security number, no driver's license.'

'Impossible! Could she have gotten out of the city?'

Officer Fontaine shook his head. 'I don't think so, Inspector. The airport closed at midnight. The last train out of Quebec City left at five-thirty-five last night. The first train this morning will be at six-thirty-nine. We have sent a description of her to the bus station, the two taxi companies and the limousine company.'

'For God's sake, we have her name, her description and her fingerprints. She can't just have disappeared.'

One hour later, a report came in from the FBI. They were unable to identify the fingerprints. There was no record of Toni Prescott.

Chapter Eight

Five days after Ashley returned from Quebec City, her father was on the telephone. 'I just got back.'

'Back?' It took Ashley a moment to remember. 'Oh. Your patient in Argentina. How is he?'

'He'll live.'

'I'm glad.'

'Can you come up to San Francisco for dinner tomorrow?'

She dreaded the thought of facing him, but she could think of no excuse. 'All right.'

'I'll see you at Restaurant Lulu. Eight o'clock.'

Ashley was waiting at the restaurant when her father walked in. Again, she saw the admiring glances of recognition on people's faces. Her father was a famous man. *Would he risk everything he had just to—?*

He was at the table.

'It's good to see you, sweetheart. Sorry about our Christmas dinner.'

She forced herself to say, 'So am I.'

She was staring at the menu, not seeing it, trying to get her thoughts together.

'What would you like?'

'I – I'm not really hungry,' she said.

'You have to eat something. You're getting too thin.'

'I'll have the chicken.'

She watched her father as he ordered, and she wondered if she dared to bring up the subject.

'How was Quebec City?'

'It was very interesting,' Ashley said. 'It's a beautiful place.'

'We must go there together sometime.'

She made a decision and tried to keep her voice as casual as possible. 'Yes. By the way . . . last June I went to my ten-year high school reunion in Bedford.'

He nodded. 'Did you enjoy it?'

'No.' She spoke slowly, choosing her words carefully. 'I – I found out that the day after you and I left for London, Jim Cleary's body . . . was found. He had been stabbed . . . and castrated.' She sat there, watching him, waiting for a reaction.

Dr Patterson frowned. 'Cleary? Oh, yes. That boy who was panting after you. I saved you from him, didn't I?'

What did that mean? Was it a confession? Had he saved her from Jim Cleary by killing him?

Ashley took a deep breath and went on. 'Dennis Tibble was murdered the same way. He was stabbed and castrated.' She watched her father pick up a roll and carefully butter it.

When he spoke, he said, 'I'm not surprised, Ashley. Bad people usually come to a bad end.'

And this was a doctor, a man dedicated to saving lives. *I'll never understand him*, Ashley thought. *I don't think I want to.*

By the time dinner was over, Ashley was no closer to the truth.

Toni said, 'I really enjoyed Quebec City, Alette. I'd like to go back someday. Did you have a good time?'

Alette said shyly, 'I enjoyed the museums.'

'Have you called your boyfriend in San Francisco yet?'

'He's not my boyfriend.'

'I'll bet you want him to be, don't you?'

'*Forse*. Perhaps.'

'Why don't you call him?'

'I don't think it would be proper to—'

'Call him.'

They arranged to meet at the De Young Museum.

'I really missed you,' Richard Melton said. 'How was Quebec?'

'*Va bene.*'

'I wish I had been there with you.'

Maybe one day, Alette thought hopefully. 'How is the painting coming along?'

'Not bad. I just sold one of my paintings to a really well-known collector.'

'Fantastic!' She was delighted. And she could not help thinking, *It's so different when I'm with him. If it were anyone else, I would have thought, Who is tasteless enough to pay money for your paintings? or Don't give up your day job or a hundred other cruel remarks. But I don't do that with Richard.*

It gave Alette an incredible feeling of freedom, as though she had found a cure for some debilitating disease.

They had lunch at the museum.

'What would you like?' Richard asked. 'They have great roast beef here.'

'I'm a vegetarian. I'll just have a salad. Thank you.'

'Okay.'

A young, attractive waitress came over to the table. 'Hello, Richard.'

'Hi, Bernice.'

Unexpectedly, Alette felt a pang of jealousy. Her reaction surprised her.

'Are you ready to order?'

'Yes. Miss Peters is going to have a salad, and I'm going to have a roast beef sandwich.'

The waitress was studying Alette. *Is she jealous of me?* Alette wondered. When the waitress left, Alette said, 'She's very pretty. Do you know her well?' Immediately she blushed. *I wish I hadn't asked that.*

Richard smiled. 'I come here a lot. When I first came here, I didn't have much money. I'd order a sandwich, and Bernice would bring me a banquet. She's great.'

'She seems very nice,' Alette said. And she thought, *She has fat thighs.*

After they had ordered, they talked about artists.

'One day I want to go to Giverny,' Alette said, 'where Monet painted.'

'Did you know Monet started out as a caricaturist?'

'No.'

'It's true. Then he met Boudin, who became his teacher and persuaded him to start painting out of doors. There's a great story about that. Monet got so hooked on painting out of doors that when he decided to paint a picture of a woman in the garden, with a canvas over eight feet high, he had a trench dug in the garden so he could raise or lower the canvas by pulleys. The picture is hanging at the Musée d'Orsay in Paris.'

The time went by swiftly and happily.

After lunch, Alette and Richard walked around looking at the various exhibits. There were more than forty thousand objects in the collection, everything from ancient Egyptian artifacts to contemporary American paintings.

Alette was filled with the wonderment of being with Richard and her complete lack of negative thoughts. *Che cosa significa?*

A uniformed guard approached them. 'Good afternoon, Richard.'

'Afternoon, Brian. This is my friend, Alette Peters. Brian Hill.'

Brian said to Alette, 'Are you enjoying the museum?'

'Oh, yes. It's wonderful.'

'Richard's teaching me to paint,' Brian said.

Alette looked at Richard. 'You are?'

Richard said modestly, 'Oh, I'm just guiding him a little bit.'

'He's doing more than that, miss. I've always wanted to be a painter. That's why I took this job at the museum, because I love art. Anyway, Richard comes here a lot and paints. When I saw his work, I thought, 'I want to be like him.' So I asked him if he'd teach me, and he's been great. Have you seen any of his paintings?'

'I have,' Alette said. 'They're wonderful.'

When they left him, Alette said, 'It's lovely of you to do that, Richard.'

'I like to do things for people,' and he was looking at Alette.

When they were walking out of the museum, Richard said, 'My roommate is at a party tonight. Why don't we stop up at my place?' He smiled. 'I have some paintings I'd like to show you.'

Alette squeezed his hand. 'Not yet, Richard.'

'Whatever you say. I'll see you next weekend?'

'Yes.'

And he had no idea how much she was looking forward to it.

Richard walked Alette to the parking lot where she had parked her car. He waved good-bye as she drove off.

As Alette was going to sleep that night, she thought, *It's like a miracle. Richard has freed me.* She fell asleep, dreaming of him.

At two o'clock in the morning, Richard Melton's roommate, Gary, returned from a birthday party. The apartment was dark. He switched on the lights in the living room. 'Richard?'

He started toward the bedroom. At the door he looked inside and was sick to his stomach.

'Calm down, son.' Detective Whittier looked at the shivering figure in the chair. 'Now, let's go over it again. Did he have any enemies, someone mad enough at him to do this?'

Gary swallowed. 'No. Everyone . . . everyone liked Richard.'

'Someone didn't. How long have you and Richard lived together?'

'Two years.'

'Were you lovers?'

'For God's sake,' Gary said indignantly. 'No. We were friends. We lived together for financial reasons.'

Detective Whittier looked around the small apartment. 'Sure as hell wasn't a burglary,' he said. 'There's nothing here to steal. Was your roommate seeing anyone romantically?'

'No – Well, yes. There was a girl he was interested in. I think he was really starting to like her.'

'Do you know her name?'

'Yes. Alette. Alette Peters. She works in Cupertino.'

Detective Whittier and Detective Reynolds looked at each other.

'Cupertino?'

'Jesus,' Reynolds said.

Thirty minutes later, Detective Whittier was on the phone with Sheriff Dowling. 'Sheriff, I thought you might be interested to know that we have a murder here that's the same M.O. as the case you had in Cupertino – multiple stab wounds and castration.'

'My God!'

'I just had a talk with the FBI. Their computer shows that there have been three previous castration killings very similar to this one. The first one happened in Bedford, Pennsylvania, about ten years ago, the next one was a man named Dennis Tibble – that was your case – then there was the same M.O. in Quebec City, and now this one.'

'It doesn't make sense. Pennsylvania . . . Cupertino . . . Quebec City . . . San Francisco . . . Is there any link?'

'We're trying to find one. Quebec requires passports. The FBI is doing a cross-check to see if anyone who was in Quebec City around Christmas was in any of the other cities at the times of the murders . . .'

When the media got wind of what was happening, their stories were splashed across the front pages across the world:

SERIAL KILLER LOOSE . . .

QUATRES HOMMES BRUTALEMENT TUÉS ET CASTRÉS . . .

WIR SUCHEN FÜR EIN MANN DER CASTRIERT SEINE HOPFER . . .

MANIAC DI HOMICIDAL SULLO SPREE CRESPO DI UCCISIÓNE.

On the networks, self-important psychologists analyzed the killings.

'. . . and all the victims were men. Because of the way

they were stabbed and castrated, it is undoubtedly the work of a homosexual who . . .'

'. . . so if the police can find a connection between the victims, they will probably discover that it was the work of a lover the men had all scorned . . .'

'. . . but I would say they were random killings committed by someone who had a dominating mother . . .'

Saturday morning, Detective Whittier called Deputy Blake from San Francisco.

'Deputy, I have an update for you.'

'Go ahead.'

'I just got a call from the FBI. Cupertino is listed as the residence of an American who was in Quebec on the date of the Parent murder.'

'That's interesting. What's his name?'

'Her. Patterson. Ashley Patterson.'

At six o'clock that evening, Deputy Sam Blake rang the bell at Ashley Patterson's apartment. Through the closed door he heard her call out cautiously, 'Who is it?'

'Deputy Blake. I'd like to talk to you, Miss Patterson.'

There was a long silence, then the door opened. Ashley was standing there, looking wary.

'May I come in?'

'Yes, of course.' *Is this about Father? I must be careful.* Ashley led the deputy to a couch. 'What can I do for you, Deputy?'

'Would you mind answering a few questions?'

Ashley shifted uncomfortably. 'I – I don't know. Am I under suspicion for something?'

He smiled reassuringly. 'Nothing like that, Miss Patterson. This is just routine. We're investigating some murders.'

'I don't know anything about any murders,' she said quickly. *Too quickly?*

'You were in Quebec City recently, weren't you?'

'Yes.'

'Are you acquainted with Jean Claude Parent?'

'Jean Claude Parent?' She thought for a moment. 'No. I've never heard of him. Who is he?'

'He owns a jewelry store in Quebec City.'

Ashley shook her head. 'I didn't do any jewelry shopping in Quebec.'

'You worked with Dennis Tibble.'

Ashley felt the fear beginning to rise again. This *was* about her father. She said cautiously, 'I didn't work with him. He worked for the same company.'

'Of course. You go into San Francisco occasionally, don't you, Miss Patterson?'

Ashley wondered where this was leading. *Careful.* 'From time to time, yes.'

'Did you ever meet an artist there named Richard Melton?'

'No. I don't know anyone by that name.'

Deputy Blake sat there studying Ashley, frustrated. 'Miss Patterson, would you mind coming down to headquarters and taking a polygraph test? If you want to, you can call your lawyer and—'

'I don't need a lawyer. I'll be glad to take a test.'

The polygraph expert was a man named Keith Rosson, and he was one of the best. He had had to cancel a dinner date, but he was happy to oblige Sam Blake.

Ashley was seated in a chair, wired to the polygraph machine. Rosson had already spent forty-five minutes chatting with her, getting background information and evaluating her emotional state. Now he was ready to begin.

'Are you comfortable?'

'Yes.'

'Good. Let's start.' He pressed a button. 'What's your name?'

'Ashley Patterson.'

Rosson's eyes kept darting between Ashley and the polygraph printout.

'How old are you, Miss Patterson?'

'Twenty-eight.'

'Where do you live?'

'10964 Via Camino Court in Cupertino.'

'Are you employed?'

'Yes.'

'Do you like classical music?'

'Yes.'

'Do you know Richard Melton?'

'No.'

There was no change on the graph.

'Where do you work?'

'At Global Computer Graphics Corporation.'

'Do you enjoy your job?'

'Yes.'

'Do you work five days a week?'

'Yes.'

'Have you ever met Jean Claude Parent?'

'No.'

Still no change on the graph.

'Did you have breakfast this morning?'

'Yes.'

'Did you kill Dennis Tibble?'

'No.'

The questions continued for another thirty minutes and were repeated three times, in a different order.

When the session was over, Keith Rosson walked into Sam Blake's office and handed him the polygraph test. 'Clean as a whistle. There's a less than one percent chance that she's lying. You've got the wrong person.'

Ashley left police headquarters, giddy with relief. *Thank God it's over.* She had been terrified that they might ask questions that would involve her father, but that had not happened. *No one can connect Father with any of this now.*

She parked her car in the garage and took the elevator up to her apartment floor. She unlocked the door, went inside and carefully locked the door behind her. She felt drained, and at the same time, elated. *A nice hot bath,* Ashley thought. She walked into the bathroom and turned dead white. On her bathroom mirror, someone had scrawled in bright red lipstick YOU WILL DIE.

Chapter Nine

She was fighting hysteria. Her fingers were trembling so hard that she dialed three times trying to reach the number. She took a deep breath and tried again. Two . . . nine . . . nine . . . two . . . one . . . zero . . . one . . . The phone began to ring.

'Sheriff's Office.'

'Deputy Blake, please. Hurry!'

'Deputy Blake has gone home. Can someone else—?'

'No! I – Would you ask him to call me? This is Ashley Patterson. I need to talk to him right away.'

'Let me put you on hold, miss, and I'll see if I can reach him.'

Deputy Sam Blake was patiently listening to his wife, Serena, screaming at him. 'My brother works you like a horse, day and night, and he doesn't give you enough money to support me decently. Why don't you demand a raise? *Why?*'

They were at the dinner table. 'Would you pass the potatoes, dear?'

Serena reached over and slammed the dish of potatoes in front of her husband. 'The trouble is that they don't appreciate you.'

'You're right, dear. May I have some gravy?'

'Aren't you listening to what I'm saying?' she yelled.

'Every word, my love. This dinner is delicious. You're a great cook.'

'How can I fight you, you bastard, if you won't fight back?'

He took a mouthful of veal. 'It's because I love you, darling.'

The telephone rang. 'Excuse me.' He got up and picked up the receiver. 'Hello . . . Yes . . . Put her through . . . Miss Patterson?' He could hear her sobbing.

'Something – something terrible has happened. You've got to come over here right away.'

'I'm on my way.'

Serena got to her feet. *'What?* You're going out? We're in the middle of dinner!'

'It's an emergency, darling. I'll be back as soon as I can.' She watched him strap on his gun. He leaned over and kissed her. 'Wonderful dinner.'

Ashley opened the door for him the instant he arrived. Her cheeks were tear stained. She was shivering.

Sam Blake stepped into the apartment, looking around warily.

'Is anyone else here?'

'S-someone *was* here.' She was fighting for self-control. 'L-look . . .' She led him to the bathroom.

Deputy Blake read the words on the mirror out loud: 'You will die.'

He turned to Ashley. 'Do you have any idea who could have written that?'

'No,' Ashley said. 'This is my apartment. No one else has a key . . . And someone has been coming in here . . . Someone's been following me. Someone's planning to kill me.' She burst into tears. 'I can't s-stand this any longer.'

She was sobbing uncontrollably. Deputy Blake put his arm around her and patted her shoulder. 'Come on. It's going to be all right. We'll give you protection, and we'll find out who's behind this.'

Ashley took a deep breath. 'I'm sorry. I – I don't usually carry on like this. It's – it's just been horrible.'

'Let's talk,' Sam Blake said.

She managed to force a smile. 'All right.'

'How about a nice cup of tea?'

They sat talking over cups of hot tea. 'When did all this start, Miss Patterson?'

'About – about six months ago. I felt I was being followed. At first it was just a vague feeling, but then it began to grow. I *knew* I was being followed, but I couldn't see anyone. Then at work, someone got into my computer and drew a picture of a hand with a knife in it trying to – to stab me.'

'And do you have any idea who it could have been?'

'No.'

'You said someone has gotten into this apartment before today?'

'Yes. Once, someone turned on all the lights when I was gone. Another time I found a cigarette butt on my dressing table. I don't smoke. And someone opened a drawer and went through my . . . my underwear.' She took a deep breath. 'And now . . . this.'

'Do you have any boyfriends who might feel rejected?'

Ashley shook her head. 'No.'

'Have you had any business dealings where somebody's lost money because of you?'

'No.'

'No threats from anyone?'

99

'No.' She thought of telling him about the lost weekend in Chicago, but that might involve mentioning her father. She decided to say nothing.

'I don't want to be alone here tonight,' Ashley said.

'All right. I'll call the station and have them send someone here to—'

'No! Please! I'm afraid to trust anyone else. Could you stay here with me, just until morning?'

'I don't think I—'

'Oh, please.' She was trembling.

He looked into her eyes and thought he had never seen anyone so terrified.

'Isn't there someplace you could stay tonight? Don't you have any friends who—?'

'What if it's one of my friends who's doing this?'

He nodded. 'Right. I'll stay. In the morning, I'll arrange for twenty-four-hour protection for you.'

'Thank you.' Her voice was filled with relief.

He patted Ashley's hand. 'And don't worry. I promise you that we'll get to the bottom of this. Let me call Sheriff Dowling and tell him what's going on.'

He spoke on the phone for five minutes, and when he hung up, he said, 'I'd better call my wife.'

'Of course.'

Deputy Blake picked up the telephone again and dialed. 'Hello, darling. I won't be home tonight, so why don't you watch some tel—?'

'You won't *what*? Where are you, with one of your cheap whores?'

Ashley could hear her screaming over the phone.

'Serena—'

'You're not fooling me.'

'Serena—'

100

'That's all you men think about – getting laid.'

'Serena—'

'Well, I won't put up with it any longer.'

'Serena—'

'That's the thanks I get for being such a good wife . . .'

The one-sided conversation went on for another ten minutes. Finally, Deputy Blake replaced the receiver and turned to Ashley, embarrassed.

'I'm sorry about that. She's not like that.'

Ashley looked at him and said, 'I understand.'

'No – I mean it. Serena acts that way because she's scared.'

Ashley looked at him curiously. 'Scared?'

He was silent for a moment. 'Serena is dying. She has cancer. It was in remission for a while. It first started about seven years ago. We've been married for five years.'

'So you knew . . . ?'

'Yes. It didn't matter. I love her.' He stopped. 'It's gotten worse lately. She's scared because she's afraid to die and she's afraid I'll leave her. All the yelling is a cover-up to hide that fear.'

'I'm – I'm so sorry.'

'She's a wonderful person. Inside, she's gentle and caring and loving. That's the Serena I know.'

Ashley said, 'I'm sorry if I caused any—'

'Not at all.' He looked around.

Ashley said, 'There's just the one bedroom. You can take it, and I'll sleep on the couch.'

Deputy Blake shook his head. 'The couch will be fine for me.'

Ashley said, 'I can't tell you how grateful I am.'

'No problem, Miss Patterson.' He watched her go into a linen closet and take out sheets and blankets.

She walked over to the couch and spread the linen out. 'I hope that you'll—'

'Perfect. I don't plan on doing much sleeping, anyway.' He checked the windows to make sure they were locked and then walked over to the door and double-bolted it. 'All right.' He placed his gun on the table next to the couch. 'You get a good night's sleep. In the morning, we'll get everything organized.'

Ashley nodded. She walked over to him and kissed him on the cheek. 'Thank you.'

Deputy Blake watched her walk into the bedroom and close the door. He walked back to the windows and checked them again. It was going to be a long night.

At FBI headquarters in Washington, Special Agent Ramirez was talking to Roland Kingsley, the chief of his section.

'We have the fingerprints and DNA reports found at the murder scenes in Bedford, Cupertino, Quebec, and San Francisco. We just got in the final DNA report. The fingerprints from the scenes all match, and the DNA traces match.'

Kingsley nodded. 'So it's definitely a serial killer.'

'No question.'

'Let's find the bastard.'

At six o'clock in the morning, Deputy Sam Blake's naked body was found by the wife of the building superintendent in the alley that ran behind Ashley Patterson's apartment building.

He had been stabbed to death and castrated.

Chapter Ten

There were five of them: Sheriff Dowling, two plainclothes detectives and two uniformed policemen. They stood in the living room watching Ashley, sitting in a chair, weeping hysterically.

Sheriff Dowling said, 'You're the only one who can help us, Miss Patterson.'

Ashley looked up at the men and nodded. She took several deep breaths. 'I'll – I'll try.'

'Let's start at the beginning. Deputy Blake spent the night here?'

'Y-yes. I asked him to. I – I was desperately afraid.'

'This apartment has one bedroom.'

'That's right.'

'Where did Deputy Blake sleep?'

Ashley pointed to the couch, which had a blanket and a pillow on it. 'He – he spent the night there.'

'What time did you go to bed?'

Ashley thought for a moment. 'It – it must have been around midnight. I was nervous. We had some tea and talked for a while, and I felt calmer. I brought out blankets and a pillow for him, then I went into my bedroom.' She was fighting for self-control.

'Was that the last time you saw him?'

'Yes.'

'And you went to sleep?'

'Not immediately. I finally took a sleeping pill. The next thing I remember, I was awakened by a woman's screams coming from the alley.' She began to tremble.

'Do you think someone came into this apartment and killed Deputy Blake?'

'I – I don't know,' Ashley said desperately. 'Someone has been getting in here. They even wrote a threatening message on my mirror.'

'He told me about that on the telephone.'

'He might have heard something and – and gone outside to investigate,' Ashley said.

Sheriff Dowling shook his head. 'I don't think he would have gone out naked.'

Ashley cried. '*I don't know! I don't know!* It's a nightmare.' She covered her eyes with her hands.

Sheriff Dowling said, 'I'd like to look around the apartment. Do I need a search warrant?'

'Of course not. G-go ahead.'

Sheriff Dowling nodded to the detectives. One of them went into the bedroom. The other one went into the kitchen.

'What did you and Deputy Blake talk about?'

Ashley took a deep breath. 'I – I told him about – about the things that have been happening to me. He was very –' She looked up at the sheriff. 'Why would anyone kill him? *Why?*'

'I don't know, Miss Patterson. We're going to find out.'

Lieutenant Elton, the detective who had gone into the kitchen, stood in the doorway. 'Could I see you for a moment, Sheriff?'

'Excuse me.'

Sheriff Dowling walked into the kitchen.

'What?'

Lieutenant Elton said, 'I found this in the sink.' He was holding up a bloodstained butcher knife by the edge of the blade. 'It hasn't been washed. I think we're going to get some prints.'

Kostoff, the second detective, came in from the bedroom and hurried into the kitchen. He was holding an emerald ring, mounted with diamonds. 'I found this in the jewelry box in the bedroom. It fits the description we got from Quebec of the ring that Jean Claude Parent gave to Toni Prescott.'

The three men were looking at one another.

'This doesn't make any sense,' the sheriff said. Gingerly, he took the butcher knife and the ring and walked back into the living room. He held out the knife and said, 'Miss Patterson, is this your knife?'

Ashley looked at it. 'I – Yes. It could be. Why?'

Sheriff Dowling held out the ring. 'Have you ever seen this ring before?'

Ashley looked at it and shook her head. 'No.'

'We found it in your jewelry box.'

They watched her expression. She was completely bewildered.

She whispered, 'I – Someone must have put it there . . .'

'Who would do a thing like that?'

Her face was pale. 'I don't know.'

A detective walked in the front door. 'Sheriff?'

'Yes, Baker?' He motioned the detective over to a corner. 'What have you got?'

'We found bloodstains on the corridor rug and in the elevator. It looks like the body was laid on a sheet, dragged into the elevator and dumped in the alley.'

'Holy shit!' Sheriff Dowling turned to Ashley. 'Miss Patterson, you're under arrest. I'm going to read you

105

your rights. You have the right to remain silent. If you give up the right to remain silent, anything you say may be used against you in a court of law. You are entitled to an attorney. If you cannot afford an attorney, one will be appointed to you by the courts.'

When they reached the sheriff's office, Sheriff Dowling said, 'Fingerprint her and book her.'

Ashley went through the procedure like an automaton. When it was finished, Sheriff Dowling said, 'You have the right to make one phone call.'

Ashley looked up at him and said dully, 'I have no one to call.' *I can't call my father.*

Sheriff Dowling watched Ashley being led into a cell.

'I'll be goddamned if I understand it. Did you see her polygraph test? I would swear she's innocent.'

Detective Kostoff walked in. 'Sam had sex before he died. We ran an ultraviolet light over his body and the sheet he was wrapped in. We got a positive result for semen and vaginal stains. We—'

Sheriff Dowling groaned. 'Hold it!' He had been putting off the moment when he would have to give his sister the news. It had to be done now. He sighed and said, 'I'll be back.'

Twenty minutes later, he was at Sam's house.

'Well, this is an unexpected pleasure,' Serena said. 'Is Sam with you?'

'No, Serena. I have to ask you a question.' This was going to be difficult.

She was looking at him curiously. 'Yes?'

'Did – did you and Sam have sex within the last twenty-four hours?'

The expression on her face changed. 'What? We . . . No. Why do you want to –? Sam's not coming back, is he?'

'I hate to tell you this, but he—'

'He left me for her, didn't he? I knew it would happen. I don't blame him. I was a terrible wife to him. I—'

'Serena, Sam's dead.'

'I was always yelling at him. I really didn't mean it. I remember—'

He took her by the arms. 'Serena, Sam's dead.'

'One time we were going out to the beach and—'

He was shaking her. 'Listen to me. Sam is dead.'

'– and we were going to have a picnic.'

As he looked at her, he realized that she had heard him.

'So we're at the beach and this man comes up and says, 'Give me your money.' And Sam says, "Let me see your gun."'

Sheriff Dowling stood there and let her talk. She was in a state of shock, in complete denial.

'. . . that was Sam. Tell me about this woman he went away with. Is she pretty? Sam tells me I'm pretty all the time, but I know I'm not. He says it to make me feel good because he loves me. He'll never leave me. He'll be back. You'll see. He loves me.' She went on talking.

Sheriff Dowling went to the phone and dialed a number. 'Get a nurse over here.' He went over and put his arms around his sister. 'Everything's going to be all right.'

'Did I tell you about the time that Sam and I—?'

Fifteen minutes later, a nurse arrived.

'Take good care of her,' Sheriff Dowling said.

There was a conference in Sheriff Dowling's office. 'There's a call for you on line one.'

Sheriff Dowling picked up the phone. 'Yeah?'

'Sheriff, this is Special Agent Ramirez at FBI headquarters in Washington. We have some information for you on the serial killer case. We didn't have any prints on file for Ashley Patterson because she had no criminal record, and before 1988, the DMV didn't require thumbprints in the state of California to get a driver's license.'

'Go ahead.'

'In the beginning, we thought it had to be a computer glitch, but we checked it out and . . .'

For the next five minutes, Sheriff Dowling sat there listening, an incredulous expression on his face. When he finally spoke, he said, 'Are you sure there's no mistake? It doesn't seem . . . All of them . . . ? I see . . . Thank you very much.'

He replaced the receiver and sat there for a long moment. Then he looked up. 'That was the FBI lab in Washington. They've finished cross-checking the fingerprints on the bodies of the victims. Jean Claude Parent in Quebec was seeing an English woman named Toni Prescott when he was murdered.'

'Yes.'

'Richard Melton in San Francisco was seeing an Italian lady named Alette Peters when he was killed.'

They nodded.

'And last night Sam Blake was with Ashley Patterson.'

'Right.'

Sheriff Dowling took a deep breath. 'Ashley Patterson . . .'

'Yes?'

'Toni Prescott . . .'

'Yes?'

'Alette Peters . . .'

'Yes?'

'They're all the same fucking person.'

Book Two

Chapter Eleven

Robert Crowther, the real estate broker from Bryant & Crowther, opened the door with a flourish and announced, 'Here's the terrace. You can look down on Coit Tower from here.'

He watched the young husband and wife step outside and walk over to the balustrade. The view from there was magnificent, the city of San Francisco spread out far below them in a spectacular panorama. Robert Crowther saw the couple exchange a glance and a secret smile, and he was amused. They were trying to hide their excitement. The pattern was always the same: Prospective buyers believed that if they showed too much enthusiasm, the price would go up.

For this duplex penthouse, Crowther thought wryly, *the price is high enough already*. He was concerned about whether the couple could afford it. The man was a lawyer, and young lawyers did not make that much.

They were an attractive couple, obviously very much in love. David Singer was in his early thirties, blond and intelligent-looking, with an engaging boyishness about him. His wife, Sandra, was lovely looking and warm.

Robert Crowther had noticed the bulge around her stomach and had said, 'The second guest room would be perfect for a nursery. There's a playground a block away and two schools in the neighborhood.' He had watched them exchange that secret smile again.

The duplex penthouse consisted of an upstairs master bedroom with a bath and a guest room. On the first floor was a spacious living room, a dining room, a library, a kitchen, a second guest bedroom and two bathrooms. Almost every room had a view of the city.

Robert watched the two of them as they walked through the apartment again. They stood in a corner whispering.

'I love it,' Sandra was saying to David. 'And it would be great for the baby. But, darling, can we afford it? It's six hundred thousand dollars!'

'Plus maintenance,' David added. 'The bad news is that we can't afford it today. The good news is that we're going to be able to afford it on Thursday. The genie is coming out of the magic bottle, and our lives are going to change.'

'I know,' she said happily. 'Isn't it wonderful!'

'Should we go ahead with it?'

Sandra took a deep breath. 'Let's go for it.'

David grinned, waved a hand and said, 'Welcome home, Mrs Singer.'

Arm in arm, they walked over to where Robert Crowther was waiting. 'We'll take it,' David told him.

'Congratulations. It's one of the choicest residences in San Francisco. You're going to be very happy here.'

'I'm sure we are.'

'You're lucky. I have to tell you, we have a few other people who are very interested in it.'

'How much of a down payment will you want?'

'A deposit of ten thousand dollars now will be fine. I'll have the papers drawn up. When you sign, we'll require another sixty thousand dollars. Your bank can work out a schedule of monthly payments on a twenty- or thirty-year mortgage.'

David glanced at Sandra. 'Okay.'

'I'll have the papers prepared.'

'Can we look around once more?' Sandra asked eagerly.

Crowther smiled benevolently. 'Take all the time you want, Mrs Singer. It's yours.'

'It all seems like a wonderful dream, David. I can't believe it's really happening.'

'It's happening.' David took her in his arms. 'I want to make all your dreams come true.'

'You do, darling.'

They had been living in a small, two-bedroom apartment in the Marina District, but with the baby coming, it was going to be crowded. Until now, they could never have afforded the duplex on Nob Hill, but Thursday was partnership day at the international law firm of Kincaid, Turner, Rose & Ripley, where David worked. Out of a possible twenty-five candidates, six would be chosen to enter the rarefied air of the firm's partnership, and everyone agreed that David was one of those who would be selected. Kincaid, Turner, Rose & Ripley, with offices in San Francisco, New York, London, Paris and Tokyo, was one of the most prestigious law firms in the world, and it was usually the number one target for graduates of all the top law schools.

The firm used the stick-and-carrot approach on their young associates. The senior partners took merciless advantage of them, disregarding their hours and illnesses and handing the younger lawyers the donkey's work that they themselves did not want to be bothered with. It was a heavy pressure, twenty-four-hour-a-day job. That was the stick. Those who stayed on did so because of the carrot. The carrot was the promise of a partnership in the firm. Becoming a partner meant a larger salary, a piece of the huge corporate-profit pie, a spacious office with a view, a private washroom, assignments overseas and myriad other perks.

David had practiced corporate law with Kincaid, Turner, Rose & Ripley for six years, and it had been a mixed blessing. The hours were horrific and the stress was enormous, but David, determined to hang in there for the partnership, had stayed and had done a brilliant job. Now the day was finally at hand.

When David and Sandra left the real estate agent, they went shopping. They bought a bassinet, high chair, stroller, playpen and clothes for the baby, whom they were already thinking of as Jeffrey.

'Let's get him some toys,' David said.

'There's plenty of time for that.' Sandra laughed.

After shopping, they wandered around the city, walking along the waterfront at Ghirardelli Square, past the Cannery to Fisherman's Wharf. They had lunch at the American Bistro.

It was Saturday, a perfect San Francisco day for monogrammed leather briefcases and power ties, dark suits and discreetly monogrammed shirts, a day for power lunches and penthouses. A lawyer's day.

David and Sandra had met three years earlier at a small dinner party. David had gone to the party with the daughter of a client of the firm. Sandra was a paralegal, working for a rival firm. At dinner, Sandra and David had gotten into an argument about a decision that had been rendered in a political case in Washington. As the others at the dinner table watched, the argument between the two of them had become more and more heated. And in the middle of it,

David and Sandra realized that neither of them cared about the court's decision. They were showing off for each other, engaged in a verbal mating dance.

David telephoned Sandra the next day. 'I'd like to finish discussing that decision,' David said. 'I think it's important.'

'So do I,' Sandra agreed.

'Could we talk about it at dinner tonight?'

Sandra hesitated. She had already made a dinner date for that evening. 'Yes,' she said. 'Tonight will be fine.'

They were together from that night on. One year from the day they met, they were married.

Joseph Kincaid, the firm's senior partner, had given David the weekend off.

David's salary at Kincaid, Turner, Rose & Ripley was $45,000 a year. Sandra kept her job as a paralegal. But now, with the baby coming, their expenses were about to go up.

'I'll have to give up my job in a few months,' Sandra said. 'I don't want a nanny bringing up our baby, darling. I want to be here for him.' The sonogram had shown that the baby was a boy.

'We'll be able to handle it,' David assured her. The partnership was going to transform their lives.

David had begun to put in even longer hours. He wanted to make sure that he was not overlooked on partnership day.

Thursday morning, as David got dressed, he was watching the news on television.

An anchorman was saying breathlessly, 'We have a breaking story . . . Ashley Patterson, the daughter of the prominent San Francisco doctor Steven Patterson, has been arrested as the suspected serial killer the police and the FBI have been searching for . . .'

David stood in front of the television set, frozen.

'. . . last night Santa Clara County Sheriff Matt Dowling announced Ashley Patterson's arrest for a series of murders that included bloody castrations. Sheriff Dowling told reporters, "There's no doubt that we have the right person. The evidence is conclusive."'

Dr Steven Patterson. David's mind went back, remembering the past . . .

He was twenty-one years old and just starting law school. He came home from class one day to find his mother on the bedroom floor, unconscious. He called 911, and an ambulance took his mother to San Francisco Memorial Hospital. David waited outside the emergency room until a doctor came to talk to him.

'Is she – Is she going to be all right?'

The doctor hesitated. 'We had one of our cardiologists examine her. She has a ruptured cord in her mitral valve.'

'What does that mean?' David demanded.

'I'm afraid there's nothing we can do for her. She's too weak to have a transplant, and mini heart surgery is new and too risky.'

David felt suddenly faint. 'How – how long can she—?'

'I'd say a few more days, maybe a week. I'm sorry, son.'

David stood there, panicky. 'Isn't there *anyone* who can help her?'

'I'm afraid not. The only one who might have been able to help is Steven Patterson, but he's a very—'

'Who's Steven Patterson?'

'Dr Patterson pioneered minimally invasive heart surgery.

116

But between his schedule and his research, there's no chance that—'

David was gone.

He called Dr Patterson's office from a pay phone in the hospital corridor. 'I'd like to make an appointment with Dr Patterson. It's for my mother. She—'

'I'm sorry. We're not accepting any new appointments. The first available time would be six months from now.'

'*She doesn't have six months,*' David shouted.

'I'm sorry. I can refer you to—'

David slammed down the phone.

The following morning David went to Dr Patterson's office. The waiting room was crowded. David walked up to the receptionist. 'I'd like to make an appointment to see Dr Patterson. My mother's very ill and—'

She looked up at him and said, 'You called yesterday, didn't you?'

'Yes.'

'I told you then. We don't have any appointments open, and we're not making any just now.'

'I'll wait,' David said stubbornly.

'You can't wait. The doctor is—'

David took a seat. He watched the people in the waiting room being called into the inner office one by one until finally he was the only one left.

At six o'clock, the receptionist said, 'There's no point in waiting any longer. Dr Patterson has gone home.'

David went to visit his mother in intensive care that evening.

'You can only stay a minute,' a nurse warned him. 'She's very weak.'

117

David stepped inside the room, and his eyes filled with tears. His mother was attached to a respirator with tubes running into her arms and through her nose. She looked whiter than the sheets she lay on. Her eyes were closed.

David moved close to her and said, 'It's me, Mom. I'm not going to let anything happen to you. You're going to be fine.' Tears were running down his cheeks. 'Do you hear me? We're going to fight this thing. Nobody can lick the two of us, not as long as we're together. I'm going to get you the best doctor in the world. You just hang in there. I'll be back tomorrow.' He bent down and gently kissed her cheek.

Will she be alive tomorrow?

The following afternoon, David went to the garage in the basement of the building where Dr Patterson had his offices. An attendant was parking cars.

He came up to David. 'May I help you?'

'I'm waiting for my wife,' David said. 'She's seeing Dr Patterson.'

The attendant smiled. 'He's a great guy.'

'He was telling us about some fancy car that he owns.' David paused, trying to remember. 'Was it a Cadillac?'

The attendant shook his head. 'Naw.' He pointed to a Rolls-Royce parked in the corner. 'It's that Rolls over there.'

David said, 'Right. I think he said he has a Cadillac, too.'

'Wouldn't surprise me,' the attendant said. He hurried off to park an incoming car.

David walked casually toward the Rolls. When he was sure no one was watching, he opened the door, slipped into the back-seat and got down on the floor. He lay there, cramped and uncomfortable, willing Dr Patterson to come out.

At 6:15, David felt a slight jar as the front door of the car opened and someone moved into the driver's seat. He heard the engine start, and then the car began to move.

'Good night, Dr Patterson.'

'Good night, Marco.'

The car left the garage, and David felt it turn a corner. He waited for two minutes, then took a deep breath and sat up.

Dr Patterson saw him in the rearview mirror. He said calmly, 'If this is a holdup, I have no cash with me.'

'Turn onto a side street and pull over to the curb.'

Dr Patterson nodded. David watched warily as the doctor turned the car onto a side street, pulled over to the curb and stopped.

'I'll give you what cash I have on me,' Dr Patterson said. 'You can take the car. There's no need for violence. If—'

David had slid into the front seat. 'This isn't a holdup. I don't want the car.'

Dr Patterson was looking at him with annoyance. 'What the hell do you want?'

'My name is Singer. My mother's dying. I want you to save her.'

There was a flicker of relief on Dr Patterson's face, replaced by a look of anger.

'Make an appointment with my—'

'There's no time to make a goddamn appointment.' David was yelling. 'She's going to *die*, and I'm not going to let that happen.' He was fighting to control himself. 'Please. The other doctors told me you're the only hope we have.'

Dr Patterson was watching him, still wary. 'What's her problem?'

'She has a – a ruptured cord in her mitral valve. The

119

doctors are afraid to operate. They say that you're the only one who can save her life.'

Dr Patterson shook his head. 'My schedule—'

'I don't give a shit about your schedule! This is my mother. You've got to save her! She's all I have . . .'

There was a long silence. David sat there, his eyes tightly shut. He heard Dr Patterson's voice.

'I won't promise a damn thing, but I'll see her. Where is she?'

David turned to look at him. 'She's in the intensive care unit at San Francisco Memorial Hospital.'

'Meet me there at eight o'clock tomorrow morning.'

David had difficulty finding his voice. 'I don't know how to—'

'Remember, I'm not promising anything. And I don't appreciate being scared out of my wits, young man. Next time, try the telephone.'

David sat there, rigid.

Dr Patterson looked at him. 'What?'

'There's another problem.'

'Oh, really?'

'I – I don't have any money. I'm a law student, and I'm working my way through law school.'

Dr Patterson was staring at him.

David said passionately, 'I swear I'll find a way to pay you back. If it takes all my life, I'll see that you get paid. I know how expensive you are, and I—'

'I don't think you do, son.'

'I have no one else to turn to, Dr Patterson. I – I'm begging you.'

There was another silence.

'How many years of law school have you had?'

'None. I'm just starting.'

'But you expect to be able to pay me back?'

'I swear it.'

'Get the hell out.'

When David got home, he was certain he was going to be picked up by the police for kidnapping, threatening bodily harm, God only knew what. But nothing happened. The question in his mind was whether Dr Patterson was going to show up at the hospital.

When David walked into the intensive care ward the next morning, Dr Patterson was there, examining David's mother.

David watched, his heart pounding, his throat dry.

Dr Patterson turned to one of a group of doctors standing there. 'Get her up to the operating room, Al. Stat!'

As they started to slide David's mother onto a gurney, David said hoarsely, 'Is she—?'

'We'll see.'

Six hours later, David was in the waiting room when Dr Patterson approached him.

David jumped to his feet. 'How is –?' He was afraid to finish the question.

'She's going to be fine. Your mother's a strong lady.'

David stood there, filled with an overpowering sense of relief. He breathed a silent prayer. *Thank you, God.*

Dr Patterson was watching him. 'I don't even know your first name.'

'David, sir.'

'Well, David sir, do you know why I decided to do this?'

'No . . .'

'Two reasons. Your mother's condition was a challenge for me. I like challenges. The second reason was you.'

'I – I don't understand.'

'What you did was the kind of thing I might have done myself when I was younger. You showed imagination. Now' – his tone changed – 'you said you were going to repay me.'

David's heart sank. 'Yes, sir. One day—'

'How about now?'

David swallowed. *'Now?'*

'I'll make you a deal. Do you know how to drive?'

'Yes, sir . . .'

'All right. I get tired of driving that big car around. You drive me to work every morning and pick me up at six or seven o'clock every evening for one year. At the end of that time, I'll consider my fee paid . . .'

That was the deal. David drove Dr Patterson to the office and back home every day, and in exchange, Dr Patterson saved the life of David's mother.

During that year, David learned to revere Dr Patterson. Despite the doctor's occasional outbursts of temper, he was the most selfless man David had ever known. He was heavily involved in charity work and donated his spare time to free clinics. Driving to and from the office or hospital, he and David had long talks.

'What kind of law are you studying, David?'

'Criminal law.'

'Why? So you can help the damn scoundrels get off scot-free?'

'No, sir. There are a lot of honest people caught up in the law who need help. I want to help them.'

When the year was up, Dr Patterson shook David's hand and said, 'We're even . . .'

*   *   *

122

David had not seen Steven Patterson in years, but he kept coming across his name.

'Dr Steven Patterson opened a free clinic for babies with AIDS . . .'

'Dr Steven Patterson arrived in Kenya today to open the Patterson Medical Center . . .'

'Work on the Patterson Charity Shelter began today . . .'

He seemed to be everywhere, donating his time and his money to those who needed him.

Sandra's voice shook David out of his reverie. 'David. Are you all right?'

He turned away from the television set. 'They've just arrested Steven Patterson's daughter for those serial killings.'

Sandra said, 'That's terrible! I'm so sorry, darling.'

'He gave Mother seven more years of a wonderful life. It's unfair that anything like that should happen to a man like him. He's the greatest gentleman I've ever known, Sandra. He doesn't deserve this. How could he have a monster like that for a daughter?' He looked at his watch. 'Damn! I'm going to be late.'

'You haven't had breakfast.'

'I'm too upset to eat.' He glanced toward the television set. 'This . . . and today's partnership day . . .'

'You're going to get it. There's no question about it.'

'There's *always* a question about it, honey. Every year, someone who's supposed to be a shoo-in winds up in the loser's box.'

She hugged him and said, 'They'll be lucky to have you.'

He leaned over and kissed her. 'Thanks, baby. I don't know what I'd do without you.'

'You'll never have to. You'll call me as soon as you get the news, won't you, David?'

'Of course I will. We'll go out and celebrate.' And the words reverberated in his mind. Years ago, he had said to someone else, *'We'll go out and celebrate.'*

And he had killed her.

The offices of Kincaid, Turner, Rose & Ripley occupied three floors in the TransAmerica Pyramid in downtown San Francisco. When David Singer walked through the doors, he was greeted with knowing smiles. It seemed to him that there was even a different quality in the 'good mornings.' They knew they were addressing a future partner in the firm.

On the way to his small office, David passed the newly decorated office that would belong to one of the chosen partners, and he could not resist looking inside. It was a large, beautiful office with a private washroom, a desk and chairs facing a picture window with a magnificent view of the Bay. He stood there a moment, drinking it in.

When David walked into his office, his secretary, Holly, said, 'Good morning, Mr Singer.' There was a lilt in her voice.

'Good morning, Holly.'

'I have a message for you.'

'Yes?'

'Mr Kincaid would like to see you in his office at five o'clock.' She broke into a broad smile.

So it was really happening. 'Great!'

She moved closer to David and said, 'I think I should also tell you, I had coffee with Dorothy, Mr Kincaid's secretary, this morning. She says you're at the top of the list.'

David grinned. 'Thanks, Holly.'

124

'Would you like some coffee?'

'Love it.'

'Hot and strong, coming up.'

David walked over to his desk. It was heaped with briefs and contracts and files.

Today was the day. Finally. *'Mr Kincaid would like to see you in his office at five o'clock ... You're at the top of the list.'*

He was tempted to telephone Sandra with the news. Something held him back. *I'll wait until it happens*, he thought.

David spent the next two hours dealing with the material on his desk. At eleven o'clock, Holly came in. 'There's a Dr Patterson here to see you. He has no app—'

He looked up in surprise. 'Dr Patterson is *here?*'

'Yes.'

David rose. 'Send him in.'

Steven Patterson came in, and David tried to conceal his reaction. The doctor looked old and tired.

'Hello, David.'

'Dr Patterson. Please, sit down.' David watched him slowly take a chair. 'I saw the news this morning. I – I can't tell you how very sorry I am.'

Dr Patterson nodded wearily. 'Yes. It's been quite a blow.' He looked up. 'I need your help, David.'

'Of course,' David said eagerly. 'Anything I can do. *Anything*.'

'I want you to represent Ashley.'

It took a moment for the words to sink in. 'I – I can't do that. I'm not a criminal defense lawyer.'

Dr Patterson looked him in the eye and said, 'Ashley's not a criminal.'

125

'I – You don't understand, Dr Patterson. I'm a corporate lawyer. I can recommend an excellent—'

'I've already had calls from half a dozen top criminal defense lawyers. They all want to represent her.' He leaned forward in his chair. 'But they're not interested in my daughter, David. This is a high-profile case, and they're looking for the limelight. They don't give a damn about her. I do. She's all I have.'

'I want you to save my mother's life. She's all I have.' David said, 'I really want to help you, but—'

'When you got out of law school, you went to work for a criminal law firm.'

David's heart began to beat faster. 'That's true, but—'

'You were a criminal defense lawyer for several years.'

David nodded. 'Yes, but I – I gave it up. That was a long time ago and—'

'Not that long ago, David. And you told me how much you loved it. Why did you quit and go into corporate law?'

David sat there, silent for a moment. 'It's not important.'

Dr Patterson took out a handwritten letter and handed it to David. David knew what it said, without reading it.

Dear Dr Patterson,

There are no words that can ever express how much I owe you and how much I appreciate your great generosity. If there's ever anything at all that I can do for you, all you have to do is ask me, and it shall be done without question.

David stared at the letter without seeing it.

'David, will you talk to Ashley?'

126

David nodded. 'Yes, of course I'll talk to her, but I—'

Dr Patterson rose. 'Thank you.'

David watched him walk out the door.

'Why did you quit and go into corporate law?'

Because I made a mistake, and an innocent woman I loved is dead. I swore I would never take anyone's life in my hands again. Ever.

I can't defend Ashley Patterson.

David pressed down the intercom button. 'Holly, would you ask Mr Kincaid if he can see me now?'

'Yes, sir.'

Thirty minutes later, David was walking into the elaborate offices of Joseph Kincaid. Kincaid was in his sixties, a gray monochrome of a man, physically, mentally and emotionally.

'Well,' he said as David walked in the door, 'you're an anxious young fellow, aren't you? Our meeting wasn't supposed to be until five o'clock.'

David approached the desk. 'I know. I came here to discuss something else, Joseph.'

Years ago, David had made the mistake of calling him Joe, and the old man had had a fit. *'Don't you ever call me Joe.'*

'Sit down, David.'

David took a seat.

'Cigar? They're from Cuba.'

'No, thanks.'

'What's on your mind?'

'Dr Steven Patterson was just in to see me.'

Kincaid said, 'He was on the news this morning. Damned shame. What did he want with you?'

'He asked me to defend his daughter.'

Kincaid looked at David, surprised. 'You're not a criminal defense lawyer.'

'I told him that.'

'Well, then.' Kincaid was thoughtful for a moment. 'You know, I'd like to get Dr Patterson as a client. He's very influential. He could bring a lot of business to this firm. He has connections with several medical organizations that—'

'There's more.'

Kincaid looked at David, quizzically. 'Oh?'

'I promised him I'd talk to his daughter.'

'I see. Well, I suppose there's no harm in that. Talk to her, and then we'll find a good defense attorney to represent her.'

'That's my plan.'

'Good. We'll be building up some points with him. You go ahead.' He smiled. 'I'll see you at five o'clock.'

'Right. Thank you, Joseph.'

As David walked back to his office, he wondered to himself, *Why in the world would Dr Patterson insist on having me represent his daughter?*

Chapter Twelve

At the Santa Clara County Jail, Ashley Patterson sat in her cell, too traumatized to try to make sense of how she got there. She was fiercely glad that she was in jail because the bars would keep out whoever was doing this to her. She wrapped the cell around herself like a blanket, trying to ward off the awful, inexplicable things that were happening to her. Her whole life had become a screaming nightmare. Ashley thought of all the mysterious events that had been happening: Someone breaking into her apartment and playing tricks on her . . . the trip to Chicago . . . the writing on her mirror . . . and now the police accusing her of unspeakable things she knew nothing about. There was some terrible conspiracy against her, but she had no idea who could be behind it or why.

Early that morning one of the guards had come to Ashley's cell. 'Visitor.'

The guard had led Ashley to the visitors' room, where her father was waiting for her.

He stood there, looking at her, his eyes grief stricken. 'Honey . . . I don't know what to say.'

Ashley whispered, 'I didn't do any of the terrible things they said I did.'

'I know you didn't. Someone's made an awful mistake, but we're going to straighten everything out.'

Ashley looked at her father and wondered how she could have ever thought he was the guilty one.

'. . . don't you worry,' he was saying. 'Everything's going to be fine. I am getting a lawyer for you. David Singer. He's one of the brightest young men I know. He'll be coming to see you. I want you to tell him everything.'

Ashley looked at her father and said hopelessly, 'Father, I – I don't know what to tell him. I don't know what's happening.'

'We'll get to the bottom of this, baby. I'm not going to let anyone hurt you. No one! Ever! You mean too much to me. You're all I have, honey.'

'And you're all I have,' Ashley whispered.

Ashley's father stayed for another hour. When he left, Ashley's world narrowed down to the small cell she was confined in. She lay on her cot, forcing herself not to think about anything. *This will be over soon, and I'll find that this is only a dream . . . Only a dream . . . Only a dream . . .* She slept.

The voice of a guard awakened her. 'You have a visitor.'

She was taken to the visitors' room, and Shane Miller was there, waiting.

He rose as Ashley entered. 'Ashley . . .'

Her heart began to pound. 'Oh, Shane!' She had never been so glad to see anyone in her life. Somehow she had known that he would come and free her, that he would arrange for them to let her go.

'Shane, I'm so glad to see you!'

'I'm glad to see you,' Shane said awkwardly. He looked around the drab visitors' room. 'Although I must say, not under these circumstances. When I heard the news, I – I couldn't believe it. What happened? What made you do it, Ashley?'

The color slowly drained from her face. 'What made me –? Do you think that I—?'

'Never mind,' Shane said quickly. 'Don't say any more. You shouldn't talk to anyone but your attorney.'

Ashley stood there, staring at him. He believed she was guilty. 'Why did you come here?'

'Well, I – I hate to do this now, but under – under the circumstances, I – the company – is terminating you. I mean . . . naturally, we can't afford to be connected with anything like this. It's bad enough that the newspapers have already mentioned that you work for Global. You understand, don't you? There's nothing personal in this.'

Driving down to San Jose, David Singer decided what he was going to say to Ashley Patterson. He would find out what he could from her and then turn the information over to Jesse Quiller, one of the best criminal defense lawyers in the country. If anyone could help Ashley, it was Jesse.

David was ushered into the office of Sheriff Dowling. He handed the sheriff his card. 'I'm an attorney. I'm here to see Ashley Patterson and—'

'She's expecting you.'

David looked at him in surprise. 'She is?'

'Yeah.' Sheriff Dowling turned to a deputy and nodded.

The deputy said to David, 'This way.' He led David into the visitors' room, and a few minutes later, Ashley was brought in from her cell.

Ashley Patterson was a complete surprise to David. He had met her once years ago, when he was in law school, chauffeuring her father. She had struck David as being an attractive, intelligent young girl. Now, he found himself

looking at a beautiful young woman with frightened eyes.
She took a seat across from him.

'Hello, Ashley. I'm David Singer.'

'My father told me you would be coming.' Her voice
was shaky.

'I just came to ask a few questions.'

She nodded.

'Before I do, I want you to know that anything you tell
me is privileged. It will just be between the two of us. But I
need to know the truth.' He hesitated. He had not intended
to go this far, but he wanted to be able to give Jesse Quiller
all the information he could, to persuade him to take the
case. 'Did you kill those men?'

'No!' Ashley's voice rang with conviction. 'I'm innocent!'

David pulled a sheet of paper from his pocket and glanced
at it. 'Were you acquainted with a Jim Cleary?'

'Yes. We – we were going to be married. I would have
had no reason to harm Jim. I loved him.'

David studied Ashley a moment, then looked at the sheet
of paper again. 'What about Dennis Tibble?'

'Dennis worked at the company I worked for. I saw him
the night he was murdered, but I had nothing to do with
that. I was in Chicago.'

David was watching Ashley's face.

'You have to believe me. I – I had no reason to kill
him.'

David said, 'All right.' He glanced at the sheet again.
'What was your relationship with Jean Claude Parent?'

'The police asked me about him. I had never even heard
of him. How could I have killed him when I didn't even
know him?' She looked at David pleadingly. 'Don't you
see? They have the wrong person. They've arrested the

132

wrong person.' She began to weep. 'I haven't killed anyone.'

'Richard Melton?'

'I don't know who he is either.'

David waited while Ashley regained control of herself. 'What about Deputy Blake?'

Ashley shook her head. 'Deputy Blake stayed at my apartment that night to watch over me. Someone had been stalking me and threatening me. I slept in my bedroom, and he slept on the couch in the living room. They – they found his body in the alley.' Her lips were trembling. 'Why would I kill him? He was *helping* me!'

David was studying Ashley, puzzled. *Something's very wrong here*, David thought. *Either she's telling the truth or she's one hell of an actress.* He stood up. 'I'll be back. I want to talk to the sheriff.'

Two minutes later, he was in the sheriff's office.

'Well, did you talk to her?' Sheriff Dowling asked.

'Yes. I think you've gotten yourself in a box, Sheriff.'

'What does that mean, Counselor?'

'It means you might have been too eager to make an arrest. Ashley Patterson doesn't even know two of the people you're accusing her of killing.'

A small smile touched Sheriff Dowling's lips. 'She fooled you, too, huh? She sure as hell fooled us.'

'What are you talking about?'

'I'll show you, mister.' He opened a file folder on his desk and handed David some papers. 'These are copies of coroner's reports, FBI reports, DNA reports and Interpol reports on the five men who were murdered and castrated. Each victim had had sex with a woman before he was murdered. There were vaginal traces and fingerprints at each of the murder scenes. There were supposed to have been three different women involved. Well, the FBI collated all this evidence, and guess what they came up with? The three women turned out to be Ashley Patterson. Her DNA and fingerprints are positive on every one of the murders.'

David was staring at him in disbelief. 'Are – are you sure?'

'Yeah. Unless you want to believe that Interpol, the FBI and five different coroner's offices are out to frame your client. It's all there, mister. One of the men she killed was my brother-in-law. Ashley Patterson's going to be tried for first-degree murder, and she's going to be convicted. Anything else?'

'Yes.' David took a deep breath. 'I'd like to see Ashley Patterson again.'

They brought her back to the visitors' room. When she walked inside, David asked angrily, 'Why did you lie to me?'

'What? I didn't lie to you. I'm innocent. I—'

'They have enough evidence against you to burn you a dozen times over. I told you I wanted the truth.'

Ashley looked at him for a full minute, and when she spoke, she said in a quiet voice, 'I told you the truth. I have nothing more to say.'

Listening to her, David thought, *She really believes what she's saying. I'm talking to a nut case. What am I going to tell Jesse Quiller?*

'Would you talk to a psychiatrist?'

'I don't – Yes. If you want me to.'

'I'll arrange it.'

On his way back to San Francisco, David thought, *I kept my end of the bargain. I talked to her. If she really thinks she's*

134

*telling the truth, then she's crazy. I'll get her to Jesse, who will
plead insanity, and that will be the end of it.*

His heart went out to Steven Patterson.

At San Francisco Memorial Hospital, Dr Patterson was
receiving the condolences of his fellow doctors.

'It's a damn shame, Steven. You sure don't deserve anything like this . . .'

'It must be a terrible burden for you. If there's anything
I can do . . .'

'I don't know what gets into kids these days. Ashley
always seemed so normal . . .'

And behind each expression of condolence was the
thought: *Thank God it's not my kid.*

When David returned to the law firm, he hurried in to see
Joseph Kincaid.

Kincaid looked up and said, 'Well, it's after six o'clock,
David, but I waited for you. Did you see Dr Patterson's
daughter?'

'Yes, I did.'

'And did you find an attorney to defend her?'

David hesitated. 'Not yet, Joseph. I'm arranging for a
psychiatrist to see her. I'll be going back in the morning
to talk to her again.'

Joseph Kincaid looked at David, puzzled. 'Oh? Frankly,
I'm surprised that you're getting this involved. Naturally,
we can't have this firm associated with anything as ugly as
this trial is going to be.'

'I'm not really involved, Joseph. It's just that I owe a
great deal to her father. I made him a promise.'

'There's nothing in writing, is there?'

'No.'

135

'So it's only a moral obligation?'

David studied him a moment, started to say something, then stopped. 'Yes. It's only a moral obligation.'

'Well, when you're through with Miss Patterson, come back and we'll talk.'

Not a word about the partnership.

When David got home that evening, the apartment was in darkness.

'Sandra?'

There was no answer. As David started to turn on the lights in the hallway, Sandra suddenly appeared from the kitchen, carrying a cake with lit candles.

'Surprise! We're having a celebration –' She saw the look on David's face and stopped. 'Is something wrong, darling? Didn't you get it, David? Did they give it to someone else?'

'No, no,' he said reassuringly. 'Everything's fine.'

Sandra put down the cake and moved closer to him. 'Something's wrong.'

'It's just that there's been a . . . a delay.'

'Wasn't your meeting with Joseph Kincaid today?'

'Yes. Sit down, honey. We have to talk.'

They sat down on the couch, and David said, 'Something unexpected has come up. Steven Patterson came to see me this morning.'

'He did? What about?'

'He wants me to defend his daughter.'

Sandra looked at him in surprise. 'But, David . . . you're not—'

'I know. I tried to tell him that. But I *have* practiced criminal law.'

'But you're not doing that anymore. Did you tell him you're about to become a partner in your firm?'

136

'No. He was very insistent that I was the only one who could defend his daughter. It doesn't make any sense, of course. I tried to suggest someone like Jesse Quiller, but he wouldn't even listen.'

'Well, he'll have to get someone else.'

'Of course. I promised to talk to his daughter, and I did.'

Sandra sat back on the couch. 'Does Mr Kincaid know about this?'

'Yes. I told him. He wasn't thrilled.' He mimicked Kincaid's voice. ' "Naturally, we can't have this firm associated with anything as ugly as this trial is going to be." '

'What's Dr Patterson's daughter like?'

'In medical terms, she's a fruitcake.'

'I'm not a doctor,' Sandra said. 'What does that mean?'

'It means that she really believes she's innocent.'

'Isn't that possible?'

'The sheriff in Cupertino showed me the file on her. Her DNA and fingerprints are all over the murder scenes.'

'What are you going to do now?'

'I've called Royce Salem. He's a psychiatrist that Jesse Quiller's office uses. I'm going to have him examine Ashley and turn the report over to her father. Dr Patterson can bring in another psychiatrist if he likes, or turn the report over to whichever attorney is going to handle the case.'

'I see.' Sandra studied her husband's troubled face. 'Did Mr Kincaid say anything about the partnership, David?'

He shook his head. 'No.'

Sandra said brightly, 'He will. Tomorrow's another day.'

Dr Royce Salem was a tall, thin man with a Sigmund Freud beard.

Maybe that's just a coincidence, David told himself. *Surely he's not trying to look like Freud.*

'Jesse talks about you often,' Dr Salem said. 'He's very fond of you.'

'I'm fond of him, Dr Salem.'

'The Patterson case sounds very interesting. Obviously the work of a psychopath. You're planning an insanity plea?'

'Actually,' David told him, 'I'm not handling the case. Before I get an attorney for her, I'd like to get an evaluation of her mental state.' David briefed Dr Salem on the facts as he knew them. 'She claims she's innocent, but the evidence shows she committed the crimes.'

'Well, let's have a look at the lady's psyche, shall we?'

The hypnotherapy session was to take place in the Santa Clara County Jail, in an interrogation room. The furniture in the room consisted of a rectangular wooden table and four wooden chairs.

Ashley, looking pale and drawn, was led into the room by a matron.

'I'll wait outside,' the matron said, and withdrew.

David said, 'Ashley, this is Dr Salem. Ashley Patterson.'

Dr Salem said, 'Hello, Ashley.'

She stood there, nervously looking from one to the other, without speaking. David had the feeling that she was ready to flee the room.

'Mr Singer tells me that you have no objection to being hypnotized.'

Silence.

Dr Salem went on. 'Would you let me hypnotize you, Ashley?'

Ashley closed her eyes for a second and nodded. 'Yes.'

'Why don't we get started?'

'Well, I'll be running along,' David said. 'If—'

'Just a moment.' Dr Salem walked over to David. 'I want you to stay.'

David stood there, frustrated. He regretted now that he had gone this far. *I'm not going to get in any deeper*, David resolved. *This will be the end of it.*

'All right,' David said reluctantly. He was eager to have it over with so he could get back to the office. The coming meeting with Kincaid loomed large in his mind.

Dr Salem said to Ashley, 'Why don't you sit in this chair?'

Ashley sat down.

'Have you ever been hypnotized before, Ashley?'

She hesitated an instant, then shook her head. 'No.'

'There's nothing to it. All you have to do is relax and listen to the sound of my voice. You have nothing to worry about. No one's going to hurt you. Feel your muscles relax. That's it. Just relax and feel your eyes getting heavy. You've been through a lot. Your body is tired, very tired. All you want to do is to go to sleep. Just close your eyes and relax. You're getting very sleepy . . . very sleepy . . .'

It took ten minutes to put her under. Dr Salem walked over to Ashley. 'Ashley, do you know where you are?'

'Yes. I'm in jail.' Her voice sounded hollow, as though coming from a distance.

'Do you know why you're in jail?'

'People think I did something bad.'

'And is it true? Did you do something bad?'

'No.'

'Ashley, did you ever kill anyone?'

'No.'

David looked at Dr Salem in surprise. *Weren't people supposed to tell the truth under hypnosis?*

'Do you have any idea who could have committed those murders?'

Suddenly, Ashley's face contorted and she began breathing hard, in short, raspy breaths. The two men watched in astonishment as her persona started changing. Her lips tightened and her features seemed to shift. She sat up straight, and there was a sudden liveliness in her face. She opened her eyes, and they were sparkling. It was an amazing transformation. Unexpectedly, she began to sing, in a sultry voice with an English accent:

> *'Half a pound of tupenny rice,*
> *Half a pound of treacle,*
> *Mix it up and make it nice,*
> *Pop! goes the weasel.'*

David listened in astonishment. *Who does she think she's fooling? She's pretending to be someone else.*

'I want to ask you some more questions, Ashley.'

She tossed her head and said in an English accent, 'I'm not Ashley.'

Dr Salem exchanged a look with David, then turned back to Ashley. 'If you're not Ashley, who are you?'

'Toni. Toni Prescott.'

And Ashley is doing this with a straight face, David thought. *How long is she going to go on with this stupid charade?* She was wasting their time.

'Ashley,' said Dr Salem.

'Toni.'

She's determined to keep it up, David thought.

'All right, Toni. What I'd like is—'

'Let me tell you what *I'd* like. I'd like to get out of this bloody place. Can you get us out of here?'

140

'That depends,' Dr Salem said. 'What do you know about—?'

'– those murders that little Goody Two-shoes is in here for? I can tell you things that—'

Ashley's expression suddenly started to change again. As David and Dr Salem watched, Ashley seemed to shrink in her chair, and her face began to soften and go through an incredible metamorphosis until she seemed to become another distinct personality.

She said in a soft voice with an Italian accent, 'Toni . . . don't say any more, *per piacere*.'

David was watching in bewilderment.

'Toni?' Dr Salem edged closer.

The soft voice said, 'I apologize for the interruption, Dr Salem.'

Dr Salem asked, 'Who are you?'

'I am Alette. Alette Peters.'

My God, it's not an act, David thought. *It's real*. He turned to Dr Salem.

Dr Salem said quietly, 'They're alters.'

David stared at him, totally confused. 'They're what?'

'I'll explain later.'

Dr Salem turned back to Ashley. 'Ashley . . . I mean Alette . . . How – how many of you are in there?'

'Beside Ashley, only Toni and me,' Alette answered.

'You have an Italian accent.'

'Yes. I was born in Rome. Have you ever been to Rome?'

'No, I've never been to Rome.'

I can't believe I'm hearing this conversation, David thought.

'*È molto bello.*'

'I'm sure. Do you know Toni?'

'*Sì, naturalmente.*'

'She has an *English* accent.'

141

'Toni was born in London.'

'Right. Alette, I want to ask you about these murders.
Do you have any idea who—?'

And David and Dr Salem watched as Ashley's face and
personality changed again before their eyes. Without her
saying a word, they knew that she had become Toni.

'You're wasting your time with her, luv.'

There was that English accent.

'Alette doesn't know anything. I'm the one you're going
to have to talk to.'

'All right, Toni. I'll talk to you. I have some questions
for you.'

'I'm sure you do, but I'm tired.' She yawned. 'Miss Tight
Ass has kept us up all night. I've got to get some sleep.'

'Not now, Toni. Listen to me. You have to help us to—'

Her face hardened. 'Why should I help you? What has
Miss Goody Two-shoes done for Alette or me? All she ever
does is keep us from having fun. Well, I'm sick of it, and
I'm sick of her. Do you hear me?' She was screaming, her
face contorted.

Dr Salem said, 'I'm going to bring her out of it.'

David was perspiring. 'Yes.'

Dr Salem leaned close to Ashley. 'Ashley . . . Ashley . . .
Everything is fine. Close your eyes now. They're very
heavy, very heavy. You're completely relaxed. Ashley,
your mind is at peace. Your body is relaxed. You're going
to wake up at the count of five, completely relaxed. One
. . .' He looked over at David and then back at Ashley.
'Two . . .'

Ashley began to stir. They watched her expression start
to change.

'Three . . .'

Her face softened.

142

'Four . . .'

They could sense her returning, and it was an eerie feeling.

'Five.'

Ashley opened her eyes. She looked around the room. 'I feel – Was I asleep?'

David stood there, staring at her, stunned.

'Yes,' Dr Salem said.

Ashley turned to David. 'Did I say anything? I mean . . . was I helpful?'

My God, David thought. *She doesn't know! She really doesn't know!* David said, 'You did fine, Ashley. I'd like to talk to Dr Salem alone.'

'All right.'

'I'll see you later.'

The men stood there, watching the matron lead Ashley away.

David sank into a chair. 'What – what the hell was that all about?'

Dr Salem took a deep breath. 'In all the years that I've been practicing, I've never seen a more clear-cut case.'

'A case of *what*?'

'Have you ever heard of multiple personality disorder?'

'What is it?'

'It's a condition where there are several completely different personalities in one body. It's also known as dissociative identity disorder. It's been in the psychiatric literature for more than two hundred years. It usually starts because of a childhood trauma. The victim shuts out the trauma by creating another identity. Sometimes a person will have dozens of different personalities or alters.'

'And they know about each other?'

'Sometimes, yes. Sometimes, no. Toni and Alette know

each other. Ashley is obviously not aware of either of them. Alters are created because the host can't stand the pain of the trauma. It's a way of escape. Every time a fresh shock occurs, a new alter can be born. The psychiatric literature on the subject shows that alters can be totally different from one another. Some alters are stupid, while others are brilliant. They can speak different languages. They have varied tastes and personalities.'

'How – how common is this?'

'Some studies suggest that one percent of the entire population suffers from multiple personality disorder, and that up to twenty percent of all patients in psychiatric hospitals have it.'

David said, 'But Ashley seems so normal and—'

'People with MPD *are* normal . . . until an alter takes over. The host can have a job, raise a family and live a perfectly ordinary life, but an alter can take over at any time. An alter can be in control for an hour, a day or even weeks, and then the host suffers a fugue, a loss of time and memory, for the period that the alter is in charge.'

'So Ashley – the host – would have no recollection of anything that the alter does?'

'None.'

David listened, spellbound.

'The most famous case of multiple personality disorder was Bridey Murphy. That's what first brought the subject to the public's attention. Since then, there have been an endless number of cases, but none as spectacular or as well publicized.'

'It – it seems so incredible.'

'It's a subject that's fascinated me for a long time. There are certain patterns that almost never change. For instance,

144

frequently, alters use the same initials as their host – Ashley Patterson . . . Alette Peters . . . Toni Prescott . . .

'Toni –?' David started to ask. Then he realized, 'Antoinette?'

'Right. You've heard the expression "alter ego."'

'Yes.'

'In a sense, we all have alter egos, or multiple personalities. A kind person can commit acts of cruelty. Cruel people can do kind things. There's no limit to the incredible range of human emotions. *Dr Jekyll and Mr Hyde* is fiction, but it's based on fact.'

David's mind was racing. 'If Ashley committed the murders . . .'

'She would not be aware of it. It was done by one of her alters.'

'My God! How can I explain that in court?'

Dr Salem looked at David curiously. 'I thought you said you weren't going to be her attorney.'

David shook his head. 'I'm not. I mean, I don't know. I – At this point, I'm a multiple personality myself.' David was silent for a moment. 'Is this curable?'

'Often, yes.'

'And if it can't be cured, what happens?'

There was a pause. 'The suicide rate is quite high.'

'And Ashley knows nothing about this?'

'No.'

'Would – would you explain it to her?'

'Yes, of course.'

'No!' It was a scream. She was cowering against the wall of her cell, her eyes filled with terror. 'You're lying! It's not true!'

Dr Salem said, 'Ashley, it is. You have to face it. I've

explained to you that what happened to you is not your fault. I—'

'Don't come near me!'

'No one's going to hurt you.'

'I want to die. Help me die!' She began sobbing uncontrollably.

Dr Salem looked at the matron and said, 'You'd better give her a sedative. And put a suicide watch on her.'

David telephoned Dr Patterson. 'I need to talk to you.'

'I've been waiting to hear from you, David. Did you see Ashley?'

'Yes. Can we meet somewhere?'

'I'll wait in my office for you.'

Driving back to San Francisco, David thought, *There's no way that I can take this case. I have too much to lose.*

I'll find her a good criminal attorney and that will be the end of it.

Dr Patterson was waiting for David in his office. 'You talked to Ashley?'

'Yes.'

'Is she all right?'

How do I answer that question? David took a deep breath. 'Have you ever heard of multiple personality disorder?'

Dr Patterson frowned. 'Vaguely . . .'

'It's when one or more personalities – or alters – exist in a person and take control from time to time, and that person is not aware of it. Your daughter has multiple personality disorder.'

Dr Patterson was looking at him, stunned. '*What?* I – I can't believe it. Are you sure?'

'I listened to Ashley while Dr Salem had her under hypnosis. She has two alters. At various times, they possess her.' David was talking more rapidly now. 'The sheriff showed me the evidence against your daughter. There's no doubt that she committed the murders.'

Dr Patterson said. 'Oh, my God! Then she's – she's guilty?'

'No. Because I don't believe she was aware that she committed the murders. She was under the influence of one of the alters. Ashley had no reason to commit those crimes. She had no motive, and she was not in control of herself. I think the state may have a difficult time proving motive or intent.'

'Then your defense is going to be that—'

David stopped him. 'I'm not going to defend her. I'm going to get you Jesse Quiller. He's a brilliant trial lawyer. I used to work with him, and he's the most—'

'No.' Dr Patterson's voice was sharp. 'You must defend Ashley.'

David said patiently, 'You don't understand. I'm not the right one to defend her. She needs—'

'I told you before that you're the only one I trust. My daughter means everything in the world to me, David. You're going to save her life.'

'I can't. I'm not qualified to—'

'Of course you are. You were a criminal attorney.'

'Yes, but I—'

'I won't have anyone else.' David could see that Dr Patterson was trying to keep his temper under control.

This makes no sense, David thought. He tried again. 'Jesse Quiller is the best—'

Dr Patterson leaned forward, the color rising in his face. 'David, your mother's life meant a lot to you. Ashley's life means as much to me. You asked for my help once, and you put your mother's life in my hands. I'm asking for your help now, and I'm putting Ashley's life in your hands. I want you to defend Ashley. You owe me that.'

He won't listen, David thought despairingly. *What's the matter with him?* A dozen objections flashed through David's mind, but they all faded before that one line: *'You owe me that'*. David tried one last time. 'Dr Patterson—'

'Yes or no, David.'

Chapter Thirteen

When David got home, Sandra was waiting for him. 'Good evening, darling.'

He took her in his arms and thought, *My God, she's lovely. What idiot said that pregnant women weren't beautiful?*

Sandra said excitedly, 'The baby kicked again today.' She took David's hand and put it on her belly. 'Can you feel him?'

After a few moments, David said, 'No. He's a stubborn little devil.'

'By the way, Mr Crowther called.'

'Crowther?'

'The real estate broker. The papers are ready to be signed.'

David felt a sudden sinking feeling. 'Oh.'

'I want to show you something,' Sandra said eagerly. 'Don't go away.'

David watched her hurry into the bedroom and thought, *What am I going to do? I have to make a decision.*

Sandra came back into the room holding up several samples of blue wallpaper. 'We're doing the nursery in blue, and we'll do the living room of the apartment in blue and white, your favorite colors. Which color wallpaper do you like, the lighter shade or the darker?'

David forced himself to concentrate. 'The lighter looks good.'

'I like it, too. The only problem is that the rug is going to be a dark blue. Do you think they should match?'

I can't give up the partnership. I've worked too hard for it. It means too much.

'David. Do you think they should match?'

He looked at her. 'What? Oh. Yes. Whatever you think, honey.'

'I'm so excited. It's going to be beautiful.'

There's no way we can afford it if I don't get the partnership.

Sandra looked around the little apartment. 'We can use some of this furniture, but I'm afraid we're going to need a lot of new things.' She looked at him anxiously. 'We can handle it, can't we, darling? I don't want to go overboard.'

'Right,' David said absently.

She snuggled against his shoulder. 'It's going to be like a whole new life, isn't it? The baby and the partnership and the penthouse. I went by there today. I wanted to see the playground and the school. The playground's beautiful. It has slides and swings and jungle gyms. I want you to come with me Saturday to look at it. Jeffrey's going to adore it.'

Maybe I can convince Kincaid that this would be a good thing for the firm.

'The school looks nice. It's just a couple blocks from our condo, and it's not too large. I think that's important.'

David was listening to her now and thought, *I can't let her down. I can't take away her dreams. I'll tell Kincaid in the morning that I'm not taking the Patterson case. Patterson will have to find someone else.*

'We'd better get ready, darling. We're due at the Quillers' at eight o'clock.'

This was the moment of truth. David felt himself tense. 'There's something we have to talk about.'

'Yes?'

'I went to see Ashley Patterson this morning.'

'Oh? Tell me about it. Is she guilty? Did she do those terrible things?'

'Yes and no.'

'Spoken like a lawyer. What does that mean?'

'She committed the murders . . . but she's not guilty.'

'David—!'

'Ashley has a medical condition called multiple personality disorder. Her personality is split, so that she does things without knowing she's doing them.'

Sandra was staring at him. 'How horrible.'

'There are two other personalities. I've heard them.'

'You've *heard* them?'

'Yes. And they're real. I mean, she's not faking.'

'And she has no idea that she—?'

'None.'

'Then is she innocent or guilty?'

'That's for the courts to decide. Her father won't talk to Jesse Quiller, so I'll have to find some other attorney.'

'But Jesse's perfect. Why won't he talk to him?'

David hesitated. 'He wants me to defend her.'

'But you told him you can't, of course.'

'Of course.'

'Then—?'

'He won't listen.'

'What did he say, David?'

He shook his head. 'It doesn't matter.'

'What did he say?'

David replied slowly, 'He said that I trusted him enough to put my mother's life in his hands, and he saved her, and now he was trusting me enough to put his daughter's life in my hands, and he is asking me to save her.'

Sandra was studying his face. 'Do you think you could?'

'I don't know. Kincaid doesn't want me to take the case. If I did take it, I could lose the partnership.'

'Oh.'

There was a long silence.

When he spoke, David said, 'I have a choice. I can say no to Dr Patterson and become a partner in the firm, or I can defend his daughter and probably go on an unpaid leave, and see what happens afterward.'

Sandra was listening quietly.

'There are people much better qualified to handle Ashley's case, but for some damn reason, her father won't hear of anyone else. I don't know why he's so stubborn about it, but he is. If I take the case and I don't get the partnership, we'll have to forget about moving. We'll have to forget about a lot of our plans, Sandra.'

Sandra said softly, 'I remember before we were married, you told me about him. He was one of the busiest doctors in the world, but he found time to help a penniless young boy. He was your hero, David. You said that if we ever had a son, you would want him to grow up to be like Steven Patterson.'

David nodded.

'When do you have to decide?'

'I'm seeing Kincaid first thing in the morning.'

Sandra took his hand and said, 'You don't need that much time. Dr Patterson saved your mother. You're going to save his daughter.' She looked around and smiled. 'Anyway, we can always do this apartment over in blue and white.'

Jesse Quiller was one of the top criminal defense attorneys

in the country. He was a tall, rugged man with a homespun touch that made jurors identify with him. They felt that he was one of them, and they wanted to help him. That was one of the reasons he seldom lost a case. The other reasons were that he had a photographic memory and a brilliant mind.

Instead of vacationing, Quiller used his summers to teach law, and years earlier David had been one of his pupils. When David graduated, Quiller invited him to join his criminal law firm, and two years later, David had become a partner. David loved practicing criminal law and excelled at it. He made sure that at least 10 percent of his cases were pro bono. Three years after becoming a partner, David had abruptly resigned and gone to work for Kincaid, Turner, Rose & Ripley to practice corporate law.

Over the years, David and Quiller had remained close friends. They, and their wives, had dinner together once a week.

Jesse Quiller had always fancied tall, sylphlike, sophisticated blondes. Then he had met Emily and fallen in love with her. Emily was a prematurely gray dumpling of a woman, from an Iowa farm – the exact opposite of other women Quiller had dated. She was a caretaker, mother earth. They made an unlikely couple, but the marriage worked because they were deeply in love with each other.

Every Tuesday, the Singers and the Quillers had dinner and then played a complicated card game called Liverpool.

When Sandra and David arrived at the Quiller's beautiful home on Hayes Street, Jesse met them at the door.

He gave Sandra a hug and said, 'Come in. We've got the champagne on ice. It's a big day for you, huh? The new

153

penthouse and the partnership. Or is it the partnership and the penthouse?'

David and Sandra looked at each other.

'Emily's in the kitchen fixing a celebration dinner.' He looked at their faces. 'I *think* it's a celebration dinner. Am I missing something?'

David said, 'No, Jesse. It's just that we may have a – a little problem.'

'Come on in. Fix you a drink?' He looked at Sandra.

'No, thanks. I don't want the baby to get into bad habits.'

'He's a lucky kid, having parents like you,' Quiller said warmly. He turned to David. 'What can I get for you?'

'I'm fine,' David said.

Sandra started toward the kitchen. 'I'll go see if I can help Emily.'

'Sit down, David. You look serious.'

'I'm in a dilemma,' David admitted.

'Let me guess. Is it the penthouse or the partnership?'

'Both.'

'*Both?*'

'Yes. You know about the Patterson case?'

'Ashley Patterson? Sure. What's that got to do with –?' He stopped. 'Wait a minute. You told me about Steven Patterson, in law school. He saved your mother's life.'

'Yes. He wants me to defend his daughter. I tried to turn the case over to you, but he won't hear of anyone but me defending her.'

Quiller frowned. 'Does he know you're not practicing criminal law anymore?'

'Yes. That's what's so damn strange. There are dozens of lawyers who can do a hell of a lot better job than I can.'

'He knows that you *were* a criminal defense lawyer?'

'Yes.'

Quiller said carefully, 'How does he feel about his daughter?'

What a strange question, David thought. 'She means more to him than anything in the world.'

'Okay. Suppose you took her case. The downside is that—'

'The downside is that Kincaid doesn't want me to take it. If I do, I have a feeling that I'll lose the partnership.'

'I see. And that's where the penthouse comes in?'

David said angrily, 'That's where my whole goddamn future comes in. It would be stupid for me to do this, Jesse. I mean really *stupid*!'

'What are you getting mad about?'

David took a deep breath. 'Because I'm going to do it.'

Quiller smiled. 'Why am I not surprised?'

David ran his hand across his forehead. 'If I turned him down, and his daughter was convicted and executed, and I did nothing to help, I – I couldn't live with myself.'

'I understand. How does Sandra feel about this?'

David managed a smile. 'You know Sandra.'

'Yeah. She wants you to go ahead with it.'

'Right.'

Quiller leaned forward. 'I'll do everything I can to help you, David.'

David sighed. 'No. That's part of my bargain. I have to handle this alone.'

Quiller frowned. 'That doesn't make any sense.'

'I know. I tried to explain that to Dr Patterson, but he wouldn't listen.'

'Have you told Kincaid about this yet?'

'I'm having a meeting with him in the morning.'

'What do you think will happen?'

'I know what's going to happen. He's going to advise me not to take the case and, if I insist, he'll ask me to take a leave of absence without pay.'

'Let's have lunch tomorrow. Rubicon, one o'clock.'

David nodded. 'Fine.'

Emily came in from the kitchen wiping her hands on a kitchen towel. David and Quiller rose.

'Hello, David.' Emily bustled up to him, and he gave her a kiss on the cheek.

'I hope you're hungry. Dinner's almost ready. Sandra's in the kitchen helping me. She's such a dear.' She picked up a tray and hurried back into the kitchen.

Quiller turned to David. 'You mean a great deal to Emily and me. I'm going to give you some advice. You've got to let go.'

David sat there, saying nothing.

'That was a long time ago, David. And what happened wasn't your fault. It could have happened to anyone.'

David looked at Quiller. 'It happened to me, Jesse. I killed her.'

It was déjà vu. All over again. And again. David sat there, transported back to another time and another place.

It had been a pro bono case, and David had said to Jesse Quiller, 'I'll handle it.'

Helen Woodman was a lovely young woman accused of murdering her wealthy stepmother. There had been bitter public quarrels between the two, but all the evidence against Helen was circumstantial. After David had gone to the jail and met with her, he was convinced she was innocent. With each meeting, he had become more

156

emotionally involved. In the end, he had broken a basic rule: Never fall in love with a client.

The trial had gone well. David had refuted the prosecutor's evidence bit by bit, and he had won the jury over to his client's side. And unexpectedly, a disaster had occurred. Helen's alibi was that at the time of the murder she had been at the theater with a friend. Under questioning in court, her friend admitted that the alibi was a lie, and a witness had come forward to say that he had seen Helen at her stepmother's apartment at the time of the murder. Helen's credibility was completely gone. The jury convicted her of first-degree murder, and the judge sentenced her to be executed. David was devastated.

'How could you have done this, Helen?' he demanded. 'Why did you lie to me?'

'I didn't kill my stepmother, David. When I got to her apartment, I found her on the floor, dead. I was afraid you wouldn't believe me, so I – I made up the story about being at the theater.'

He stood there, listening, a cynical expression on his face.

'I'm telling you the truth, David.'

'Are you?' He turned and stormed out.

Sometime during the night, Helen committed suicide.

One week later, an ex-convict caught committing a burglary confessed to the murder of Helen's stepmother.

The next day, David quit Jesse Quiller's firm. Quiller had tried to dissuade him.

'It wasn't your fault, David. She lied to you and—'

'That's the point. I let her. I didn't do my job. I didn't make sure she was telling me the truth. I wanted to believe her, and because of that, I let her down.'

Two weeks later, David was working for Kincaid, Turner, Rose & Ripley.

'I'll never be responsible for another person's life,' David had sworn.

And now he was defending Ashley Patterson.

Chapter Fourteen

At ten o'clock the following morning, David walked into Joseph Kincaid's office. Kincaid was signing some papers and he glanced up as David entered.

'Ah. Sit down, David. I'll be through in a moment.'

David sat down and waited.

When Kincaid had finished, he smiled and said, 'Well! You have some good news, I trust?'

Good news for whom? David wondered.

'You have a very bright future here, David, and I'm sure you wouldn't want to do anything to spoil that. The firm has big plans for you.'

David was silent, trying to find the right words.

Kincaid said, 'Well? Have you told Dr Patterson that you'd find another lawyer for him?'

'No. I've decided that I'm going to defend her.'

Kincaid's smile faded. 'Are you really going to defend that woman, David? She's a vicious, sick murderer. Anyone who defends her will be tarred with the same brush.'

'I'm not doing this because I want to, Joseph. I'm obligated. I owe Dr Patterson a great deal, and this is the only way I can ever repay him.'

Kincaid sat there, silent. When he finally spoke, he said, 'If you've really decided to go ahead with this, then I suggest that it would be appropriate for you to take a leave of absence. Without pay, of course.'

Good-bye, partnership.

'After the trial, naturally, you'll come back to us and the partnership will be waiting for you.'

David nodded. 'Naturally.'

'I'll have Collins take over your workload. I'm sure you'll want to begin concentrating on the trial.'

Thirty minutes later, the partners of Kincaid, Turner, Rose & Ripley were in a meeting.

'We can't afford to have this firm be involved in a trial like that,' Henry Turner objected.

Joseph Kincaid was quick to respond. 'We're not really involved, Henry. We're giving the boy a leave of absence.'

Albert Rose spoke up. 'I think we should cut him loose.'

'Not yet. That would be shortsighted. Dr Patterson could be a cash cow for us. He knows everybody, and he'll be grateful to us for letting him borrow David. No matter what happens at the trial, it's a win-win situation. If it goes well, we get the doctor as a client and make Singer a partner. If the trial goes badly, we'll drop Singer and see if we can't keep the good doctor. There's really no downside.'

There was a moment of silence, then John Ripley grinned. 'Good thinking, Joseph.'

When David left Kincaid's office, he went to see Steven Patterson. He had telephoned ahead, and the doctor was waiting for him.

'Well, David?'

My answer is going to change my life, David thought. *And not for the better.* 'I'm going to defend your daughter, Dr Patterson.'

Steven Patterson took a deep breath. 'I knew it. I would

160

have bet my life on it.' He hesitated a moment. 'I'm betting my daughter's life on it.'

'My firm has given me a leave of absence. I'm going to get help from one of the best trial lawyers in the—'

Dr Patterson raised a hand. 'David, I thought I made it clear to you that I don't want anyone else involved in this case. She's in your hands and your hands only.'

'I understand,' David said. 'But Jesse Quiller is—'

Dr Patterson got to his feet. 'I don't want to hear anything more about Jesse Quiller or any of the rest of them. I know trial lawyers, David. They're interested in the money and the publicity. This isn't about money or publicity. This is about Ashley.'

David started to speak, then stopped. There was nothing he could say. The man was fanatic on the subject. *I can use all the help I can get*, David thought. *Why won't he let me?*

'Have I made myself clear?'

David nodded. 'Yes.'

'I'll take care of your fee and your expenses, of course.'

'No. This is pro bono.'

Dr Patterson studied him a moment, then nodded. 'Quid pro quo?'

'Quid pro quo.' David managed a smile. 'Do you drive?'

'David, if you're on a leave of absence, you'll need some expense money to keep you going. I insist.'

'As you wish,' David said.

At least we'll eat during the trial.

Jesse Quiller was waiting for David at Rubicon.

'How did it go?'

David sighed. 'It was predictable. I'm on a leave of absence, no salary.'

'Those bastards. How can they—?'

'I can't blame them,' David interrupted. 'They're a very conservative firm.'

'What are you going to do now?'

'What do you mean?'

'What do I *mean*? You're handling the trial of the century. You don't have an office to work in anymore; you don't have access to research files or case files, criminal law books or a fax machine, and I've seen that outdated computer that you and Sandra have. It won't be able to run the legal software you'll need or get you on the Internet.'

'I'll be all right,' David said.

'You're damn right you will. There's an empty office in my suite that you're going to use. You'll find everything you need there.'

It took David a moment to find his voice. 'Jesse, I can't—'

'Yes, you can.' Quiller grinned. 'You'll find a way to pay me back. You always pay people back, don't you, Saint David?' He picked up a menu. 'I'm starved.' He looked up. 'By the way, lunch is on you.'

David went to visit Ashley in the Santa Clara County Jail.

'Good morning, Ashley.'

'Good morning.' She looked even paler than usual. 'Father was here this morning. He told me that you're going to get me out of here.'

I wish I were that optimistic, David thought. He said carefully, 'I'm going to do everything I can, Ashley. The trouble is that not many people are familiar with the problem you have. We're going to let them know about it. We're going to get the finest doctors in the world to come here and testify for you.'

'It scares me,' Ashley whispered.

'What does?'

162

'It's as though two different people are living inside me, and I don't even know them.' Her voice was trembling. 'They can take over anytime they want to, and I have no control over them. I'm so frightened.' Her eyes filled with tears.

David said quietly, 'They're not people, Ashley. They're in your mind. They're part of you. And with the proper treatment, you're going to be well.'

When David got home that evening, Sandra gave him a hug and said, 'Did I ever tell you how proud I am of you?'

'Because I'm out of a job?' David asked.

'That, too. By the way, Mr Crowther called. The real estate broker. He said the papers are ready to sign. They want the down payment of sixty thousand dollars. I'm afraid we'll have to tell him we can't afford—'

'Wait! I have that much in the company pension plan. With Dr Patterson giving us some expense money, maybe we can still swing this.'

'It doesn't matter, David. We don't want to spoil the baby with a penthouse, anyway.'

'Well, I have some good news. Jesse is going to let me—'

'I know. I talked to Emily. We're moving into Jesse's offices.'

David said, 'We?'

'You forget, you married a paralegal. Seriously, darling, I can be very helpful. I'll work with you until' – she touched her stomach – 'Jeffrey comes along, and then we'll see.'

'Mrs Singer, do you have any idea how much I love you?'

'No. But take your time. Dinner's not for another hour.'

'An hour isn't enough time,' David told her.

163

She put her arms around him and murmured, 'Why don't you get undressed, Tiger?'

'What?' He pulled back and looked at her, worried. 'What about the – What does Dr Bailey say?'

'The doctor says if you don't get undressed in a hurry, I should attack you.'

David grinned. 'His word's good enough for me.'

The following morning, David moved into the back office of Jesse Quiller's suite. It was a serviceable office, part of a five-office suite.

'We've expanded a little since you were here,' Jesse explained to David. 'I'm sure you'll find everything. The law library is next door; you've got faxes, computers, everything you need. If there's anything you don't see, just ask.'

'Thanks,' David said. 'I – I can't tell you how much I appreciate this, Jesse.'

Jesse smiled. 'You're going to pay me back. Remember?'

Sandra arrived a few minutes later. 'I'm ready,' she said. 'Where do we begin?'

'We begin by looking up every case we can find on multiple personality trials. There's probably a ton of stuff on the Internet. We'll try the California Criminal Law Observer, the Court TV site and some other criminal law links, and we'll gather whatever useful information we can get from Westlaw and Lexis-Nexis. Next, we get hold of doctors who specialize in multiple personality problems, and we contact them as possible expert witnesses. We'll need to interview them and see if we can use their testimony to strengthen our case. I'll have to brush up on criminal court procedures and get ready for voir dire. We've also got to get a list of the district attorney's witnesses and the witnesses' statements. I want his whole discovery package.'

'And we have to send him ours. Are you going to call Ashley to the stand?'

David shook his head. 'She's much too fragile. The prosecution would tear her apart.' He looked up at Sandra. 'This is going to be a hard one to win.'

Sandra smiled. 'But you're going to win it. I know you are.'

David put in a call to Harvey Udell, the accountant at Kincaid, Turner, Rose & Ripley.

'Harvey. David Singer.'

'Hello, David. I hear you're leaving us for a little while.'

'Yes.'

'That's an interesting case you're taking on. The papers are full of it. What can I do for you?'

David said, 'I have sixty thousand dollars in my pension plan there, Harvey. I wasn't going to take it out this early, but Sandra and I just bought a penthouse, and I'm going to need the money for a down payment.'

'A penthouse. Well, congratulations.'

'Thanks. How soon can I get the money?'

There was a brief hesitation. 'Can I get back to you?'

'Of course.' David gave him his telephone number.

'I'll call you right back.'

'Thanks.'

Harvey Udell replaced the receiver and then picked up the telephone again. 'Tell Mr Kincaid I'd like to see him.'

Thirty minutes later he was in Joseph Kincaid's office. 'What is it, Harvey?'

'I got a call from David Singer, Mr Kincaid. He's bought

a penthouse, and he needs the sixty thousand he has in his pension fund for a down payment. In my opinion, we're not obligated to give him the money now. He's on leave, and he's not—'

'I wonder if he knows how expensive it is to maintain a penthouse?'

'Probably not. I'll just tell him we can't—'

'Give him the money.'

Harvey looked at him in surprise. 'But we don't have to—'

Kincaid leaned forward in his chair. 'We're going to help him dig a hole for himself, Harvey. Once he puts a down payment on that penthouse . . . we own him.'

Harvey Udell telephoned David. 'I've good news for you, David. That money you have in the pension plan, you're taking it out early, but there's no problem. Mr Kincaid says to give you anything you want.'

'Mr Crowther. David Singer.'

'I've been waiting to hear from you, Mr Singer.'

'The down payment on the penthouse is on its way. You'll have it tomorrow.'

'Wonderful. As I told you, we have some other folks who are anxious to get it, but I have the feeling that you and your wife are the right owners for it. You're going to be very happy there.'

All it will take, David thought, *is a few dozen miracles.*

Ashley Patterson's arraignment took place in the Superior Court of the County of Santa Clara on North First Street in San Jose. The legal wrangling about jurisdiction had gone on for weeks. It had been complicated, because the

166

murders had taken place in two countries and two different states. A meeting was held in San Francisco, attended by Officer Guy Fontaine from the Quebec Police Department, Sheriff Dowling from Santa Clara County, Detective Eagan from Bedford, Pennsylvania, Captain Rudford from the San Francisco Police Department, and Roger Toland, the chief of police in San Jose.

Fontaine said, 'We would like to try her in Quebec because we have absolute evidence of her guilt. There's no way she can win a trial there.'

Detective Eagan said, 'For that matter, so do we, Officer Fontaine. Jim Cleary's was the first murder she committed, and I think that should take precedence over the others.'

Captain Rudford of the San Francisco police said, 'Gentlemen, there's no doubt that we can all prove her guilt. But three of these murders took place in California, and she should be tried here for all of them. That gives us a much stronger case.'

'I agree,' Sheriff Dowling said. 'And two of them took place in Santa Clara County, so this is where the jurisdiction should lie.'

They spent the next two hours arguing the merits of their positions, and in the end, it was decided that the trial for the murders of Dennis Tibble, Richard Melton and Deputy Sam Blake would be held at the Hall of Justice in San Jose. They agreed that the murders in Bedford and Quebec would be put on hold.

On the day of arraignment, David stood at Ashley's side.

The judge on the bench said, 'How do you plead?'

'Not guilty and not guilty by reason of insanity.'

The judge nodded. 'Very well.'

'Your Honor, we're requesting bail at this time.'

The attorney from the prosecutor's office jumped in. 'Your Honor, we strongly object. The defendant is accused of three savage murders and faces the death penalty. If she were given the opportunity, she would flee the country.'

'That's not true,' David said. 'There's no—'

The judge interrupted. 'I've reviewed the file and the prosecutor's affidavit in support of no bail. Bail denied. This case is assigned to Judge Williams for all purposes. The defendant will be held in custody at the Santa Clara County Jail until trial.'

David sighed. 'Yes, Your Honor.' He turned to Ashley. 'Don't worry. Everything's going to work out. Remember . . . you're not guilty.'

When David returned to the office, Sandra said, 'Have you seen the headlines? The tabloids are calling Ashley "the Butcher Bitch." The story is all over television.'

'We knew this was going to be rough,' David said. 'And this is only the beginning. Let's go to work.'

The trial was eight weeks away.

The next eight weeks were filled with feverish activity. David and Sandra worked all day and far into the night, digging up transcripts of trials of defendants with multiple personality disorder. There were dozens of cases. The various defendants had been tried for murder, rape, robbery, drug dealing, arson . . . Some had been convicted, some had been acquitted.

'We're going to get Ashley acquitted,' David told Sandra.

Sandra gathered the names of prospective witnesses and telephoned them.

'Dr Nakamoto, I'm working with David Singer. I believe

you testified in *The State of Oregon Versus Bohannan*. Mr Singer is representing Ashley Patterson . . . Oh, you did? Yes. Well, we would like you to come to San Jose and testify in her behalf . . .'

'Dr Booth, I'm calling from David Singer's office. He's defending Ashley Patterson. You testified in the *Dickerson* case. We're interested in your expert testimony . . . We would like you to come to San Jose and testify for Miss Patterson. We need your expertise . . .'

'Dr Jameson, this is Sandra Singer. We need you to come to . . .'

And so it went, from morning until midnight. Finally, a list of a dozen witnesses was compiled. David looked at it and said, 'It's pretty impressive. Doctors, a dean . . . heads of law schools.' He looked up at Sandra and smiled. 'I think we're in good shape.'

From time to time, Jesse Quiller came into the office David was using. 'How are you getting along?' he asked. 'Anything I can do to help?'

'I'm fine.'

Quiller looked around the office. 'Do you have everything you need?'

David smiled. 'Everything, including my best friend.'

On a Monday morning, David received a package from the prosecutor's office listing the state's discovery. As David read it, his spirits sank.

Sandra was watching him, concerned. 'What is it?'

'Look at this. He's bringing in a lot of heavyweight medical experts to testify against MPD.'

'How are you going to handle that?' Sandra asked.

'We're going to admit that Ashley was at the scenes

when the murders took place, but that the murders were actually committed by an alter ego.' *Can I persuade a jury to believe that?*

Five days before the trial was to begin, David received a telephone call saying that Judge Williams wanted to meet with him.

David walked into Jesse Quiller's office. 'Jesse, what can you tell me about Judge Williams?'

Jesse leaned back in his chair and laced his fingers behind his head. 'Tessa Williams . . . Were you ever a Boy Scout, David?'

'Yes . . .'

'Do you remember the Boy Scout motto, – "be prepared"?'

'Sure.'

'When you walk into Tessa Williams's courtroom, be prepared. She's brilliant. She came up the hard way. Her folks were Mississippi sharecroppers. She went through college on a scholarship, and the people in her hometown were so proud of her, they raised the money to put her through law school. There's a rumor that she turned down a big appointment in Washington because she likes it where she is. She's a legend.'

'Interesting,' David said.

'The trial is going to be in Santa Clara County?'

'Yes.'

'Then you'll have my old friend Mickey Brennan prosecuting.'

'Tell me about him.'

'He's a feisty Irishman, tough on the inside, tough on the outside. Brennan comes from a long line of overachievers. His father runs a huge publishing business; his mother's

170

a doctor; his sister is a college professor. Brennan was a football star in his college days, and he was at the top of his law class.' He leaned forward. 'He's good, David. Be careful. His trick is to disarm witnesses and then move in for the kill. He likes to blindside them . . . Why does Judge Williams want to see you?'

'I have no idea. The call just said she wants to discuss the Patterson case with me.'

Jesse Quiller frowned. 'That's unusual. When are you meeting with her?'

'Wednesday morning.'

'Watch your back.'

'Thanks, Jesse. I will.'

The superior courthouse in Santa Clara County is a white, four-story building on North First Street. Directly inside the courthouse entrance is a desk manned by a uniformed guard; there is a metal detector, a railing alongside and an elevator. There are seven courtrooms in the building, each one presided over by a judge and staff.

At ten o'clock Wednesday morning, David Singer was ushered into the chambers of Judge Tessa Williams. In the room with her was Mickey Brennan. The leading prosecutor from the district attorney's office was in his fifties, a short, burly man with a slight brogue. Tessa Williams was in her late forties, a slim, attractive African-American woman with a crisp, authoritative manner.

'Good morning, Mr Singer. I'm Judge Williams. This is Mr Brennan.'

The two men shook hands.

'Sit down, Mr Singer. I want to talk about the Patterson case. According to the records, you've filed a plea of not guilty and not guilty by reason of insanity?'

'Yes, Your Honor.'

Judge Williams said, 'I brought you two together because I think we can save a lot of time and save the state a great deal of expense. I'm usually against plea bargaining, but in this case, I think it's justified.'

David was listening, puzzled.

The judge turned to Brennan. 'I've read the preliminary hearing transcript, and I see no reason for this case to go to trial. I'd like the state to waive the death penalty and accept a guilty plea with no chance of parole.'

David said, 'Wait a minute. That's out of the question!'

They both turned to look at him.

'Mr Singer—'

'My client is not guilty. Ashley Patterson passed a lie detector test that proves—'

'That doesn't prove anything, and as you well know it's not admissible in court. Because of all the publicity, this is going to be a long and messy trial.'

'I'm sure that—'

'I've been practicing law a long time, Mr Singer. I've heard the whole basket of legal pleas. I've heard pleas of self-defense – that's an acceptable plea; murder by reason of temporary insanity – that's a reasonable plea; diminished capacity . . . But I'll tell you what I don't believe in, Counselor. "Not guilty because I didn't commit the crime, my alter ego did it." To use a term you might not find in *Blackstone*, that's "bullshit." Your client either committed the crimes or she didn't. If you change your plea to guilty, we can save a lot of—'

'No, Your Honor, I won't.'

Judge Williams studied David a moment. 'You're very stubborn. A lot of people find that an admirable quality.' She leaned forward in her chair. 'I don't.'

'Your Honor—'

'You're forcing us into a trial that's going to last at least three months – maybe longer.'

Brennan nodded. 'I agree.'

'I'm sorry that you feel—'

'Mr Singer, I'm here to do you a favor. If we try your client, she's going to die.'

'Hold on! You're prejudging this case without—'

'Prejudging it? Have you seen the evidence?'

'Yes, I—'

'For God's sake, Counselor, Ashley Patterson's DNA and fingerprints are at every crime scene. I've never seen a more clear-cut case of guilt. If you insist on going ahead with this, it could turn into a circus. Well, I'm not going to let that happen. I don't like circuses in my court. Let's dispose of this case here and now. I'm going to ask you once more, will you plead your client to life without parole?'

David said stubbornly, 'No.'

She was glaring at him. 'Right. I'll see you next week.'

He had made an enemy.

Chapter Fifteen

San Jose had quickly taken on the atmosphere of a carnival town. Media from all over the world were pouring in. Every hotel was booked, and some of the members of the press were forced to take rooms in the outlying towns of Santa Clara, Sunnyvale and Palo Alto. David was besieged by reporters.

'Mr Singer, tell us about the case. Are you pleading your client not guilty . . . ?'

'Are you going to put Ashley Patterson on the stand . . . ?'

'Is it true that the district attorney was willing to plea-bargain?'

'Is Dr Patterson going to testify for his daughter . . . ?'

'My magazine will pay fifty thousand dollars for an interview with your client . . .'

Mickey Brennan was also pursued by the media.

'Mr Brennan, would you say a few words about the trial?'

Brennan turned and smiled at the television cameras. 'Yes. I can sum up the trial in five words. "We're going to win it." No further comment.'

'Wait! Do you think she's insane . . . ?'

'Is the state going to ask for the death penalty . . . ?'

'Did you call it an open-and-shut case . . . ?'

*   *   *

David rented an office in San Jose close to the courthouse, where he could interview his witnesses and prepare them for the trial. He had decided that Sandra would work out of Quiller's office in San Francisco until the trial started. Dr Salem had arrived in San Jose.

'I want you to hypnotize Ashley again,' David said. 'Let's get all the information we can from her and the alters before the trial starts.'

They met Ashley in a holding room at the county detention center. She was trying hard to conceal her nervousness. To David, she looked like a deer trapped in the headlights of a juggernaut.

'Morning, Ashley. You remember Dr Salem?'

Ashley nodded.

'He's going to hypnotize you again. Will that be all right?'

Ashley said, 'He's going to talk to the . . . the others?'

'Yes. Do you mind?'

'No. But I – I don't want to talk to them.'

'That's all right. You don't have to.'

'I hate this!' Ashley burst out angrily.

'I know,' David said soothingly. 'Don't worry. It's going to be over soon.' He nodded to Dr Salem.

'Make yourself comfortable, Ashley. Remember how easy this was. Close your eyes and relax. Just try to clear your mind. Feel your body relaxing. Listen to the sound of my voice. Let everything else go. You're getting very sleepy. Your eyes are getting very heavy. You want to go to sleep . . . Go to sleep . . .'

In ten minutes, she was under. Dr Salem signaled to David. David walked over to Ashley.

'I'd like to talk to Alette. Are you in there, Alette?'

And they watched Ashley's face soften and go through

the same transformation they had seen earlier. And then, that soft, mellifluous Italian accent.

'*Buon giorno.*'

'Good morning, Alette. How do you feel?'

'*Male.* This is a very difficult time.'

'It's difficult for all of us,' David assured her, 'but everything's going to be all right.'

'I hope so.'

'Alette, I'd like to ask you a few questions.'

'*Sì . . .*'

'Did you know Jim Cleary?'

'No.'

'Did you know Richard Melton?'

'Yes.' There was a deep sadness in her voice. 'It was . . . it was terrible what happened to him.'

David looked over at Dr Salem. 'Yes, it was terrible. When was the last time you saw him?'

'I visited him in San Francisco. We went to a museum and then had dinner. Before I left, he asked me to go to his apartment with him.'

'And did you go?'

'No. I wish I had,' Alette said regretfully. 'I might have saved his life.' There was a short silence. 'We said good-bye, and I drove back to Cupertino.'

'And that was the last time you saw him?'

'Yes.'

'Thank you, Alette.'

David moved closer to Ashley and said, 'Toni? Are you there, Toni? I'd like to talk to you.'

As they watched, Ashley's face went through another remarkable transformation. Her persona changed before their eyes. There was a new assurance, a sexual awareness. She began to sing in that clear, throaty voice:

> *'Up and down the city road,*
> *In and out of the Eagle.*
> *That's the way the money goes,*
> *Pop! goes the weasel.'*

She looked at David. 'Do you know why I like to sing that song, luv?'

'No.'

'Because my mother hated it. She hated me.'

'Why did she hate you?'

'Well, we can't ask her now, can we?' Toni laughed. 'Not where she is. I couldn't do anything right for her. What kind of mother did you have, David?'

'My mother was a wonderful person.'

'You're lucky then, aren't you? It's really the luck of the draw, I suppose. God plays games with us, doesn't he?'

'Do you believe in God? Are you a religious person, Toni?'

'I don't know. Maybe there's a God. If there is, he has a strange sense of humor, doesn't he? Alette is the religious one. She goes to church regularly, that one.'

'And do you?'

Toni gave a short laugh. 'Well, if she's there, I'm there.'

'Toni, do you believe it's right to kill people?'

'No, of course not.'

'Then—'

'Not unless you have to.'

David and Dr Salem exchanged a look.

'What do you mean by that?'

Her tone of voice changed. She suddenly sounded defensive. 'Well, you know, like if you have to protect yourself. If someone's hurting you.' She was getting agitated. 'If some git is trying to do dirty things to you.' She was becoming hysterical.

'Toni—'

She started sobbing. 'Why can't they leave me alone? Why did they have to –?' She was screaming.

'Toni—'

Silence.

'Toni . . .'

Nothing.

Dr Salem said, 'She's gone. I'd like to wake Ashley up.'

David sighed. 'All right.'

A few minutes later, Ashley was opening her eyes.

'How do you feel?' David asked.

'Tired. Did it . . . did it go all right?'

'Yes. We talked to Alette and Toni. They—'

'I don't want to know.'

'All right. Why don't you go rest now, Ashley? I'll be back to see you this afternoon.'

They watched a female jailer lead her away.

Dr Salem said, 'You have to put her on the stand, David. That will convince any jury in the world that—'

'I've given it a lot of thought,' David said. 'I don't think I can.'

Dr Salem looked at him a moment. 'Why not?'

'Brennan, the prosecuting attorney, is a killer. He would tear her apart. I can't take that chance.'

David and Sandra were having dinner with the Quillers two days before the preliminaries of the trial were to begin.

'We've checked into the Wyndham Hotel,' David said. 'The manager did me a special favor. Sandra's coming down with me. The town is crowded beyond belief.'

'And if it's that bad now,' Emily said, 'imagine what it's going to be like when the trial starts.'

Quiller looked at David. 'Anything I can do to help?'

David shook his head. 'I have a big decision to make. Whether to put Ashley on the stand or not.'

'It's a tough call,' Jesse Quiller said. 'You're damned if you do and damned if you don't. The problem is that Brennan is going to build Ashley Patterson up as a sadistic, murdering monster. If you don't put her on the stand, that's the image the jurors will carry in their minds when they go into the jury room to reach a verdict. On the other hand, from what you tell me, if you do put Ashley on the stand, Brennan can destroy her.'

'Brennan's going to have all his medical experts there to discredit multiple personality disorder.'

'You've got to convince them that it's real.'

'And I intend to,' David said. 'Do you know what bothers me, Jesse? The jokes. The latest one going around is that I wanted to ask for a change of venue, but I decided not to because there are no places left where Ashley hasn't murdered someone. Do you remember when Johnny Carson was on television? He was funny and he always remained a gentleman. Now, the hosts on the late-night shows are all malicious. Their humor at the expense of other people is savage.'

'David?'

'Yes.'

Jesse Quiller said quietly, 'It's going to get worse.'

David Singer was unable to sleep the night before he was to go into court. He could not stem the negative thoughts swirling through his head. When he finally fell asleep, he heard a voice saying, *You let your last client die. What if you let this one die?*

He sat up in bed, bathed in perspiration.

Sandra opened her eyes. 'Are you all right?'

'Yes. No. What the hell am I doing here? All I had to do was say no to Dr Patterson.'

Sandra squeezed his arm and said softly, 'Why didn't you?'

He grunted. 'You're right. I couldn't.'

'All right then. Now, how about getting some sleep so you'll be nice and fresh in the morning?'

'Great idea.'

He was awake the rest of the night.

Judge Williams had been correct about the media. The reporters were relentless. Journalists were swarming in from around the world, avid to cover the story of a beautiful young woman being tried as a serial killer who sexually mutilated her victims.

The fact that Mickey Brennan was forbidden to bring the names of Jim Cleary or Jean Claude Parent into the trial had been frustrating, but the media had solved the problem for him. Television talk shows, magazines and newspapers all carried lurid stories of the five murders and castrations. Mickey Brennan was pleased.

When David arrived at the courtroom, the press was out in full force. David was besieged.

'Mr Singer, are you still employed by Kincaid, Turner, Rose & Ripley . . . ?'

'Look this way, Mr Singer . . .'

'Is it true you were fired for taking this case . . . ?'

'Can you tell us about Helen Woodman? Didn't you handle her murder trial . . . ?'

'Did Ashley Patterson say why she did it . . . ?'

'Are you going to put your client on the stand . . . ?'

'No comment,' David said curtly.

*   *   *

When Mickey Brennan drove up to the courthouse, he was instantly surrounded by the media.

'Mr Brennan, how do you think the trial is going to go . . . ?'

'Have you ever tried an alter ego defense before . . . ?'

Brennan smiled genially. 'No. I can't wait to talk to all the defendants.' He got the laugh that he wanted. 'If there are enough of them, they can have their own ball club.' Another laugh. 'I've got to get inside. I don't want to keep any of the defendants waiting.'

The voir dire started with Judge Williams asking general questions of the potential jurors. When she had finished, it was the defense's turn and then the prosecution's.

To laymen, the selection of a jury seems simple: *Choose the prospective juror who seemed friendly and dismiss the others.* In fact, voir dire was a carefully planned ritual. Skilled trial lawyers did not ask direct questions that would bring yes or no answers. They asked general questions that would encourage the jurors to talk and reveal something of themselves and their true feelings.

Mickey Brennan and David Singer had different agendas. In this case, Brennan wanted a preponderance of men on the jury, men who would be disgusted and shocked at the idea of a woman stabbing and castrating her victims. Brennan's questions were meant to pinpoint people who were traditional in their thinking, who would be less likely to believe in spirits and goblins and people who claimed they were inhabited by alters. David took the opposite approach.

'Mr Harris, is it? I'm David Singer. I'm representing the

defendant. Have you ever served on a jury before, Mr Harris?'

'No.'

'I appreciate your taking the time and trouble to do this.'

'It should be interesting, a big murder trial like this.'

'Yes. I think it will be.'

'In fact, I've been looking forward to it.'

'Have you?'

'Yeah.'

'Where do you work, Mr Harris?'

'At United Steel.'

'I imagine you and your fellow workers have talked about the Patterson case.'

'Yes. As a matter of fact, we have.'

David said, 'That's understandable. Everyone seems to be talking about it. What's the general opinion? Do your fellow workers think Ashley Patterson is guilty?'

'Yeah. I have to say they do.'

'And do you think so?'

'Well, it sure looks like it.'

'But you're willing to listen to the evidence before making up your mind?'

'Yeah. I'll listen to it.'

'What do you like to read, Mr Harris?'

'I'm not a big reader. I like to camp out and hunt and fish.'

'An outdoorsman. When you're camping out at night and you look at the stars, do you ever wonder if there are other civilizations up there?'

'You mean that crazy UFO stuff? I don't believe in all that nonsense.'

David turned to Judge Williams. 'Pass for cause, Your Honor.'

* * *

Another juror interrogation:

'What do you like to do in your spare time, Mr Allen?'

'Well, I like to read and watch television.'

'I like to do the same things. What do you watch on television?'

'There's some great shows on Thursday nights. It's hard to choose. The damn networks put all the good shows on at the same time.'

'You're right. It's a shame. Do you ever watch the *X-Files*?'

'Yeah. My kids love it.'

'What about *Sabrina, the Teenage Witch*?'

'Yeah. We watch that. That's a good show.'

'What do you like to read?'

'Anne Rice, Stephen King . . .'

Yes.

Another juror interrogation:

'What do you like to watch on television, Mr Mayer?'

'*Sixty Minutes*, the *NewsHour* with Jim Lehrer, documentaries . . .'

'What do you like to read?'

'Mainly history and political books.'

'Thank you.'

No.

Judge Tessa Williams sat on the bench, listening to the questioning, her face betraying nothing. But David could feel her disapproval every time she looked at him.

When the last juror was finally selected, the panel consisted of seven men and five women. Brennan glanced at David triumphantly. *This is going to be a slaughter.*

Chapter Sixteen

Early on the morning the trial of Ashley Patterson was to begin, David went to see Ashley at the detention center. She was near hysteria.

'I can't go through with this. I can't! Tell them to leave me alone.'

'Ashley, it's going to be all right. We're going to face them, and we're going to win.'

'You don't know – You don't know what this is like. I feel as though I'm in some kind of hell.'

'We're going to get you out of it. This is the first step.'

She was trembling. 'I'm afraid they're – they're going to do something terrible to me.'

'I won't let them,' David said firmly. 'I want you to believe in me. Just remember, you're not responsible for what happened. You haven't done anything wrong. They're waiting for us.'

She took a deep breath. 'All right. I'm going to be fine. I'm going to be fine. I'm going to be fine.'

Seated in the spectators' section was Dr Steven Patterson. He had responded to the barrage of reporters' questions outside the courtroom with one answer: 'My daughter is innocent.'

Several rows away were Jesse and Emily Quiller, there for moral support.

At the prosecutor's table were Mickey Brennan and two associates, Susan Freeman and Eleanor Tucker.

Sandra and Ashley were seated at the defendant's table, with David between them. The two women had met the previous week.

'David, you can *look* at Ashley and know she's innocent.'

'Sandra, you can look at the evidence she left on her victims and know she killed them. But killing them and being guilty are two different things. Now all I have to do is convince the jury.'

Judge Williams entered the courtroom and moved to the bench. The court clerk announced, 'All rise. Court is now in session. The Honorable Judge Tessa Williams presiding.'

Judge Williams said, 'You may be seated. This is the case of *The People of the State of California Versus Ashley Patterson*. Let's get started.' Judge Williams looked at Brennan. 'Would the prosecutor like to make an opening statement?'

Mickey Brennan rose. 'Yes, Your Honor.' He turned to the jury and moved toward them. 'Good morning. As you know, ladies and gentlemen, the defendant is on trial, accused of committing three bloody murders. Murderers come in many disguises.' He nodded toward Ashley. 'Her disguise is that of an innocent, vulnerable young woman. But the state will prove to you beyond a reasonable doubt that the defendant willfully and knowingly murdered and mutilated three innocent men.

'She used an alias to commit one of these murders, hoping not to get caught. She knew exactly what she was doing. We're talking calculated, cold-blooded murder. As the trial goes on, I will show you all the strands, one by one, that tie this case to the defendant sitting there. Thank you.'

He returned to his seat.

Judge Williams looked at David. 'Does the defense have an opening statement?'

'Yes, Your Honor.' David stood and faced the jury. He took a deep breath. 'Ladies and gentlemen, in the course of this trial, I will prove to you that Ashley Patterson is not responsible for what happened. She had no motive for any of the murders, nor any knowledge of them. My client is a victim. She is a victim of MPD – multiple personality disorder, which in the course of this trial will be explained to you.'

He glanced at Judge Williams and said firmly, 'MPD is an established medical fact. It means that there are other personalities, or alters, that take over their hosts and control their actions. MPD has a long history. Benjamin Rush, a physician and signer of the Declaration of Independence, discussed case histories of MPD in his lectures. Many incidents of MPD were reported throughout the nineteenth century and in this century of people taken over by alters.'

Brennan was listening to David, a cynical smile on his face.

'We will prove to you that it was an alter who took command and committed the murders that Ashley Patterson had absolutely no reason to commit. None. She had no control over what happened, and therefore is not responsible for what happened. During the course of the trial, I will bring in eminent doctors who will explain in greater detail about MPD. Fortunately, it is curable.'

He looked into the faces of the jurors. 'Ashley Patterson had no control over what she did, and in the name of justice, we ask that Ashley Patterson not be convicted of crimes for which she is not responsible.'

David took his seat.

Judge Williams looked at Brennan. 'Is the state ready to proceed?'

Brennan rose. 'Yes, Your Honor.' He flashed a smile at his associates and moved in front of the jury box. Brennan stood there a moment and deliberately let out a loud burp. The jurors were staring at him, surprised.

Brennan looked at them a moment as though puzzled and then his face cleared. 'Oh, I see. You were waiting for me to say "excuse me." Well, I didn't say it because I didn't do that. My alter ego, Pete, did it.'

David was on his feet, furious. 'Objection. Your Honor, this is the most outrageous—'

'Sustained.'

But the damage had already been done.

Brennan gave David a patronizing smile and then turned back to the jury. 'Well, I guess there hasn't been a defense like this since the Salem witch trials three hundred years ago.' He turned to look at Ashley. 'I didn't do it. No, sir. The devil made me do it.'

David was on his feet again. 'Objection. The—'

'Overruled.'

David slammed back into his seat.

Brennan stepped closer to the jury box. 'I promised you that I was going to prove that the defendant willfully and cold-bloodedly murdered and mutilated three men – Dennis Tibble, Richard Melton and Deputy Samuel Blake. *Three men!* In spite of what the defense says' – he turned and pointed to Ashley again – 'there's only *one* defendant sitting there, and she's the one who committed the murders. What did Mr Singer call it? Multiple personality disorder? Well, I'm going to bring some prominent doctors here who will tell you, under oath, that there is no such thing! But first, let's hear from some experts who are going to tie the defendant to the crimes.'

Brennan turned to Judge Williams. 'I would like to call my first witness, Special Agent Vincent Jordan.'

A short bald man stood up and moved toward the witness box.

The clerk said, 'Please state your full name and spell it for the record.'

'Special Agent Vincent Jordan, *J-o-r-d-a-n*.'

Brennan waited until he was sworn in and took a seat. 'You are with the Federal Bureau of Investigation in Washington, D.C.?'

'Yes, sir.'

'And what do you do with the FBI, Special Agent Jordan?'

'I'm in charge of the fingerprints section.'

'How long have you had that job?'

'Fifteen years.'

'Fifteen years. In all that time have you ever come across a duplicate set of fingerprints from different people?'

'No, sir.'

'How many sets of fingerprints are currently on file with the FBI?'

'At last count, just over two hundred and fifty million, but we receive over thirty-four thousand fingerprint cards a day.'

'And none of them matches any others?'

'No, sir.'

'How do you identify a fingerprint?'

'We use seven different fingerprint patterns for identification purposes. Fingerprints are unique. They're formed before birth and last throughout one's life. Barring accidental or intentional mutilation, no two patterns are alike.'

'Special Agent Jordan, you were sent the fingerprints

found at the scenes of the three victims who the defendant is accused of murdering?'

'Yes, sir. We were.'

'And you were also sent the fingerprints of the defendant, Ashley Patterson?'

'Yes, sir.'

'Did you personally examine those prints?'

'I did.'

'And what was your conclusion?'

'That the prints left at the murder scenes and the prints that were taken from Ashley Patterson were identical.'

There was a loud buzz in the courtroom.

'Order! Order!'

Brennan waited until the courtroom quieted down. 'They were identical? Is there any doubt in your mind, Agent Jordan? Could there be any mistake?'

'No, sir. All the prints were clear and easily identifiable.'

'Just to clarify this . . . we're talking about the fingerprints left at the murder scenes of Dennis Tibble, Richard Melton and Deputy Samuel Blake?'

'Yes, sir.'

'And the fingerprints of the defendant, Ashley Patterson, were found at all the scenes of the murders?'

'That is correct.'

'And what would you say was the margin of error?'

'None.'

'Thank you, Agent Jordan.' Brennan turned to David Singer. 'Your witness.'

David sat there a moment, then rose and walked over to the witness box. 'Agent Jordan, when you examine fingerprints, do you ever find that some have been deliberately smudged, or damaged in some way, in order for the felon to conceal his crime?'

190

'Yes, but we're usually able to correct them with high-intensity laser techniques.'

'Did you have to do that in the case of Ashley Patterson?'

'No, sir.'

'Why was that?'

'Well, like I said . . . the fingerprints were all clear.'

David glanced at the jury. 'So what you're saying is that the defendant made no attempt to erase or disguise her fingerprints?'

'That is correct.'

'Thank you. No further questions.' He turned to the jury. 'Ashley Patterson made no attempt to conceal her prints because she was innocent and—'

Judge Williams snapped, 'That's enough, Counselor! You'll have your chance to plead your case later.'

David resumed his seat.

Brennan turned to Special Agent Jordan. 'You're excused.' The FBI agent stepped down.

Brennan said, 'I would like to call as my next witness, Stanley Clarke.'

A young man with long hair was ushered into the court-room. He walked toward the witness stand. The courtroom was still as he was sworn in and took his seat.

Brennan said, 'What is your occupation, Mr Clarke?'

'I'm with National Biotech Laboratory. I work with deoxyribonucleic acid.'

'More commonly known to us simple nonscientists as DNA?'

'Yes, sir.'

'How long have you worked at National Biotech Laboratory?'

'Seven years.'

'And what is your position?'

'I'm a supervisor.'

'So, in that seven years, I assume that you've had a lot of experience with testing DNA?'

'Sure. I do it every day.'

Brennan glanced at the jury. 'I think we're all familiar with the importance of DNA.' He pointed to the spectators. 'Would you say that perhaps half a dozen people in this courtroom have identical DNA?'

'Hell no, sir. If we took a profile of DNA strands and assigned it a frequency based on collected databases, only one in five hundred billion unrelated Caucasians would have the same DNA profile.'

Brennan looked impressed. 'One in five hundred billion. Mr Clarke, how do you obtain DNA from a crime scene?'

'Lots of ways. We find DNA in saliva or semen or vaginal discharge, blood, a strand of hair, teeth, bone marrow . . .'

'And from any *one* of those things you can match it to a specific person?'

'That's correct.'

'Did you personally compare the DNA evidence in the murders of Dennis Tibble, Richard Melton and Samuel Blake?'

'I did.'

'And were you later given several strands of hair from the defendant, Ashley Patterson?'

'I was.'

'When you compared the DNA evidence from the various murder scenes with the strands of hair from the defendant, what was your conclusion?'

'They were identical.'

This time the reaction from the spectators was even noisier.

Judge Williams slammed down her gavel. 'Order! Be quiet, or I'll have the courtroom cleared.'

Brennan waited until the room was still. 'Mr Clarke, did you say that the DNA taken from every one of the three murder scenes and the DNA of the accused were *identical?*' Brennan leaned on the word.

'Yes, sir.'

Brennan glanced over at the table where Ashley was sitting, then turned back to the witness. 'What about contamination? We're all aware of a famous criminal trial where the DNA evidence was supposedly contaminated. Could the evidence in this case have been mishandled so that it was no longer valid or—?'

'No, sir. The DNA evidence in these murder cases was very carefully handled and sealed.'

'So there's no doubt about it. The defendant murdered the three—?'

David was on his feet. 'Objection, Your Honor. The prosecutor is leading the witness and—'

'Sustained.'

David took his seat.

'Thank you, Mr Clarke.' Brennan turned to David. 'Nothing further.'

Judge Williams said, 'Your witness, Mr Singer.'

'No questions.'

The jurors were staring at David.

Brennan acted surprised. *'No questions?'* He turned to the witness. 'You may step down.'

Brennan looked at the jurors and said, 'I'm amazed that the defense is not questioning the evidence, because it proves beyond a doubt that the defendant murdered and castrated three innocent men and—'

David was on his feet. 'Your Honor—'

'Sustained. You're stepping over the boundaries, Mr Brennan!'

'Sorry, Your Honor. No more questions.'

Ashley was looking at David, frightened.

He whispered, 'Don't worry. It will be our turn soon.'

The afternoon consisted of more witnesses for the prosecution, and their testimony was devastating.

'The building superintendent summoned you to Dennis Tibble's apartment, Detective Lightman?'

'Yes.'

'Would you tell us what you found there?'

'It was a mess. There was blood all over the place.'

'What was the condition of the victim?'

'He had been stabbed to death and castrated.'

Brennan glanced at the jury, a look of horror on his face. 'Stabbed to death and castrated. Did you find any evidence at the scene of the crime?'

'Oh, yes. The victim had had sex before he died. We found some vaginal discharge and fingerprints.'

'Why didn't you arrest someone immediately?'

'The fingerprints we found didn't match any that we had on record. We were waiting for a match on the prints we had.'

'But when you finally got Ashley Patterson's fingerprints and her DNA, it all came together?'

'It sure did. It all came together.'

Dr Steven Patterson was at the trial every day. He sat in the spectators' section just behind the defendant's table. Whenever he entered or left the courtroom, he was besieged by reporters.

'Dr Patterson, how do you think the trial is going?'

'It's going very well.'

'What do you think is going to happen?'

'My daughter is going to be found innocent.'

Late one afternoon when David and Sandra got back to the hotel, there was a message waiting for them. 'Please call Mr Kwong at your bank.'

David and Sandra looked at each other. 'Is it time for another payment already?' Sandra asked.

'Yes. Time flies when you're having fun,' he said dryly. David was thoughtful for a moment. 'The trial's going to be over soon, honey. We have enough left in our bank account to give them this month's payment.'

Sandra looked at him, worried. 'David, if we can't make all the payments . . . do we lose everything we've put in?'

'We do. But don't worry. Good things happen to good people.'

And he thought about Helen Woodman.

Brian Hill was sitting in the witness box after being sworn in. Mickey Brennan gave him a friendly smile.

'Would you tell us what you do, Mr Hill?'

'Yes, sir. I'm a guard at the De Young Museum in San Francisco.'

'That must be an interesting job.'

'It is, if you like art. I'm a frustrated painter.'

'How long have you worked there?'

'Four years.'

'Do a lot of the same people visit the museum? That is, do people come again and again?'

'Oh, yes. Some people do.'

'So I suppose that over a period of time, they would become familiar to you, or at least they would be familiar faces?'

'That's true.'

'And I'm told that artists are permitted to come in to copy some of the museum's paintings?'

'Oh, yes. We have a lot of artists.'

'Did you ever meet any of them, Mr Hill?'

'Yes, we – You kind of become friendly after a while.'

'Did you ever meet a man named Richard Melton?'

Brian Hill sighed. 'Yes. He was very talented.'

'So talented, in fact, that you asked him to teach you to paint?'

'That's right.'

David got to his feet. 'Your Honor, this is fascinating, but I don't see what it has to do with the trial. If Mr Brennan—'

'It's relevant, Your Honor. I'm establishing that Mr Hill could identify the victim by sight and by name and tell us who the victim associated with.'

'Objection overruled. You may go ahead.'

'And did he teach you to paint?'

'Yes, he did, when he had time.'

'When Mr Melton was at the museum, did you ever see him with any young ladies?'

'Well, not in the beginning. But then he met somebody he was kind of interested in, and I used to see him with her.'

'What was her name?'

'Alette Peters.'

Brennan looked puzzled. 'Alette Peters? Are you sure you have the right name?'

'Yes, sir. That's the way he introduced her.'

'You don't happen to see her in this courtroom right now, do you, Mr Hill?'

'Yes, sir.' He pointed to Ashley. 'That's her sitting there.'

Brennan said, 'But that's not Alette Peters. That's the defendant, Ashley Patterson.'

David was on his feet. 'Your Honor, we have already said

that Alette Peters is a part of this trial. She is one of the alters who controls Ashley Patterson and—'

'You're getting ahead of yourself, Mr Singer. Mr Brennan, please continue.'

'Now, Mr Hill, you're sure that the defendant, who's here under the name of Ashley Patterson, was known to Richard Melton as Alette Peters?'

'That's right.'

'And there's no doubt that this is the same woman?'

Brian Hill hesitated. 'Well . . . Yeah, it's the same woman.'

'And you saw her with Richard Melton the day that Melton was murdered?'

'Yes, sir.'

'Thank you.' Brennan turned to David. 'Your witness.'

David got up and slowly walked over to the witness box. 'Mr Hill, I would think it's a big responsibility being a guard in a place where so many hundreds of millions of dollars' worth of art was being exhibited.'

'Yes, sir. It is.'

'And to be a good guard, you have to be on the alert all the time.'

'That's right.'

'You have to be aware of what's going on all the time.'

'You bet.'

'Would you say that you're a trained observer, Mr Hill?'

'Yes, I would.'

'I ask that because I noticed when Mr Brennan asked you if you had any doubts about whether Ashley Patterson was the woman who was with Richard Melton, you hesitated. Weren't you sure?'

There was a momentary pause. 'Well, she looks a lot like the same woman, but in a way she seems different.'

'In what way, Mr Hill?'

'Alette Peters was more Italian, and she had an Italian accent . . . and she seemed younger than the defendant.'

'That's exactly right, Mr Hill. The person you saw in San Francisco was an alter of Ashley Patterson. She was born in Rome, she was eight years younger—'

Brennan was on his feet, furious. 'Objection.'

David turned to Judge Williams. 'Your Honor, I was—'

'Will counsel approach the bench, please?' David and Brennan walked over to Judge Williams. 'I don't want to have to tell you this again, Mr Singer. The defense will have its chance when the prosecution rests. Until then, stop pleading your case.'

Bernice Jenkins was on the stand.

'Would you tell us your occupation, Miss Jenkins?'

'I'm a waitress.'

'And where do you work?'

'The café at the De Young Museum.'

'What was your relationship with Richard Melton?'

'We were good friends.'

'Could you elaborate on that?'

'Well, at one time we had a romantic relationship and then things kind of cooled off. Those things happen.'

'I'm sure they do. And then what?'

'Then we became like brother and sister. I mean, I – I told him about all my problems, and he told me about all his problems.'

'Did he ever discuss the defendant with you?'

'Well, yeah, but she called herself by a different name.'

'And that name was?'

'Alette Peters.'

'But he knew her name was really Ashley Patterson?'

'No. He thought her name was Alette Peters.'

'You mean she deceived him?'

David sprang to his feet, furious. 'Objection.'

'Sustained. You will stop leading the witness, Mr Brennan.'

'Sorry, Your Honor.' Brennan turned back to the witness box. 'He spoke to you about this Alette Peters, but did you ever see the two of them together?'

'Yes, I did. He brought her into the restaurant one day and introduced us.'

'And you're speaking of the defendant, Ashley Patterson?'

'Yeah. Only she called herself Alette Peters.'

Gary King was on the stand.

Brennan asked, 'You were Richard Melton's roommate?'

'Yes.'

'Were you also friends? Did you go out with him socially?'

'Sure. We double-dated a lot together.'

'Was Mr Melton interested in any young lady in particular?'

'Yeah.'

'Do you know her name?'

'She called herself Alette Peters.'

'Do you see her in this courtroom?'

'Yeah. She's sitting over there.'

'For the record, you are pointing to the defendant, Ashley Patterson?'

'Right.'

'When you came home on the night of the murder, you found Richard Melton's body in the apartment?'

'I sure did.'

'What was the condition of the body?'

'Bloody.'

199

'The body had been castrated?'

A shudder. 'Yeah. Man, it was awful.'

Brennan looked over at the jury for their reaction. It was exactly what he hoped for.

'What did you do next, Mr King?'

'I called the police.'

'Thank you.' Brennan turned to David. 'Your witness.'

David rose and walked over to Gary King.

'Tell us about Richard Melton. What kind of man was he?'

'He was great.'

'Was he argumentative? Did he like to get into fights?'

'Richard? No. Just the opposite. He was very quiet, laid back.'

'But he liked to be around women who were tough and kind of physical?'

Gary was looking at him strangely. 'Not at all. Richard liked nice, quiet women.'

'Did he and Alette have a lot of fights? Did she yell at him a lot?'

Gary was puzzled. 'You've got it all wrong. They never yelled at each other. They were great together.'

'Did you ever see anything that would lead you to believe that Alette Peters would do anything to harm—?'

'Objection. He's leading the witness.'

'Sustained.'

'No more questions,' David said.

When David sat down, he said to Ashley, 'Don't worry. They're building up our case for us.'

He sounded more confident than he felt.

David and Sandra were having dinner at San Fresco, the restaurant in the Wyndham Hotel, when the maître d' came up to David and said, 'There's an urgent telephone call for you, Mr Singer.'

'Thank you.' David said to Sandra, 'I'll be right back.'

He followed the maître d' to a telephone. 'This is David Singer.'

'David – Jesse. Go up to your room and call me back. The goddamn roof is falling in!'

Chapter Seventeen

Jesse—?'

'David, I know I'm not supposed to interfere, but I think you should ask for a mistrial.'

'What's happened?'

'Have you been on the Internet in the past few days?'

'No. I've been a little busy.'

'Well, the trial is all over the damned Internet. That's all they're talking about in the chat rooms.'

'That figures,' David said. 'But what's the—?'

'It's all negative, David. They're saying that Ashley is guilty and that she should be executed. And they're saying it in very colorful ways. You can't believe how vicious they are.'

David, suddenly realizing, said, 'Oh, my God! If any of the jurors are on the Internet—'

'The odds are pretty good that some of them are, and they'll be influenced. I would ask for a mistrial, or at the very least, to have the jurors sequestered.'

'Thanks, Jesse. Will do.' David replaced the receiver. When he returned to the restaurant where Sandra was waiting, she asked, 'Bad?'

'Bad.'

Before court convened the following morning, David asked to see Judge Williams. He was ushered into her chambers, along with Mickey Brennan.

'You asked to see me?'

'Yes, Your Honor. I learned last night that this trial is the number one subject on the Internet. It's what all the chat rooms are discussing, and they've already convicted the defendant. It's very prejudicial. And since I'm sure that some of the jurors have computers with on-line access, or talk to friends who have online access, it could seriously damage the defense. Therefore, I'm making a motion for a mistrial.'

She was thoughtful for a moment. 'Motion denied.'

David sat there, fighting to control himself. 'Then I make a motion to immediately sequester the jury so that—'

'Mr Singer, every day the press is at this courtroom in full force. This trial is the number one topic on television, on radio and in the newspapers all over the world. I warned you that this was going to turn into a circus, and you wouldn't listen.' She leaned forward. 'Well, it's *your* circus. If you wanted the jury sequestered, you should have made that motion before the trial. And I probably would not have granted it. Is there anything else?'

David sat there, his stomach churning. 'No, Your Honor.'

'Then let's get into the courtroom.'

Mickey Brennan was questioning Sheriff Dowling.

'Deputy Sam Blake called to tell you that he was going to spend the night at the defendant's apartment in order to protect her? She told him that someone was threatening her life?'

'That is correct.'

'When did you hear from Deputy Blake again?'

'I – I didn't. I got a call in the morning that his – his body had been found in the alley in back of Miss Patterson's apartment building.'

'And of course you went there immediately?'

'Of course.'

'And what did you find?'

He swallowed. 'Sam's body was wrapped in a bloody sheet. He had been stabbed to death and castrated like the other two victims.'

'Like the *other* two victims. So all those murders were carried out in a similar fashion?'

'Yes, sir.'

'As though they were killed by the same person?'

David was on his feet. 'Objection!'

'Sustained.'

'I'll withdraw that. What did you do next, Sheriff?'

'Well, up until that time, Ashley Patterson wasn't a suspect. But after this happened, we took her in and had her fingerprints taken.'

'And then?'

'We sent them to the FBI, and we got a positive make on her.'

'Would you explain to the jury what you mean by a positive make?'

Sheriff Dowling turned to the jury. 'Her fingerprints matched other fingerprints on file that they were trying to identify from the previous murders.'

'Thank you, Sheriff.' Brennan turned to David. 'Your witness.'

David got up and walked over to the witness box. 'Sheriff, we've heard testimony in this courtroom that a bloody knife was found in Miss Patterson's kitchen.'

'That's right.'

'How was it hidden? Wrapped up in something? Stashed away where it couldn't be found?'

'No. It was right out in the open.'

205

'Right out in the open. Left there by someone who had nothing to hide. Someone who was innocent because—'

'Objection!'

'Sustained.'

'No more questions.'

'The witness is dismissed.'

Brennan said, 'If it pleases the court . . .' He signaled someone at the back of the courtroom, and a man in overalls came in, carrying the mirror from Ashley Patterson's medicine cabinet. On it, in red lipstick, was written YOU WILL DIE.

David rose. 'What is this?'

Judge Williams turned to Mickey Brennan. 'Mr Brennan?'

'This is the bait the defendant used to get Deputy Blake to come to her apartment so she could murder him. I would like this marked as exhibit D. It came from the medicine chest of the defendant.'

'Objection, Your Honor. It has no relevance.'

'I will prove that there is a relevance.'

'We'll see. In the meantime, you may proceed.'

Brennan placed the mirror in full view of the jury. 'This mirror was taken from the defendant's bathroom.' He looked at the jurors. 'As you can see, scrawled across it is "You Will Die." This was the defendant's pretext for having Deputy Blake come to her apartment that night to protect her.' He turned to Judge Williams. 'I would like to call my next witness, Miss Laura Niven.'

A middle-aged woman walking with a cane approached the witness box and was sworn in.

'Where do you work, Miss Niven?'

'I'm a consultant for the County of San Jose.'

'And what do you do?'

'I'm a handwriting expert.'

'How long have you worked for the county, Miss Niven?'

'Twenty-two years.'

Brennan nodded toward the mirror. 'You have been shown this mirror before?'

'Yes.'

'And you've examined it?'

'I have.'

'And you've been shown an example of the defendant's handwriting?'

'Yes.'

'And had a chance to examine that?'

'Yes.'

'And you've compared the two?'

'I have.'

'And what is your conclusion?'

'They were written by the same person.'

There was a collective gasp from the courtroom.

'So what you're saying is that Ashley Patterson wrote this threat to herself?'

'That is correct.'

Mickey Brennan looked over at David. 'Your witness.'

David hesitated. He glanced at Ashley. She was staring down at the table, shaking her head. 'No questions.'

Judge Williams was studying David. 'No questions, Mr Singer?'

David rose to his feet. 'No. All this testimony is meaningless.' He turned to the jury. 'The prosecution will have to prove that Ashley Patterson knew the defendants and had a motive to—'

Judge Williams said angrily, 'I've warned you before. It is not your place to instruct the jury on the law. If—'

'Someone has to,' David exploded. 'You're letting him get away with—'

'That's enough, Mr Singer. Approach the bench.'

David walked to the bench.

'I'm citing you for contempt of court and sentencing you to a night here in our nice jail the day this trial is over.'

'Wait, Your Honor. You can't—'

She said grimly, 'I've sentenced you to one night. Would you like to try for two?'

David stood there, glaring at her, taking deep breaths. 'For the sake of my client, I'll – I'll keep my feelings to myself.'

'A wise decision,' Judge Williams said curtly. 'Court is adjourned.' She turned to a bailiff. 'When this trial is ended, I want Mr Singer taken into custody.'

'Yes, Your Honor.'

Ashley turned to Sandra. 'Oh, my God! What's happening?'

Sandra squeezed her arm. 'Don't worry. You have to trust David.'

Sandra telephoned Jesse Quiller.

'I heard,' he said. 'It's all over the news, Sandra. I don't blame David for losing his temper. She's been goading him from the beginning. What did David do to get her so down on him?'

'I don't know, Jesse. It's been horrible. You should see the faces of the jurors. They hate Ashley. They can't wait to convict her. Well, it's the defense's turn next. David will change their minds.'

'Hold the thought.'

'Judge Williams hates me, Sandra, and it's harming Ashley. If I don't do something about this, Ashley is going to die. I can't let that happen.'

'What can you do?' Sandra asked.

David took a deep breath. 'Resign from the case.'

Both of them knew what that meant. The media would be full of his failure.

'I never should have agreed to take on the trial,' David said bitterly. 'Dr Patterson trusted me to save his daughter's life, and I've –' He could not go on.

Sandra put her arms around him and held him close. 'Don't worry, darling. Everything's going to turn out fine.'

I've let everyone down, David thought. *Ashley, Sandra . . . I'm going to be kicked out of the firm, I won't have a job and the baby is due soon. 'Everything's going to turn out fine.'*

Right.

In the morning, David asked to see Judge Williams in her chambers. Mickey Brennan was there.

Judge Williams said, 'You asked to see me, Mr Singer?'

'Yes, Your Honor. I want to resign from the case.'

Judge Williams said, 'On what grounds?'

David spoke carefully. 'I don't believe I'm the right lawyer for this trial. I think I'm hurting my client. I would like to be replaced.'

Judge Williams said quietly, 'Mr Singer, if you think I'm going to let you walk away from this and then have to start this trial all over again and waste even more time and money, you're quite mistaken. The answer is no. Do you understand me?'

David closed his eyes for an instant, forcing himself to stay calm. He looked up and said, 'Yes, Your Honor. I understand you.'

He was trapped.

Chapter Eighteen

More than three months had gone by since the beginning of the trial, and David could not remember when he had last had a full night's sleep.

One afternoon, when they returned from the courtroom, Sandra said, 'David, I think I should go back to San Francisco.'

David looked at her in surprise. 'Why? We're right in the middle of – Oh, my God.' He put his arms around her. 'The baby. Is it coming?'

Sandra smiled. 'Anytime now. I'd feel safer if I were back there, closer to Dr Bailey. Mother said she'd come and stay with me.'

'Of course. You have to go back,' David said. 'I lost track of time. He's due in three weeks, isn't he?'

'Yes.'

He grimaced. 'And I can't be there with you.'

Sandra took his hand. 'Don't be upset, darling. This trial's going to be over soon.'

'This goddamn trial is ruining our lives.'

'David, we're going to be fine. My old job's waiting for me. After the baby comes, I can—'

David said, 'I'm so sorry, Sandra. I wish—'

'David, don't ever be sorry for doing something you believe is right.'

'I love you.'

'I love you.'

He stroked her stomach. 'I love you both.' He sighed. 'All right. I'll help you pack. I'll drive you back to San Francisco tonight and—'

'No,' Sandra said firmly. 'You can't leave here. I'll ask Emily to come and pick me up.'

'Ask her if she can join us here for dinner tonight.'

'All right.'

Emily had been delighted. 'Of course I'll come to pick you up.' And she had arrived in San Jose two hours later.

The three of them had dinner that evening at Chai Jane.

'It's terrible timing,' Emily said. 'I hate to see you two away from each other right now.'

'The trial's almost over,' David said hopefully. 'Maybe it will end before the baby comes.'

Emily smiled. 'We'll have a double celebration.'

It was time to go. David held Sandra in his arms. 'I'll talk to you every night,' he said.

'Please don't worry about me. I'll be fine. I love you very much.' Sandra looked at him and said, 'Take care of yourself, David. You look tired.'

It wasn't until Sandra left that David realized how utterly alone he was.

Court was in session.

Mickey Brennan rose and addressed the court. 'I would like to call Dr Lawrence Larkin as my next witness.'

A distinguished gray-haired man was sworn in and took the stand.

'I want to thank you for being here, Dr Larkin. I know

your time is very valuable. Would you tell us a little about your background?'

'I have a successful practice in Chicago. I'm a past president of the Chicago Psychiatric Association.'

'How many years have you been in practice, Doctor?'

'Approximately thirty years.'

'And as a psychiatrist, I imagine you've seen many cases of multiple personality disorder?'

'No.'

Brennan frowned. 'When you say no, you mean you haven't seen a lot of them? Maybe a dozen?'

'I've never seen one case of multiple personality disorder.'

Brennan looked at the jury in mock dismay, then back at the doctor. 'In thirty years of working with mentally disturbed patients, you have never seen a *single* case of multiple personality disorder?'

'That's correct.'

'I'm amazed. How do you explain that?'

'It's very simple. I don't think that multiple personality disorder exists.'

'Well, I'm puzzled, Doctor. Haven't cases of multiple personality disorder been reported?'

Dr Larkin snorted. 'Being reported doesn't mean they're real. You see, what some doctors believe is MPD, they're confusing with schizophrenia, depressions and various other anxiety disorders.'

'That's very interesting. So in your opinion, as an expert psychiatrist, you don't believe that multiple personality disorder even exists?'

'That is correct.'

'Thank you, Doctor.' Mickey Brennan turned to David. 'Your witness.'

213

David rose and walked over to the witness box. 'You are a past president of the Chicago Psychiatric Association, Dr Larkin?'

'Yes.'

'You must have met a great many of your peers.'

'Yes. I'm proud to say that I have.'

'Do you know Dr Royce Salem?'

'Yes. I know him very well.'

'Is he a good psychiatrist?'

'Excellent. One of the best.'

'Did you ever meet Dr Clyde Donovan?'

'Yes. Many times.'

'Would you say that he's a good psychiatrist?'

'I would use him' – a small chuckle – 'if I needed one.'

'And what about Dr Ingram? Do you know him?'

'Ray Ingram? Indeed, I do. Fine man.'

'Competent psychiatrist?'

'Oh, yes.'

'Tell me, do all psychiatrists agree on every mental condition?'

'No. Of course we have some disagreements. Psychiatry is not an exact science.'

'That's interesting, Doctor. Because Dr Salem, Dr Donovan and Dr Ingram are going to come here and testify that they have treated cases of multiple personality disorder. Perhaps none of them is as competent as you are. That's all. Dismissed.'

Judge Williams turned to Brennan. 'Redirect?'

Brennan got to his feet and walked over to the witness box.

'Dr Larkin, do you believe that because these other doctors disagree with your opinion about MPD that that makes them right and you wrong?'

'No. I could produce dozens of psychiatrists who don't believe in MPD.'

'Thank you, Doctor. No more questions.'

Mickey Brennan said, 'Dr Upton, we've heard testimony that sometimes what is thought to be multiple personality disorder is really confused with other disorders. What are the tests that prove multiple personality disorder isn't one of those other conditions?'

'There is no test.'

Brennan's mouth dropped open in surprise as he glanced at the jury. 'There *is* no test? Are you saying that there's *no* way to tell whether someone who claims he has MPD is lying or malingering or using it to excuse some crime he or she doesn't want to be held responsible for?'

'As I said, there is no test.'

'So it's simply a matter of opinion? Some psychiatrists believe in it and some don't?'

'That's right.'

'Let me ask you this, Doctor. If you hypnotize someone, surely you can tell whether they really have MPD or they're pretending to have it?'

Dr Upton shook his head. 'I'm afraid not. Even under hypnosis or with sodium amytal, there is no way of exposing someone if he or she is faking.'

'That's very interesting. Thank you, Doctor. No more questions.' Brennan turned to David. 'Your witness.'

David rose and walked over to the witness box. 'Dr Upton, have you ever had patients come to you, having been diagnosed by other doctors as having MPD?'

'Yes. Several times.'

'And did you treat those patients?'

'No, I didn't.'

'Why not?'

'I can't treat conditions that don't exist. One of the patients was an embezzler who wanted me to testify that he wasn't responsible because he had an alter who did it. Another patient was a housewife who was arrested for beating her children. She says that someone inside her made her do it. There were a few more like that with different excuses, but they were all trying to hide from something. In other words, they were faking.'

'You seem to have a very definite opinion about this, Doctor.'

'I do. I know I'm right.'

David said, 'You know you're right?'

'Well, I mean—'

'– that everyone else must be wrong? All the doctors who believe in MPD are all wrong?'

'I didn't mean that—'

'And you're the only one who's right. Thank you, Doctor. That's all.'

Dr Simon Raleigh was on the stand. He was a short, bald man in his sixties.

Brennan said, 'Thank you for coming here, Doctor. You've had a long and illustrious career. You're a doctor, you're a professor, you went to school at—'

David stood up. 'The defense will stipulate to the witness's distinguished background.'

'Thank you.' Brennan turned back to the witness. 'Dr Raleigh, what does *iatrogenicity* mean?'

'That's when there's an existing illness, and medical treatment of psychotherapy aggravates it.'

'Would you be more specific, Doctor?'

'Well, in psychotherapy, very often the therapist influences the patient with his questions or attitude. He might make the patient feel that he has to meet the expectations of the therapist.'

'How would that apply to MPD?'

'If the psychiatrist is questioning the patient about different personalities within him, the patient might make up some in order to please the therapist. It's a very tricky area. Amytal and hypnosis can mimic MPD in patients who are otherwise normal.'

'So what you're saying is that under hypnosis the psychiatrist himself can alter the condition of the patient so that the patient believes something that is not true?'

'That has happened, yes.'

'Thank you, Doctor.' He looked at David. 'Your witness.'

David said, 'Thank you.' He rose and walked over to the witness box. David said disarmingly, 'Your credentials are very impressive. You're not only a psychiatrist, but you teach at a university.'

'Yes.'

'How long have you been teaching, Doctor?'

'More than fifteen years.'

'That's wonderful. How do you divide your time? By that I mean, do you spend half of your time teaching and the other half working as a doctor?'

'Now, I teach full-time.'

'Oh? How long has it been since you actually practiced medicine?'

'About eight years. But I keep up on all the current medical literature.'

'I have to tell you, I find that admirable. So you read up on everything. That's how you're so familiar with iatrogenicity?'

'Yes.'

'And in the past, a lot of patients came to you claiming they had MPD?'

'Well, no . . .'

'Not a lot? In the years you were practicing as a doctor, would you say you had a dozen cases who claimed they had MPD?'

'No.'

'Six?'

Dr Raleigh shook his head.

'Four?'

There was no answer.

'Doctor, have you *ever* had a patient who came to you with MPD?'

'Well, it's hard to—'

'Yes or no, Doctor?'

'No.'

'So all you really know about MPD is what you've read? No further questions.'

The prosecution called six more witnesses, and the pattern was the same with each. Mickey Brennan had assembled nine top psychiatrists from around the country, all united in their belief that MPD did not exist.

The prosecution's case was winding to a close.

When the last witness on the prosecution's list had been excused, Judge Williams turned to Brennan. 'Do you have any more witnesses to call, Mr Brennan?'

'No, Your Honor. But I would like to show the jury police photographs of the death scenes from the murders of—'

David said furiously, 'Absolutely not.'

Judge Williams turned to David. 'What did you say, Mr Singer?'

'I said' – David caught himself – 'objection. The prosecution is trying to inflame the jury by—'

'Objection overruled. The foundation was laid in a pretrial motion.' Judge Williams turned to Brennan. 'You may show the photographs.'

David took his seat, furious.

Brennan walked back to his desk and picked up a stack of photographs and handed them out to the jurors. 'These are not pleasant to look at, ladies and gentlemen, but this is what the trial is about. It's not about words or theories or excuses. It's not about mysterious alter egos killing people. It's about three real people who were savagely and brutally murdered. The law says that someone has to pay for those murders. It's up to each one of you to see that justice is done.'

Brennan could see the horror on the faces of the jurors as they looked at the photographs.

He turned to Judge Williams. 'The prosecution rests.'

Judge Williams looked at her watch. 'It's four o'clock. The court will recess for the day and begin again at ten o'clock Monday morning. Court adjourned.'

•

Chapter Nineteen

Ashley Patterson was on the gallows being hanged, when a policeman ran up and said, 'Wait a minute. She's supposed to be electrocuted.'

The scene changed, and she was in the electric chair. A guard reached up to pull the switch, and Judge Williams came running in screaming, 'No. We're going to kill her with a lethal injection.'

David woke up and sat upright in bed, his heart pounding. His pajamas were wet with perspiration. He started to get up and was suddenly dizzy. He had a pounding headache, and he felt feverish. He touched his forehead. It was hot.

As David started to get out of bed, he was overcome by a wave of dizziness. 'Oh, no,' he groaned. 'Not today. Not now.'

This was the day he had been waiting for, the day the defense would begin to present its case. David stumbled into the bathroom and bathed his face in cold water. He looked in the mirror. 'You look like hell.'

When David arrived in court, Judge Williams was already on the bench. They were all waiting for him.

'I apologize for being late,' David said. His voice was a croak. 'May I approach the bench?'

'Yes.'

David walked up to the bench, with Mickey Brennan

close behind him. 'Your Honor,' David said, 'I'd like to ask for a one-day stay.'

'On what grounds?'

'I – I'm not feeling very well, Your Honor. I'm sure a doctor can give me something and tomorrow I'll be fine.'

Judge Williams said, 'Why don't you have your associate take over for you?'

David looked at her in surprise. 'I don't have an associate.'

'Why don't you, Mr Singer?'

'Because . . .'

Judge Williams leaned forward. 'I've never seen a murder trial conducted like this. You're a one-man show looking for glory, aren't you? Well, you won't find it in this court. I'll tell you something else. You probably think I should recuse myself because I don't believe in your devil-made-me-do-it defense, but I'm not recusing myself. We're going to let the jury decide whether they think your client is innocent or guilty. Is there anything else, Mr Singer?'

David stood there looking at her, and the room was swimming. He wanted to tell her to go fuck herself. He wanted to get on his knees and beg her to be fair. He wanted to go home to bed. He said in a hoarse voice, 'No. Thank you, Your Honor.'

Judge Williams nodded. 'Mr Singer, you're on. Don't waste any more of this court's time.'

David walked over to the jury box, trying to forget about his headache and fever. He spoke slowly.

'Ladies and gentlemen, you have listened to the prosecution ridiculing the facts of multiple personality disorder. I'm sure that Mr Brennan wasn't being deliberately malicious. His statements were made out of ignorance. The fact is that he obviously knows nothing about multiple personality

222

disorder, and the same is true of some of the witnesses he has put on the stand. But I'm going to have some people talk to you who *do* know about it. These are reputable doctors, who are experts in this problem. When you have heard their testimony, I'm sure that it will cast a whole different light on what Mr Brennan has had to say.

'Mr Brennan has talked about my client's guilt in committing these terrible crimes. That's a very important point. *Guilt.* For murder in the first degree to be proved, there must be not only a guilty act, but a guilty intention. I will show you that there was no guilty intention, because Ashley Patterson was not in control at the time the crimes occurred. She was totally unaware that they were taking place. Some eminent doctors are going to testify that Ashley Patterson has two additional personalities, or alters, one of them a controlling one.'

David looked into the faces of the jurors. They seemed to be swaying in front of him. He squeezed his eyes shut for an instant.

'The American Psychiatric Association recognizes multiple personality disorder. So do prominent physicians around the world who have treated patients with this problem. One of Ashley Patterson's personalities committed murder, but it was a *personality* – an *alter* – over which she had no control.' His voice was getting stronger. 'To see the problem clearly, you must understand that the law does not punish an innocent person. So there is a paradox here. Imagine that a Siamese twin is being tried for murder. The law says that you cannot punish the guilty one because you would then have to punish the innocent one.' The jury was listening intently.

David nodded toward Ashley. 'In this case, we have not two but three personalities to deal with.'

He turned to Judge Williams. 'I would like to call my first witness. Dr Joel Ashanti.'

'Dr Ashanti, where do you practice medicine?'

'At Madison Hospital in New York.'

'And did you come here at my request?'

'No. I read about the trial, and I wanted to testify. I've worked with patients who have multiple personality disorder, and I wanted to be helpful, if I could. MPD is much more common than the public realizes, and I want to try to clear up any misunderstandings about it.'

'I appreciate that, Doctor. In cases like these, is it usual to find a patient with two personalities or alters?'

'In my experience, people with MPD usually have many more alters, sometimes as many as a hundred.'

Eleanor Tucker turned to whisper something to Mickey Brennan. Brennan smiled.

'How long have you been dealing with multiple personality disorder, Dr Ashanti?'

'For the past fifteen years.'

'In a patient with MPD, is there usually one alter who dominates?'

'Yes.'

Some of the jurors were making notes.

'And is the host – the person who has those personalities within him or her – aware of the other alters?'

'It varies. Sometimes some of the alters know all the other alters, sometimes they know only some of them. But the host is usually not aware of them, not until psychiatric treatment.'

'That's very interesting. Is MPD curable?'

'Often, yes. It requires psychiatric treatment over long periods. Sometimes up to six or seven years.'

'Have you ever been able to cure MPD patients?'

'Oh, yes.'

'Thank you, Doctor.'

David turned to study the jury for a moment. *Interested, but not convinced*, he thought.

He looked over at Mickey Brennan. 'Your witness.'

Brennan rose and walked over to the witness box. 'Dr Ashanti, you testified that you flew here all the way from New York because you wanted to be helpful?'

'That's correct.'

'Your coming here couldn't have anything to do with the fact that this is a high-profile case and that the publicity would be beneficial to—'

David was on his feet. 'Objection. Argumentative.'

'Overruled.'

Dr Ashanti said calmly, 'I stated why I came here.'

'Right. Since you've been practicing medicine, Doctor, how many patients would you say you've treated for mental disorders?'

'Oh, perhaps two hundred.'

'And of those cases, how many would you say suffered from multiple personality disorder?'

'A dozen . . .'

Brennan looked at him in feigned astonishment. 'Out of two hundred patients?'

'Well, yes. You see—'

'What I don't see, Dr Ashanti, is how you can consider yourself an expert if you've dealt with only those few cases. I would appreciate it if you would give us some evidence that would prove or disprove the existence of multiple personality disorder.'

'When you say proof—'

'We're in a court of law, Doctor. The jury is not going

225

to make decisions based on theory and "what if." What if, for example, the defendant hated the men she murdered, and after killing them, decided to use the excuse of an alter inside her so that she—'

David was on his feet. 'Objection! That's argumentative and leading the witness.'

'Overruled.'

'Your Honor—'

'Sit down, Mr Singer.'

David glared at Judge Williams and angrily took his seat.

'So what you're telling us, Doctor, is that there's no evidence that will prove or disprove the existence of MPD?'

'Well, no. But—'

Brennan nodded. 'That's all.'

Dr Royce Salem was on the witness stand.

David said, 'Dr Salem, you examined Ashley Patterson?'

'I did.'

'And what was your conclusion?'

'Miss Patterson is suffering from MPD. She has two alters who call themselves Toni Prescott and Alette Peters.'

'Does she have any control over them?'

'None. When they take over, she is in a state of fugue amnesia.'

'Would you explain that, Dr Salem?'

'Fugue amnesia is a condition where the victim loses consciousness of where he is, or what he is doing. It can last for a few minutes, days or sometimes weeks.'

'And during that time would you say that that person is responsible for his or her actions?'

'No.'

'Thank you, Doctor.' He turned to Brennan. 'Your witness.'

Brennan said, 'Dr Salem, you are a consultant at several hospitals and you give lectures all around the world?'

'Yes, sir.'

'I assume that your peers are gifted, capable doctors?'

'Yes, I would say they are.'

'So, they all agree about multiple personality disorder?'

'No.'

'What do you mean, no?'

'Some of them don't agree.'

'You mean, they don't believe it exists?'

'Yes.'

'But they're wrong and you're right?'

'I've treated patients, and I *know* that there is such a thing. When—'

'Let me ask you something. If there *were* such a thing as multiple personality disorder, would one alter always be in charge of telling the host what to do? The alter says, "Kill," and the host does it?'

'It depends. Alters have various degrees of influence.'

'So the host *could* be in charge?'

'Sometimes, of course.'

'The majority of times?'

'No.'

'Doctor, where is the proof that MPD exists?'

'I have witnessed complete physical changes in patients under hypnosis, and I know—'

'And that's a basis of truth?'

'Yes.'

'Dr Salem, if I hypnotized you in a warm room and told you that you were at the North Pole naked in a snowstorm, would your body temperature drop?'

'Well, yes, but—'

'That's all.'

David walked over to the witness stand. 'Dr Salem, is there any doubt in your mind that these alters exist in Ashley Patterson?'

'None. And they are absolutely capable of taking over and dominating her.'

'And she would not be aware of it?'

'She would not be aware of it.'

'Thank you.'

'I would like to call Shane Miller to the stand.' David watched him being sworn in. 'What do you do, Mr Miller?'

'I'm a supervisor at Global Computer Graphics Corporation.'

'And how long have you worked there?'

'About seven years.'

'And was Ashley Patterson employed there?'

'Yes.'

'And did she work under your supervision?'

'She did.'

'So you got to know her pretty well?'

'That's right.'

'Mr Miller, you've heard doctors testify that some of the symptoms of multiple personality disorder are paranoia, nervousness, distress. Have you ever noticed any of those symptoms in Miss Patterson?'

'Well, I—'

'Didn't Miss Patterson tell you that she felt someone was stalking her?'

'Yes. She did.'

'And that she had no idea who it could be or why anyone would do that?'

'That's right.'

'Didn't she once say that someone used her computer to threaten her with a knife?'

'Yes.'

'And didn't things get so bad that you finally sent her to the psychologist who works at your company, Dr Speakman?'

'Yes.'

'So Ashley Patterson did exhibit the symptoms we're talking about?'

'That's right.'

'Thank you, Mr Miller.' David turned to Mickey Brennan. 'Your witness.'

'How many employees do you have directly under you, Mr Miller?'

'Thirty.'

'And out of thirty employees, Ashley Patterson is the only one you've ever seen get upset?'

'Well, no . . .'

'Oh, really?'

'Everyone gets upset sometimes.'

'You mean other employees had to go and see your company psychologist?'

'Oh, sure. They keep him pretty busy.'

Brennan seemed impressed. 'Is that so?'

'Yeah. A lot of them have problems. Hey, they're all human.'

'No further questions.'

'Redirect.'

David approached the witness stand. 'Mr Miller, you said that some of the employees under you had problems. What kind of problems?'

'Well, it could be about an argument with a boyfriend or a husband . . .'

'Yes?'

'Or it could be about a financial problem . . .'

'Yes?'

'Or their kids bugging them . . .'

'In other words, the ordinary kinds of domestic problems that any of us might face?'

'Yes.'

'But no one went to see Dr Speakman because they thought they were being stalked or because they thought someone was threatening to kill them?'

'No.'

'Thank you.'

The trial was recessed for lunch.

David got into his car and drove through the park, depressed. The trial was going badly. The doctors couldn't make up their minds whether MPD existed or not. *If they can't agree,* David thought, *how am I going to get a jury to agree? I can't let anything happen to Ashley. I can't.* He was approaching Harold's Café, a restaurant near the courthouse. He parked the car and went inside. The hostess smiled at him.

'Good afternoon, Mr Singer.'

He was famous. *Infamous?*

'Right this way, please.' He followed her to a booth and sat down. The hostess handed him the menu, gave him a lingering smile and walked away, her hips moving provocatively. *The perks of fame,* David thought wryly.

He was not hungry, but he could hear Sandra's voice saying, 'You have to eat to keep up your strength.'

There were two men and two women seated in the booth next to him. One of the men was saying, 'She's a hell of a lot worse than Lizzie Borden. Borden killed only two people.'

The other man added, 'And *she* didn't castrate them.'

'What do you think they'll do to her?'

'Are you kidding? She'll get the death sentence.'

'Too bad the Butcher Bitch can't get three death sentences.'

That's the public speaking, David thought. He had the depressing feeling that if he walked around the restaurant, he would hear variations of the same comments. Brennan had built her up as a monster. He could hear Quiller's voice. *'If you don't put her on the stand, that's the image the jurors will carry in their minds when they go into the jury room to reach a verdict.'*

I've got to take the chance. I've got to let the jurors see for themselves that Ashley's telling the truth.

The waitress was at his side. 'Are you ready to order, Mr Singer?'

'I've changed my mind,' David said. 'I'm not hungry.' As he got up and walked out of the restaurant, he could feel baleful eyes following him. *I hope they're not armed,* David thought.

Chapter Twenty

When David returned to the courthouse, he visited Ashley in her cell. She was seated on the little cot, staring at the floor.

'Ashley.'

She looked up, her eyes filled with despair.

David sat next to her. 'We have to talk.'

She watched him, silent.

'These terrible things they're saying about you . . . none of them are true. But the jurors don't know that. They don't know you. We've got to let them see what you're really like.'

Ashley looked at him and said dully, 'What am I really like?'

'You're a decent human being who has an illness. They'll sympathize with that.'

'What do you want me to do?'

'I want you to get on the witness stand and testify.'

She was staring at him, horrified. 'I – I can't. I don't know anything. I can't tell them anything.'

'Let me handle that. All you have to do is answer my questions.'

A guard came up to the cell. 'Court's coming into session.'

David rose and squeezed Ashley's hand. 'It's going to work. You'll see.'

* * *

'All rise. Court is now in session. The Honorable Judge Tessa Williams presiding in the case of *The People of the State of California Versus Ashley Patterson*.'

Judge Williams took her seat on the bench.

David said, 'May I approach the bench?'

'You may.'

Mickey Brennan walked to the bench with David.

'What is it, Mr Singer?'

'I'd like to call a witness who's not on the discovery list.'

Brennan said, 'It's awfully late in the trial to introduce new witnesses.'

'I would like to call Ashley Patterson as my next witness.'

Judge Williams said, 'I don't—'

Mickey Brennan said quickly, 'The state has no objection, Your Honor.'

Judge Williams looked at the two attorneys. 'Very well. You may call your witness, Mr Singer.'

'Thank you, Your Honor.' He walked over to Ashley and held out his hand. 'Ashley . . .'

She sat there in a panic.

'You must.'

She rose, her heart palpitating, and slowly made her way to the witness stand.

Mickey Brennan whispered to Eleanor, 'I was praying that he'd call her.'

Eleanor nodded. 'It's over.'

Ashley Patterson was being sworn in by the court clerk. 'You do solemnly swear to tell the truth, the whole truth and nothing but the truth, so help you God?'

'I do.' Her voice was a whisper. Ashley took her seat in the witness box.

David walked over to her. He said gently, 'I know this

is very difficult for you. You've been accused of horrible crimes that you did not commit. All I want is for the jury to know the truth. Do you have any memory of committing any of those crimes?'

Ashley shook her head. 'No.'

David glanced at the jury, then went on. 'Did you know Dennis Tibble?'

'Yes. We worked together at Global Computer Graphics Corporation.'

'Did you have any reason to kill Dennis Tibble?'

'No.' It was difficult for her to speak. 'I – I went to his apartment to give him some advice that he had asked me for, and that was the last time I saw him.'

'Did you know Richard Melton?'

'No . . .'

'He was an artist. He was murdered in San Francisco. The police found evidence of your DNA and fingerprints there.'

Ashley was shaking her head from side to side. 'I – I don't know what to say. I didn't know him!'

'You knew Deputy Sam Blake?'

'Yes. He was helping me. I didn't kill him!'

'Are you aware that you have two other personalities, or alters, within you, Ashley?'

'Yes.' Her voice was strained.

'When did you learn this?'

'Before the trial. Dr Salem told me about it. I couldn't believe it. I – I still can't believe it. It's – it's too awful.'

'You had no previous knowledge of these alters.'

'No.'

'You had never heard of Toni Prescott or Alette Peters?'

'No!'

'Do you believe now that they exist within you?'

235

'Yes . . . I have to believe it. They must have done all these – these horrible things . . .'

'So you have no recollection of ever having met Richard Melton, you had no motive for killing Dennis Tibble or for killing Deputy Sam Blake, who was at your apartment to protect you?'

'That's right.' Her eyes swept over the crowded courtroom, and she felt a sense of panic.

'One last question,' David said. 'Have you ever been in trouble with the law?'

'Never.'

David put his hand on hers. 'That's all for now.' He turned to Mickey Brennan. 'Your witness.'

Brennan rose, a big smile on his face. 'Well, Miss Patterson, we finally get to talk to all of you. Did you ever, at any time, have sexual intercourse with Dennis Tibble?'

'No.'

'Did you ever have sexual intercourse with Richard Melton?'

'No.'

'Did you ever, at any time, have sexual intercourse with Deputy Samuel Blake?'

'No.'

'That's very interesting.' Brennan glanced at the jury. 'Because traces of a vaginal discharge were found on the bodies of all three men. The DNA tests matched your DNA.'

'I . . . I don't know anything about that.'

'Maybe you've been framed. Maybe some fiend got hold of it—'

'Objection! It's argumentative.'

'Overruled.'

'– and planted it on those three mutilated bodies.

236

Do you have any enemies who would do such a thing to you?'

'I . . . don't know.'

'The FBI's fingerprint lab checked the fingerprints the police found at the scenes of the crimes. And I'm sure this will surprise you—'

'Objection.'

'Sustained. Be careful, Mr Brennan.'

'Yes, Your Honor.'

Satisfied, David slowly sat down.

Ashley was on the verge of hysteria. 'The alters must have—'

'The fingerprints at the scenes of the three murders were yours, and yours alone.'

Ashley sat there, silent.

Brennan walked over to a table, picked up a butcher knife wrapped in cellophane and held it up. 'Do you recognize this?'

'It – it could be one of . . . one of my—'

'One of your knives? It is. It has already been admitted into evidence. The stains on it match the blood of Deputy Blake. Your fingerprints are on this murder weapon.'

Ashley was mindlessly shaking her head from side to side.

'I've never seen a clearer case of cold-blooded murder or a more feeble defense. Hiding behind two nonexistent, imaginary characters is the most—'

David was on his feet again. 'Objection.'

'Sustained. I've already warned you, Mr Brennan.'

'Sorry, Your Honor.'

Brennan went on. 'I'm sure that the jury would like to meet the characters you're talking about. You are Ashley Patterson, correct?'

'Yes . . .'

'Fine. I would like to talk to Toni Prescott.'

'I . . . I can't bring her out.'

Brennan looked at her in surprise. 'You *can't*? *Really*? Well, then, how about Alette Peters?'

Ashley shook her head despairingly. 'I . . . I don't control them.'

'Miss Patterson, I'm trying to help you,' Brennan said. 'I want to show the jury your alters who killed and mutilated three innocent men. Bring them out!'

'I . . . I can't.' She was sobbing.

'You can't because they don't exist! You're hiding behind phantoms. You're the only one sitting in that box, and you're the only one who's guilty. They don't exist, but *you* do, and I'll tell you what else exists – irrefutable, undeniable proof that you murdered three men and cold-bloodedly emasculated them.' He turned to Judge Williams. 'Your Honor, the state rests.'

David turned to look at the jury. They were all staring at Ashley and their faces were filled with repulsion.

Judge Williams turned to David. 'Mr Singer?'

David rose. 'Your Honor, I would like permission to have the defendant hypnotized so that—'

Judge Williams said curtly, 'Mr Singer, I warned you before that I will not have this trial turned into a sideshow. You can't hypnotize her in *my* courtroom. The answer is no.'

David said fiercely, 'You *have* to let me do this. You don't know how important—'

'That's enough, Mr Singer.' Her voice was ice. 'I'm citing you a second time for contempt. Do you want to reexamine the witness or don't you?'

David stood there, frustrated. 'Yes, Your Honor.' He

walked over to the witness box. 'Ashley, you know you're under oath?'

'Yes.' She was taking deep breaths, fighting to control herself.

'And everything you've said is the truth as you know it?'

'Yes.'

'You know that there are two alters in your mind and body and soul who you have no control over?'

'Yes.'

'Toni and Alette?'

'Yes.'

'You didn't commit any of those terrible murders?'

'No.'

'One of them did, and you're not responsible.'

Eleanor looked at Brennan questioningly, but he smiled and shook his head. 'Let him hang himself,' he whispered.

'Helen –' David stopped, white-faced at his slip. 'I mean, Ashley . . . I want you to have Toni come out.'

Ashley looked at David and shook her head helplessly. 'I – I can't,' she whispered.

David said, 'Yes, you can. Toni is listening to us right now. She's enjoying herself, and why shouldn't she? She got away with three murders.' He raised his voice. 'You're very clever, Toni. Come on out and take a bow. No one can touch you. They can't punish you because Ashley is innocent, and they'd have to punish her to get at you.'

Everyone in the courtroom was staring at David. Ashley sat there, frozen.

David moved closer to her. 'Toni! Toni, can you hear me? I want you to come out. *Now!*'

He waited a moment. Nothing happened. He raised his

voice. 'Toni! Alette! Come out! Come on out. We all know you're in there!'

There was not a sound in the courtroom.

David lost control. He was yelling, 'Come out. Show your faces . . . *Damn it! Now! Now!*'

Ashley dissolved in tears.

Judge Williams said furiously, 'Approach the bench, Mr Singer.'

Slowly, David walked over to the bench.

'Are you through badgering your client, Mr Singer? I'm going to send a report of your behavior to the state bar association. You're a disgrace to your profession, and I'm going to recommend that you're disbarred.'

David had no answer.

'Do you have any more witnesses to call?'

David shook his head defeated. 'No, Your Honor.'

It was over. He had lost. Ashley was going to die.

'The defense rests.'

Joseph Kincaid was seated in the last row of the courtroom, watching, his face grim. He turned to Harvey Udell. 'Get rid of him.' Kincaid got up and left.

Udell stopped David as he was leaving the courtroom. 'David . . .'

'Hello, Harvey.'

'Sorry about the way this turned out.'

'It's not—'

'Mr Kincaid hates to do this, but, well, he thinks it would be better if you didn't come back to the firm. Good luck.'

The moment David stepped outside the courtroom, he was surrounded by television cameras and shouting reporters.

'Do you have a statement, Mr Singer . . . ?'

'We hear Judge Williams says you're going to be disbarred . . .'

'Judge Williams says she's going to hold you for contempt of court. Do you think you—?'

'The experts feel you've lost this case. Do you plan to appeal . . . ?'

'Our network legal experts say that your client will get the death penalty . . .'

'Have you made any plans for the future . . . ?'

David got into his car without a word and drove away.

Chapter Twenty-one

He rewrote the scenes in his mind, over and over again, endlessly.

I saw the news this morning, Dr Patterson. I can't tell you how very sorry I am.

Yes. It's been quite a blow. I need your help, David.

Of course. Anything I can do.

I want you to represent Ashley.

I can't do that. I'm not a criminal defense lawyer. But I can recommend a great attorney, Jesse Quiller.

That will be fine. Thank you, David . . .

You're an anxious young fellow, aren't you? Our meeting wasn't supposed to be until five o'clock. Well, I have good news for you. We're making you a partner.

You asked to see me?

Yes, Your Honor. They're talking about this trial on the Internet, and they've already convicted the defendant. This could seriously damage the defense. Therefore, I'm making a motion for a mistrial.

I think those are excellent grounds for a mistrial, Mr Singer. I'm going to grant it . . .

The bitter-tasting game of 'What if.' . . .

*   *   *

The following morning, the court was in session.

'Is the prosecution ready to make its closing argument?' Brennan stood up. He walked over to the jury box and looked at the jurors one by one.

'You're in a position to make history here. If you believe that the defendant is really a lot of different people and she's not responsible for what she's done, for the terrible crimes she committed, and you let her go, then you're saying that anybody can get away with murder by simply claiming that they didn't do it, that some mysterious alter ego did it. They can rob, rape and kill, and are they guilty? No. "I didn't do it. My alter ego did it." Ken or Joe or Suzy or whatever they want to call themselves. Well, I think you're all too intelligent to fall for that fantasy. The reality is in those photographs you looked at. Those people weren't murdered by any alter egos. They were all deliberately, calculatedly, cruelly murdered by the defendant sitting at that table, Ashley Patterson. Ladies and gentlemen of the jury, what the defense has tried to do in this court has been tried before. In *Mann Versus Teller*, the decision was that a finding of MPD does not, per se, require a finding of acquittal. In *United States Versus Whirley*, a nurse who murdered a baby pleaded that she had MPD. The court found her guilty.

'You know, I almost feel sorry for the defendant. All those characters living in that poor girl. I'm sure none of us would want a bunch of crazy strangers moving around inside us, would we? Going around murdering and castrating men. I'd be scared.'

He turned to look at Ashley. 'The defendant doesn't seem scared, does she? Not too scared to put on a pretty dress and comb her hair nicely and apply makeup. She doesn't seem scared at all. She thinks you're going to believe her story and let her go. No one can prove whether this multiple personality disorder really exists at all, so we're going to have to make our own judgments.

'The defense claims that these characters come out and take over. Let's see – there's Toni; she was born in England. And Alette; she was born in Italy. They're all the same person. They were just born in different countries at different times. Does that confuse you? I know it confuses me. I offered the defendant a chance to let us see her alters, but she didn't take me up on it. I wonder why? Could it be because they don't exist . . . ? Does California law recognize MPD as a mental condition? No. Colorado law? No. Mississippi? No. Federal law? No. As a matter of fact, *no* state has a law confirming MPD as a legal defense. And why? Because it *isn't* a defense. Ladies and gentlemen, it's a fictitious alibi to escape punishment . . .'

'What the defense is asking you to believe is that there are two people inside the defendant, so no one bears any responsibility for her criminal actions. But there is only one defendant sitting in this courtroom – Ashley Patterson. We have proved beyond a shadow of a doubt that she is a murderer. But she claims she didn't commit the crimes. That was done by someone else, someone who borrowed her body to kill innocent people – her alters. Wouldn't it be wonderful if we all had alters, someone to carry out anything we secretly wanted done that society doesn't permit? Or maybe not. Would you like to live in a world where people could go around murdering others and say, "You can't touch me, my alter did it" and "You can't punish my alter because my alter is really me"?

'But this trial is not about some mythical characters who don't exist. The defendant, Ashley Patterson, is on trial

245

for three vicious, cold-blooded murders, and the state is asking the death penalty. Thank you.'

Mickey Brennan returned to his seat.

'Is the defense ready to present its closing argument?'

David rose. He walked to the jury box and looked into the faces of the jurors, and what he saw there was disheartening. 'I know that this has been a very difficult case for all of us. You've heard experts testify that they've treated multiple personality disorder, and you've heard other experts testify that there is no such thing. You're not doctors, so no one expects you to make your judgment based on medical knowledge. I want to apologize to all of you if my behavior yesterday seemed boorish. I yelled at Ashley Patterson only because I wanted to force her alters to come out. I've talked to those alters. I know they exist. There really is an Alette and a Toni, and they can control Ashley anytime they want to. She has no knowledge of committing any murders.

'I told you at the beginning of this trial that for someone to be convicted of first-degree murder, there has to be physical evidence and a motive. There is no motive here, ladies and gentlemen. None. And the law says that the prosecution must prove a defendant is guilty beyond a reasonable doubt. I'm sure you'll agree that in this case, there *is* a reasonable doubt.

'As far as proof is concerned, the defense does not question it. There are Ashley Patterson's fingerprints and traces of DNA at each of the crime scenes. But the very fact that they are there should give us pause. Ashley Patterson is an intelligent young woman. If she committed a murder and did not want to be caught, would she have been stupid enough to leave her fingerprints at each one of the scenes? The answer is no.'

246

David went on for another thirty minutes. At the end, he looked at their faces and was not reassured. He sat down.

Judge Williams turned to the jurors. 'I want to instruct you now on the applicable law to this case. I want you to listen carefully.' She talked for the next twenty minutes, detailing what was admissible and allowable by law.

'If you have any questions, or want any part of the testimony read back to you, the court reporter will do so. The jury is excused to go deliberate. Court is adjourned until they return with their verdict.'

David watched the jury file out of the box and into the jury room. *The longer the jurors take, the better our chances*, David thought.

The jurors returned forty-five minutes later.

David and Ashley watched as the jurors filed in and took their seats in the jury box. Ashley was stone-faced. David found that he was perspiring.

Judge Williams turned to the jury foreman. 'Have the jurors reached a verdict?'

'We have, Your Honor.'

'Would you please hand it to the bailiff.'

The bailiff carried the piece of paper to the judge. Judge Williams unfolded it. There was not a sound in the courtroom.

The bailiff returned the paper to the jury foreman.

'Would you read the verdict, please?'

In a slow, measured tone, he read, 'In the case of *The People of the State of California Versus Ashley Patterson*, we, the jury, in the above entitled action, find the defendant, Ashley Patterson, guilty of the murder of Dennis Tibble, a violation of Penal Code Section 187.'

There was a gasp in the courtroom. Ashley shut her eyes tightly.

'In the case of *The People of the State of California Versus Ashley Patterson*, we, the jury, in the above entitled action, find the defendant, Ashley Patterson, guilty of the murder of Deputy Samuel Blake, a violation of Penal Code Section 187.

'In the case of *The People of the State of California Versus Ashley Patterson*, we, the jury, in the above entitled action, find the defendant, Ashley Patterson, guilty of the murder of Richard Melton, a violation of Penal Code Section 187. We, the jury, in all the verdicts, further fix the degree at first degree.'

David was finding it difficult to breathe. He turned to Ashley, but he had no words. He leaned over and put his arms around her.

Judge Williams said, 'I would like to have the jury polled.'

One by one, each juror stood up.

'Was the verdict read, your verdict?'

And when each one had affirmed it, Judge Williams said, 'The verdict will be recorded and entered into the minutes.' She went on. 'I want to thank the jury for their time and service in this case. You're dismissed. Tomorrow the court will take up the issue of sanity.'

David sat there, numb, watching Ashley being led away.

Judge Williams got up and walked to her chambers without looking at David. Her attitude told David more clearly than words what her decision was going to be in the morning. Ashley was going to be sentenced to die.

* * *

Sandra called from San Francisco. 'Are you all right, David?'

He tried to sound cheerful. 'Yes, I'm great. How are you feeling?'

'I'm fine. I've been watching the news on television. The judge wasn't fair to you. She can't have you disbarred. You were only trying to help your client.'

He had no answer.

'I'm so sorry, David. I wish I were with you. I could drive down and—'

'No,' David said. 'We can't take any chances. Did you see the doctor today?'

'Yes.'

'What did he say?'

'Very soon now. Any day.'

Happy birthday, Jeffrey.

Jesse Quiller called.

'I bungled it,' David said.

'Like hell you did. You got the wrong judge. What did you ever do to get her so down on you?'

David said, 'She wanted me to plea-bargain. She didn't want this to go to trial. Maybe I should have listened to her.'

All the television channels were full of the news of his disgrace. He watched one of the network's legal experts discussing the case.

'I've never heard of a defending attorney screaming at his own client before. I must tell you, the courtroom was stunned. It was one of the most outrageous—'

David switched off the station. *Where did it all go wrong? Life is supposed to have a happy ending. Because I've bungled*

249

everything, Ashley's going to die, I'm going to be disbarred, the baby's going to be born any minute and I don't even have a job.

He sat in his hotel room in the middle of the night, staring into the darkness. It was the lowest moment of his life. Playing over and over again in his mind was the final courtroom scene. *'You can't hypnotize her in my courtroom. The answer is no.'*

If only she had let me hypnotize Ashley on the stand, I know she would have convinced the jury. Too late. It's all over now.

And a small, nagging voice in his mind said, *Who says it's over? I don't hear the fat lady singing.*

There's nothing more I can do.

Your client is innocent. Are you going to let her die?

Leave me alone.

Judge Williams's words kept echoing in his mind. *'You can't hypnotize her in my courtroom.'*

And three words kept repeating themselves – *in my courtroom.'*

At five o'clock in the morning, David made two excited, urgent phone calls. As he finished, the sun was just beginning to appear over the horizon. *It's an omen*, David thought. *We're going to win.*

A little later, David hurried into an antiques store.

The clerk approached him. 'May I help you, sir?' He recognized David. 'Mr Singer.'

'I'm looking for a folding Chinese screen. Do you have something like that?'

'Yes, we do. We don't have any real antique screens, but—'

'Let's see what you have.'

'Certainly.' He led David over to the section where there were several Chinese folding screens. The clerk pointed to the first one. 'Now, this one—'

'That's fine,' David said.

'Yes, sir. Where shall I send it?'

'I'll take it with me.'

David's next stop was at a hardware store, where he bought a Swiss Army knife. Fifteen minutes later, he was walking into the lobby of the courthouse carrying the screen. He said to the guard at the desk, 'I made arrangements to interview Ashley Patterson. I have permission to use Judge Goldberg's chambers. He's not here today.'

The guard said, 'Yes, sir. It's all set. I'll have the defendant brought up. Dr Salem and another man are already up there, waiting.'

'Thank you.'

The guard watched David carry the Chinese screen into the elevator. *Crazy as a loon*, he thought.

Judge Goldberg's chamber was a comfortable-looking room with a desk facing the window, a swivel chair, and near one wall a couch and several chairs. Dr Salem and another man were standing in the room when David entered.

'Sorry I'm late,' David said.

Dr Salem said, 'This is Hugh Iverson. He's the expert you asked for.'

The two men shook hands. 'Let's get set up fast,' David said. 'Ashley's on her way here.'

He turned to Hugh Iverson and pointed to a corner of the room. 'How's that for you?'

'Fine.'

He watched Iverson go to work. A few minutes later, the door opened and Ashley entered with a guard.

'I'll have to stay in the room,' the guard said.

David nodded. 'That's all right.' He turned to Ashley. 'Sit down, please.'

He watched her take a seat. 'First of all, I want to tell you how terribly sorry I am about the way things went.'

She nodded, almost dazed.

'But it's not over yet. We still have a chance.'

She looked at him with disbelieving eyes.

'Ashley, I would like Dr Salem to hypnotize you again.'

'No. What's the point in—'

'Do it for me. Will you?'

She shrugged.

David nodded to Dr Salem.

Dr Salem said to Ashley, 'We've done this before, so you know that all you have to do is close your eyes and relax. Just relax. Feel all the muscles in your body letting go of all the tension. All you want to do is sleep. You're getting very drowsy . . .'

Ten minutes later, Dr Salem looked at David and said, 'She's completely under.'

David moved toward Ashley, and his heart was pounding.

'I want to talk to Toni.'

There was no reaction.

David raised his voice. 'Toni. I want you to come out. Do you hear me? Alette . . . I want you both to talk to me.'

Silence.

David was yelling now. 'What's the matter with you? Are you too frightened? That's what happened in the courtroom, isn't it? Did you hear what the jury said?

Ashley's guilty. You were afraid to come out. You're a coward, Toni!'

They looked at Ashley. There was no reaction. David looked at Dr Salem in despair. It was not going to work.

'Court is now in session. The Honorable Judge Tessa Williams presiding.'

Ashley was seated at the defendant's table next to David. David's hand was wrapped in a large bandage.

David rose. 'May I approach the bench, Your Honor?'

'You may.'

David walked toward the bench. Brennan followed him.

David said, 'I would like to present new evidence to this case.'

'Absolutely not,' Brennan objected.

Judge Williams turned to him and said, 'Let me make that decision, Mr Brennan.' She turned back to David. 'The trial is over. Your client has been convicted and—'

'This concerns the insanity plea,' David said. 'All I'm asking for is ten minutes of your time.'

Judge Williams said angrily, 'Time doesn't mean much to you, does it, Mr Singer? You have already wasted a great deal of everyone's time.' She made her decision. 'All right. I hope this is the last request you'll ever be able to make in a court of law. The court is recessed for ten minutes.'

David and Brennan followed the judge to her chambers.

She turned to David. 'I'm giving you your ten minutes. What is it, Counselor?'

'I want to show you a piece of film, Your Honor.'

Brennan said, 'I don't see what this has to do with—'

Judge Williams said to Brennan, 'I don't, either.' She turned to David. 'You now have nine minutes.'

David hurried over to the door leading to the hallway and opened it. 'Come in.'

Hugh Iverson walked in, carrying a sixteen-millimeter projector and a portable screen. 'Where should I set it up?'

David pointed to a corner of the room. 'Over there.'

They watched as the man set up the equipment and plugged in the projector.

'May I pull down the shades?' David asked.

It was all Judge Williams could do to hold back her anger. 'Yes, you go right ahead, Mr Singer.' She looked at her watch. 'You have seven minutes.'

The projector was turned on. Judge Goldberg's chambers flickered onto the screen. David and Dr Salem were watching Ashley, who was seated in a chair.

On the screen, Dr Salem said, 'She's completely under.'

David walked up to Ashley. 'I want to talk to Toni . . . Toni, I want you to come out. Do you hear me? Alette . . . I want you both to talk to me.'

Silence.

Judge Williams sat there, her face tight, watching the film.

David was yelling now. 'What's the matter with you? Are you too frightened? That's what happened in the courtroom, isn't it? Did you hear what the jury said? Ashley's guilty. You were afraid to come out. You're a coward, Toni!'

Judge Williams got to her feet. 'I've had enough of this! I've seen this disgusting performance before. Your time is up, Mr Singer.'

'Wait,' David said. 'You haven't—'

'It's finished,' Judge Williams told him and started for the door.

Suddenly, a song began to fill the room.

'A penny for a spool of thread.
A penny for a needle.
That's the way the money goes,
Pop! goes the weasel.'

Puzzled, Judge Williams turned around. She looked at the picture on the screen.

Ashley's face had completely changed. It was Toni.

Toni said angrily, 'Too frightened to come out in court? Did you really think I would come out just because you ordered me to? What do you think I am, a trained pony?'

Judge Williams slowly moved back into the room, staring at the film.

'I listened to all those bloody gits making fools of themselves.' She mimicked one of their voices. '"I don't think that multiple personality disorder exists." What idiots. I've never seen such—'

As they watched, Ashley's face changed again. She seemed to relax in her chair, and her face took on a shy look. In her Italian accent, Alette said, 'Mr Singer, I know you did the best you could. I wanted to appear in court and help you, but Toni wouldn't let me.'

Judge Williams was watching, her face blank.

The face and voice changed again. 'You're bleeding right I wouldn't,' Toni said.

David said, 'Toni, what do you think is going to happen to you if the judge gives Ashley the death sentence?'

'She's not going to give her the death sentence. Ashley didn't even know one of the men. Remember?'

255

David said, 'But Alette knew them all. You committed those murders, Alette. You had sex with those men and then you stabbed them to death and castrated them . . .'

Toni said, 'You bloody idiot! You don't know anything, do you? Alette would never have had the nerve to do that. *I* did it. They deserved to die. All they wanted to do was have sex.' She was breathing hard. 'But I made them all pay for it, didn't I? And no one can ever prove I did it. Let little Miss Goody Two-shoes take the blame. We'll all go to a nice cozy asylum and—'

In the background, behind the Chinese screen in the corner, there was a loud click.

Toni turned. 'What was that?'

'Nothing,' David said quickly. 'It was just—'

Toni rose and started running toward the camera until her face filled the screen. She pushed against something, and the scene tilted; part of the folding Chinese screen fell into the picture. A small hole had been cut in the center.

'You've got a fucking camera behind here,' Toni screamed. She turned to David. 'You son of a bitch, what are you trying to do? You tricked me!'

On the desk was a letter opener. Toni grabbed it and lunged at David, screaming, 'I'm going to kill you. I'm going to kill you!'

David tried to hold her, but he was no match for her. The letter opener sliced into his hand.

Toni raised her arm to strike again, and the guard ran to her and tried to grab her. Toni knocked him to the floor. The door opened and a uniformed officer ran in. When he saw what was happening, he lunged at Toni. She kicked him in the groin, and he went down. Two more officers came running in. It took three of them to pin Toni to the chair, and all the time she was yelling and screaming at them.

Blood was pouring from David's hand. He said to Dr Salem, 'For God's sake, wake her up.'

Dr Salem said, 'Ashley . . . Ashley . . . listen to me. You're going to come out now. Toni is gone. It's safe to come out now, Ashley. I'm going to count to three.'

And as the group watched, Ashley's body became quiet and relaxed.

'Can you hear me?'

'Yes.' It was Ashley's voice, sounding far away.

'You'll awaken at the count of three. One . . . two . . . three . . . How do you feel?'

Her eyes opened. 'I feel so tired. Did I say anything?'

The screen in Judge Williams's office went blank. David walked over to the wall and turned on the lights.

Brennan said, 'Well! What a performance. If they were giving out Oscars for the best—'

Judge Williams turned to him. 'Shut up.'

Brennan looked at her, in shock.

There was a momentary silence. Judge Williams turned to David. 'Counselor.'

'Yes?'

There was a pause. 'I owe you an apology.'

Seated on the bench, Judge Tessa Williams said, 'Both counsels have agreed that they will accept the opinion of a psychiatrist who has already examined the defendant, Dr Salem. The decision of this court is that the defendant is not guilty by reason of insanity. She will be ordered to a mental health facility, where she can be treated. The court is now adjourned.'

David stood up, drained. *It's over*, he thought. *It's finally over*. He and Sandra could start living their lives again.

He looked at Judge Williams and said happily, 'We're having a baby.'

Dr Salem said to David, 'I would like to make a suggestion. I'm not sure it can be done, but if you can arrange it, I think it would be helpful to Ashley.'

'What is it?'

'The Connecticut Psychiatric Hospital back east has handled more cases of MPD than any other place in the country. A friend of mine, Dr Otto Lewison, is in charge of it. If you could arrange for the court to have Ashley sent there, I think it would be very beneficial.'

'Thanks,' David said. 'I'll see what I can do.'

Dr Steven Patterson said to David, 'I – I don't know how to thank you.'

David smiled. 'You don't have to. It was quid pro quo. Remember?'

'You did a brilliant job. For a while I was afraid—'

'So was I.'

'But justice has been served. My daughter's going to be cured.'

'I'm sure of it,' David said. 'Dr Salem suggested a psychiatric hospital in Connecticut. Their doctors are trained in MPD.'

Dr Patterson was silent for a moment. 'You know, Ashley didn't deserve any of this. She's such a beautiful person.'

'I agree. I'll talk to Judge Williams and try to get the transfer.'

*   *   *

Judge Williams was in her chambers. 'What can I do for you, Mr Singer?'

'I'd like to ask a favor.'

She smiled. 'I hope I can grant it. What is it?'

David explained to the judge what Dr Salem had told him.

'Well, that's a rather unusual request. We have some fine psychiatric facilities right here in California.'

David said, 'All right. Thank you, Your Honor.' He turned to leave, disappointed.

'I haven't said no, Mr Singer.' David stopped. 'It's an unusual request, but this has been an unusual case.'

David waited.

'I think I can arrange for her to be transferred.'

'Thank you, Your Honor. I appreciate it.'

In her cell, Ashley thought, *They've sentenced me to death. A long death in an asylum filled with crazy people. It would have been kinder to kill me now.* She thought of the endless, hopeless years ahead of her, and she began to sob.

The cell door opened, and her father came in. He stood there a moment, looking at her, his face filled with anguish.

'Honey . . .' He sat down opposite her. 'You're going to live,' he said.

She shook her head. 'I don't want to live.'

'Don't say that. You have a medical problem, but it can be cured. And it's going to be. When you're better, you're going to come and live with me, and I'll take care of you. No matter what happens, we'll always have each other. They can't take that away from us.'

Ashley sat there, saying nothing.

'I know how you're feeling right now, but believe me,

that's going to change. My girl is going to come home to me, cured.' He slowly got to his feet. 'I'm afraid I have to get back to San Francisco.' He waited for Ashley to say something.

She was silent.

'David told me that he thinks you're going to be sent to one of the best psychiatric centers in the world. I'll come and visit you. Would you like that?'

She nodded, dully. 'Yes.'

'All right, honey.' He kissed her on the cheek and gave her a hug. 'I'm going to see to it that you have the best care in the world. I want my little girl back.'

Ashley watched her father leave, and she thought, *Why can't I die now? Why won't they let me die?*

One hour later, David came to see her.

'Well, we did it,' he said. He looked at her in concern. 'Are you all right?'

'I don't want to go to an insane asylum. I want to die. I can't stand living like this. Help me, David. Please help me.'

'Ashley, you're going to get help. The past is over. You have a future now. The nightmare is going to be finished.' He took her hand. 'Look, you've trusted me this far. Keep trusting me. You're going to live a normal life again.'

She sat there, silent.

'Say "I believe you, David."'

She took a deep breath. 'I – I believe you, David.'

He grinned. 'Good girl. This is a new beginning for you.'

The moment the ruling was made public, the media went crazy. Overnight, David was a hero. He had taken an impossible case and won it.

He called Sandra. 'Honey, I—'

'I know, darling. I know. I just saw it on television. Isn't it wonderful? I'm so proud of you.'

'I can't tell you how glad I am that it's over. I'll be coming back tonight. I can't wait to see—'

'David . . . ?'

'Yes?'

'David . . . oooh . . .'

'Yes? What's wrong, honey?'

'. . . Oooh . . . We're having a baby . . .'

'Wait for me!' David shouted.

Jeffrey Singer weighed eight pounds, ten ounces, and was the most beautiful baby David had ever seen.

'He looks just like you, David,' Sandra said.

'He does, doesn't he?' David beamed.

'I'm glad everything turned out so well,' Sandra said.

David sighed. 'There were times when I wasn't so sure.'

'I never doubted you.'

David hugged Sandra and said, 'I'll be back, honey. I have to clean out my things at the office.'

When David arrived at the offices of Kincaid, Turner, Rose & Ripley, he was greeted warmly.

'Congratulations, David . . .'

'Good job . . .'

'You really showed them . . .'

David walked into his office. Holly was gone. David started cleaning out his desk.

'David—'

David turned around. It was Joseph Kincaid.

Kincaid walked up to him and said, 'What are you doing?'

'I'm cleaning out my office. I was fired.'

Kincaid smiled. 'Fired? Of course not. No, no, no. There was some kind of a misunderstanding.' He beamed. 'We're making you a partner, my boy. In fact, I've set up a press conference for you here this afternoon at three o'clock.'

David looked at him. 'Really?'

Kincaid nodded. 'Absolutely.'

David said, 'You'd better cancel it. I've decided to go back into criminal law. I've been offered a partnership by Jesse Quiller. At least when you're dealing with that part of the law, you know who the criminals really are. So, Joey, baby, you take your partnership and shove it where the sun don't shine.'

And David walked out of the office.

Jesse Quiller looked around the penthouse and said, 'This is great. It really becomes you two.'

'Thank you,' Sandra said. She heard a sound from the nursery. 'I'd better check on Jeffrey.' She hurried off to the next room.

Jesse Quiller walked over to admire a beautiful sterling silver picture frame with Jeffrey's first photograph already in it. 'This is lovely. Where did it come from?'

'Judge Williams sent it.'

Jesse said, 'I'm glad to have you back, partner.'

'I'm glad to be back, Jesse.'

'You'll probably want a little time to relax now. Rest up a little . . .'

'Yes. We thought we'd take Jeffrey and drive up to Oregon to visit Sandra's parents and—'

'By the way, an interesting case came into the office this morning, David. This woman is accused of murdering her two children. I have a feeling she's innocent. Unfortunately, I'm going to Washington on another case, but I thought that you might just talk to her and see what you think . . .'

Book Three

Book Three

Chapter Twenty-two

The Connecticut Psychiatric Hospital, fifteen miles north of Westport, was originally the estate of Wim Boeker, a wealthy Dutchman, who built the house in 1910. The forty lush acres contained a large manor house, a workshop, stable and swimming pool. The state had bought the property in 1925 and had refitted the manor house to accommodate a hundred patients. A tall chain-link fence had been erected around the property, with a manned guard post at the entrance. Metal bars had been placed on all the windows, and one section of the house had been fortified as a security area to hold dangerous inmates.

In the office of Dr Otto Lewison, head of the psychiatric clinic, a meeting was taking place. Dr Gilbert Keller and Dr Craig Foster were discussing a new patient who was about to arrive.

Gilbert Keller was a man in his forties, medium height, blond hair and intense gray eyes. He was a renowned expert on multiple personality disorder.

Otto Lewison, the superintendent of the Connecticut Psychiatric Hospital, was in his seventies, a neat, dapper little man with a full beard and pince-nez glasses.

Dr Craig Foster had worked with Dr Keller for years and was writing a book on multiple personality disorder. All were studying Ashley Patterson's records.

Otto Lewison said, 'The lady has been busy. She's only

twenty-eight and she's murdered five men.' He glanced at the paper again. 'She also tried to murder her attorney.'

'Everyone's fantasy,' Gilbert Keller said dryly.

Otto Lewison said, 'We're going to keep her in security ward A until we can get a full evaluation.'

'When is she arriving?' Dr Keller asked.

The voice of Dr Lewison's secretary came over the intercom. 'Dr Lewison, they're bringing Ashley Patterson in. Would you like to have them bring her into your office?'

'Yes, please.' Lewison looked up. 'Does that answer your question?'

The trip had been a nightmare. At the end of her trial, Ashley Patterson had been taken back to her cell and held there for three days while arrangements were made to fly her back east.

A prison bus had driven her to the airport in Oakland, where a plane was waiting for her. It was a converted DC-6, part of the huge National Prisoner Transportation System run by the U.S. Marshals Service. There were twenty-four prisoners aboard, all manacled and shackled.

Ashley was wearing handcuffs, and when she sat down, her feet were shackled to the bottom of the seat.

Why are they doing this to me? I'm not a dangerous criminal. I'm a normal woman. And a voice inside her said, *Who murdered five innocent people.*

The prisoners on the plane were hardened criminals, convicted of murder, rape, armed robbery and a dozen other crimes. They were on their way to top security prisons around the country. Ashley was the only woman on board.

One of the convicts looked at her and grinned. 'Hi, baby. How would you like to come over and warm up my lap?'

'Cool it,' a guard warned.

'Hey! Don't you have any romance in your soul? This bitch ain't going to get laid for – What's your sentence, baby?'

Another convict said, 'Are you horny, honey? How about me movin' into the seat next to you and slippin' you—?'

Another convict was staring at Ashley. 'Wait a minute!' he said. 'That's the broad who killed five men and castrated them.'

They were all looking at Ashley now.

That was the end of the badgering.

On the way to New York, the plane made two landings to discharge or pick up passengers. It was a long flight, the air was turbulent and by the time they landed at La Guardia Airport, Ashley was airsick.

Two uniformed police officers were waiting for her on the tarmac when the plane landed. She was unshackled from the plane seat and shackled again in the interior of a police van. She had never felt so humiliated. The fact that she felt so normal made it all the more unbearable. Did they think she was going to try to escape or murder someone? All that was over, in the past. Didn't they know that? She was sure it would never happen again. She wanted to be away from there. Anywhere.

Sometime during the long, dreary drive to Connecticut, she dozed off. She was awakened by a guard's voice.

'We're here.'

They had reached the gates of the Connecticut Psychiatric Hospital.

* * *

When Ashley Patterson was ushered into Dr Lewison's office, he said, 'Welcome to Connecticut Psychiatric Hospital, Miss Patterson.'

Ashley stood there, pale and silent.

Dr Lewison made the introductions and held out a chair. 'Sit down, please.' He looked at the guard. 'Take off the handcuffs and shackles.'

The restraints were removed, and Ashley took a seat.

Dr Foster said, 'I know this must be very difficult for you. We're going to do everything we can to make it as easy as possible. Our goal is to see that one day you will leave this place, cured.'

Ashley found her voice. 'How – how long could that take?'

Otto Lewison said, 'It's too soon to answer that yet. If you *can* be cured, it could take five or six years.'

Each word hit Ashley like a thunderbolt. *'If you can be cured, it could take five or six years . . .'*

'The therapy is nonthreatening. It will consist of a combination of sessions with Dr Keller – hypnotism, group therapy, art therapy. The important thing to remember is that we're not your enemies.'

Gilbert Keller was studying her face. 'We're here to help you, and we want you to help us do that.'

There was nothing more to say.

Otto Lewison nodded to the attendant, and he walked over to Ashley and took her arm.

Craig Foster said, 'He'll take you to your quarters now. We'll talk again later.'

When Ashley had left the room, Otto Lewison turned to Gilbert Keller. 'What do you think?'

'Well, there's one advantage. There are only two alters to work on.'

Keller was trying to remember. 'What's the most we've had?'

'The Beltrand woman – ninety alters.'

Ashley had not known what to expect, but somehow she had envisioned a dark, dreary prison. The Connecticut Psychiatric Hospital was more like a pleasant clubhouse – with metal bars.

As the attendant escorted Ashley through the long, cheerful corridors, Ashley watched the inmates freely walking back and forth. There were people of every age, and all of them seemed normal. *Why are they here?* Some of them smiled at her and said, 'Good morning,' but Ashley was too bewildered to answer. Everything seemed surreal. She was in an insane asylum. *Am I insane?*

They reached a large steel door that closed off a part of the building. There was a male attendant behind the door. He pressed a red button and the huge door opened.

'This is Ashley Patterson.'

The second attendant said, 'Good morning, Miss Patterson.' They made everything seem so normal. *But nothing is normal anymore*, Ashley thought. *The world is upside down.*

'This way, Miss Patterson.' He walked her to another door and opened it. Ashley stepped inside. Instead of a cell, she was looking at a pleasant, medium-size room with pastel blue walls, a small couch and a comfortable-looking bed.

'This is where you'll be staying. They'll be bringing your things in a few minutes.'

Ashley watched the guard leave and close the door behind him. *This is where you'll be staying.*

She began to feel claustrophobic. *What if I don't want to stay? What if I want to get out of here?*

She walked over to the door. It was locked. Ashley sat down on the couch, trying to organize her thoughts. She tried to concentrate on the positive. *We're going to try to cure you.*

We're going to try to cure you.

We're going to cure you.

Chapter Twenty-three

Dr Gilbert Keller was in charge of Ashley's therapy. His specialty was treating multiple personality disorder, and while he had had failures, his success rate was high. In cases like this, there were no easy answers. His first job was to get the patient to trust him, to feel comfortable with him, and then to bring out the alters, one by one, so that in the end they could communicate with one another and understand why they existed, and finally, why there was no more need for them. That was the moment of blending, when the personality states came together as a single entity.

We're a long way from that, Dr Keller thought.

The following morning, Dr Keller had Ashley brought to his office. 'Good morning, Ashley.'

'Good morning, Dr Keller.'

'I want you to call me Gilbert. We're going to be friends. How do you feel?'

She looked at him and said, 'They tell me I've killed five people. How should I feel?'

'Do you remember killing any of them?'

'No.'

'I read the transcript of your trial, Ashley. You didn't kill them. One of your alters did. We're going to get acquainted

with your alters, and in time, with your help, we'll make
them disappear.'

'I – I hope you can—'

'I can. I'm here to help you, and that's what I'm going
to do. The alters were created in your mind to save you
from an unbearable pain. We have to find out what caused
that pain. I need to find out when those alters were born
and why.'

'How – how do you do that?'

'We'll talk. Things will come to you. From time to time,
we'll use hypnotism or Sodium Amytal. You've been hypnotized before, haven't you?'

'Yes.'

'No one's going to pressure you. We're going to take our
time.' He added reassuringly, 'And when we're through,
you're going to be well.'

They talked for almost an hour. At the end of that time,
Ashley felt much more relaxed. Back in her room, she
thought, *I really think he can do it.* And she said a little
prayer.

Dr Keller had a meeting with Otto Lewison. 'We talked
this morning,' Dr Keller said. 'The good news is that Ashley
admits she has a problem, and she's willing to be helped.'

'That's a beginning. Keep me informed.'

'I will, Otto.'

Dr Keller was looking forward to the challenge ahead
of him. There was something very special about Ashley
Patterson. He was determined to help her.

They talked every day, and a week after Ashley arrived,
Dr Keller said, 'I want you to be comfortable and relaxed.
I'm going to hypnotize you.' He moved toward her.

'No! Wait!'

He looked at her, surprised. 'What's the matter?'

A dozen terrible thoughts flashed through Ashley's head. He was going to bring out her alters. She was terrified of the idea. 'Please,' she said. 'I – I don't want to meet them.'

'You won't,' Dr Keller assured her. 'Not yet.'

She swallowed. 'All right.'

'Are you ready?'

She nodded. 'Yes.'

'Good. Here we go.'

It took fifteen minutes to hypnotize her. When she was under, Gilbert Keller glanced at a piece of paper on his desk. *Toni Prescott and Alette Peters.* It was time for switching, the process of changing from one dominating personality state to another.

He looked at Ashley, asleep in her chair, then leaned forward. 'Good morning, Toni. Can you hear me?'

He watched Ashley's face transform, taken over by an entirely different personality. There was a sudden vivacity in her face. She began to sing:

> *'Half a pound of tupenny rice,*
> *Half a pound of treacle,*
> *Mix it up and make it nice,*
> *Pop! goes the weasel . . .'*

'That was very nice, Toni. I'm Gilbert Keller.'

'I know who you are,' Toni said.

'I'm glad to meet you. Did anyone ever tell you that you have a beautiful singing voice?'

'Sod off.'

'I mean it. Did you ever take singing lessons? I'll bet you did.'

'No, I didn't. As a matter of fact, I wanted to, but my' – *For God's sakes, will you stop that terrible noise! Whoever told you you could sing?* – 'never mind.'

'Toni, I want to help you.'

'No, you don't, Dockie baby. You want to lay me.'

'Why do you think that, Toni?'

'That's all you bloody men ever want to do. Ta.'

'Toni . . . ? Toni . . . ?'

Silence.

Gilbert Keller looked at Ashley's face again. It was serene. Dr Keller leaned forward. 'Alette?'

There was no change in Ashley's expression.

'Alette . . . ?'

Nothing.

'I want to speak to you, Alette.'

Ashley began to stir uneasily.

'Come out, Alette.'

Ashley took a deep breath, and then there was a sudden explosion of words spoken in Italian.

'*C'è qualcuno che parla Italiano?*'

'Alette—'

'*Non so dove mi travo.*'

'Alette, listen to me. You're safe. I want you to relax.'

'*Mi sento stanca* . . . I'm tired.'

'You've been through a terrible time, but all that is behind you. Your future is going to be very peaceful. Do you know where you are?'

His voice was white.

'*Sì.* It's some kind of place for people who are *pazzo.*' *That's why you're here, Doctor. You're the crazy one.*

'It's a place where you're going to be cured. Alette, when you close your eyes and visualize this place, what comes to your mind?'

'Hogarth. He painted insane asylums and scenes that are terrifying.' *You're too ignorant ever to have heard of him.*

'I don't want you to think of this place as terrifying. Tell me about yourself, Alette. What do you like to do? What would you like to do while you're here?'

'I like to paint.'

'We'll have to get you some paints.'

'No!'

'Why?'

'I don't want to.' *'What do you call that, child? It looks like an ugly blob to me.'*

Leave me alone.

'Alette?' Gilbert Keller watched Ashley's face change again. Alette was gone. Dr Keller awakened Ashley.

She opened her eyes and blinked. 'Have you started?'

'We've finished.'

'How did I do?'

'Toni and Alette talked to me. We've made a good beginning, Ashley.'

The letter from David Singer read:

Dear Ashley,

Just a note to let you know that I'm thinking about you and hoping that you're making good progress. As a matter of fact, I think about you often. I feel as though we've gone through the wars together. It was a tough fight, but we won. And I have good news. I've been assured that the murder charges against you in Bedford and Quebec will be dropped. If there is anything I can do for you, let me know.

Warmest wishes,
David

The following morning, Dr Keller was talking to Toni while Ashley was under hypnosis.

'What is it now, Dockie?'

'I just want to have a little chat with you. I'd like to help you.'

'I don't need your bloody help. I'm doing fine.'

'Well, I need *your* help, Toni. I want to ask you a question. What do you think of Ashley?'

'Miss *Tight Ass*? Don't get me started.'

'You don't like her?'

'In spades.'

'What don't you like about her?'

There was a pause. 'She tries to keep everybody from having fun. If I didn't take over once in a while, our lives would be boring. *Boring*. She doesn't like to go to parties or travel or do any fun things.'

'But you do?'

'You bet I do. That's what life's all about, isn't it, luv?'

'You were born in London, weren't you, Toni? Do you want to tell me about it?'

'I'll tell you one thing. I wish I were there now.'

Silence.

'Toni . . . ? Toni . . . ?'

She was gone.

Gilbert Keller said to Ashley, 'I'd like to speak to Alette.' He watched the expression on Ashley's face change. He leaned forward and said softly, 'Alette.'

'*Sì.*'

'Did you hear my conversation with Toni?'

'Yes.'

'Do you and Toni know each other?'

'Yes.' *Of course we do, stupid.*

'But Ashley doesn't know either of you?'

278

'No.'

'Do you like Ashley?'

'She's all right.' *Why are you asking me all these foolish questions?*

'Why don't you talk to her?'

'Toni does not want me to.'

'Does Toni always tell you what to do?'

'Toni is my friend.' *It's none of your business.*

'I want to be your friend, Alette. Tell me about yourself. Where were you born?'

'I was born in Rome.'

'Did you like Rome?'

Gilbert Keller watched the expression on Ashley's face change, and she began to weep.

Why? Dr Keller leaned forward and said soothingly, 'It's all right. You're going to awaken now, Ashley . . .'

She opened her eyes.

'I talked to Toni and Alette. They're friends. I want you all to be friends.'

While Ashley was at lunch, a male nurse walked into her room and saw a painting of a landscape on the floor. He studied it a moment, then took it to Dr Keller's office.

There was a meeting in Dr Lewison's office.

'How's it going, Gilbert?'

Dr Keller said thoughtfully, 'I've talked to the two alters. The dominant one is Toni. She has an English background and won't talk about it. The other one, Alette, was born in Rome, and she doesn't want to talk about it, either. So that's where I'm going to concentrate. That's where the traumas occurred. Toni is the more aggressive one. Alette is sensitive and withdrawn. She's interested in painting, but she's afraid to pursue it. I have to find out why.'

'So you think Toni dominates Ashley?'

'Yes. Toni takes over. Ashley wasn't aware that she exists, or for that matter, that Alette existed. But Toni and Alette know each other. It's interesting. Toni has a lovely singing voice, and Alette is a talented painter.' He held up the painting that the male nurse had brought him. 'I think their talents may be the key to getting through to them.'

Ashley received a letter from her father once a week. After she read them, she would sit in her room quietly, not wanting to talk to anyone.

'They're her only link to home,' Dr Keller said to Otto Lewison. 'I think it increases her desire to get out of here and start leading a normal life. Every little bit helps . . .'

Ashley was becoming used to her surroundings. The patients seemed to walk about, although there were attendants at every door and in the corridors. The gates to the grounds were always locked. There was a recreation room where they could gather and watch television, a gymnasium where inmates could work out and a common dining room. There were many kinds of people there: Japanese, Chinese, French, Americans . . . Every effort had been made to make the hospital as ordinary-looking as possible, but when Ashley went to her room, the doors were always locked behind her.

'This isn't a hospital,' Toni complained to Alette. 'It's a bloody prison.'

'But Dr Keller thinks he can cure Ashley. Then we can get out of here.'

'Don't be stupid, Alette. Don't you see? The only way he can cure Ashley is to get rid of us, make us disappear.

In other words, to cure her, we have to die. Well, I'm not going to let that happen.'

'What are you going to do?'

'I'm going to find a way for us to escape.'

Chapter Twenty-four

The following morning a male nurse was escorting Ashley back to her room. He said, 'You seem different today.'

'Do I, Bill?'

'Yeah. Almost like another person.'

Toni said softly, 'That's because of you.'

'What do you mean?'

'You make me feel different.' She touched his arm and looked into his eyes. 'You make me feel wonderful.'

'Come on.'

'I mean it. You're very sexy. Do you know that?'

'No.'

'Well, you are. Are you married, Bill?'

'I was, once.'

'Your wife was mad to ever let you go. How long have you worked here, Bill?'

'Five years.'

'That's a long time. Do you ever feel you want to get out of here?'

'Sometimes, sure.'

Toni lowered her voice. 'You know there's nothing really wrong with me. I admit I had a little problem when I came in, but I'm cured now. I'd like to get out of here, too. I'll bet you could help me. The two of us could leave here together. We'd have a wonderful time.'

He studied her a moment. 'I don't know what to say.'

'Yes, you do. Look how simple it would be. All you have to do is let me out of here one night when everyone's asleep, and we'll be on our way.' She looked over at him and said softly, 'I'll make it worth your while.'

He nodded. 'Let me think about it.'

'You do that,' Toni said confidently.

When Toni returned to the room, she said to Alette, 'We're getting out of this place.'

The following morning, Ashley was escorted into Dr Keller's office.

'Good morning, Ashley.'

'Good morning, Gilbert.'

'We're going to try some Sodium Amytal this morning. Have you ever had it?'

'No.'

'Well, you'll find it's very relaxing.'

Ashley nodded. 'All right. I'm ready.'

Five minutes later, Dr Keller was talking to Toni. 'Good morning, Toni.'

'Hi, Dockie.'

'Are you happy here, Toni?'

'It's funny you should ask that. To tell you the truth, I'm really beginning to like this place. I feel at home here.'

'Then why do you want to escape?'

Toni's voice hardened. 'What?'

'Bill tells me that you asked him to help you escape from here.'

'That son of a bitch!' There was fury in her voice. She flew out of the chair, ran over to the desk, picked up a paperweight and flung it at Dr Keller's head.

He ducked.

'I'll kill you, and I'll kill him!'

Dr Keller grabbed her. 'Toni—'

He watched the expression on Ashley's face change. Toni had gone. He found that his heart was pounding.

'Ashley!'

When Ashley awakened, she opened her eyes, looked around, puzzled, and said, 'Is everything all right?'

'Toni attacked me. She was angry because I found out she was trying to escape.'

'I – I'm sorry. I had a feeling that something bad was happening.'

'It's all right. I want to bring you and Toni and Alette together.'

'No!'

'Why not?'

'I'm afraid. I – I don't want to meet them. Don't you understand? They're not *real*. They're my imagination.'

'Sooner or later, you're going to have to meet them, Ashley. You have to get to know one another. It's the only way you're going to be cured.'

Ashley stood up. 'I want to go back to my room.'

When she was returned to her room, Ashley watched the attendant leave. She was filled with a deep sense of despair. She thought, *I'm never going to get out of here. They're lying to me. They can't cure me.* She could not face the reality that other personalities were living inside of her . . . Because of them, people had been murdered, families destroyed. *Why me, God?* She began to weep. *What did I ever do to you?* She sat down on the bed and thought, *I can't go on like this. There's only one way to end it. I have to do it now.*

She got up and walked around the small room, looking for something sharp. There was nothing. The rooms had been carefully designed so that there was nothing in them that would allow the patients to harm themselves.

As her eyes darted around the room, she saw the paints and canvas and paintbrushes and walked over to them. The handles of the paintbrushes were wooden. Ashley snapped one in half, exposing sharp, jagged edges. Slowly, she took the sharp edge and placed it on her wrist. In one fast, deep movement, she cut into her veins and her blood began to pour out. Ashley placed the jagged edge on her other wrist and repeated the movement. She stood there, watching the blood stain the carpet. She began to feel cold. She dropped to the floor and curled up into a fetal position.

And then the room went dark.

When Dr Gilbert Keller heard the news, he was shocked. He went to visit Ashley in the infirmary. Her wrists were heavily bandaged. Watching her lying there, Dr Keller thought, *I can't ever let this happen again.*

'We almost lost you,' he said. 'It would have made me look bad.'

Ashley managed a wry smile. 'I'm sorry. But everything seems so – so hopeless.'

'That's where you're wrong,' Dr Keller assured her. 'Do you want to be helped, Ashley?'

'Yes.'

'Then you have to believe in me. You have to work with me. I can't do it alone. What do you say?'

There was a long silence. 'What do you want me to do?'

'First, I want a promise from you that you'll never try to harm yourself again.'

'All right. I promise.'

'I'm going to get the same promise now from Toni and Alette. I'm going to put you to sleep now.'

A few minutes later, Dr Keller was speaking to Toni.

'That selfish bitch tried to kill us all. She thinks only about herself. Do you see what I mean?'

'Toni—'

'Well, I'm not having it. I—'

'Will you be quiet and listen to me?'

'I'm listening.'

'I want you to promise that you'll never harm Ashley.'

'Why should I promise?'

'I'll tell you why. Because you're part of her. You were born out of her pain. I don't know yet what you've had to go through, Toni, but I know that it must have been terrible. But you have to realize that she went through the same thing, and Alette was born for the same reason as you. The three of you have a lot in common. You should help each other, not hate each other. Will you give me your word?'

Nothing.

'Toni?'

'I suppose so,' she said grudgingly.

'Thank you. Do you want to talk about England now?'

'No.'

'Alette. Are you there?'

'Yes.' *Where do you think I am, stupid?*

'I want you to make me the same promise that Toni did. Promise never to harm Ashley.'

That's the only one you care about, isn't it? Ashley, Ashley, Ashley. What about us?

'Alette?'

'Yes. I promise.'

* * *

287

The months were going by, and there were no signs of progress. Dr Keller sat at his desk, reviewing notes, recalling sessions, trying to find a clue to what was wrong. He was taking care of half a dozen other patients, but he found that it was Ashley he was most concerned about. There was such an incredible chasm between her innocent vulnerability and the dark forces that were able to take over her life. Every time he talked to Ashley, he had an over-powering urge to try to protect her. *She's like a daughter to me*, he thought. *Who am I kidding? I'm falling in love with her.*

Dr Keller went to see Otto Lewison. 'I have a problem, Otto.'

'I thought that was reserved for our patients.'

'This involves one of our patients. Ashley Patterson.'

'Oh?'

'I find that I'm – I'm very attracted to her.'

'Reverse transference?'

'Yes.'

'That could be very dangerous for both of you, Gilbert.'

'I know.'

'Well, as long as you're aware of it . . . Be careful.'

'I intend to.'

NOVEMBER

    I gave Ashley a diary this morning.

'I want you and Toni and Alette to use this, Ashley. You can keep it in your room. Anytime that any of you has any thoughts or ideas that you prefer to write down instead of talking to me, just put them down.'

'All right, Gilbert.'

*   *   *

A month later, Dr Keller wrote in his diary:

DECEMBER
The treatment is at a standstill. Toni and Alette refuse to discuss the past. It is becoming more difficult to persuade Ashley to undergo hypnosis.

MARCH
The diary is still blank. I'm not sure whether the most resistance is coming from Ashley or Toni. When I do hypnotize Ashley, Toni and Alette come out very briefly. They are adamant about not discussing the past.

JUNE
I meet with Ashley regularly, but I feel there's no progress. The diary is still untouched. I have given Alette an easel and a set of paints. I am hoping that if she begins to paint, there may be a breakthrough.

JULY
Something happened, but I'm not sure if it's a sign of progress. Alette painted a beautiful picture of the hospital grounds. When I complimented her on it, she seemed pleased. That evening the painting was torn to shreds.

Dr Keller and Otto Lewison were having coffee.

'I think I'm going to try a little group therapy,' Dr Keller said. 'Nothing else seems to be working.'

'How many patients did you have in mind?'

'Not more than half a dozen. I want her to start

interacting with other people. Right now she's living in a world of her own. I want her to break out of that.'

'Good idea. It's worth a try.'

Dr Keller led Ashley into a small meeting room. There were six people in the room.

'I want you to meet some friends,' Dr Keller said.

He took Ashley around the room introducing them, but Ashley was too self-conscious to listen to their names. One name blurred into the next. There was Fat Woman, Bony Man, Bald Woman, Lame Man, Chinese Woman and Gentle Man. They all seemed very pleasant.

'Sit down,' Bald Woman said. 'Would you like some coffee?'

Ashley took a seat. 'Thank you.'

'We've heard about you,' Gentle Man said. 'You've been through a lot.'

Ashley nodded.

Bony Man said, 'I guess we've all been through a lot, but we're being helped. This place is wonderful.'

'They have the best doctors in the world,' Chinese Woman said.

They all seem so normal, Ashley thought.

Dr Keller sat to one side, monitoring the conversations. Forty-five minutes later he rose. 'I think it's time to go, Ashley.'

Ashley stood up. 'It was nice meeting all of you.'

Lame Man walked up to her and whispered, 'Don't drink the water here. It's poisoned. They want to kill us and still collect the money from the state.'

Ashley gulped. 'Thanks. I'll – I'll remember.'

As Ashley and Dr Keller walked down the corridor, she said, 'What are their problems?'

290

'Paranoia, schizophrenia, MPD, compulsive disorders. But, Ashley, their improvement since they came here has been remarkable. Would you like to chat with them regularly?'

'No.'

Dr Keller walked into Otto Lewison's office.

'I'm not getting anywhere,' he confessed. 'The group therapy didn't work, and the hypnotism sessions aren't working at all. I want to try something different.'

'What?'

'I need your permission to take Ashley to dinner off the grounds.'

'I don't think that's a good idea, Gilbert. It could be dangerous. She's already—'

'I know. But right now I'm the enemy. I want to become a friend.'

'Her alter, Toni, tried to kill you once. What if she tries again?'

'I'll handle it.'

Dr Lewison thought about it. 'All right. Do you want someone to go with you?'

'No. I'll be fine, Otto.'

'When do you want to start this?'

'Tonight.'

'You want to take me out to dinner?'

'Yes. I think it would be good for you to get away from this place for a while, Ashley. What do you say?'

'Yes.'

Ashley was surprised at how excited she was at the thought of going out to dinner with Gilbert Keller. *It will be fun to get out of here for an evening*, Ashley thought. But she knew that it was more than that. The thought of being with Gilbert Keller on a date was exhilarating.

They were having dinner at a Japanese restaurant called Otani Gardens, five miles from the hospital. Dr Keller knew that he was taking a risk. At any moment, Toni or Alette could take over. He had been warned. *It's more important that Ashley learns to trust me so that I can help her.*

'It's funny, Gilbert,' Ashley said, looking around the crowded restaurant.

'What is?'

'These people don't look any different from the people at the hospital.'

'They aren't really different, Ashley. I'm sure they all have problems. The only difference is the people at the hospital aren't able to cope with them as well, so we help them.'

'I didn't know I had any problems until – Well, you know.'

'Do you know why, Ashley? Because you buried them. You couldn't face what happened to you, so you built the fences in your mind and shut the bad things away. To one degree or another, a lot of people do that.' He deliberately changed the subject. 'How's your steak?'

'Delicious, thank you.'

From then on, Ashley and Dr Keller had meals away from the hospital once a week. They had lunch at an excellent little Italian restaurant called Banducci's and dinners at The Palm, Eveleene's and The Gumbo Pot. Neither Toni nor Alette made an appearance.

One night, Dr Keller took Ashley dancing. It was at a small nightclub with a wonderful band.

'Are you enjoying yourself?' he asked.

'Very much. Thank you.' She looked at him and said, 'You're not like other doctors.'

'They don't dance?'

'You know what I mean.'

He was holding her close, and both of them felt the urgency of the moment.

That could be very dangerous for both of you, Gilbert . . .

293

Dr X ... was looking over his notes with Dr Lewison.

Chapter Twenty-five

I know what the bloody hell you're trying to do, Dockie.
You're trying to make Ashley think you're her friend.'

'I am her friend, Toni, and yours.'

'No, you're not. You think she's great, and I'm nothing.'

'You're wrong. I respect you and Alette as much as I
respect Ashley. You're all equally important to me.'

'Is that true?'

'Yes. Toni, when I told you that you had a beautiful
singing voice, I meant it. Do you play an instrument?'

'Piano.'

'If I could arrange for you to use the piano in the
recreation hall so you can play and sing, would you be
interested?'

'I might be.' She sounded excited.

Dr Keller smiled. 'Then I'll be happy to do it. It will be
there for you to use.'

'Thanks.'

Dr Keller arranged for Toni to have private access to
the recreation room for one hour every afternoon. In the
beginning, the doors were closed, but as other inmates
heard the piano music and the singing from inside, they
opened the door to listen. Soon, Toni was entertaining
dozens of patients.

Dr Keller was looking over his notes with Dr Lewison.

Dr Lewison said, 'What about the other one – Alette?'

'I've set it up for her to paint in the garden every afternoon. She'll be watched, of course. I think it's going to be good therapy.'

But Alette refused. In a session with her, Dr Keller said, 'You don't use the paints I gave you, Alette. It's a shame to let them go to waste. You're so talented.'

How would you know?

'Don't you enjoy painting?'

'Yes.'

'Then why don't you do it?'

'Because I'm no good.' *Stop pestering me.*

'Who told you that?'

'My – my mother.'

'We haven't talked about your mother. Do you want to tell me about her?'

'There's nothing to tell.'

'She died in an accident, didn't she?'

There was a long pause. 'Yes. She died in an accident.'

The following day, Alette started to paint. She enjoyed being in the garden with her canvas and brushes. When she painted, she was able to forget everything else. Some of the patients would gather around her and watch. They talked in multicolored voices.

'Your paintings should be in a gallery.' Black.

'You're really good.' Yellow.

'Where did you learn to do that?' Black.

'Can you paint a picture of me sometime?' Orange.

'I wish *I* knew how to do that.' Black.

She was always sorry when her time was up and she had to go back into the big building.

* * *

296

'I want you to meet someone, Ashley. This is Lisa Garrett.'
She was a woman in her fifties, small and wraithlike. 'Lisa
is going home today.'

The woman beamed. 'Isn't that wonderful? And I owe
it all to Dr Keller.'

Gilbert Keller looked at Ashley and said, 'Lisa suffered
from MPD and had thirty alters.'

'That's right, dear. And they're all gone.'

Dr Keller said pointedly, 'She's the third MPD patient
leaving us this year.'

And Ashley felt a surge of hope.

Alette said, 'Dr Keller is sympathetic. He really seems to
like us.'

'You're bloody stupid,' Toni scoffed. 'Don't you see
what's happening? I told you once. He's pretending to
like us so we'll do what he wants us to do. And do you
know what that is? He wants to bring us all together, luv,
and then convince Ashley that she doesn't need us. And
do you know what happens then? You and I die. Is that
what you want? I don't.'

'Well, no,' Alette said hesitantly.

'Then listen to me. We go along with the doctor. We
make him believe that we're really trying to help him.
We string him along. We're in no hurry. And I promise
you that one day I'll get us out of here.'

'Whatever you say, Toni.'

'Good. So we'll let old Dockie think he's doing just
great.'

A letter arrived from David. In the envelope was a photograph of a small boy. The letter read:

297

Dear Ashley,

I hope that you're coming along well and that the therapy is progressing. Everything's fine here. I'm working hard and enjoying it. Enclosed is a photograph of our two-year-old, Jeffrey. At the rate he's growing, in a few minutes, he'll be getting married. There's no real news to report. I just wanted you to know that I was thinking about you.

Sandra joins me in sending our warm regards,
David

Ashley studied the photograph. *He's a beautiful little boy*, she thought. *I hope he has a happy life.*

She went to lunch, and when she returned, the photograph was on the floor of her room, torn to bits.

June 15, 1:30 P.M.

Patient: Ashley Patterson. Therapy session using Sodium Amytal. Alter, Alette Peters.

'Tell me about Rome, Alette.'

'It's the most beautiful city in the world. It's filled with great museums. I used to visit all of them.' *What would you know about museums?*

'And you wanted to be a painter?'

'Yes.' *What did you think I wanted to be, a firefighter?*

'Did you study painting?'

'No, I didn't.' *Can't you go bother someone else?*

'Why not? Because of what your mother told you?'

'Oh, no. I just decided that I wasn't good enough.' *Toni, get him away from me!*

'Did you have any traumas during that period? Did any terrible things happen to you that you can recall?'

'No. I was very happy.' *Toni!*

298

August 15, 9:00 A.M.

Patient: Ashley Patterson. Hypnotherapy session with alter, Toni Prescott.

'Do you want to talk about London, Toni?'

'Yes. I had a lovely time there. London is so civilized. There's so much to do there.'

'Did you have any problems?'

'Problems? No. I was very happy in London.'

'Nothing bad happened there at all that you remember?'

'Of course not.' *What are you going to make of that, you willy?*

Each session brought back memories to Ashley. When she went to bed at night, she dreamed that she was at Global Computer Graphics. Shane Miller was there, and he was complimenting her on some work she had done. *'We couldn't get along without you, Ashley. We're going to keep you here forever.'* Then the scene shifted to a prison cell, and Shane Miller was saying, *'Well, I hate to do this now, but under the circumstances, the company is terminating you. Naturally, we can't afford to be connected with anything like this. You understand, don't you? There's nothing personal in this.'*

In the morning, when Ashley awakened, her pillow was wet with tears.

Alette was saddened by the therapy sessions. They reminded her of how much she missed Rome and how happy she had been with Richard Melton. *We could have had such a happy life together, but now it is too late. Too late.*

*   *   *

Toni hated the therapy sessions because they brought back too many bad memories for her, too. Everything she had done had been to protect Ashley and Alette. But did anybody appreciate her? No. She was locked away as though she were some kind of criminal. *But I'll get out of here*, Toni promised herself. *I'll get out of here.*

The pages of the calendar were wiped away by time, and another year came and went. Dr Keller was getting more and more frustrated.

'I've read your latest report,' Dr Lewison told Gilbert Keller. 'Do you think there's a genuine lacuna, or are they playing games?'

'They're playing games, Otto. It's as though they know what I'm trying to do, and they won't let me. I think Ashley genuinely wants to help, but they won't allow her to. Usually under hypnosis you can get through to them, but Toni is very strong. She takes complete control, and she's dangerous.'

'Dangerous?'

'Yes. Imagine how much hatred she must have in her to murder and castrate five men.'

The rest of the year went no better.

Dr Keller was having success with his other patients, but Ashley, the one he was most concerned about, was making no progress. Dr Keller had a feeling that Toni enjoyed playing games with him. She was determined that he was not going to succeed. And then, unexpectedly, there was a breakthrough.

It started with another letter from Dr Patterson.

June 5

Dear Ashley,

I'm on my way to New York to take care of some
business, and I would like very much to stop by
and see you. I will call Dr Lewison, and if there's
no objection, you can expect me around the 25th.

Much love,
Father

Three weeks later, Dr Patterson arrived with an attractive,
dark-haired woman in her early forties and her three-year-
old daughter, Katrina.

They were ushered into Dr Lewison's office. He rose as
they entered. 'Dr Patterson, I'm delighted to meet you.'

'Thank you. This is Miss Victoria Aniston and her daughter, Katrina.'

'How do you do, Miss Aniston? Katrina.'

'I brought them along to meet Ashley.'

'Wonderful. She's with Dr Keller right now, but they
should be finished soon.'

Dr Patterson said, 'How is Ashley doing?'

Otto Lewison hesitated. 'I wonder if I could speak to
you alone for a few minutes?'

'Certainly.'

Dr Patterson turned to Victoria and Katrina. 'It looks
like there's a beautiful garden out there. Why don't you
wait for me, and I'll join you with Ashley.'

Victoria Aniston smiled. 'Fine.' She looked over at Otto
Lewison. 'It was nice to meet you, Doctor.'

'Thank you, Miss Aniston.'

Dr Patterson watched the two of them leave. He turned
to Otto Lewison. 'Is there a problem?'

'I'll be frank with you, Dr Patterson. We're not making

301

as much progress as I had hoped we would. Ashley says she wants to be helped, but she's not cooperating with us. In fact, she's fighting the treatment.'

Dr Patterson was studying him, puzzled. 'Why?'

'It's not that unusual. At some stage, patients with MPD are afraid of meeting their alters. It terrifies them. The very thought that other characters can be living in their mind and body and take over at will – Well, you can imagine how devastating that can be.'

Dr Patterson nodded. 'Of course.'

'There's something that puzzles us about Ashley's problem. Almost always, these problems start with a history of molestation when the patient is very young. We have no record of anything like that in Ashley's case, so we have no idea how or why this trauma began.'

Dr Patterson sat there silently for a moment. When he spoke, he said heavily, 'I can help you.' He took a deep breath. 'I blame myself.'

Otto Lewison was watching intently.

'It happened when Ashley was six. I had to go to England. My wife couldn't go. I took Ashley with me. My wife had an elderly cousin over there named John. I didn't realize it at the time, but John had . . . emotional problems. I had to leave to give a lecture one day, and John offered to baby-sit. When I got back that evening, he was gone. Ashley was in a state of complete hysteria. It took a long, long time to calm her down. After that, she wouldn't let anyone come near her, she became timid and withdrawn and a week later, John was arrested as a serial child molester.' Dr Patterson's face was filled with pain. 'I never forgave myself. I never left Ashley alone with anyone after that.'

There was a long silence. Otto Lewison said, 'I'm terribly

sorry. But I think you've given us the answer to what we've been looking for, Dr Patterson. Now Dr Keller will have something specific to work on.'

'It's been too painful for me even to discuss before.'

'I understand.' Otto Lewison looked at his watch. 'Ashley's going to be a little while. Why don't you join Miss Aniston in the garden, and I'll send Ashley out when she comes.'

Dr Patterson rose. 'Thank you. I will.'

Otto Lewison watched him leave. He could not wait to tell Dr Keller what he had learned.

Victoria Aniston and Katrina were waiting for him. 'Did you see Ashley?' Victoria asked.

'They'll send her out in a few minutes,' Dr Patterson said. He looked around the spacious grounds. 'This is lovely, isn't it?'

Katrina ran up to him, 'I want to go up to the sky again.'

He smiled. 'All right.' He picked her up, threw her into the air and caught her as she came down.

'Higher!'

'Hang on. Here we go.' He threw her up again and caught her, and she was screaming with delight.

'Again!'

Dr Patterson's back was to the main building, so he did not see Ashley and Dr Keller come out.

'Higher!' Katrina screamed.

Ashley stopped in the doorway, frozen. She watched her father playing with the little girl, and time seemed to fragment. Everything after that happened in slow motion.

There were flashes of a little girl being thrown into the air . . . 'Higher, Papa!'

'Hang on. Here we go.'

And then the girl being tossed onto a bed . . .

A voice saying, 'You'll like this . . .'

An image of the man getting into bed beside her. The little girl was screaming, 'Stop it. No. Please, no.'

The man was in the shadow. He was holding her down, and he was stroking her body. 'Doesn't that feel good?'

And suddenly the shadow lifted, and Ashley could see the man's face. It was her father.

Looking at him now, in the garden, playing with the little girl, Ashley opened her mouth and began to scream, and could not stop.

Dr Patterson, Victoria Aniston and Katrina turned around, startled.

Dr Keller said quickly, 'I'm terribly sorry. This is a bad day. Could you come back another time?' And he carried Ashley inside.

They had her in one of the emergency rooms.

'Her pulse is abnormally high,' Dr Keller said. 'She's in a fugue state.' He moved close to her and said, 'Ashley, you have nothing to be frightened about. You're safe here. No one's going to hurt you. Just listen to my voice and relax . . . relax . . . relax . . .'

It took half an hour. 'Ashley, tell me what happened. What upset you?'

'Father and the little girl . . .'

'What about them?'

It was Toni who answered. 'She can't face it. She's afraid he's going to do to the little girl what he did to her.'

Dr Keller stared at her a moment. 'What – what did he do to her?'

304

It was in London. She was in bed. He sat down next to
her and said, 'I'm going to make you very happy, baby,'
and began tickling her, and she was laughing. And then
. . . he took her pajamas off, and he started playing with
her. 'Don't my hands feel good?' Ashley started screaming,
'Stop it. Don't do that.' But he wouldn't stop. He held her
down and went on and on . . .

Dr Keller asked, 'Was that the first time it happened,
Toni?'

'Yes.'

'How old was Ashley?'

'She was six.'

'And that's when you were born?'

'Yes. Ashley was too terrified to face it.'

'What happened after that?'

'Father came to her every night and got into bed with
her.' The words were pouring out now. 'She couldn't
stop him. When they got home, Ashley told Mother what
happened, and Mother called her a lying little bitch.

'Ashley was afraid to go to sleep at night because she
knew Papa was going to come to her room. He used
to make her touch him and then play with himself.
And he said to her, "Don't tell anyone about this or
I won't love you anymore." She couldn't tell anyone.
Mama and Papa were yelling at each other all the time,
and Ashley thought it was her fault. She knew she had
done something wrong, but she didn't know what. Mama
hated her.'

'How long did this go on?' Dr Keller asked.

'When I was eight . . .' Toni stopped.

'Go on, Toni.'

Ashley's face changed, and it was Alette sitting in the

305

chair. She said, 'We moved to Roma, where he did research at Policlinico Umberto Primo.'

'And that's where you were born?'

'Yes. Ashley couldn't stand what happened one night, so I came to protect her.'

'What happened, Alette?'

'Papa came into her room while she was asleep, and he was naked. And he crawled into her bed, and this time he forced himself inside her. She tried to stop him, but she couldn't. She begged him never to do it again, but he came to her every night. And he always said, "This is how a man shows a woman he loves her, and you're my woman, and I love you. You must never tell anyone about this." And she could never tell anyone.'

Ashley was sobbing, tears running down her cheeks.

It was all Gilbert Keller could do not to take her in his arms and hold her and tell her that he loved her and everything was going to be all right. But, of course, it was impossible. *I'm her doctor.*

When Dr Keller returned to Dr Lewison's office, Dr Patterson, Victoria Aniston and Katrina had left.

'Well, this is what we've been waiting for,' Dr Keller told Otto Lewison. 'We finally got a breakthrough. I know when Toni and Alette were born and why. We should see a big change from now on.'

Dr Keller was right. Things began to move.

Chapter Twenty-six

The hypnotherapy session had begun. Once Ashley was under, Dr Keller said, 'Ashley, tell me about Jim Cleary.'

'I loved Jim. We were going to run away together and get married.'

'Yes . . . ?'

'At the graduation party, Jim asked me if I would go to his house with him, and I . . . I said no. When he brought me home, my father was waiting up for us. He was furious. He told Jim to get out and stay out.'

'What happened then?'

'I decided to go to Jim. I packed a suitcase and I started toward his house.' She hesitated. 'Halfway to his house, I changed my mind and I went back home. I—'

Ashley's expression started to change. She began to relax in her chair, and it was Toni sitting there.

'Like hell she did. She went to his house, Dockie.'

When she reached Jim Cleary's house, it was dark. 'My folks will be away for the weekend.' Ashley rang the doorbell. A few minutes later, Jim Cleary opened the door. He was in his pajamas.

'Ashley.' His face lit up in a grin. 'You decided to come.' He pulled her inside.

'I came because I—'

307

'I don't care why you came. You're here.' He put his
arms around her and kissed her. *'How about a drink?'*

'No. Maybe some water.' She was suddenly apprehensive.

'Sure. Come on.' He took her hand and led her into the
kitchen. He poured a glass of water for her and watched
her drink it. *'You look nervous.'*

'I – I am.'

*'There's nothing to be nervous about. There's no chance
that my folks will come back. Let's go upstairs.'*

'Jim, I don't think we should.'

He came up behind her, his arms reaching for her
breasts. She turned. *'Jim . . .'*

His lips were on hers, and he was forcing her against
the kitchen counter.

'I'm going to make you happy, honey.' It was her father
saying, 'I'm going to make you happy, honey.'

She froze. She felt him pulling her clothes off and
entering her as she stood there naked, silently screaming.

And the feral rage took over.

She saw the large butcher knife sticking out of a wooden
block. She picked it up and began stabbing him in the chest,
screaming, 'Stop it, Father . . . Stop it . . . Stop it . . .
Stop it . . .'

She looked down, and Jim was lying on the floor, blood
spurting out of him.

'You animal,' she screamed. *'You won't do this to
anyone again.'* She reached down and plunged the knife
into his testicles.

At six o'clock in the morning, Ashley went to the railroad
station to wait for Jim. There was no sign of him.

308

She was beginning to panic. What could have happened? Ashley heard the train whistle in the distance. She looked at her watch: 7:00. The train was pulling into the station. Ashley rose to her feet and looked around frantically. *Something terrible has happened to him.* A few minutes later, she stood there watching the train pull out of the station, taking her dreams with it.

She waited another half hour and then slowly headed home. That noon, Ashley and her father were on a plane to London . . .

The session was ending.

Dr Keller counted, '. . . four . . . five. You're awake now.'

Ashley opened her eyes. 'What happened?'

'Toni told me how she killed Jim Cleary. He was attacking you.'

Ashley's face went white. 'I want to go to my room.'

Dr Keller reported to Otto Lewison. 'We're really beginning to make some advances, Otto. Up to now, it's been a logjam, with each one of them afraid to make the first move. But they're getting more relaxed. We're going in the right direction, but Ashley is still afraid to face reality.'

Dr Lewison said, 'She has no idea how these murders took place?'

'Absolutely none. She's completely blanked it out. Toni took over.'

It was two days later.

'Are you comfortable, Ashley?'

'Yes.' Her voice sounded far away.

'I want us to talk about Dennis Tibble. Was he a friend of yours?'

'Dennis and I worked for the same company. We weren't really friends.'

'The police report says that your fingerprints were found at his apartment.'

'That's right. I went there because he wanted me to give him some advice.'

'And what happened?'

'We talked for a few minutes, and he gave me a glass of wine with a drug in it.'

'What's the next thing you remember?'

'I – I woke up in Chicago.'

Ashley's expression began to change.

In an instant, it was Toni talking to him. 'Do you want to know what really happened . . . ?'

'Tell me, Toni.'

Dennis Tibble picked up the bottle of wine and said, 'Let's get comfortable.' He started leading her toward the bedroom.

'Dennis, I don't want to—'

And they were in the bedroom, and he was taking off her clothes.

'I know what you want, baby. You want me to screw you. That's why you came up here.'

She was fighting to get free. 'Stop it, Dennis!'

'Not until I give you what you came here for. You're going to love it, baby.'

He pushed her onto the bed, holding her tightly, his hands moving down to her groin. It was her father's voice. 'You're going to love it, baby.' And he was forcing himself into her, again and again, and she was silently screaming, 'No, Father. Stop!' And then the unspeakable fury took over. She saw the wine bottle. She reached for it, smashed it against the edge of the table and jammed the ragged edge of the bottle into his back. He screamed and tried to get up, but she held him tightly while she kept ramming the broken bottle into him. She watched him roll onto the floor.

'Stop it,' he whimpered.

'Do you promise to never do that again? Well, we'll make sure.' She picked up the broken glass and reached for his groin.

Dr Keller let a moment of silence pass. 'What did you do after that, Toni?'

'I decided I'd better get out of there before the police came. I have to admit I was pretty excited. I wanted to get away from Ashley's boring life for a while, and I had a friend in Chicago, so I decided to go there. It turned out he wasn't home, so I did a little shopping, hit some of the bars and had a good time.'

'And what happened next?'

'I checked into a hotel and fell asleep.' She shrugged. 'From then on it was Ashley's party.'

She awakened slowly, knowing something was wrong, terribly wrong. She felt as though she had been drugged. Ashley looked around the room and began to panic. She was lying in bed, naked, in some cheap hotel room. She had no idea where she was or how she had gotten there. She managed to sit up, and her head started to pound.

She got out of bed, walked into the tiny bathroom and stepped into the shower. She let the stream of hot water pound against her body, trying to wash away whatever

311

terrible, dirty things had happened to her. What if he had gotten her pregnant? The thought of having his child was sickening. Ashley got out of the shower, dried herself and walked over to the closet. Her clothes were missing. The only things inside the closet were a black leather miniskirt, a cheap-looking tube top and a pair of spiked high-heeled shoes. She was repelled by the thought of putting the clothes on, but she had no choice. She dressed quickly and glanced in the mirror. She looked like a prostitute.

'Father, I—'

'What's wrong?'

'I'm in Chicago and—'

'What are you doing in Chicago?'

'I can't go into it now. I need an airline ticket to San Jose. I don't have any money with me. Can you help me?'

'Of course. Hold on . . . There's an American Airlines plane leaving O'Hare at ten-forty A.M. Flight 407. There will be a ticket waiting for you at the check-in counter.'

'Alette, can you hear me? Alette.'

'I'm here, Dr Keller.'

'I want us to talk about Richard Melton. He was a friend of yours, wasn't he?'

'Yes. He was very . . . *simpático*. I was in love with him.'

'Was he in love with you?'

'I think so, yes. He was an artist. We would go to museums together and look at all of the wonderful paintings. When I was with Richard I felt . . . alive. I think if someone had not killed him, then one day we would have been married.'

'Tell me about the last time you were together.'

'When we were walking out of a museum, Richard said, "My roommate is at a party tonight. Why don't we stop at my place? I have some paintings I'd like to show you."'

'"Not yet, Richard."'

'"Whatever you say. I'll see you next weekend?"'

'"Yes."'

'I drove away,' Alette said. 'And that was the last time I—'

Dr Keller watched her face begin to take on Toni's animation.

'That's what she wants to think,' Toni said. 'That's not what happened.'

'What did happen?' Dr Keller asked.

She went to his apartment on Fell Street. It was small, but Richard's paintings made it look beautiful.

'It makes the room come alive, Richard.'

'Thank you, Alette.' He took her in his arms. 'I want to make love to you. You're beautiful.'

'You're beautiful,' her father said. And she froze. Because she knew the terrible thing that was going to happen. She was lying on the bed, naked, feeling the familiar pain of him entering her, tearing her apart.

And she was screaming, 'No! Stop it, Father! Stop it!' And then the manic-depressive frenzy took over. She had no recollection of where she got the knife, but she was stabbing his body over and over, yelling at him, 'I told you to stop it! Stop it!'

Ashley was writhing in her chair, screaming.

'It's all right, Ashley,' Dr Keller said. 'You're safe. You're going to wake up now, at the count of five.'

Ashley awoke, trembling. 'Is everything all right?'

313

'Toni told me about Richard Melton. He made love to you. You thought it was your father, so you—'

She put her hands over her ears. 'I don't want to hear any more!'

Dr Keller went to see Otto Lewison.

'I think we're finally making the breakthrough. It's very traumatic for Ashley, but we're nearing the end. We still have two murders to retrieve.'

'And then?'

'I'm going to bring Ashley, Toni and Alette together.'

Chapter Twenty-seven

Toni? Toni, can you hear me?' Dr Keller watched Ashley's expression change.

'I hear you, Dockie.'

'Let's talk about Jean Claude Parent.'

'I should have known he was too good to be true.'

'What do you mean?'

'In the beginning, he seemed like a real gentleman. He took me out every day, and we really had a good time. I thought he was different, but he was like all the others. All he wanted was sex.'

'I see.'

'He gave me a beautiful ring, and I guess he thought that he owned me. I went with him to his house.'

The house was a beautiful two-story, redbrick house filled with antiques.

'It's lovely.'

'There's something special I want to show you upstairs in the bedroom.' And he was taking her upstairs, and she was powerless to stop him. They were in the bedroom, and he took her in his arms and whispered, 'Get undressed.'

'I don't want to—'

'Yes, you do. We both want it.' He undressed her quickly, then laid her down on the bed and got on top of her. She was moaning, 'Don't. Please don't, Father!'

But he paid no attention. He kept plunging into her until suddenly he said, 'Ah,' and then stopped. 'You're wonderful,' he said.

And the malevolent explosion shook her. She grabbed the sharp letter opener from the desk and plunged it into his chest, up and down and up and down.

'You won't do that to anyone again.' She reached for his groin.

Afterward, she took a leisurely shower, dressed and went back to the hotel.

'Ashley . . .' Ashley's face began to change. 'Wake up now.'

Ashley slowly came awake. She looked at Dr Keller and said, 'Toni again?'

'Yes. She met Jean Claude on the Internet. Ashley, when you were in Quebec, were there periods when you seemed to lose time? When suddenly it was hours later or a day later, and you didn't know where the time had gone?'

She nodded slowly. 'Yes. It – it happened a lot.'

'That's when Toni took over.'

'And that's when . . . when she—?'

'Yes.'

The next few months were uneventful. In the afternoons, Dr Keller would listen to Toni play the piano and sing, and he would watch Alette painting in the garden. There was one more murder to discuss, but he wanted Ashley to be relaxed before he started talking about it.

It had been five years now since she had come to the hospital. *She's almost cured*, Dr Keller thought.

On a Monday morning, he sent for Ashley and watched

her walk into the office. She was pale, as though she knew what she was facing.

'Good morning, Ashley.'

'Good morning, Gilbert.'

'How are you feeling?'

'Nervous. This is the last one, isn't it?'

'Yes. Let's talk about Deputy Sam Blake. What was he doing in your apartment?'

'I asked him to come. Someone had written on my bathroom mirror, "You Will Die." I didn't know what to do. I thought someone was trying to kill me. I called the police, and Deputy Blake came over. He was very sympathetic.'

'Did you ask him to stay with you?'

'Yes. I was afraid to be alone. He said that he would spend the night and then in the morning he would arrange for twenty-four-hour protection for me. I offered to sleep on the couch and let him sleep in the bedroom, but he said he would sleep on the couch. I remember he checked the windows to make sure they were locked, and then he double-bolted the door. His gun was on the table next to the couch. I said good night and went into the bedroom and closed the door.'

'And then what happened?'

'I – The next thing I remember is being awakened by someone screaming in the alley. Then the sheriff came in to tell me that Deputy Blake had been found dead.' She stopped, her face pale.

'All right. I'm going to put you to sleep now. Just relax . . . Close your eyes and relax . . .' It took ten minutes. Dr Keller said, 'Toni . . .'

'I'm here. You want to know what really happened, don't you? Ashley was a fool to invite Sam to stay at the apartment. I could have told her what he would do.'

He heard a cry from the bedroom, quickly rose from the couch and scooped up his gun. He hurried over to the bedroom door and listened a moment. Silence. He had imagined it. As he started to turn away, he heard it again. He pushed the door open, gun in hand. Ashley was in bed, naked, asleep. There was no one else in the room. She was making little moaning sounds. He moved to her bedside. She looked beautiful lying there, curled up in a fetal position. She moaned again, trapped in some terrible dream. He meant only to comfort her, to take her in his arms and hold her. He lay down at her side and gently pulled her toward him, and he felt the heat of her body and began to be aroused.

She was awakened by his voice saying, 'It's all right now. You're safe.' And his lips were on hers, and he was moving her legs apart and was inside her.

And she was screaming, 'No, Father!'

And he moved faster and faster in a primal urgency, and then the savage revenge took over. She grabbed the knife from the dresser drawer at her bedside and began to slash into his body.

'What happened after you killed him?'

'She wrapped his body in the sheets and dragged him to the elevator and then through the garage to the alley in back.'

'. . . and then,' Dr Keller told Ashley, 'Toni wrapped his body in the sheets and dragged him into the elevator and through the garage to the alley in back.'

Ashley sat there, her face dead white. 'She's a mon – I'm a monster.'

Gilbert Keller said, 'No. Ashley, you must remember

that Toni was born out of your pain, to protect you. The same is true of Alette. It's time to bring this to a closure. I want you to meet them. It's the next step to your getting well.'

Ashley's eyes were tightly shut. 'All right. When do we . . . do this?'

'Tomorrow morning.'

Ashley was in a deep hypnotic state. Dr Keller started with Toni.

'Toni, I want you and Alette to talk to Ashley.'

'What makes you think she can handle us?'

'I think she can.'

'All right Dockie. Whatever you say.'

'Alette, are you ready to meet Ashley?'

'If Toni says it's all right.'

'Sure, Alette. It's about time.'

Dr Keller took a deep breath and said, 'Ashley, I want you to say hello to Toni.'

There was a long silence. Then, a timid, 'Hello, Toni . . .'

'Hello.'

'Ashley, say hello to Alette.'

'Hello, Alette . . .'

'Hello, Ashley . . .'

Dr Keller breathed a deep sigh of relief. 'I want you all to get to know one another. You've suffered through the same terrible traumas. They've separated you from one another. But there's no reason for that separation anymore. You're going to become one whole, healthy person. It's a long journey, but you've begun it. I promise you, the most difficult part is over.'

From that point on, Ashley's treatment moved swiftly.

Ashley and her two alters talked to one another every day.

'I had to protect you,' Toni explained. 'I suppose every time I killed one of those men, I was killing Father for what he had done to you.'

'I tried to protect you, too,' Alette said.

'I – I appreciate that. I'm grateful to both of you.'

Ashley turned to Dr Keller and said wryly, 'It's really all me, isn't it? I'm talking to myself.'

'You're talking to two other parts of yourself,' he corrected her gently. 'It's time for all of you to unify and become one again.'

That afternoon, Dr Keller went to see Otto Lewison.

Dr Lewison said, 'I hear good reports, Gilbert.'

Dr Keller nodded. 'Ashley's made remarkable progress. In another few months, I think she can be released and go on with her treatment as an outpatient.'

'That's wonderful news. Congratulations.'

I'll miss her, Dr Keller thought. *I'll miss her terribly*.

'Dr Salem is on line two for you, Mr Singer.'

'Right.' David reached for the phone, puzzled. Why would Dr Salem be calling? It had been years since the two men had talked. 'Royce?'

'Good morning, David. I have some interesting information for you. It's about Ashley Patterson.'

David felt a sudden sense of alarm. 'What about her?'

'Do you remember how hard we tried to find the trauma that had caused her condition, and we failed?'

David remembered it well. It had been a major weakness in their case. 'Yes.'

'Well, I just learned the answer. My friend, Dr Lewison,

320

who's head of the Connecticut Psychiatric Hospital, just called. The missing piece of the puzzle is Dr Steven Patterson. He's the one who molested Ashley when she was a child.'

David asked incredulously, *'What?'*

'Dr Lewison just learned about it.'

David sat listening as Dr Salem went on, but his mind was elsewhere. He was recalling Dr Patterson's words. *'You're the only one I trust, David. My daughter means everything in the world to me. You're going to save her life . . . I want you to defend Ashley, and I won't have anyone else involved in this case . . .'*

And David suddenly realized why Dr Patterson had been so insistent on his representing Ashley alone. The doctor was sure that if David had ever discovered what he had done, he would have protected him. Dr Patterson had had to decide between his daughter and his reputation, and he had chosen his reputation. *The son of a bitch!*

'Thanks, Royce.'

That afternoon, as Ashley passed the recreation room, she saw a copy of the *Westport News* that someone had left there. On the front page of the newspaper was a photograph of her father with Victoria Aniston and Katrina. The beginning of the story read, 'Dr Steven Patterson is to be married to socialite Victoria Aniston, who has a three-year-old daughter from a previous marriage. Dr Patterson is joining the staff of St John's Hospital in Manhattan, and he and his future wife have bought a house on Long Island . . .'

Ashley stopped and her face contorted into a mask of rage. 'I'll kill the son of a bitch,' Toni screamed. 'I'll kill him!'

She was completely out of control. They had to put

her in a padded room where she could not hurt herself, restrained by handcuffs and leg-irons. When the attendants came to feed her, she tried to grab them, and they had to be careful not to get too close to her. Toni had taken total possession of Ashley.

When she saw Dr Keller, she screamed, 'Let me out of here, you bastard. Now!'

'We're going to let you out of here,' Dr Keller said soothingly, 'but first you have to calm down.'

'I'm calm,' Toni yelled. 'Let me go!'

Dr Keller sat on the floor beside her and said, 'Toni, when you saw that picture of your father, you said you were going to hurt him, and—'

'You're a liar! I said I was going to *kill* him!'

'There's been enough killing. You don't want to stab anyone else.'

'I'm not going to stab him. Have you heard of hydrochloric acid? It will eat through anything, including skin. Wait until I—'

'I don't want you to think like that.'

'You're right. Arson! Arson is better. He won't have to wait until hell to burn to death. I can do it so they'll never catch me if—'

'Toni, forget about this.'

'All right. I can think of some other ways that are even better.'

He studied her a moment, frustrated. 'Why are you so angry?'

'Don't you know? I thought you were supposed to be such a great doctor. He's marrying a woman with a three-year-old daughter. What's going to happen to that little girl, Mr Famous Doctor? I'll tell you what. The same thing that happened to us. Well, I'm going to stop it!'

'I'd hoped we'd gotten rid of all that hate.'
'Hate? You want to hear about hate?'

It was raining, a steady downpour of raindrops hitting the roof of the speeding car. She looked at her mother sitting at the wheel, squinting at the road ahead, and she smiled, in a happy mood. She began to sing:

> *'All around the mulberry bush,*
> *The monkey chased—'*

Her mother turned to her and screamed, 'Shut up. I told you I detest that song. You make me sick, you miserable little—'

After that, everything seemed to happen in slow motion. The curve ahead, the car skidding off the road, the tree. The crash flung her out of the car. She was shaken, but unhurt. She got to her feet. She could hear her mother, trapped in the car, screaming, 'Get me out of here. Help me! Help me!'

And she stood there watching until the car finally exploded.

'Hate? Do you want to hear more?'

Walter Manning said, 'This has to be a unanimous decision. My daughter's a professional artist, not a dilettante. She did this as a favor. We can't turn her down . . . This has to be unanimous. We're either giving him my daughter's painting or we don't give him anything at all.'

She was parked at the curb, with the motor running.

323

She watched Walter Manning cross the street, headed for the garage where he kept his car. She put the car in gear and slammed her foot down on the accelerator. At the last moment, he heard the sound of the car coming toward him, and he turned. She watched the expression on his face as the car smashed into him and then hurled his broken body aside. She kept driving. There were no witnesses. God was on her side.

'*That's* hate, Dockie! That's real hate!'

Gilbert Keller listened to her recital, appalled, shaken by the cold-blooded viciousness of it. He canceled the rest of his appointments for the day. He needed to be alone.

The following morning when Dr Keller walked into the padded cell, Alette had taken over.

'Why are you doing this to me, Dr Keller?' Alette asked. 'Let me out of here.'

'I will,' Dr Keller assured her. 'Tell me about Toni. What has she told you?'

'She said we have to escape from here and kill Father.'

Toni took over. 'Morning, Dockie. We're fine now. Why don't you let us go?'

Dr Keller looked into her eyes. There was cold-blooded murder there.

Dr Otto Lewison sighed. 'I'm terribly sorry about what's happened, Gilbert. Everything was going so well.'

'Right now, I can't even reach Ashley.'

'I suppose this means having to start the treatment all over.'

Dr Keller was thoughtful. 'Not really, Otto. We've arrived at the point where the three alters have gotten

324

to know one another. That was a big breakthrough. The next step was to get them to integrate. I have to find a way to do that.'

'That damned article—'

'It's fortunate for us that Toni saw that article.'

Otto Lewison looked at him in surprise. 'Fortunate?'

'Yes. Because there's that residual hate in Toni. Now that we know it's there, we can work on it. I want to try an experiment. If it works, we'll be in good shape. If it doesn't' – he paused and added quietly – 'then I think Ashley may have to be confined here for the rest of her life.'

'What do you want to do?'

'I think it's a bad idea for Ashley's father to see her again, but I want to hire a national clipping service, and I want them to send me every article that appears about Dr Patterson.'

Otto Lewison blinked. 'What's the point?'

'I'm going to show them all to Toni. Eventually, her hate has to burn itself out. That way I can monitor it and try to control it.'

'It may take a long time, Gilbert.'

'At least a year, maybe longer. But it's the only chance Ashley has.'

Five days later Ashley had taken over.

When Dr Keller walked into the padded cell, Ashley said, 'Good morning, Gilbert. I'm sorry that all this happened.'

'I'm glad it did, Ashley. We're going to get all of our feelings out in the open.' He nodded to the guard to remove the leg-irons and handcuffs.

Ashley stood up and rubbed her wrists. 'That wasn't very

comfortable,' she said. They walked out into the corridor. 'Toni's very angry.'

'Yes, but she's going to get over it. Here's my plan . . .'

There were three or four articles about Dr Steven Patterson every month. One read: 'Dr Steven Patterson is to wed Victoria Aniston in an elaborate wedding ceremony on Long Island this Friday. Dr Patterson's colleagues will fly in to attend . . .'

Toni was hysterical when Dr Keller showed the story to her.

'That marriage isn't going to last long.'

'Why do you say that, Toni?'

'Because he's going to be dead!'

'Dr Steven Patterson has resigned from St John's Hospital and will head the cardiac staff at Manhattan Methodist Hospital . . .'

'So he can rape all the little girls there,' Toni screamed.

'Dr Steven Patterson received the Lasker Award for his work in medicine and is being honored at the White House . . .'

'They should hang the bastard!' Toni yelled.

Gilbert Keller saw to it that Toni received all the articles written about her father. And as time went by, with each new item, Toni's rage seemed to be diminishing. It was as though her emotions had been worn out. She went from hatred to anger and, finally, to a resigned acceptance.

There was a mention in the real estate section. 'Dr Steven Patterson and his new bride have moved into a home in

Manhattan, but they plan to purchase a second home in the Hamptons and will be spending their summers there with their daughter, Katrina.'

Toni started sobbing. 'How could he do that to us?'

'Do you feel that that little girl has taken your place, Toni?'

'I don't know. I'm – I'm confused.'

Another year went by. Ashley had therapy sessions three times a week. Alette painted almost every day, but Toni refused to sing or play the piano.

At Christmas, Dr Keller showed Toni a new clipping. There was a picture of her father and Victoria and Katrina. The caption read: THE PATTERSONS CELEBRATE CHRISTMAS IN THE HAMPTONS.

Toni said wistfully, 'We used to spend Christmases together. He always gave me wonderful gifts.' She looked at Dr Keller. 'He wasn't all bad. Aside from the – you know – he was a good father. I think he really loved me.'

It was the first sign of a new breakthrough.

One day, as Dr Keller passed the recreation room, he heard Toni singing and playing the piano. Surprised, he stepped into the room and watched her. She was completely absorbed in the music.

The next day, Dr Keller had a session with Toni.

'Your father's getting older, Toni. How do you think you'll feel when he dies?'

'I – I don't want him to die. I know I said a lot of stupid things, but I said them because I was angry with him.'

'You're not angry anymore?'

She thought about it. 'I'm not angry, I'm hurt. I think you were right. I did feel that the little girl was taking my place.' She looked up at Dr Keller and said, 'I was confused. But my father has a right to get on with his life, and Ashley has a right to get on with hers.'

Dr Keller smiled. *We're back on track.*

The three of them talked to one another freely now.

Dr Keller said, 'Ashley, you needed Toni and Alette because you couldn't stand the pain. How do you feel about your father now?'

There was a brief silence. She said slowly, 'I can never forget what he did to me, but I can forgive him. I want to put the past behind me and start my future.'

'To do that, we must make you all one again. How do you feel about that, Alette?'

Alette said, 'If I'm Ashley, can I still go on painting?'

'Of course you can.'

'Well, then, all right.'

'Toni?'

'Will I still be able to sing and play the piano?'

'Yes,' he said.

'Then, why not?'

'Ashley?'

'I'm ready for all of us to be one. I – I want to thank them for helping me when I needed them.'

'My pleasure, luv.'

'*Minièra anche,*' Alette said.

It was time for the final step: integration.

'All right. I'm going to hypnotize you now, Ashley. I want you to say good-bye to Toni and Alette.'

Ashley took a deep breath. 'Good-bye, Toni. Good-bye, Alette.'

'Good-bye, Ashley.'

'Take care of yourself, Ashley.'

328

Ten minutes later, Ashley was in a deep hypnotic state. 'Ashley, there's nothing more to be afraid of. All your problems are behind you. You don't need anyone to protect you anymore. You're able to handle your life without help, without shutting out any bad experiences. You're able to face whatever happens. Do you agree with me?'

'Yes, I do. I'm ready to face the future.'

'Good. Toni?'

There was no answer.

'Toni?'

There was no answer.

'Alette?'

Silence.

'Alette?'

Silence.

'They're gone, Ashley. You're whole now and you're cured.'

He watched Ashley's face light up.

'You'll awaken at the count of three. One ... two ... three ...'

Ashley opened her eyes and a beatific smile lit her face. 'It – it happened, didn't it?'

He nodded. 'Yes.'

She was ecstatic. 'I'm free. Oh, thank you, Gilbert! I feel – I feel as though a terrible dark curtain has been taken away.'

Dr Keller took her hand. 'I can't tell you how pleased I am. We'll be doing some more tests over the next few months, but if they turn out as I think they will, well, we'll be sending you home. I'll arrange for some outpatient treatment for you wherever you are.'

Ashley nodded, too overcome with emotion to speak.

Chapter Twenty-eight

Over the next few months, Otto Lewison had three psychiatrists examine Ashley. They used hypnotherapy and Sodium Amytal.

'Hello, Ashley. I'm Dr Montfort, and I need to ask you some questions. How do you feel about yourself?'

'I feel wonderful, Doctor. It's as though I've just gotten over a long illness.'

'Do you think you're a bad person?'

'No. I know some bad things have happened, but I don't believe I'm responsible for them.'

'Do you hate anyone?'

'No.'

'What about your father? Do you hate him?'

'I did. I don't hate him anymore. I don't think he could help what he did. I just hope he's all right now.'

'Would you like to see him again?'

'I think it would be better if I didn't. He has his life. I want to start a new life for myself.'

'Ashley?'

'Yes.'

'I'm Dr Vaughn. I'd like to have a little chat with you.'

'All right.'

'Do you remember Toni and Alette?'

'Of course. But they're gone.'

'How do you feel about them?'

'In the beginning, I was terrified, but now I know I needed them. I'm grateful to them.'

'Do you sleep well at night?'

'Now I do, yes.'

'Tell me your dreams.'

'I used to have terrible dreams; something was always chasing me. I thought I was going to be murdered.'

'Do you still have those dreams?'

'Not anymore. My dreams are very peaceful. I see bright colors and smiling people. Last night, I dreamed I was at a ski resort, flying down the slopes. It was wonderful. I don't mind cold weather at all anymore.'

'How do you feel about your father?'

'I want him to be happy, and I want to be happy.'

'Ashley?'

'Yes.'

'I'm Dr Hoelterhoff.'

'How do you do, Doctor?'

'They didn't tell me how beautiful you were. Do you think you're beautiful?'

'I think I'm attractive . . .'

'I hear that you have a lovely voice. Do you think you do?'

'It's not a trained voice, but, yes' – she laughed – 'I do manage to sing on key.'

'And they tell me you paint. Are you good?'

'For an amateur, I think I'm quite good. Yes.'

He was studying her thoughtfully. 'Do you have any problems that you would like to discuss with me?'

'I can't think of any. I'm treated very well here.'

'How do you feel about leaving here and getting out into the world?'

'I've thought a lot about it. It's scary, but at the same time it's exciting.'

'Do you think you would be afraid out there?'

'No. I want to build a new life. I'm good with computers. I can't go back to the company I worked for, but I'm sure I can get a job at another company.'

Dr Hoelterhoff nodded. 'Thank you, Ashley. It was a pleasure talking to you.'

Dr Montfort, Dr Vaughn, Dr Hoelterhoff and Dr Keller were gathered in Otto Lewison's office. He was studying their reports. When he finished, he looked up at Dr Keller and smiled.

'Congratulations,' he said. 'These reports are all positive. You've done a wonderful job.'

'She's a wonderful woman. Very special, Otto. I'm glad she's going to have her life back again.'

'Has she agreed to outpatient treatment when she leaves here?'

'Absolutely.'

Otto Lewison nodded. 'Very well. I'll have the release papers drawn up.' He turned to the other doctors. 'Thank you, gentlemen. I appreciate your help.'

Chapter Twenty-nine

Two days later, she was called into Dr Lewison's office. Dr Keller was there. Ashley was to be discharged and would return to her home in Cupertino, where regular therapy and evaluation sessions had been arranged with a court-approved psychiatrist.

Dr Lewison said, 'Well, today's the day. Are you excited?'

Ashley said, 'I'm excited, I'm frightened, I'm – I don't know. I feel like a bird that's just been set free. I feel like I'm flying.' Her face was glowing.

'I'm glad you're leaving, but I'm – I'm going to miss you,' Dr Keller said.

Ashley took his hand and said warmly, 'I'm going to miss you, too. I don't know how I . . . how I can ever thank you.' Her eyes filled with tears. 'You've given me my life back.'

She turned to Dr Lewison. 'When I'm back in California, I'll get a job at one of the computer plants there. I'll let you know how it works out and how I get on with the outpatient therapy. I want to make sure that what happened before never happens to me again.'

'I don't think you have anything to worry about,' Dr Lewison assured her.

When she left, Dr Lewison turned to Gilbert Keller. 'This makes up for a lot of the ones that didn't succeed, doesn't it, Gilbert?'

*　　*　　*

It was a sunny June day, and as she walked down Madison Avenue in New York City, her radiant smile made people turn back to look at her. She had never been so happy. She thought of the wonderful life ahead of her, and all that she was going to do. There could have been a terrible ending for her, she thought, but this was the happy ending she had prayed for.

She walked into Pennsylvania Station. It was the busiest train station in America, a charmless maze of airless rooms and passages. The station was crowded with people. *And each person has an interesting story to tell,* she thought. *They're all going to different places, living their own lives, and now, I'm going to live my own life.*

She purchased a ticket from one of the machines. Her train was just pulling in. *Serendipity,* she thought.

She boarded the train and took a seat. She was filled with excitement at what was about to happen. The train gave a jerk and then started picking up speed. *I'm on my way at last.* And as the train headed toward the Hamptons, she began to sing softly:

> *'All around the mulberry bush,*
> *The monkey chased the weasel.*
> *The monkey thought 'twas all in fun,*
> *Pop! goes the weasel . . .'*

Author's Note

During the past twenty years, there have been doz-
criminal trials involving defendants claiming to have
multiple personalities. The charges covered a wide range
of activities, including murder, kidnapping, rape and
arson.

Multiple personality disorder (MPD), also known as dissociative identity disorder (DID), is a controversial topic
among psychiatrists. Some psychiatrists believe that it does
not exist. On the other hand, for years many reputable
doctors, hospitals and social services organizations have
been treating patients who suffer from MPD. Some studies estimate that between 5 and 15 percent of psychiatric
patients are afflicted with it.

Current statistics from the Department of Justice indicate
that approximately one-third of juvenile victims of sexual
abuse are children under six years of age, and that one
out of three girls are sexually abused before the age of
eighteen.

Most reported cases of incest involve a father and
daughter.

A research project in three countries suggests that MPD
affects one percent of the general population.

Dissociative disorders are often misdiagnosed, and studies have shown that, on average, people with MPD have
spent seven years, prior to an accurate diagnosis.

Two-thirds of the cases of multiple personality disorder are treatable. Following is a list of some of the organizations devoted to helping and treating patients. In addition, I have included a list of books and articles that may be of interest.

Organizations

UNITED KINGDOM
British Dissociative Disorders Professional Study Group
c/o Jeannie McIntee, Msc
Chester Therapy Centre
Weldon House
20 Walpole Street
Chester CH1 4HG
England
Tel: 01244 390121

ARGENTINA
Grupo de Estudio de
Trastornos de disociacion y trauma de Argentina
Dra. Graciela Rodriguez
Federico Lacroze 1820 7mo.A
(1426) Buenos Aires
Argentina
Tel-Fax: 541 775 2792

AUSTRALIA
Australian Association for Trauma and Dissociation (AATD)
PO Box 85
Brunswick
Melbourne, Victoria 3056
Australia
Tel: (03) 9663 6225

Beyond Survival: A Magazine on Abuse, Trauma and Dissociation
PO Box 85
Annandale, NSW 2038
Australia
Tel: (02) 9566 2045

CANADA
Canadian Society for the Study of Dissociation
c/o John O'Neil, MD FRCPC
4064 Wilson Ave
Montreal, QC H4A 2T9
Canada
Tel: 514 485 9529

ISRAEL
Maytal – Israel Institute for Treatment & Research on Stress
Eli Somer, PhD, Clinical Director
3 Maayan St
Haifa 34484
Israel
Tel: 972 4 8381999 Fax: 972 4 8386369

NETHERLANDS
Praktijk voor psychotherapie
en hypnose
Els Grimminck, MD
Wielewaal 17
1902 KE Castricum
The Netherlands
Tel: (31 0) 25 1650264 Fax: (31 0) 25 1653306

Nederlands-Vlaamse Vereniging voor de bestudering van Dissociatieve
Stoornissen (NVVDS)
(Netherlands-Flemish Society for the Study of Dissociative Disorders)
c/o Stichting RBC, location PC Bloemendaal
Kliniek voor Intensieve Behandeling Atlantis
Fenny ten Boschstraat 23
2555 PT Den Haag
The Netherlands
Tel: 31 (070) 391 6117 Fax: 31 (070) 391 6115

Books

Calof, David L. with Mary Leloo. *Multiple Personality and Dissociation: Understanding Incest, Abuse, and MPD.* Park Ridge, Ill.: Parkside Publishing.

Putnam, Frank. *Diagnosis and Treatment of Multiple Personality Disorder.* New York: Guilford Press, 1989.

Putnam, F. W. *Dissociation in Children and Adolescents: A Developmental Perspective.* New York: Guilford Press, 1997.

Roseman, Mark, Gini Scott, and William Craig. *You the Jury.* Santa Ana, Cal.: Seven Locks Press, 1997.

Saks, Elyn R., with Stephen H. Behnke. *Jekyll on Trial.* New York: New York University Press, 1997.

Schreiber, Flora *Sybil.* New York: Warner Books, 1995

Thigpen, Corbett H., and Hervey M. Cleckley. *Three Faces of Eve.* Revised. Three Faces of Eve, 1992.

*   *   *

Articles

Abrams S. 'The Multiple Personality: A Legal Defense.'
American Journal of Clinical Hypnosis 25 (1983): 225–31.
Allison, R. B. 'Multiple Personality and Criminal Behaviour.'
American Journal of Forensic Psychiatry 2 (1981–1982): 32–38

On the Internet

The Sidran Foundation Online
http://www.sidran.org

Pat McClendon's Home Page
http://www.users.mis.net7patmc/

ISTSS Home Page
http://www.issd.org

International Society for the Study of Dissociation
E-mail: into@issd.org